AF290915

AUBEY LLC - WASHINGTON, DC

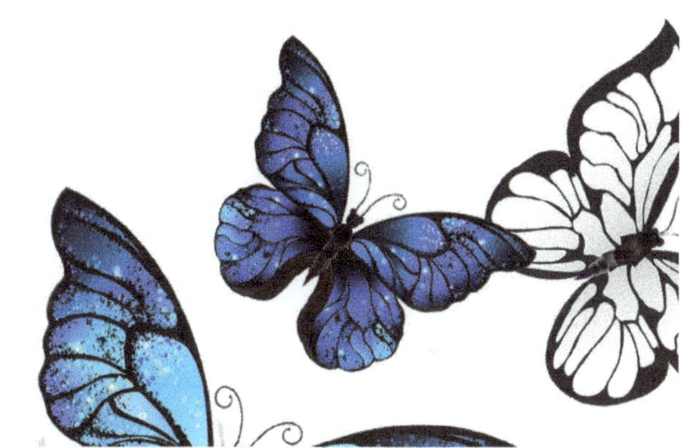

TO OTHER WORLDS

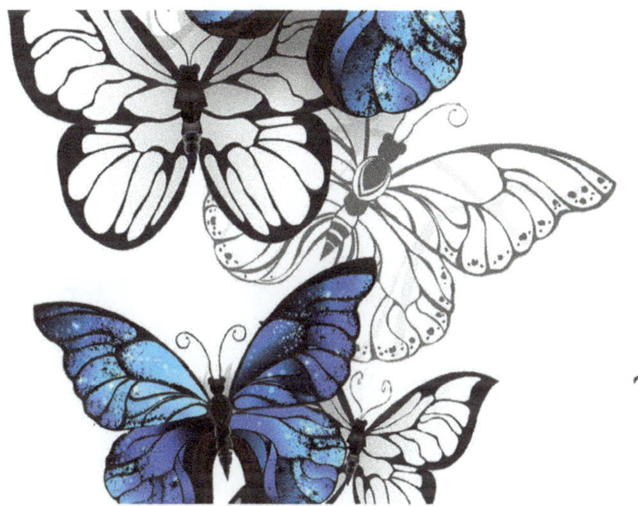

Magical photos to awaken your imagination

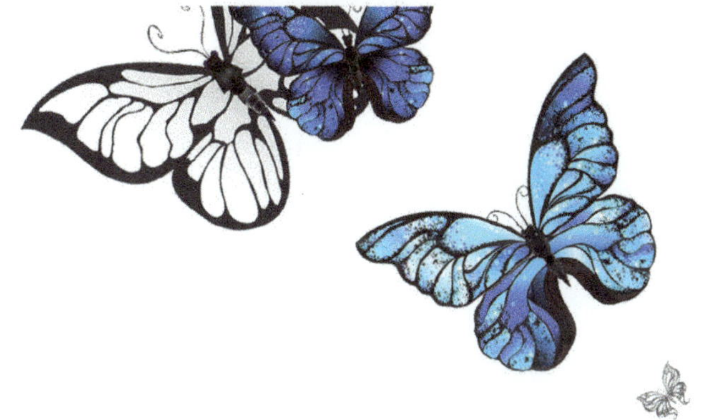

AUDEN JOHNSON

FORWARD

A natural scene can conjure tales of magical fortresses, fairy tale houses and treks across rich terrain in search of a priceless treasure. Imagination is a funny thing. It seems so much easier to grasp as a child. Then, reality gets in the way. You have trouble letting your mind wander. You can't see the castle in the cardboard box. Nature's magic can revive your imagination. It can inspire an adventure.

Ever hear how long walks are great for curing a creative block? Miles of empty road surrounded by nothing but trees. Your mind has no choice but to dive into your imagination.

I've been fortunate enough to have visited diverse places in the last decade. Bermuda, Hawaii, Florida and Brooklyn, Beacon, Peekskill and Cold Spring in New York. Each location blends together and comes out as I write and create fantasy worlds.

Annissa is a fictional location in one of my stories. I've used real world inspiration from Bermuda and Kauai, Hawaii. Those photos, even the bad ones, have been essential in making Annissa seem real. They've even given me inspiration on things to add and change.

Amazing the kind of stories that can grow out of just one photo.

Recently, I started a blog series called Story and Photos. I take a series of photos with a related theme like a foggy day and write a story inspired by those images. I don't plot it out beforehand. I collect the photos and just start writing. After a while, the story grows legs and starts running ahead of me. A few want to be novels.

nages can give nearly any muse a nice kick to get it going.

ou know how some people make up stories of the people they see on the
reet? I weave stories in my head about places and things I photograph.

o Other Worlds takes you on a photo journey with a fictional narrator who
ts out to find better worlds beyond the horizon. Maybe some of these pho-
s will inspire you as well.

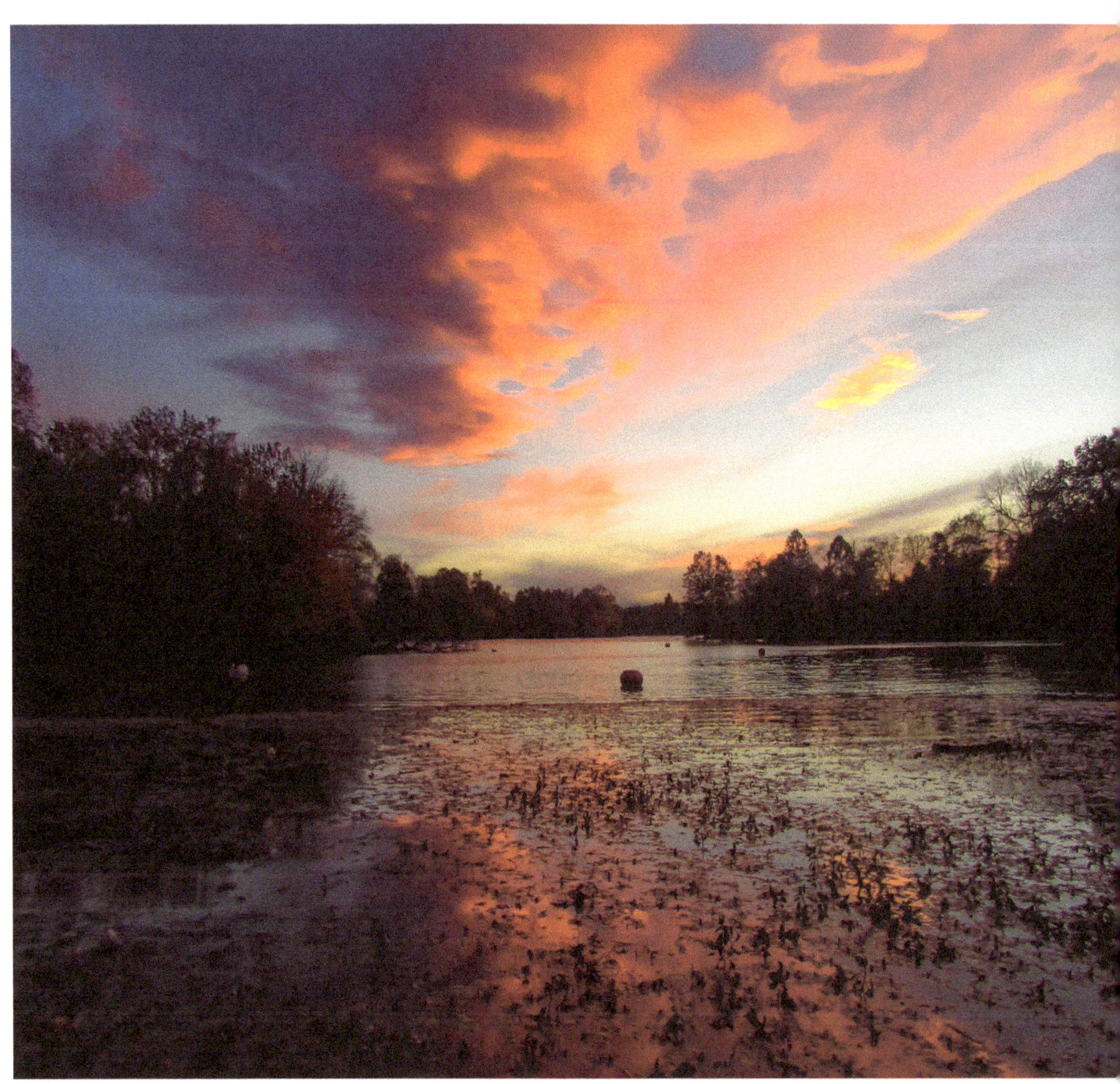

THE DREAM

The sun glided down the landscape as it dropped behind the horizon.
The waning light painted a masterpiece in the sky. Mesmerizing as colors
shifted and textures changed.

He never grew tired of watching the sun as it rose and set each day.
What caused the sky to take on such striking colors? He could find logical explanations through research. But, he liked magic the best.

It was magic.

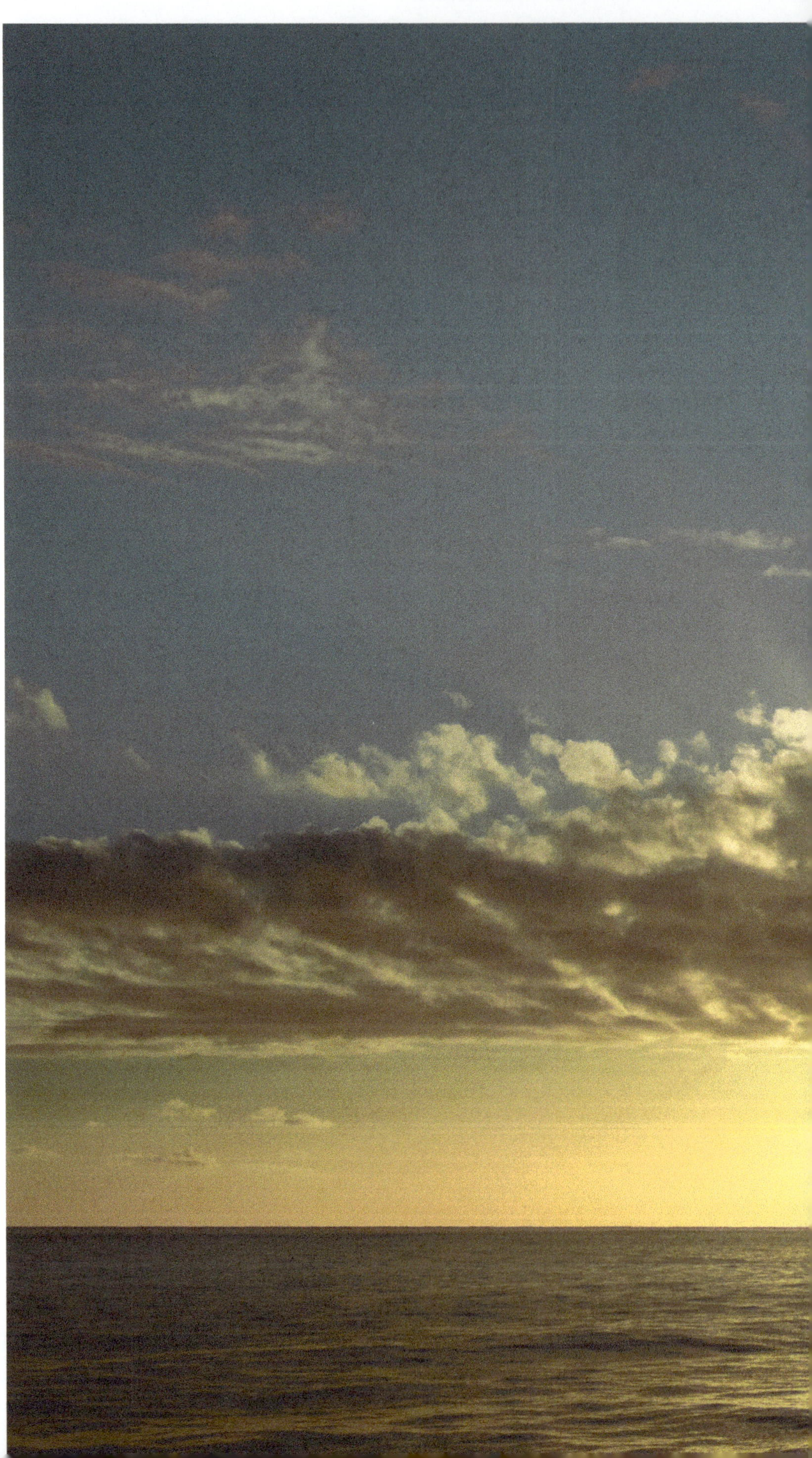

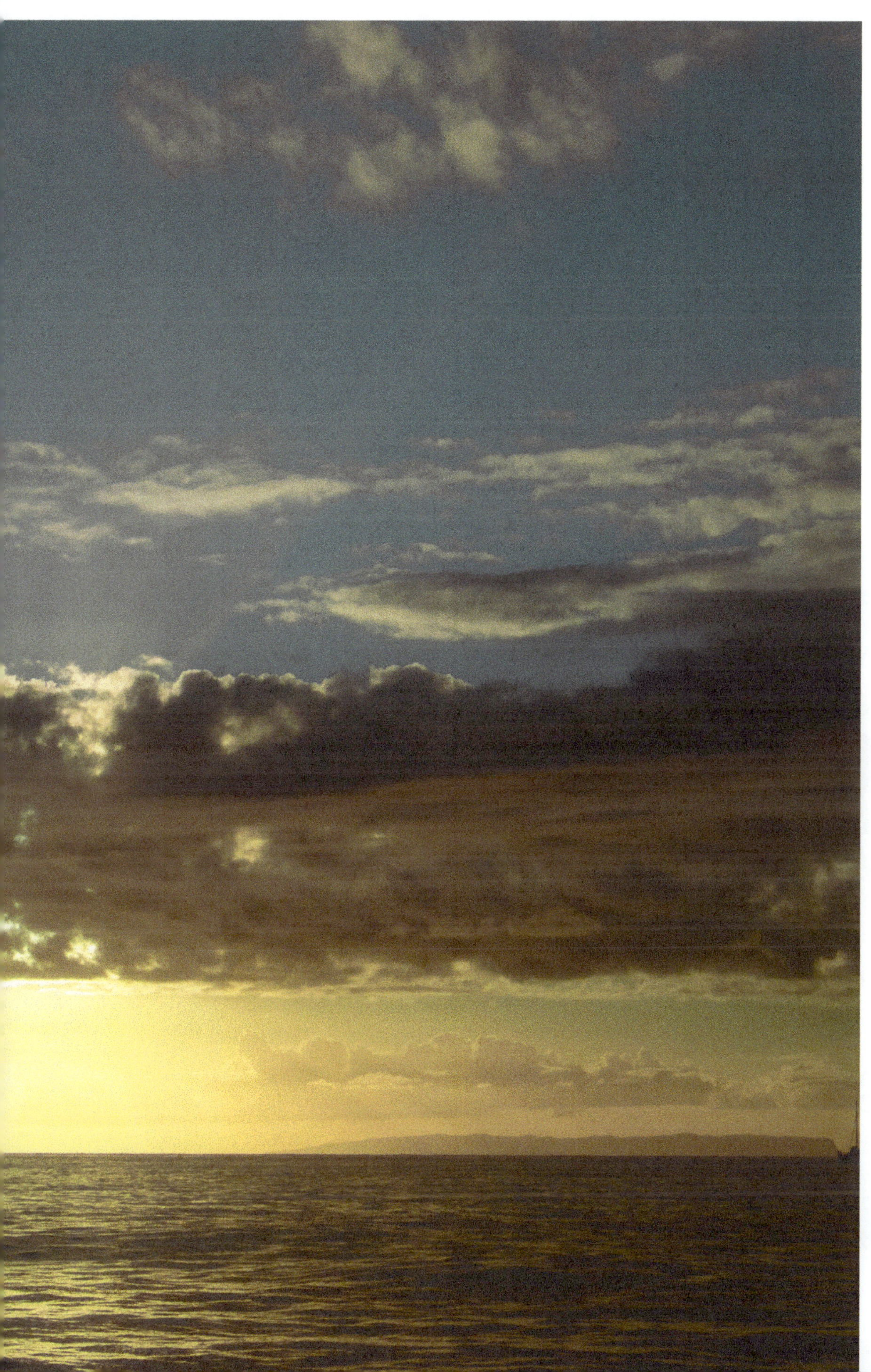

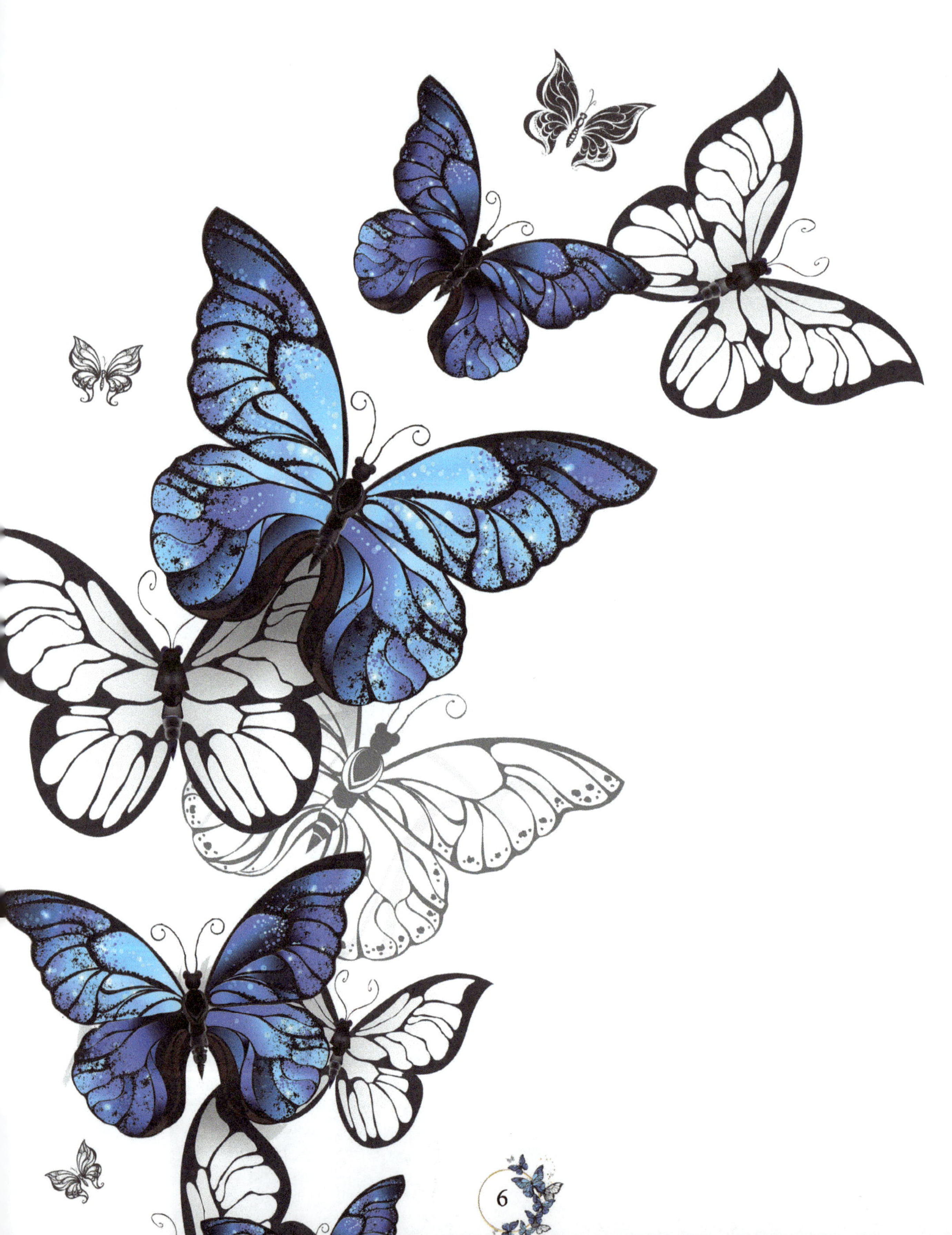

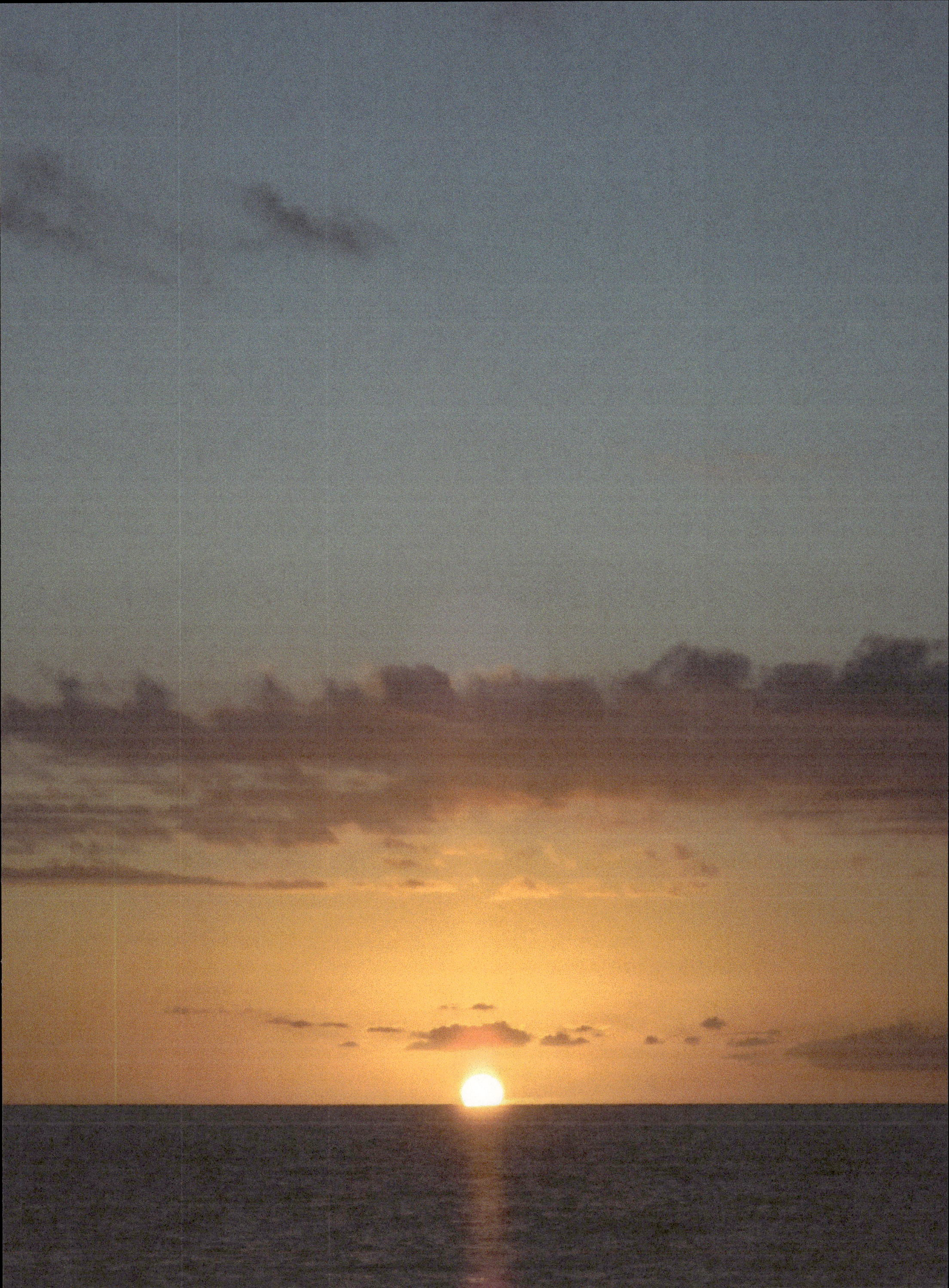

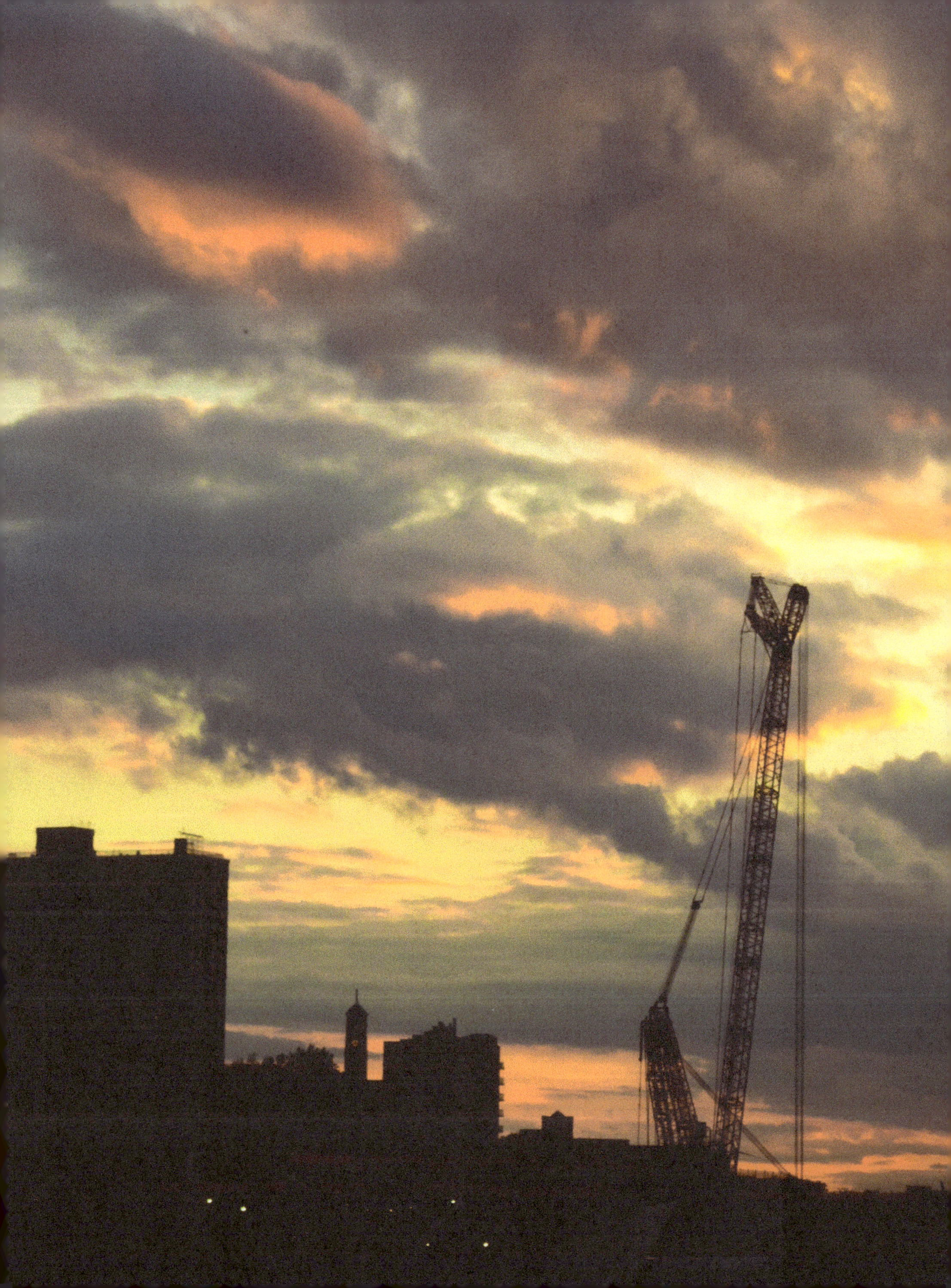

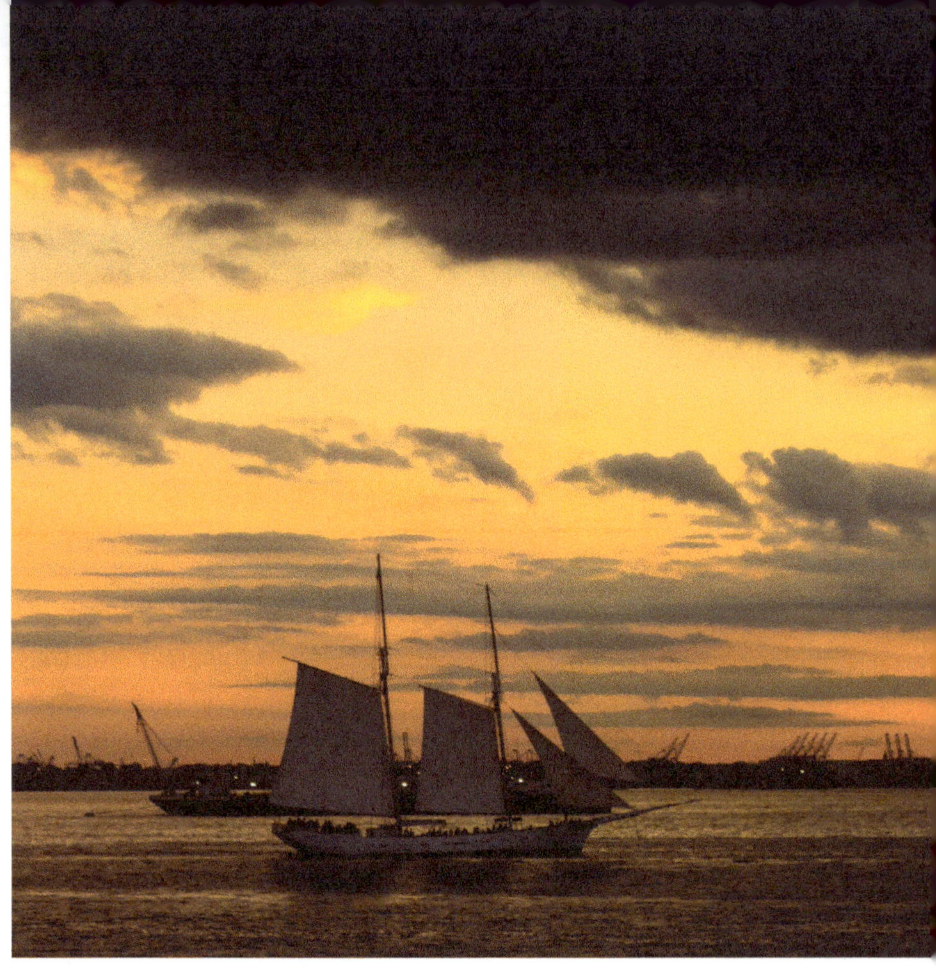

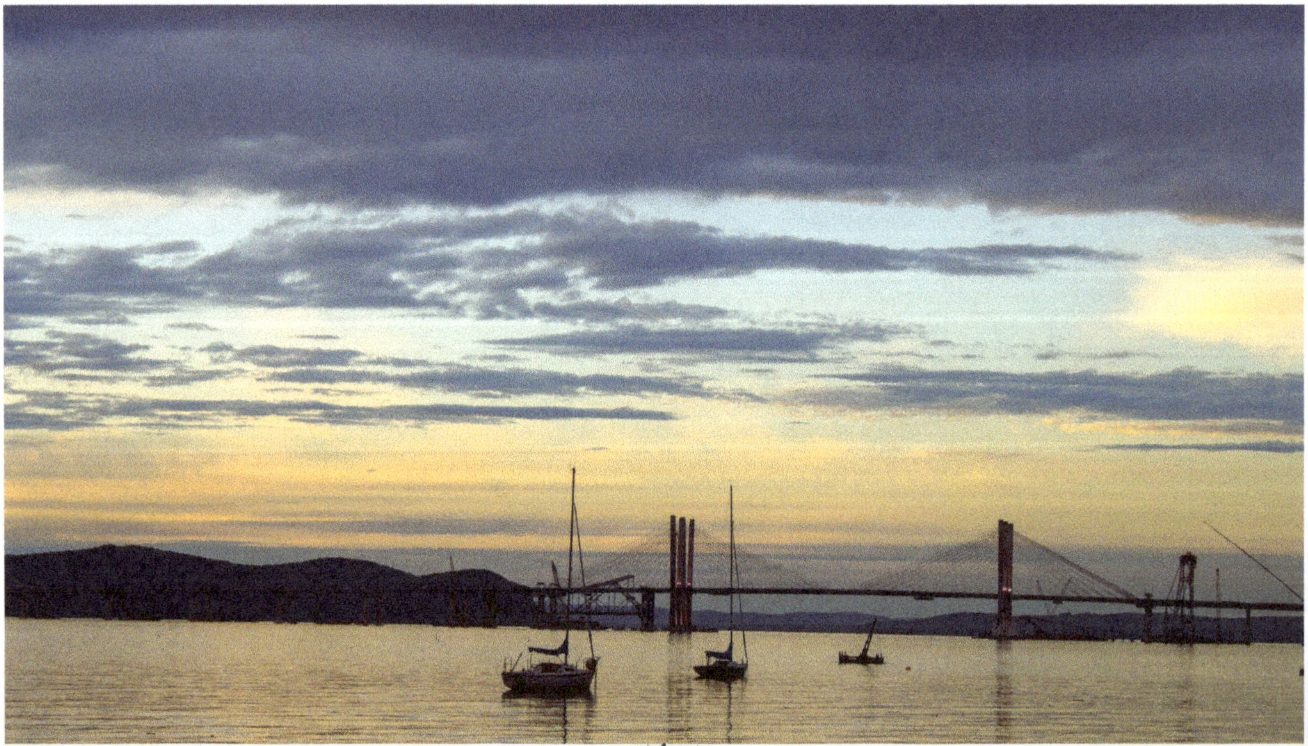

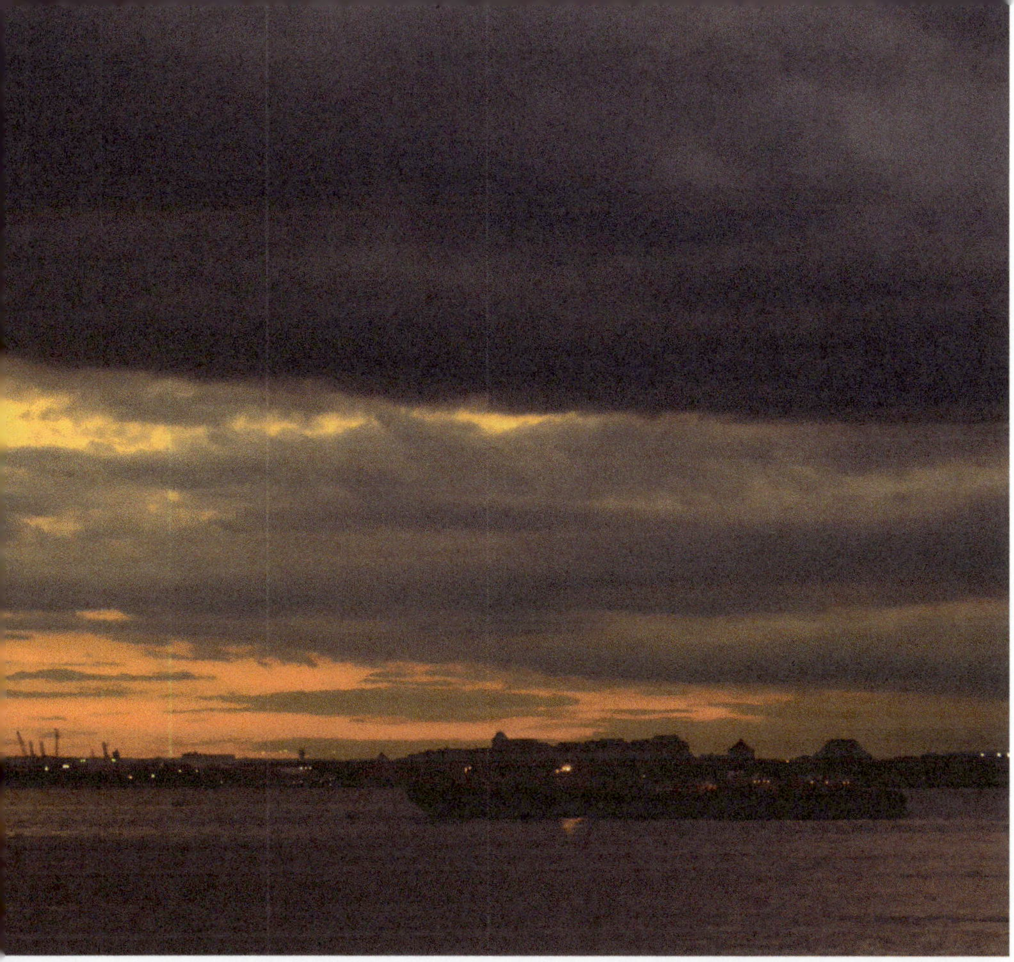

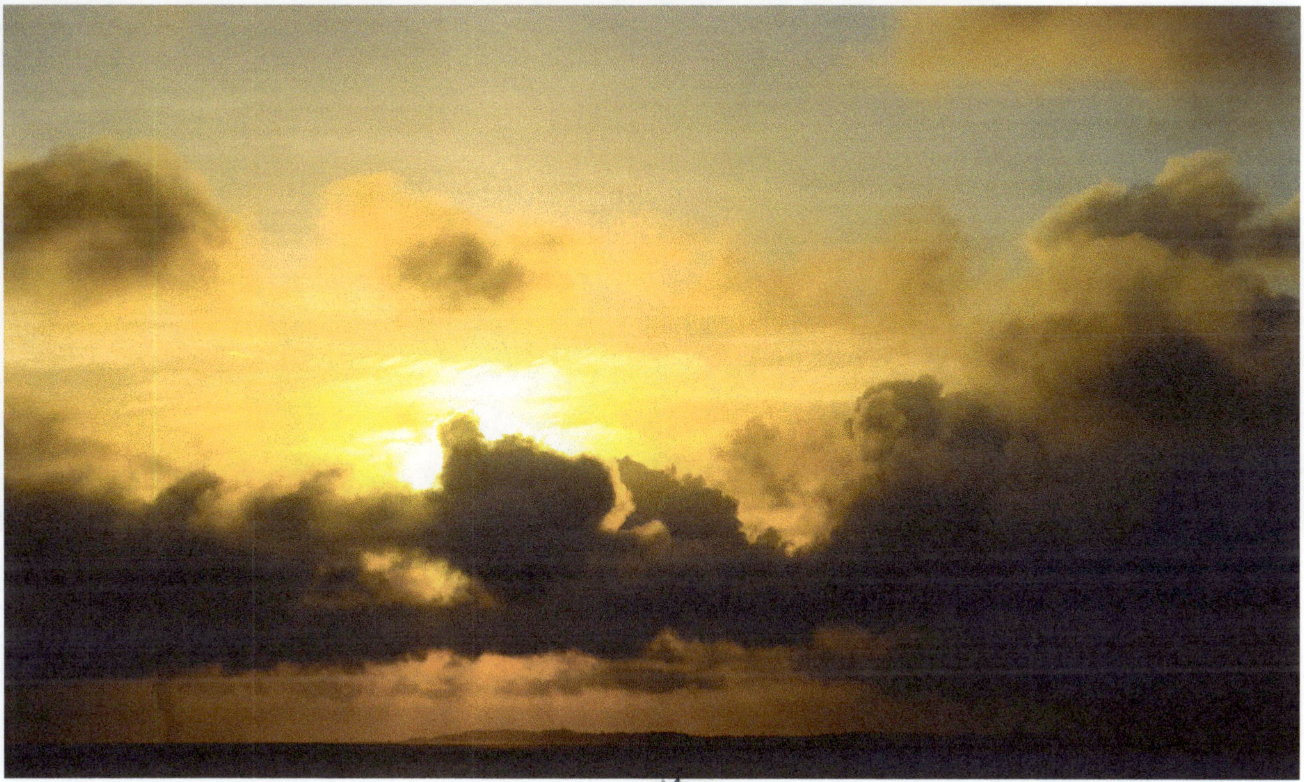

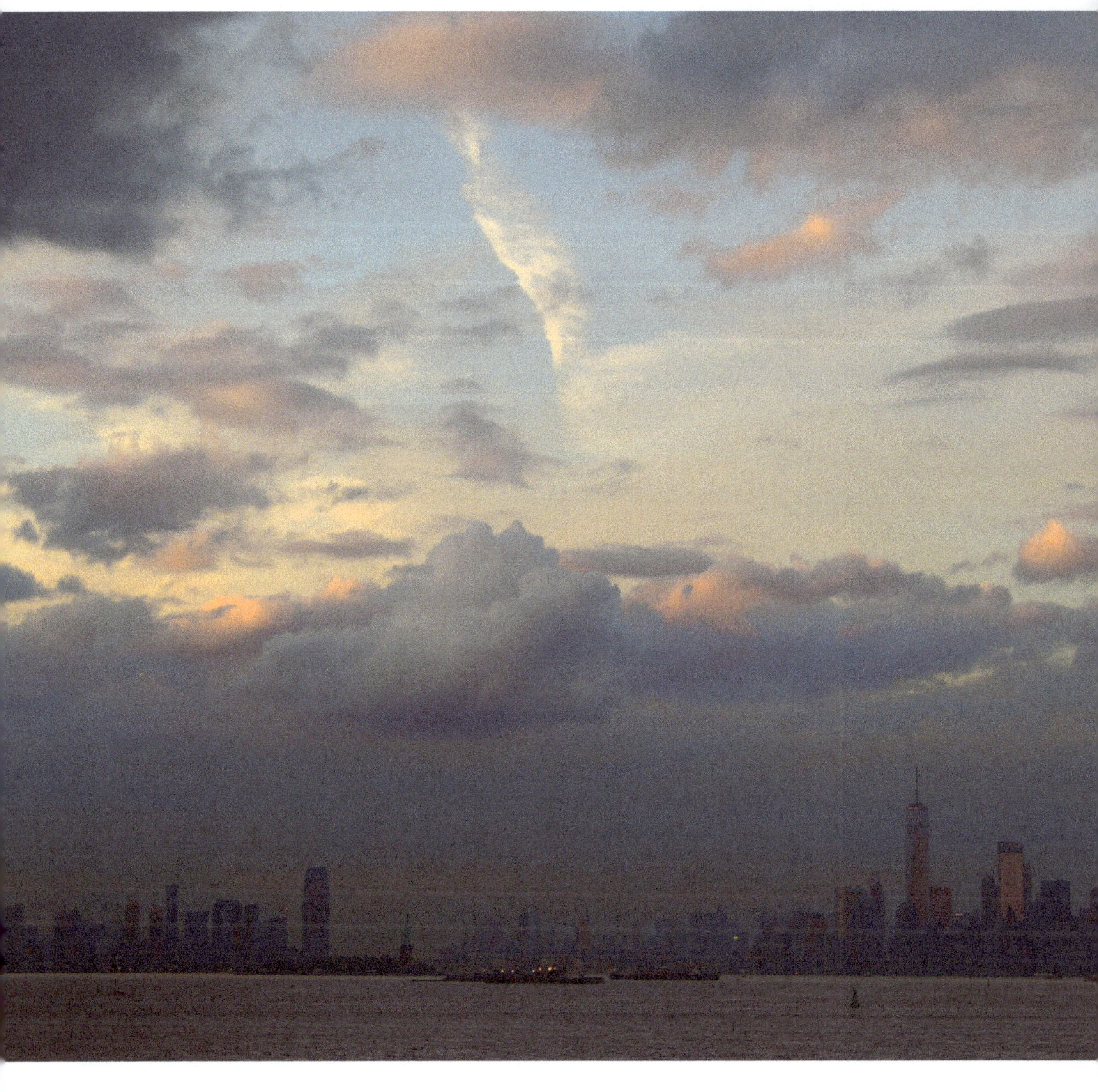

e chased the sun across his homeland. He had to see every shape, every way
transformed the world as it rose and set each day. He would not look away
d risk missing a single detail.

s completion left him feeling both refreshed and sad. In the midst of such
agic and beauty, it didn't matter that people didn't see him, really see him.
didn't matter that he often felt invisible and misunderstood.

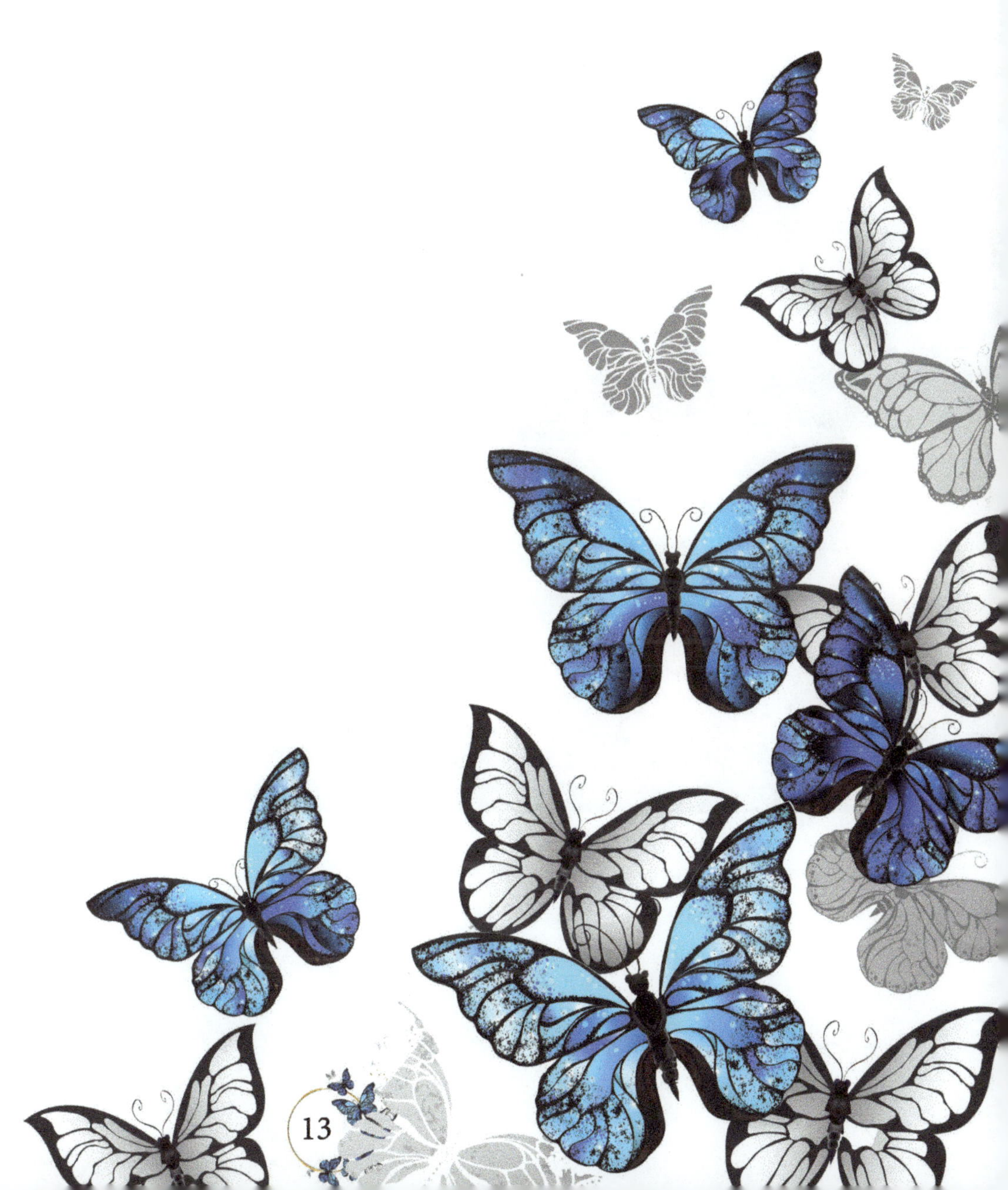

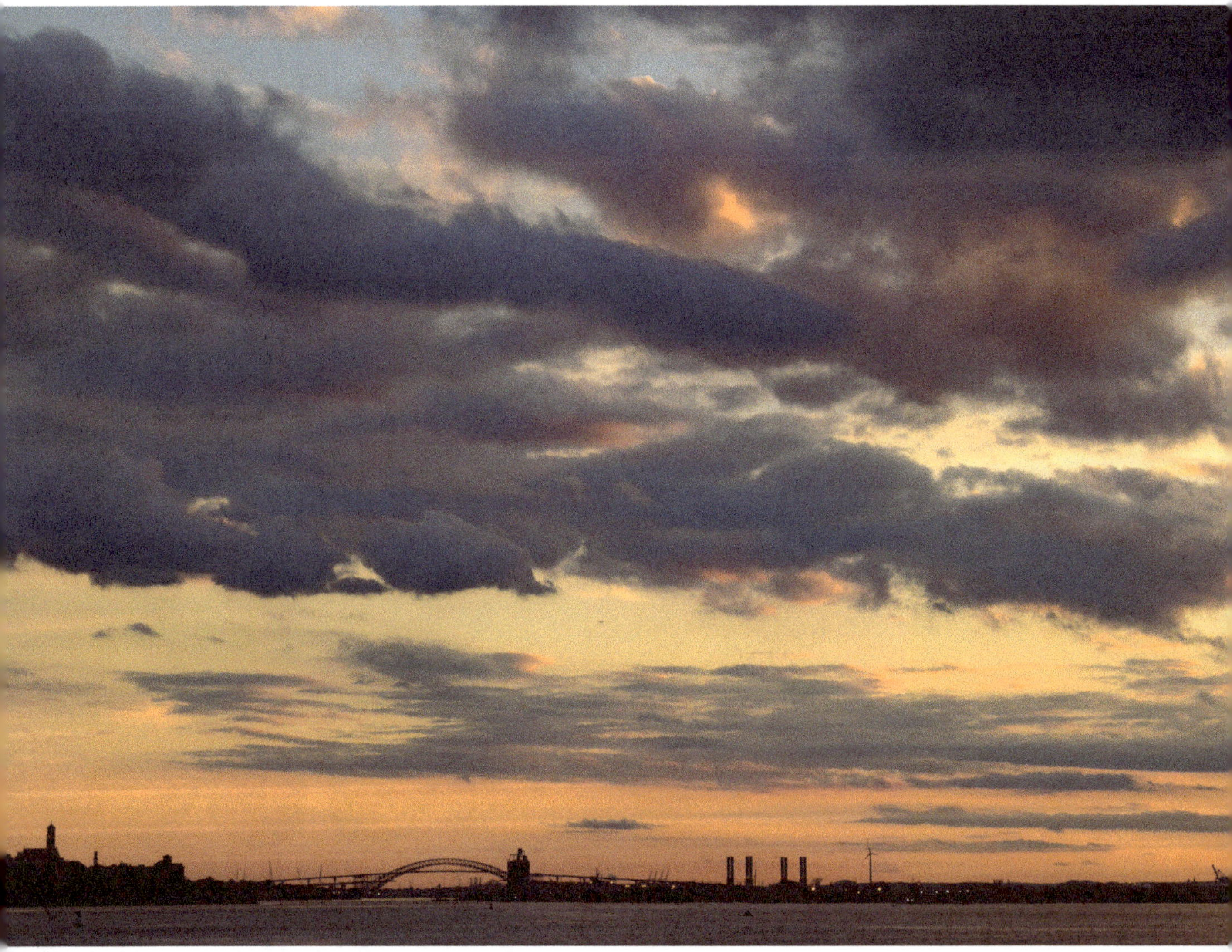

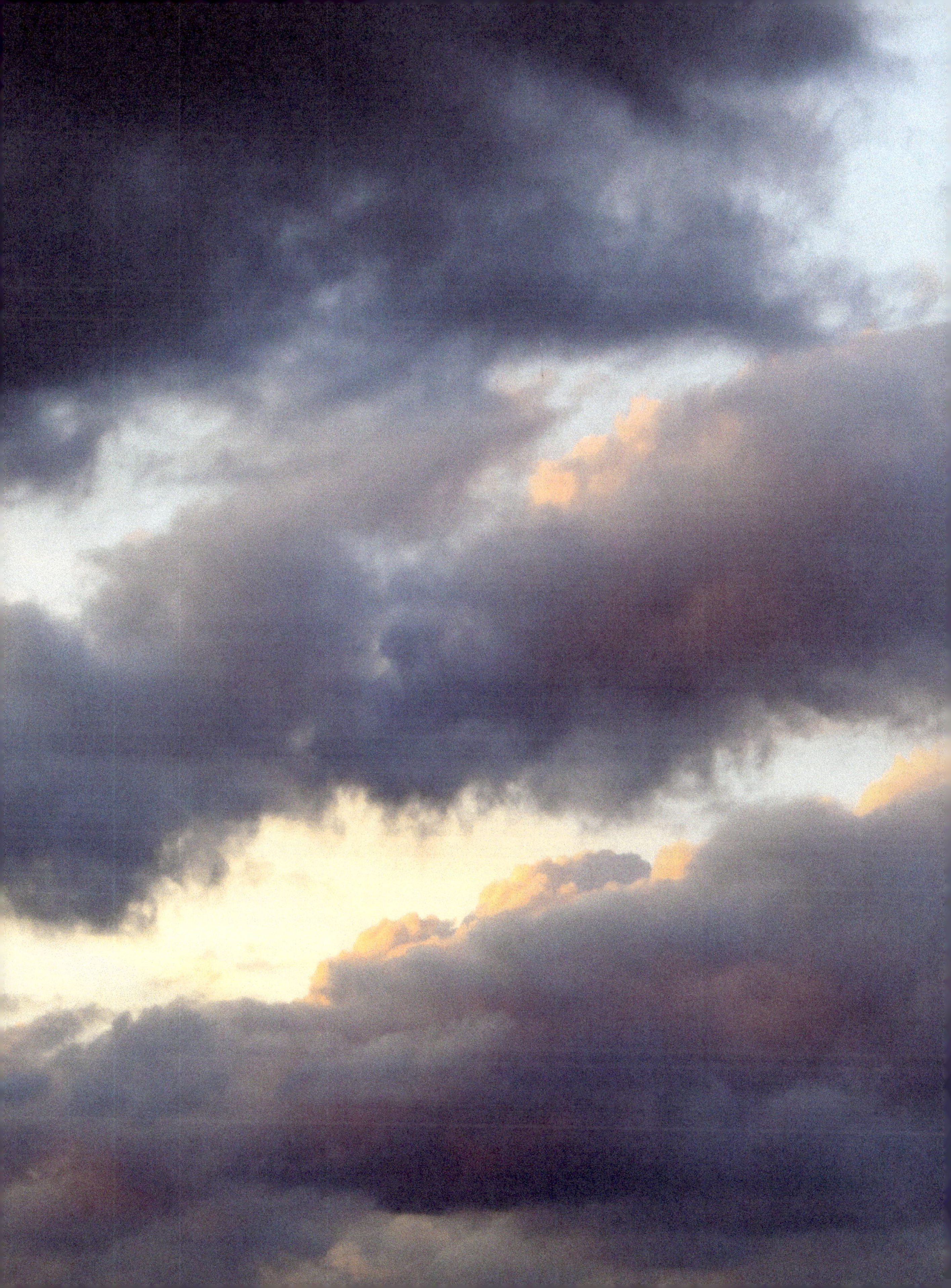

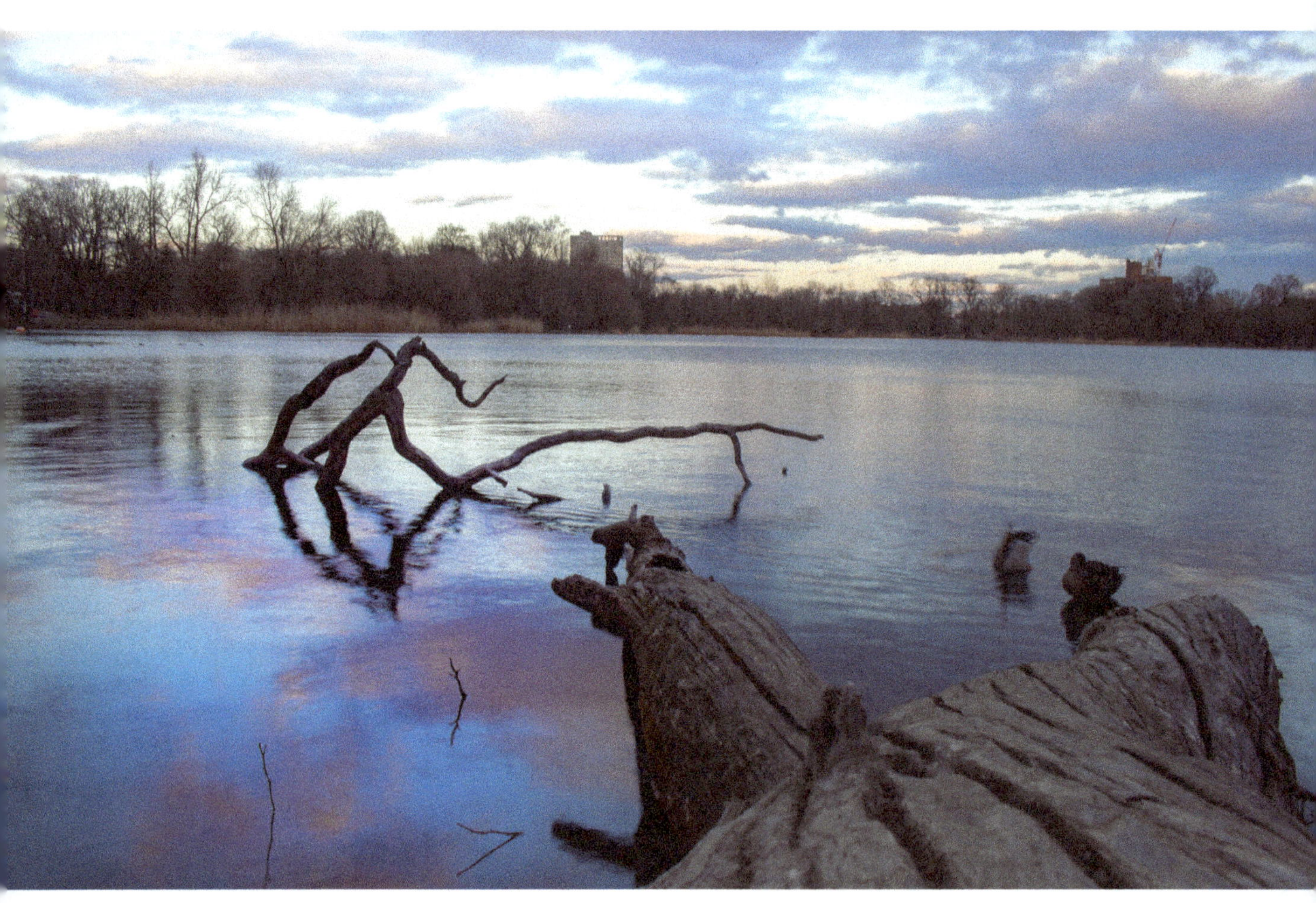

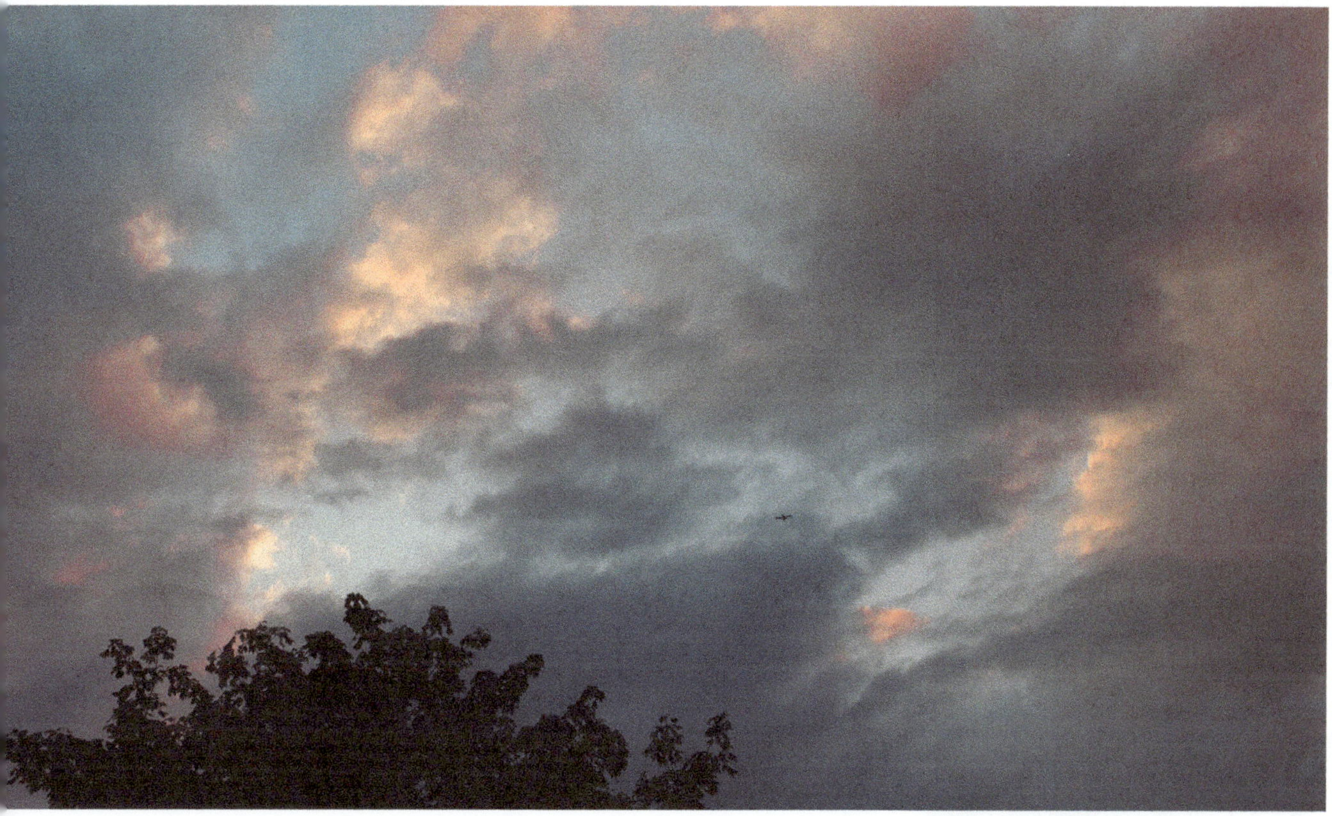

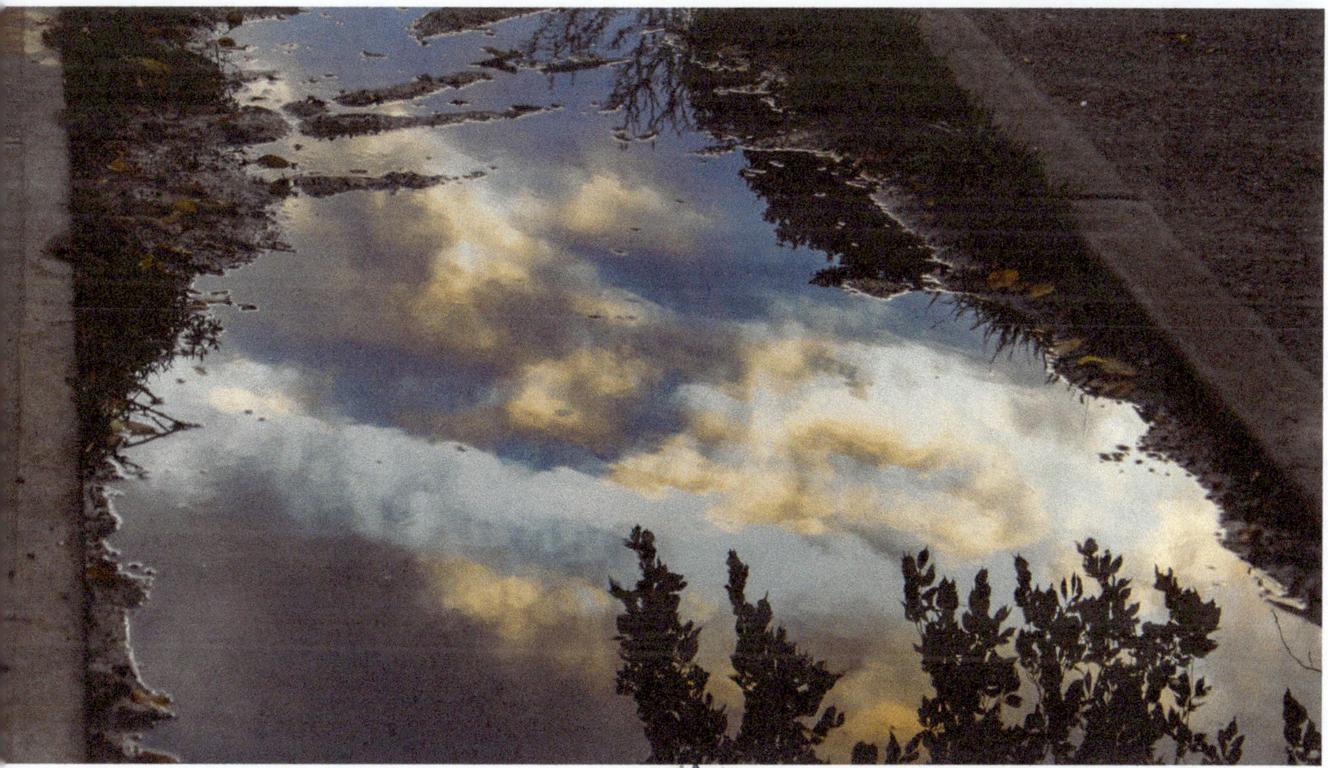

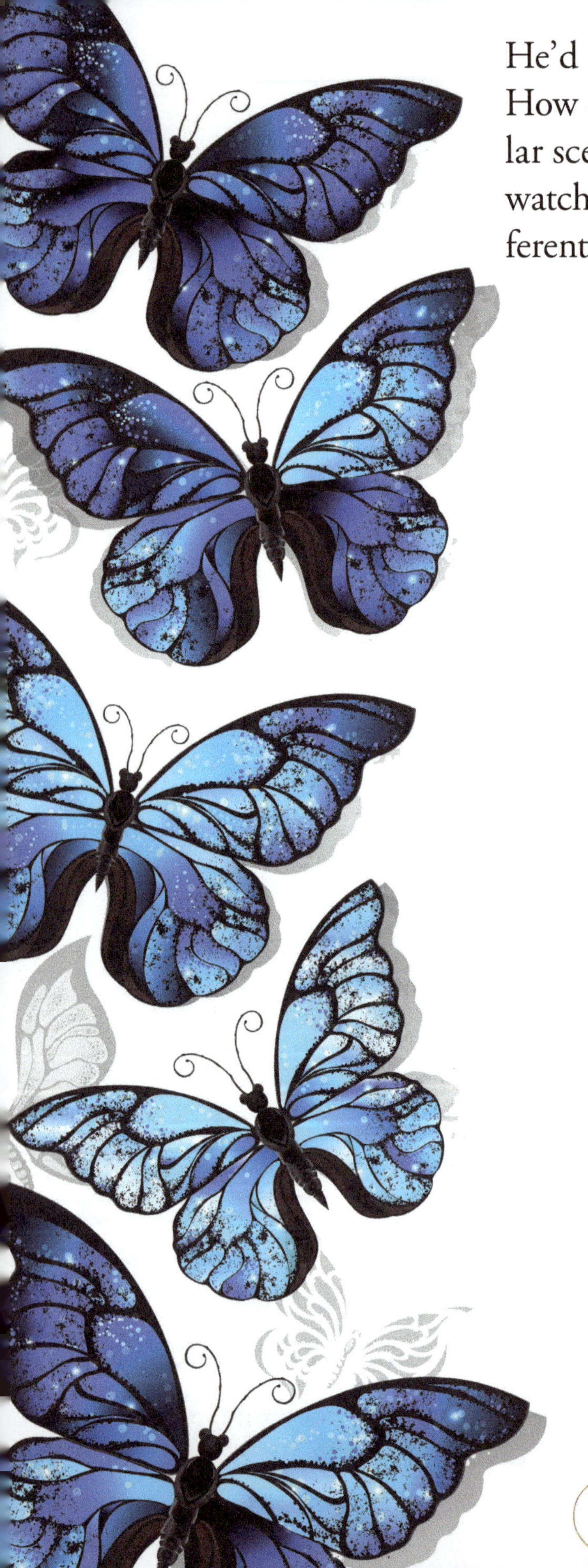

He'd get lost in its endless array of colors. How could anyone look at such a spectacular scene and not think of magic? You could watch the same sky for months and see a different sunset each time.

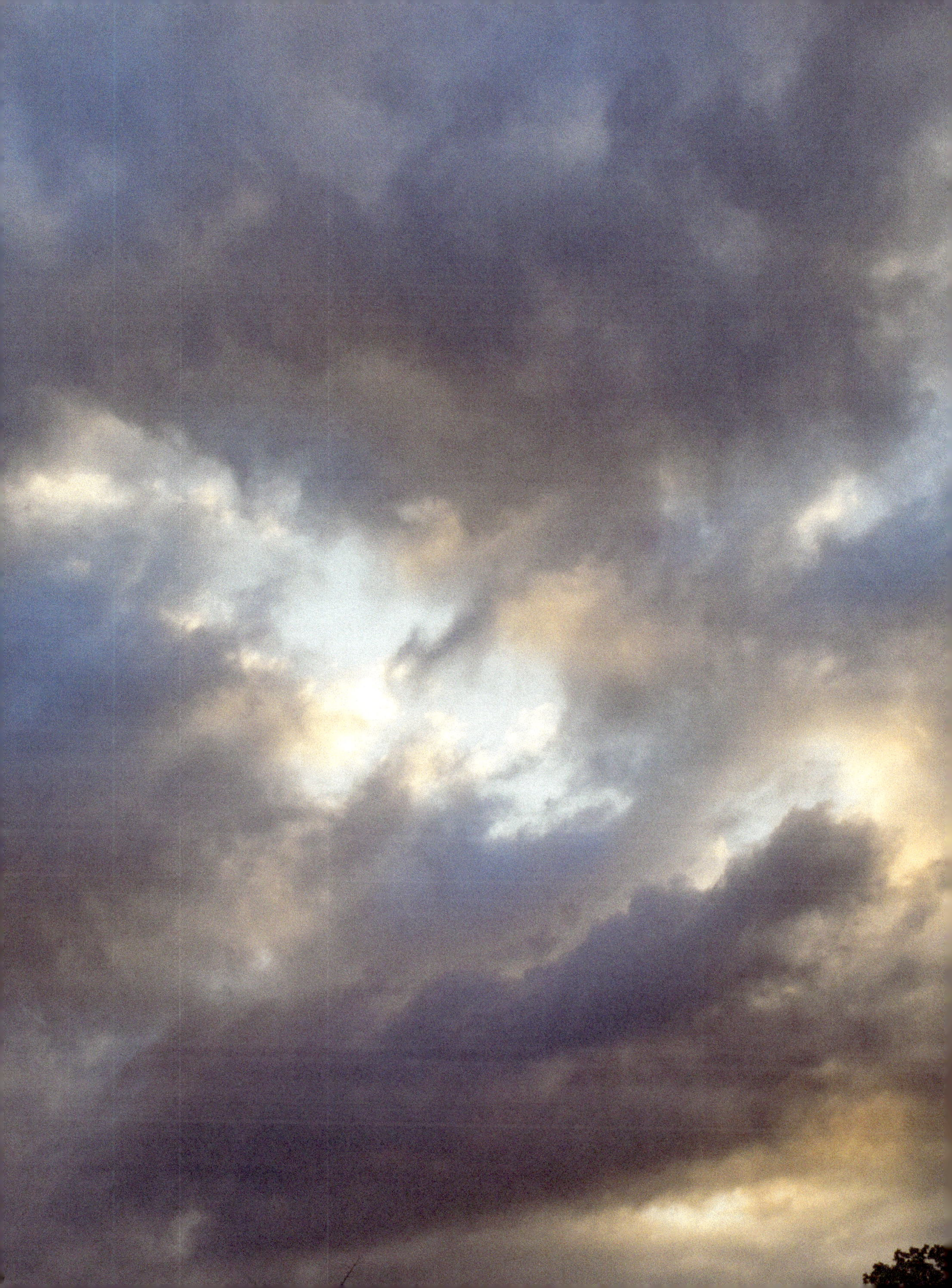

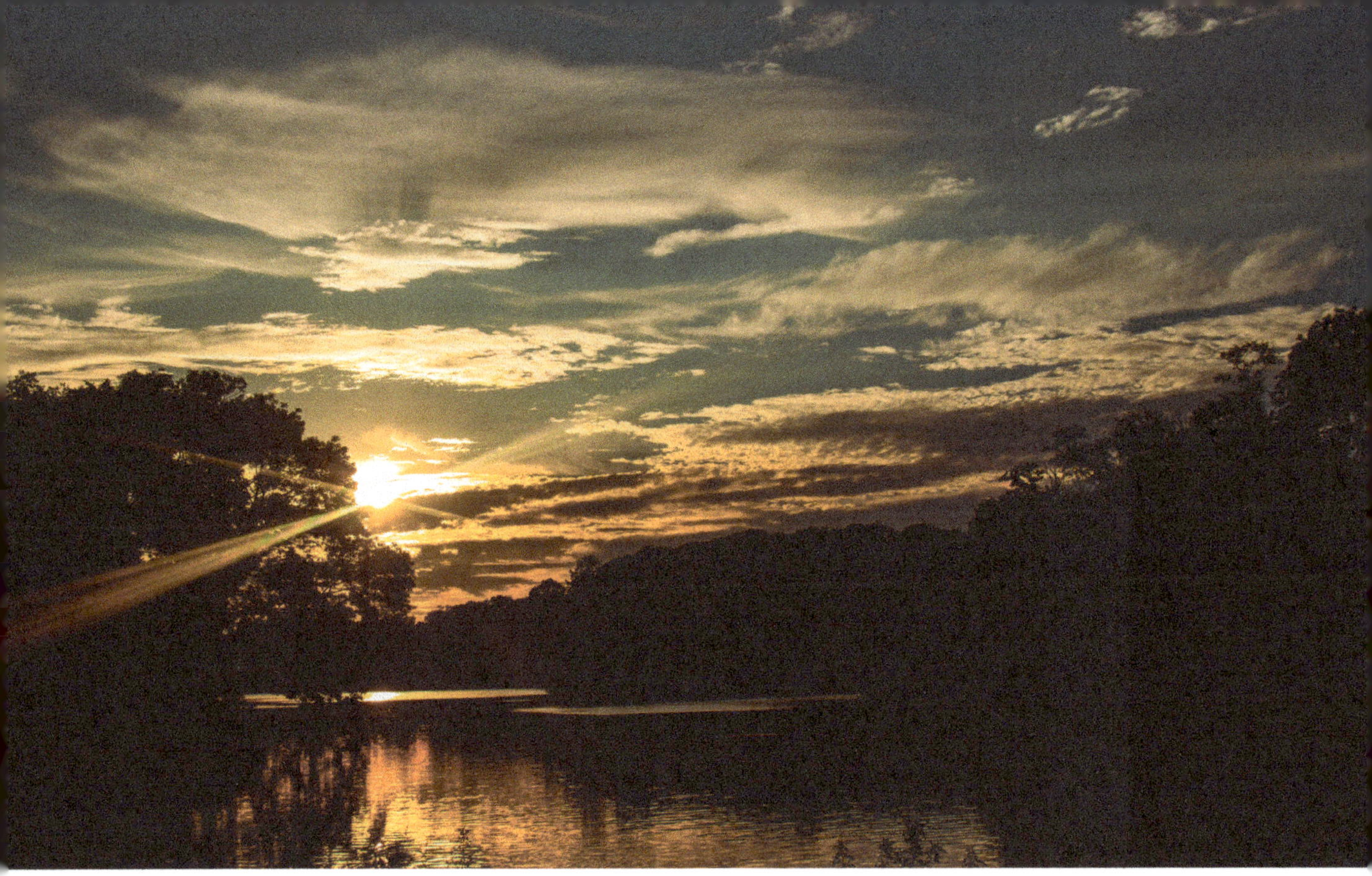

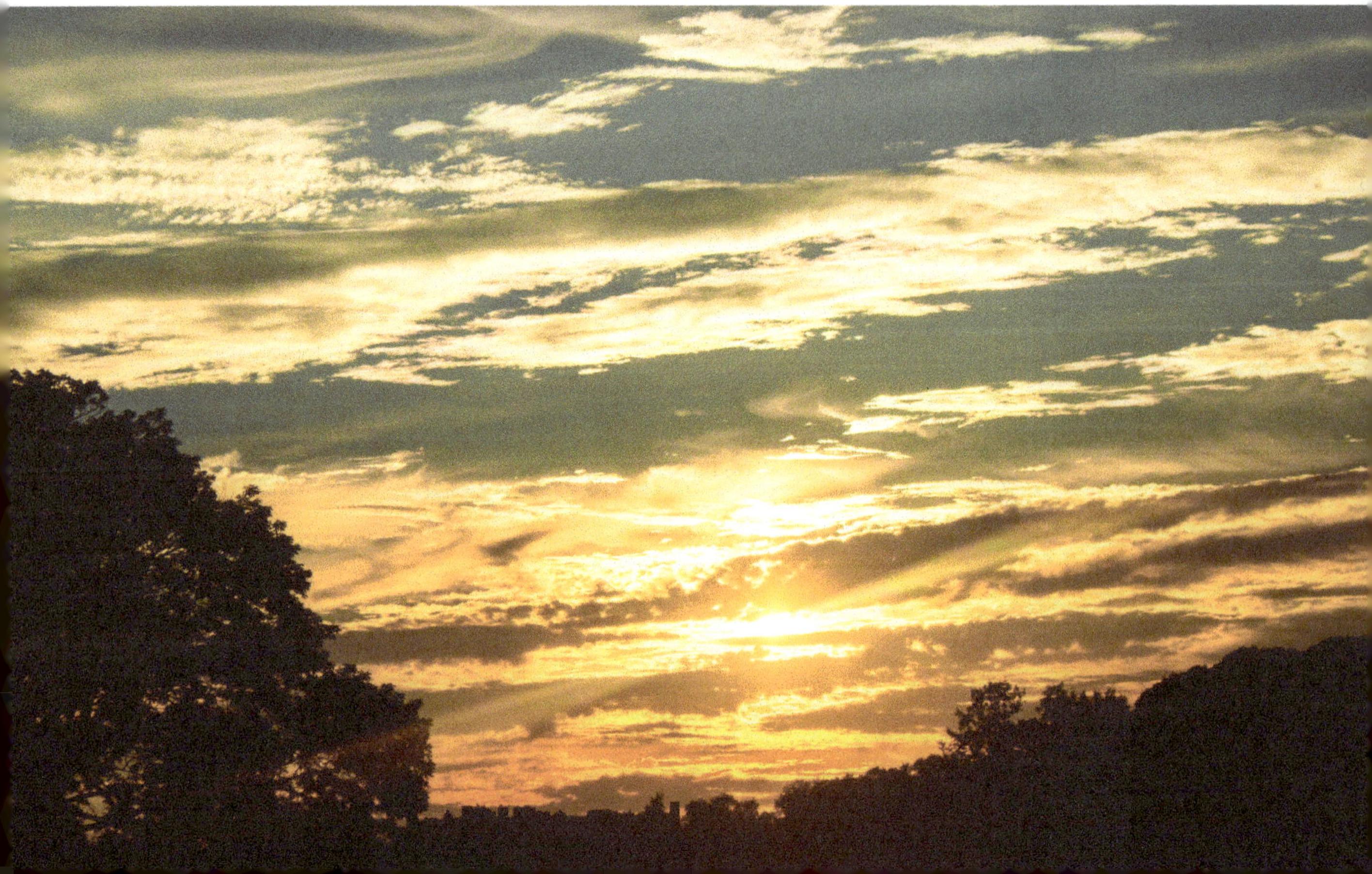

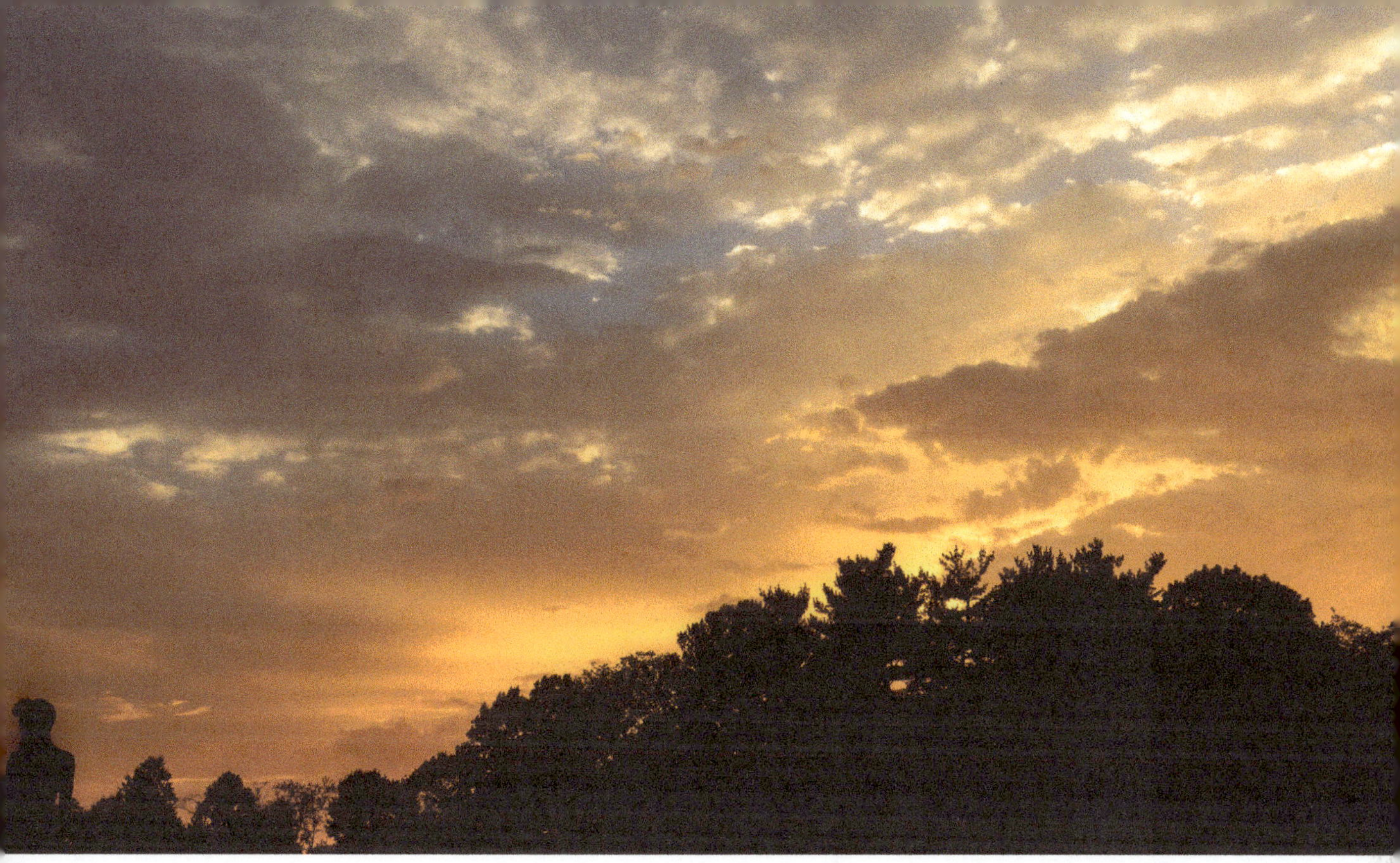

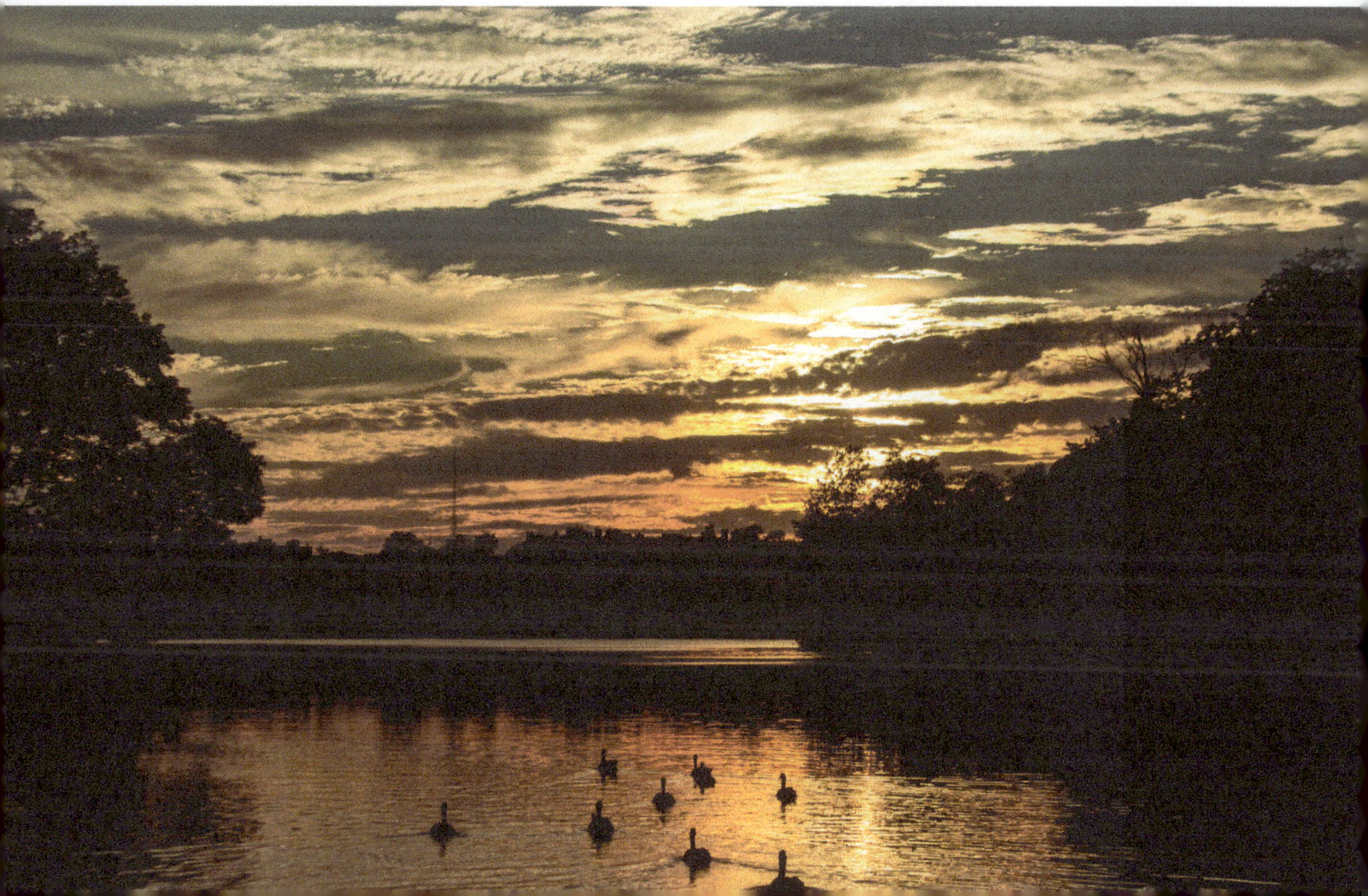

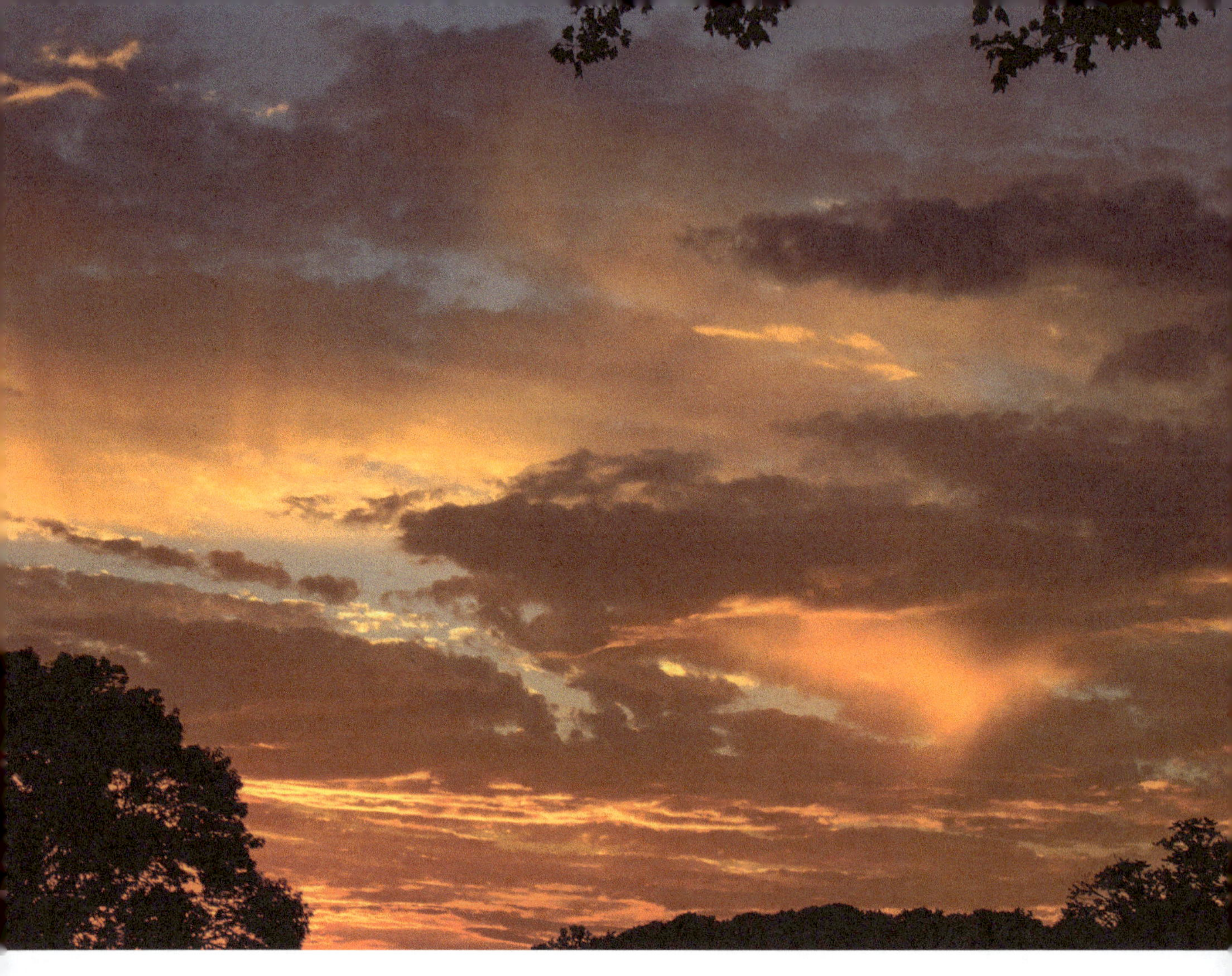

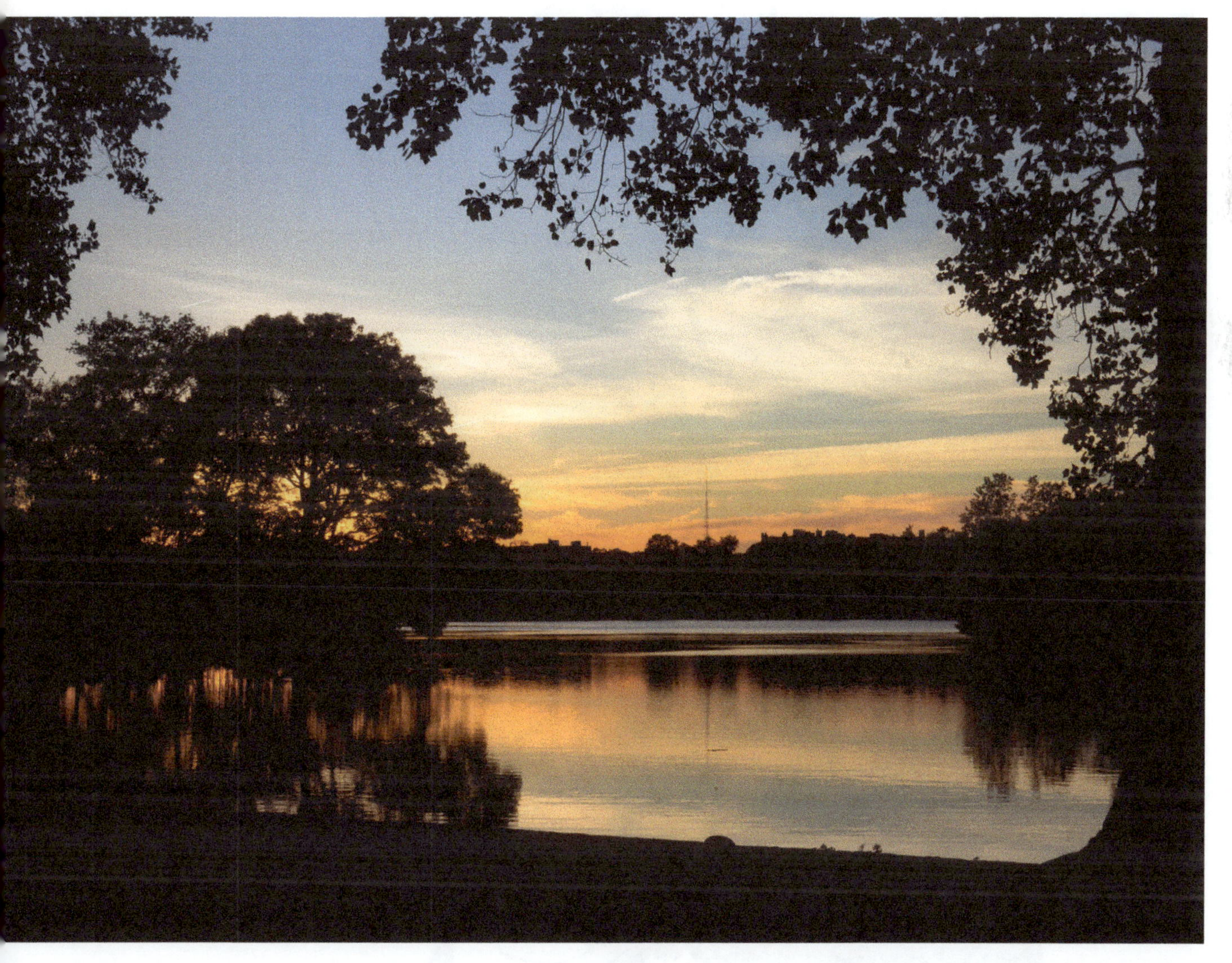

He loved folktales about the power living between dark and light. He especially enjoyed ones about doors to other worlds opening at sunrise or sunset.

What if those stories were true?

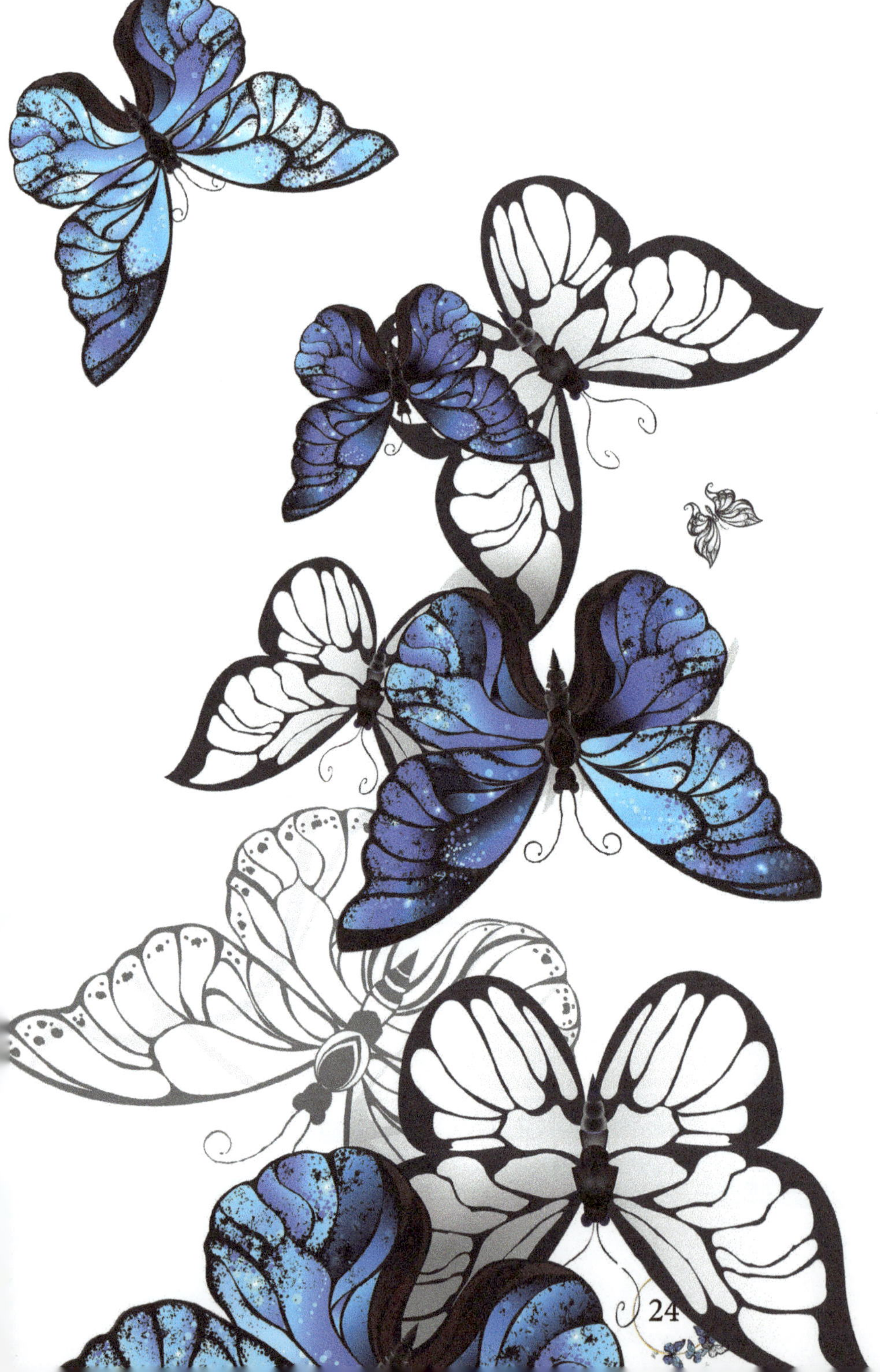

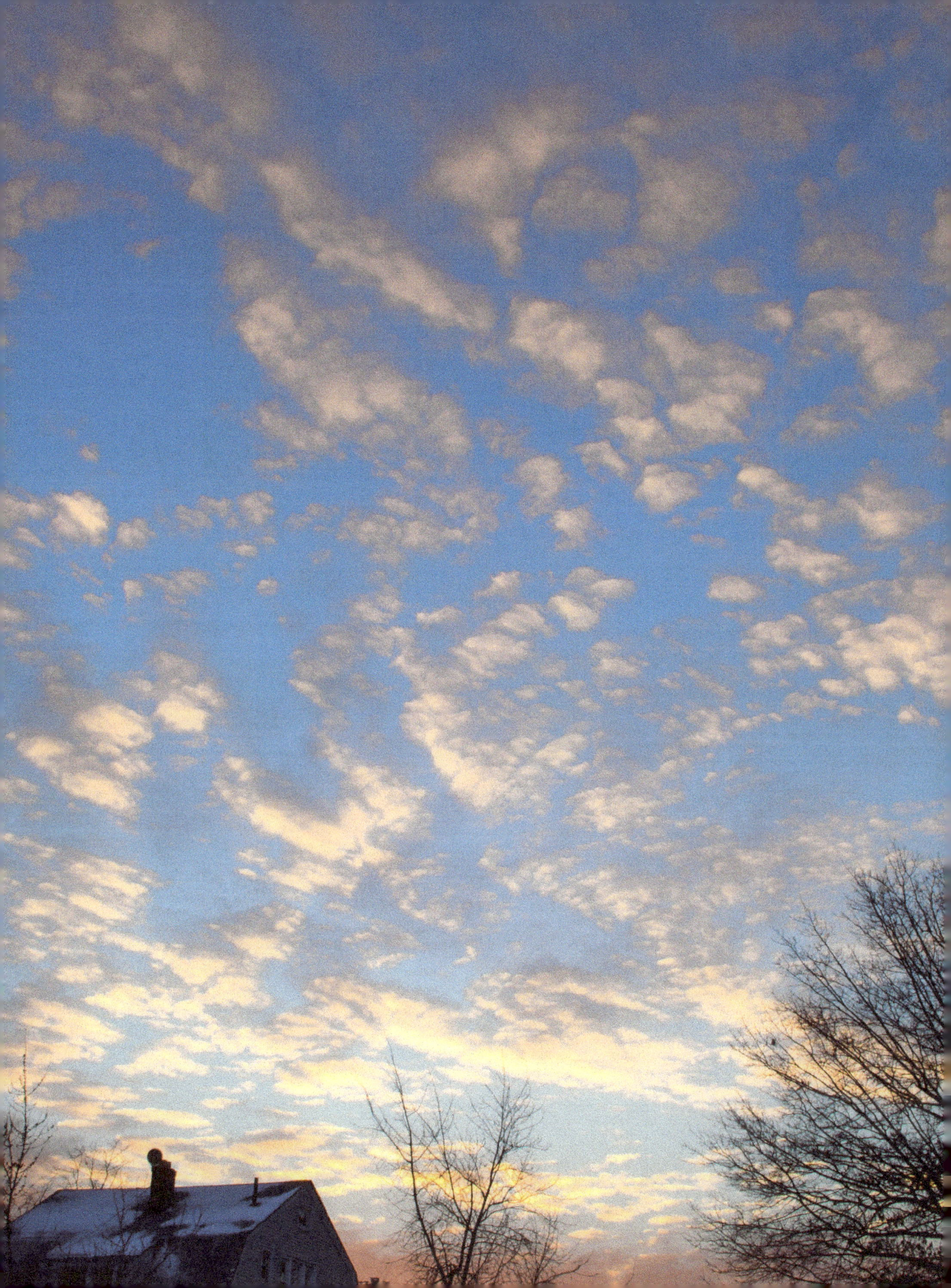

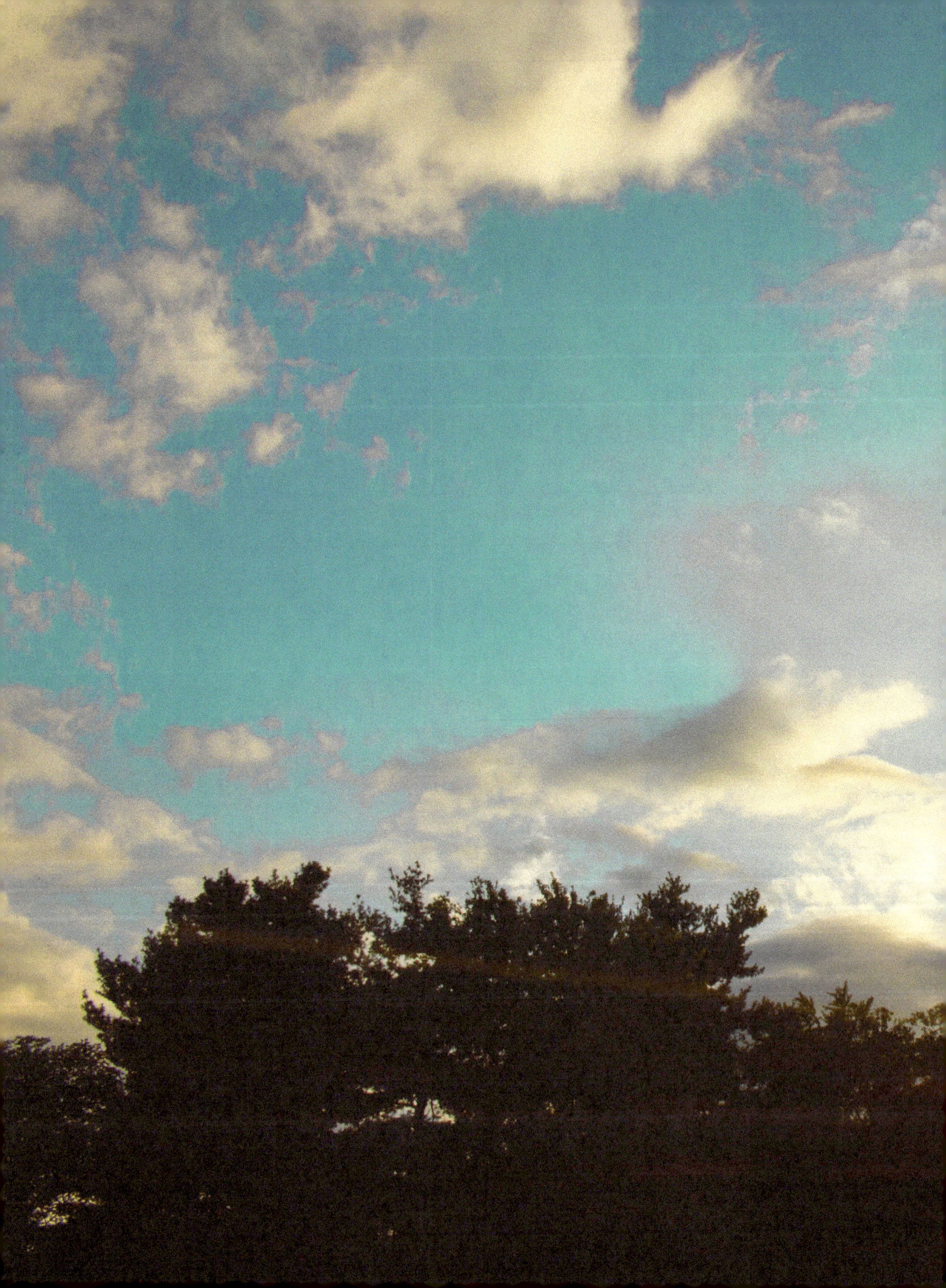

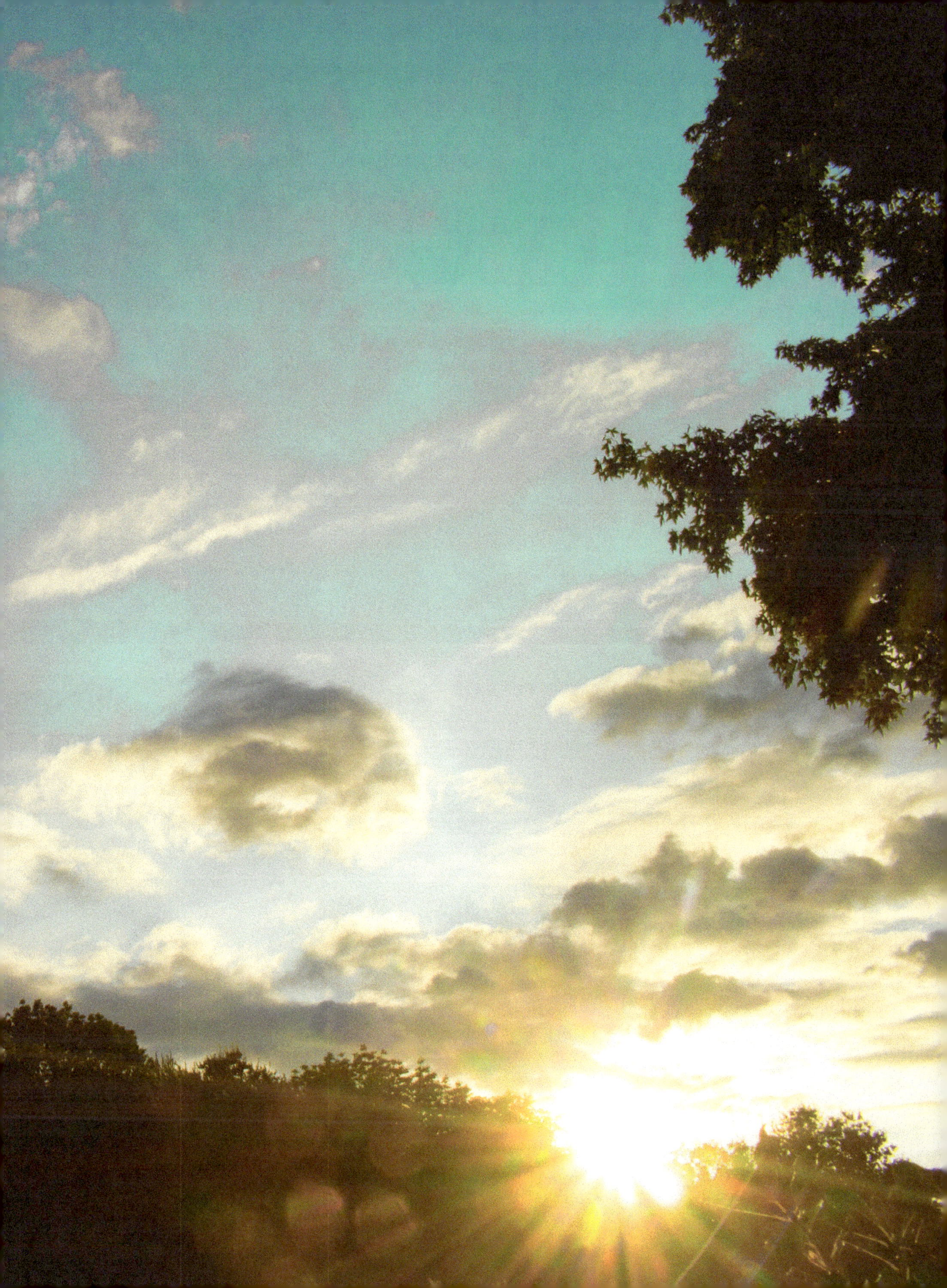

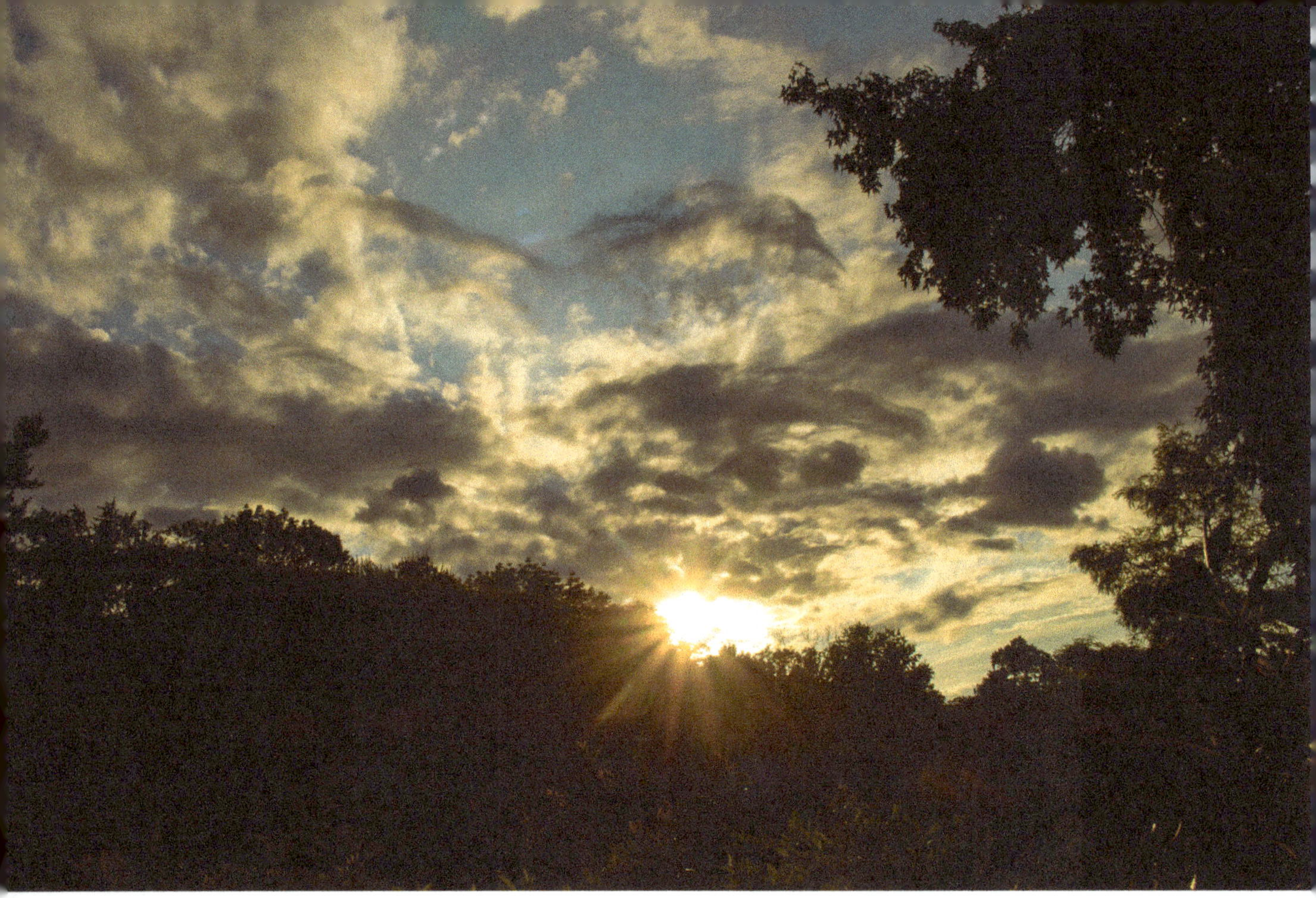

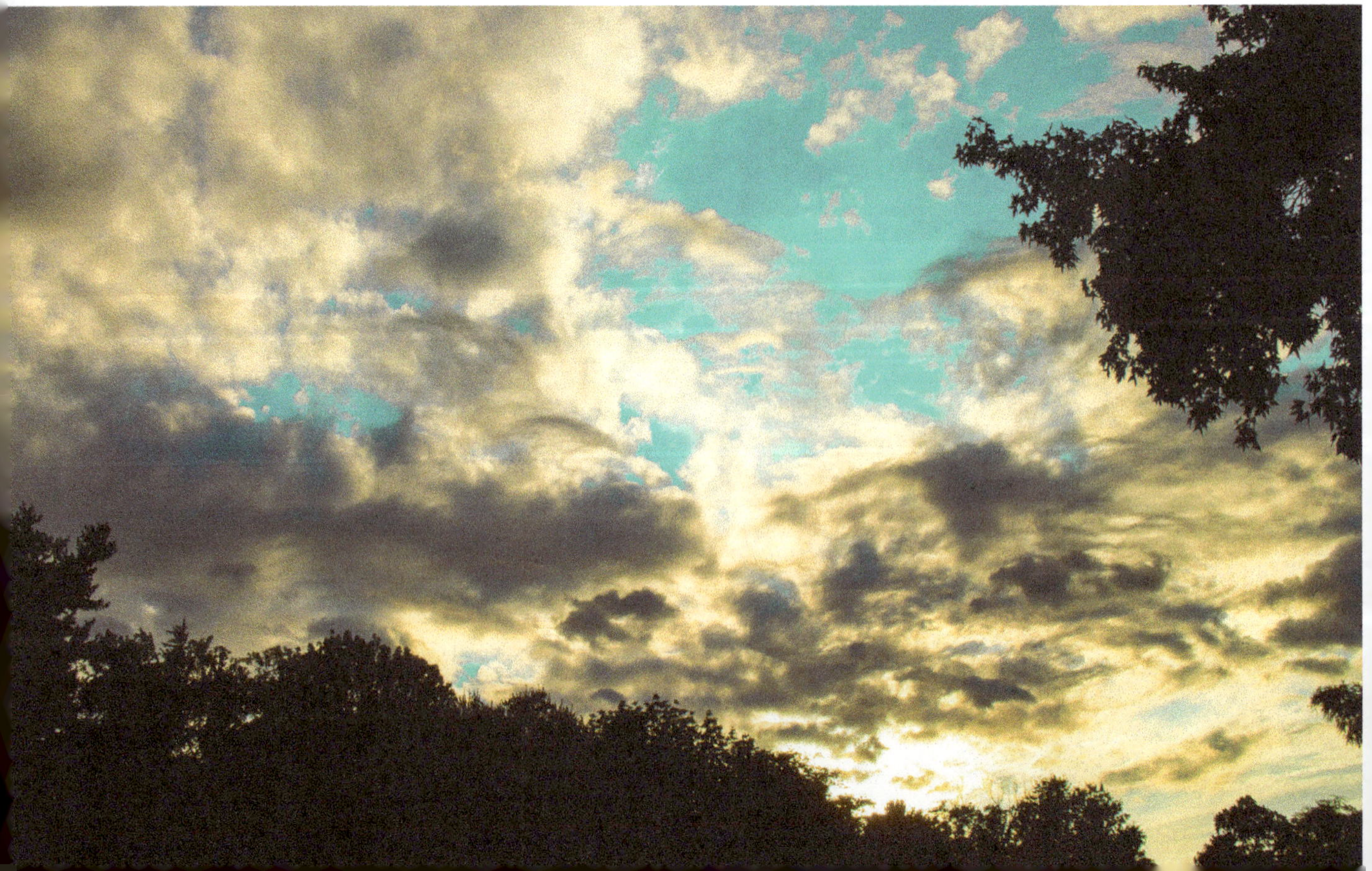

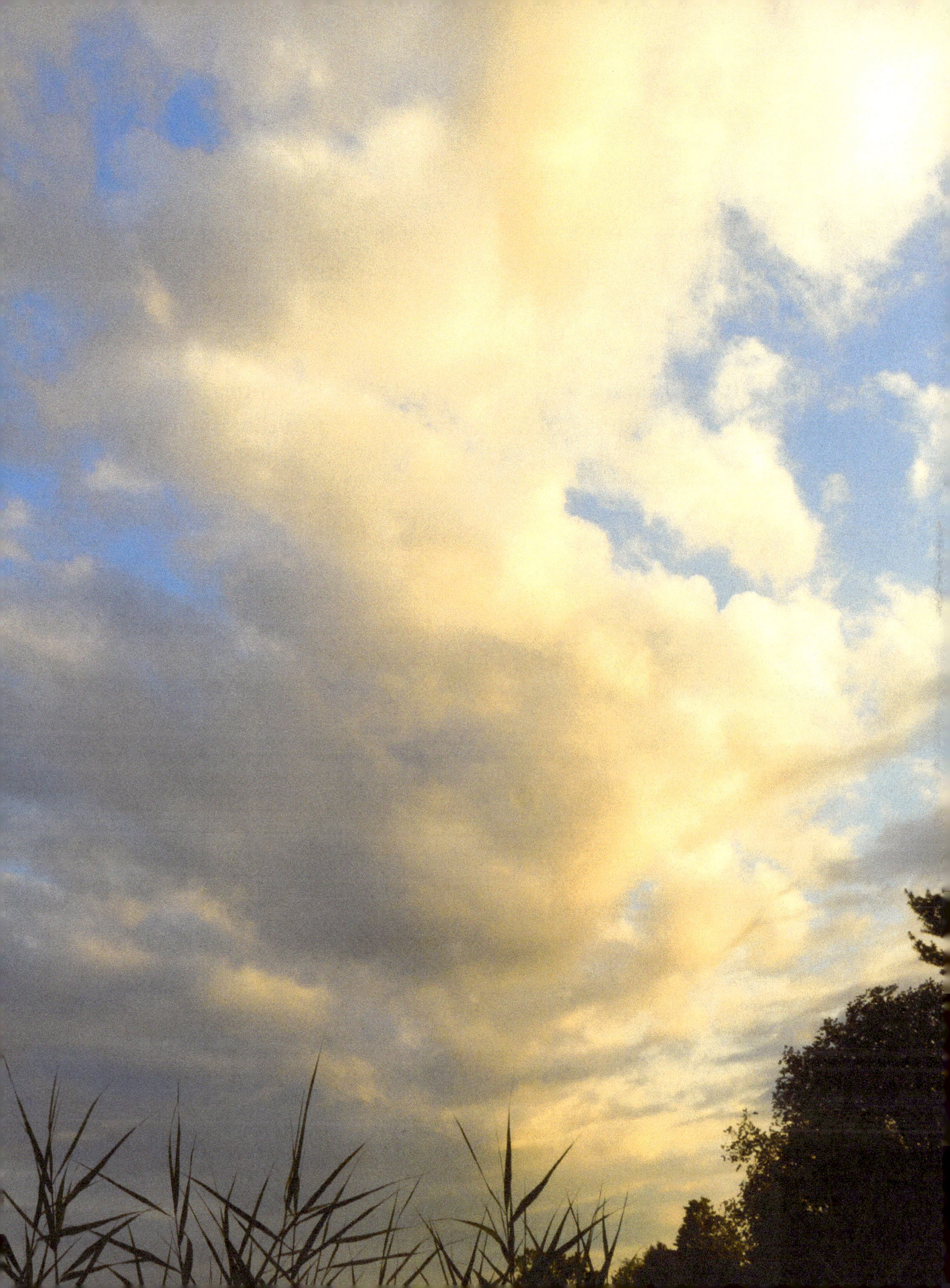

What if—what if— he wasn't looking at a natural phenomenon with a logical explanation? What if, during those times when dark and light mixed, he peeked into another world?

Some truth had to be buried in those old stories. People believed in other worlds, places they could only see when night and day overlapped.

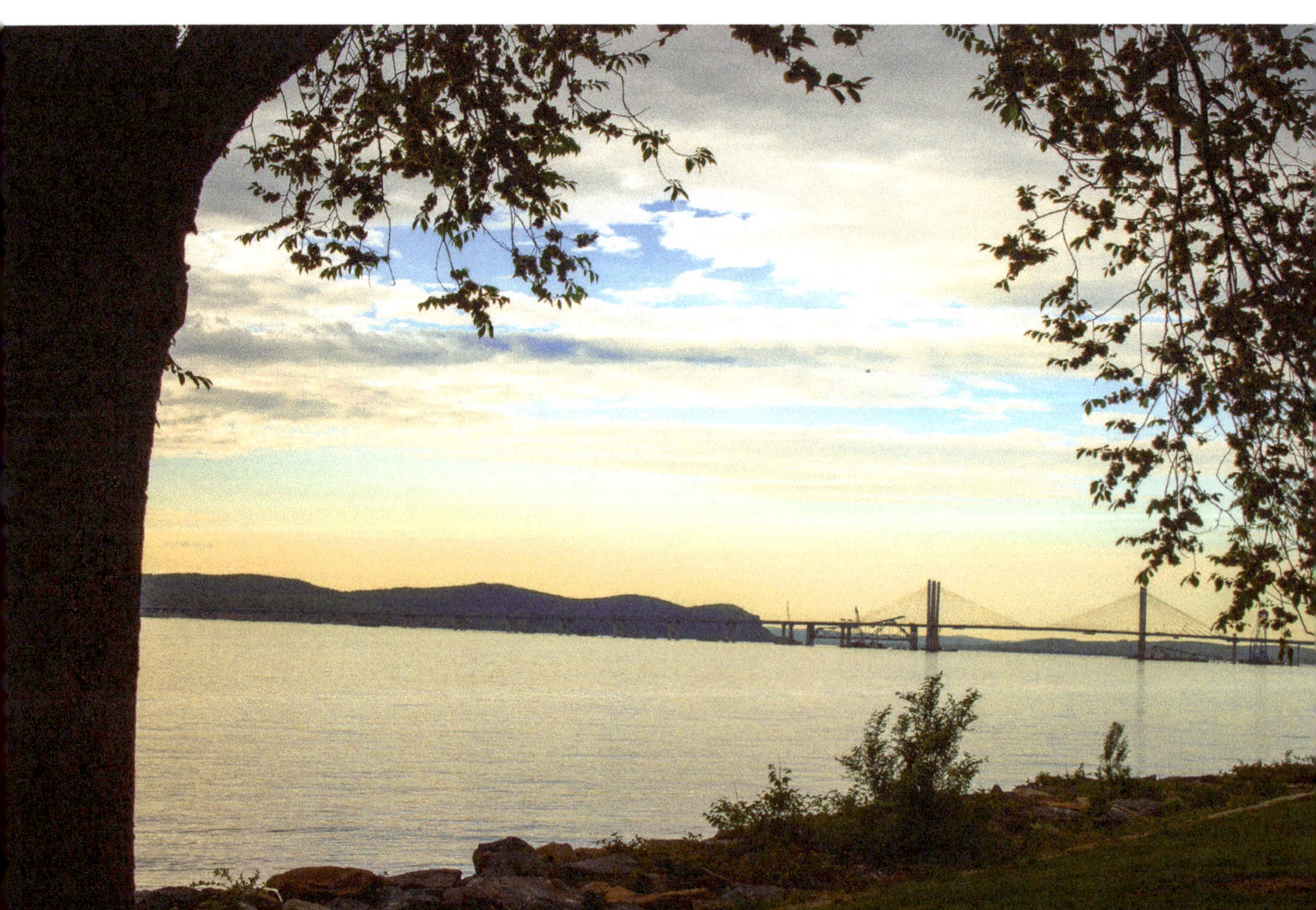

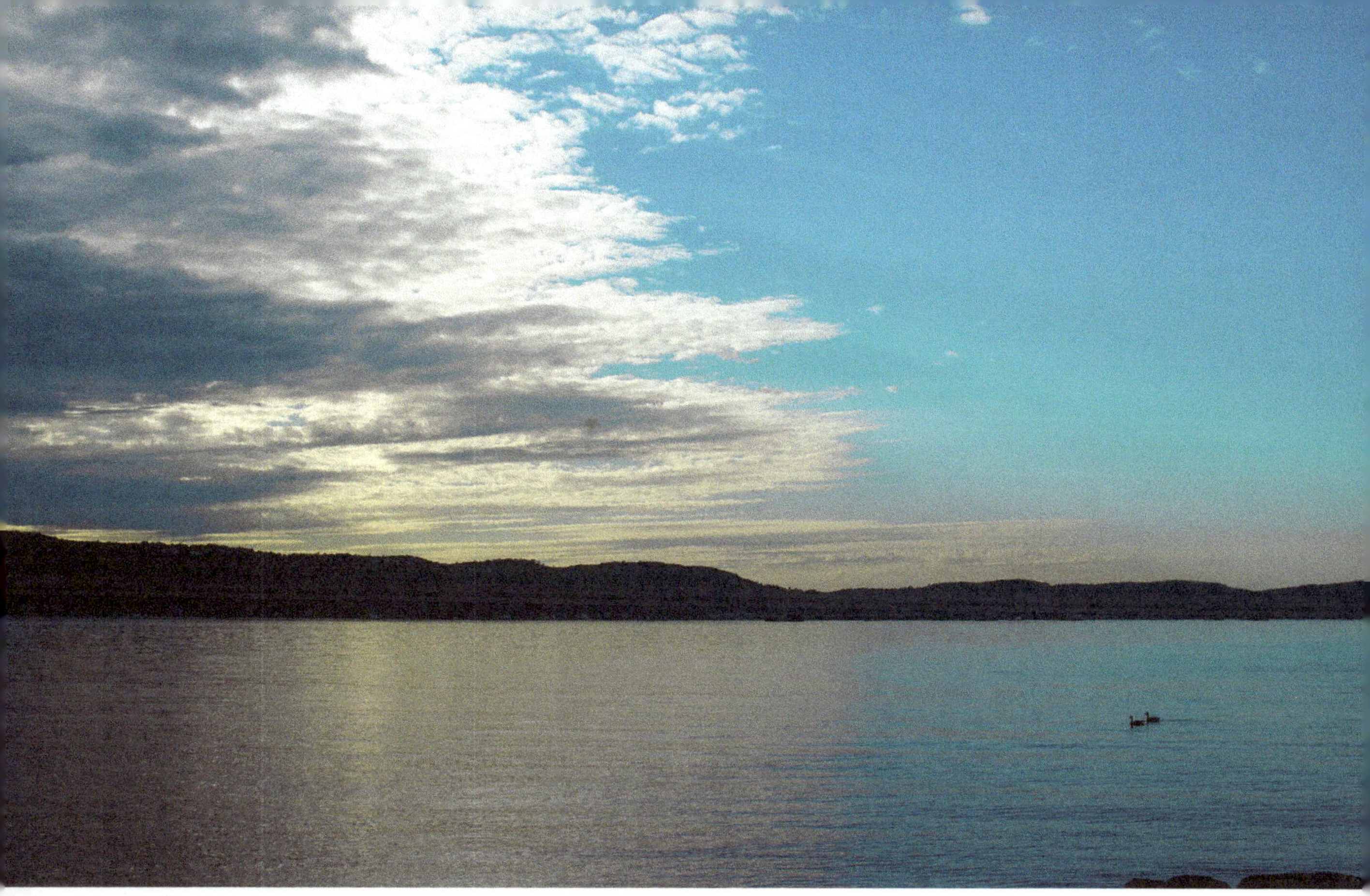

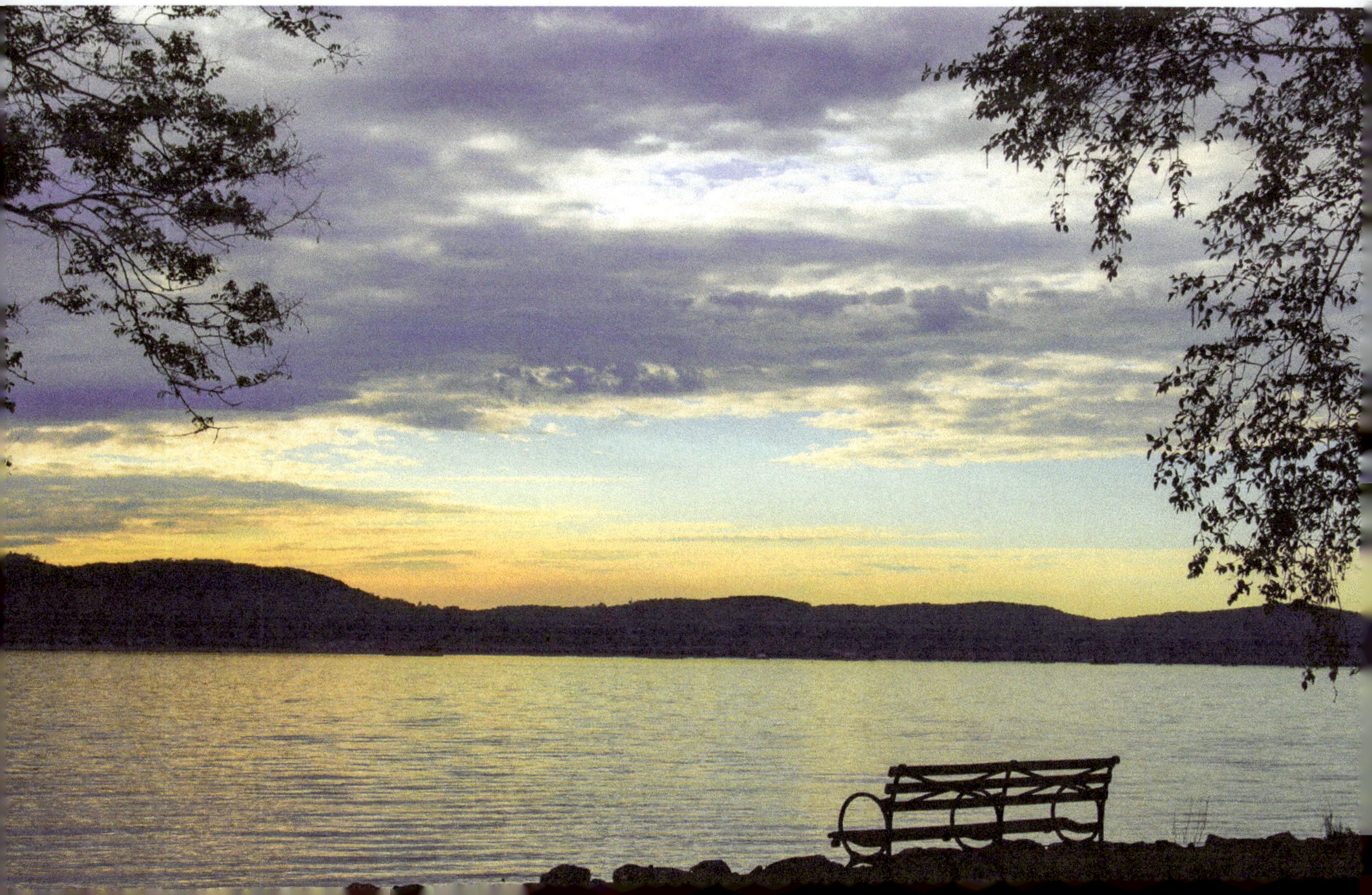

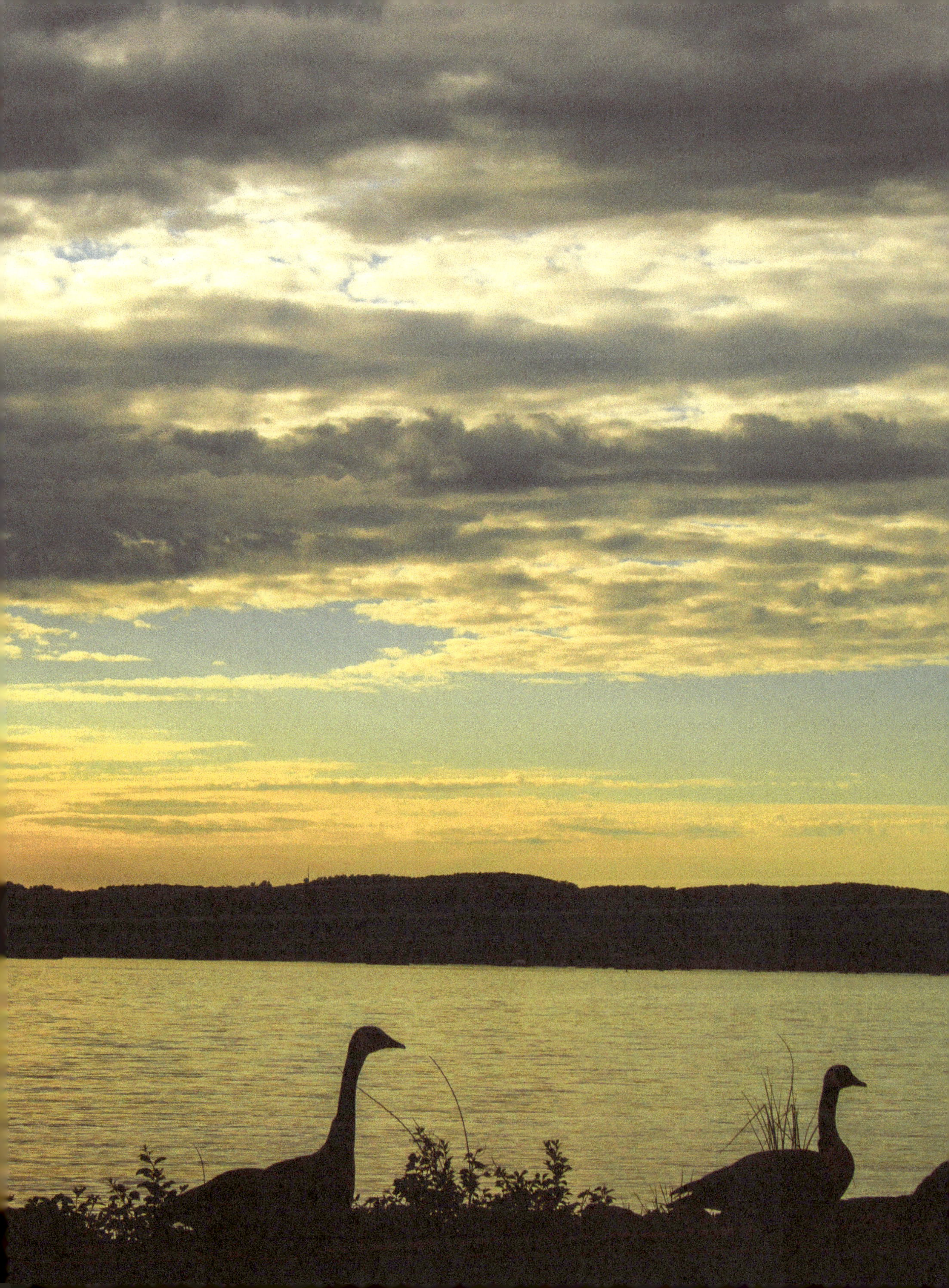

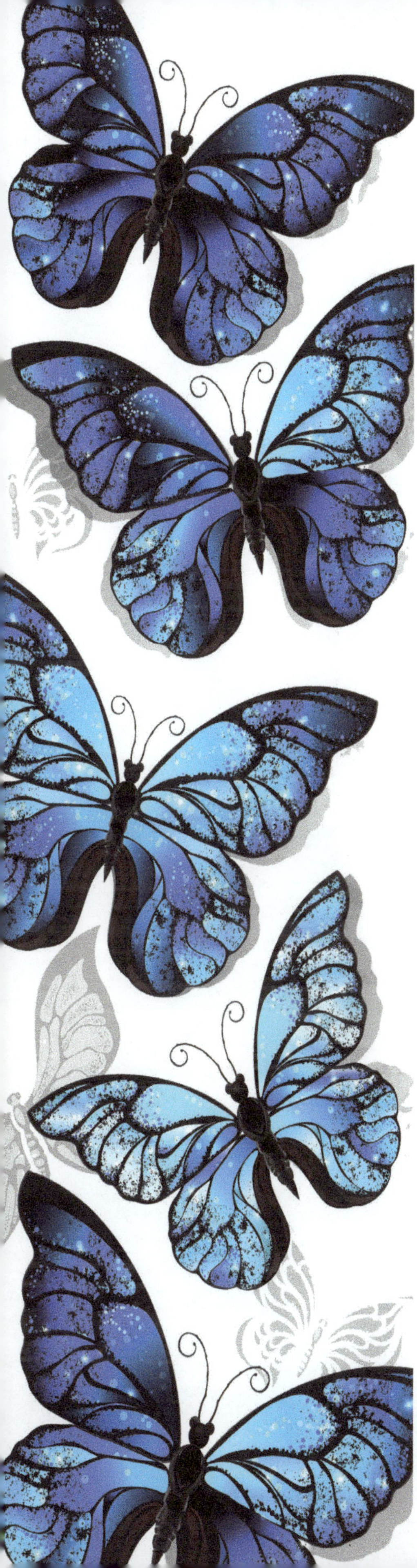

It was a nice dream. Who didn't sometimes wish to escape to another world, if only for a moment? Those people didn't drown in such imaginings, didn't plot courses and examine maps and stories for potential locations.

He had to be normal. He had to chase what normal people pursued. He needed to be realistic.

But, but, was it so wrong to dream?

What if—

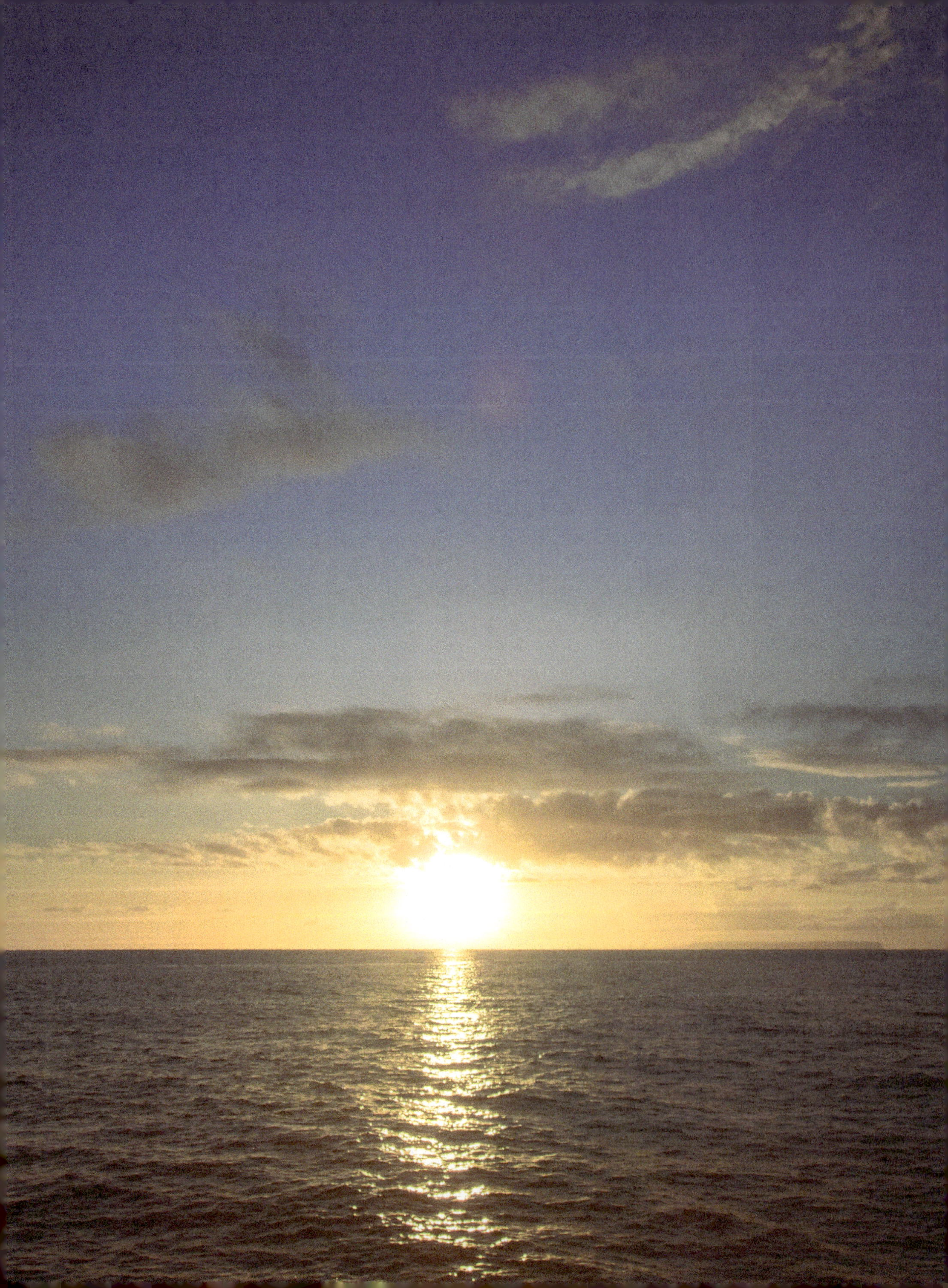

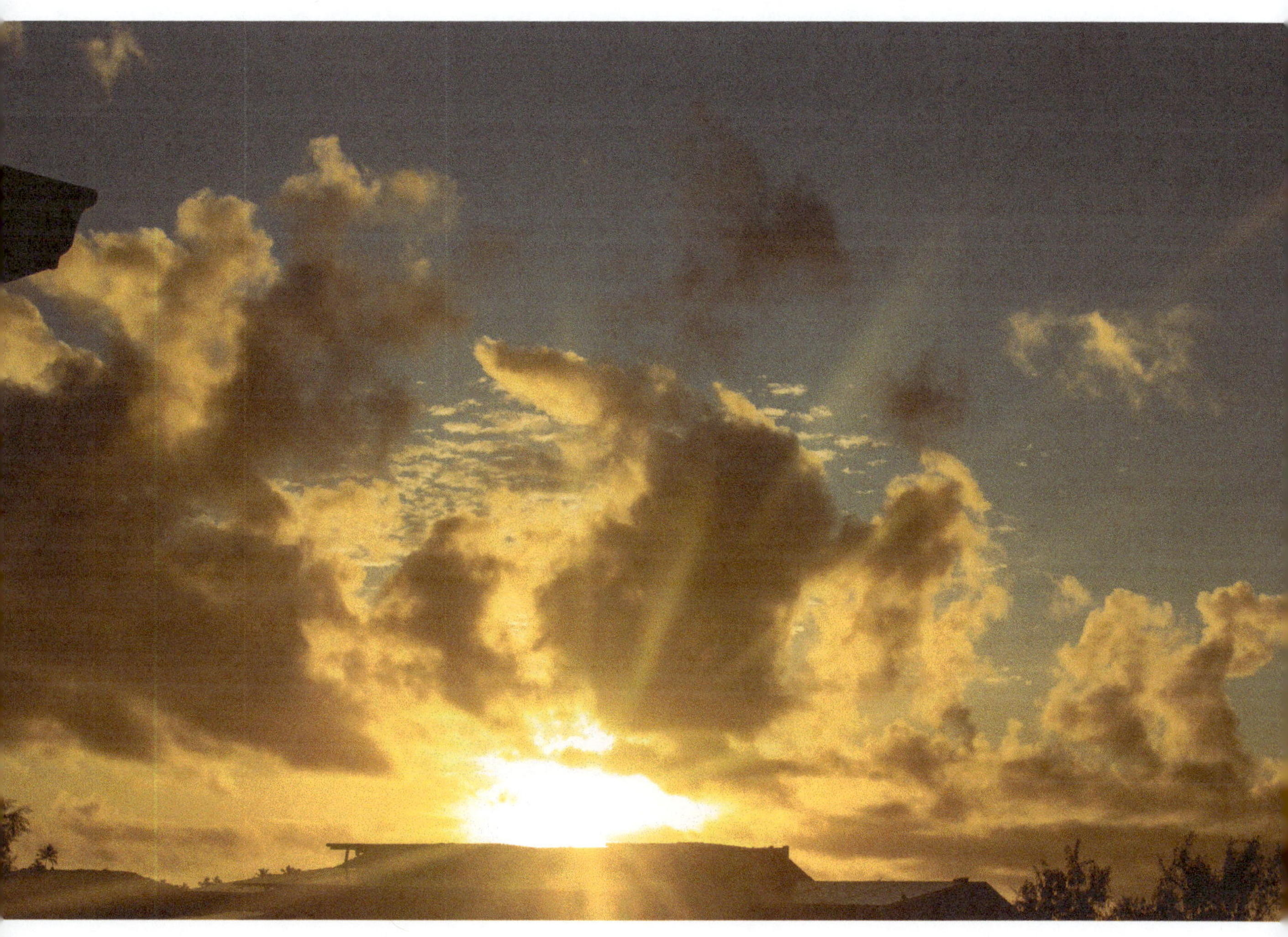

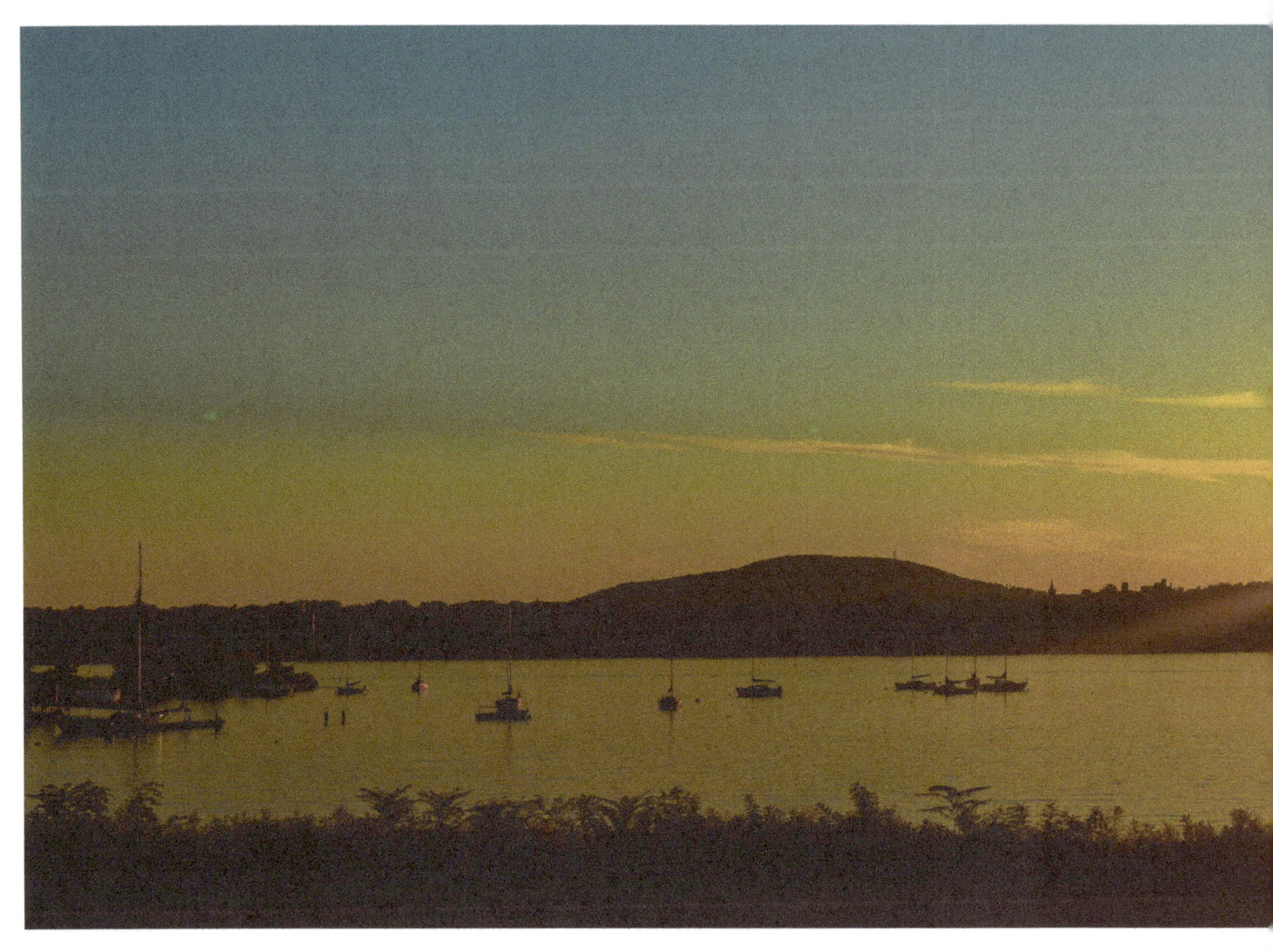

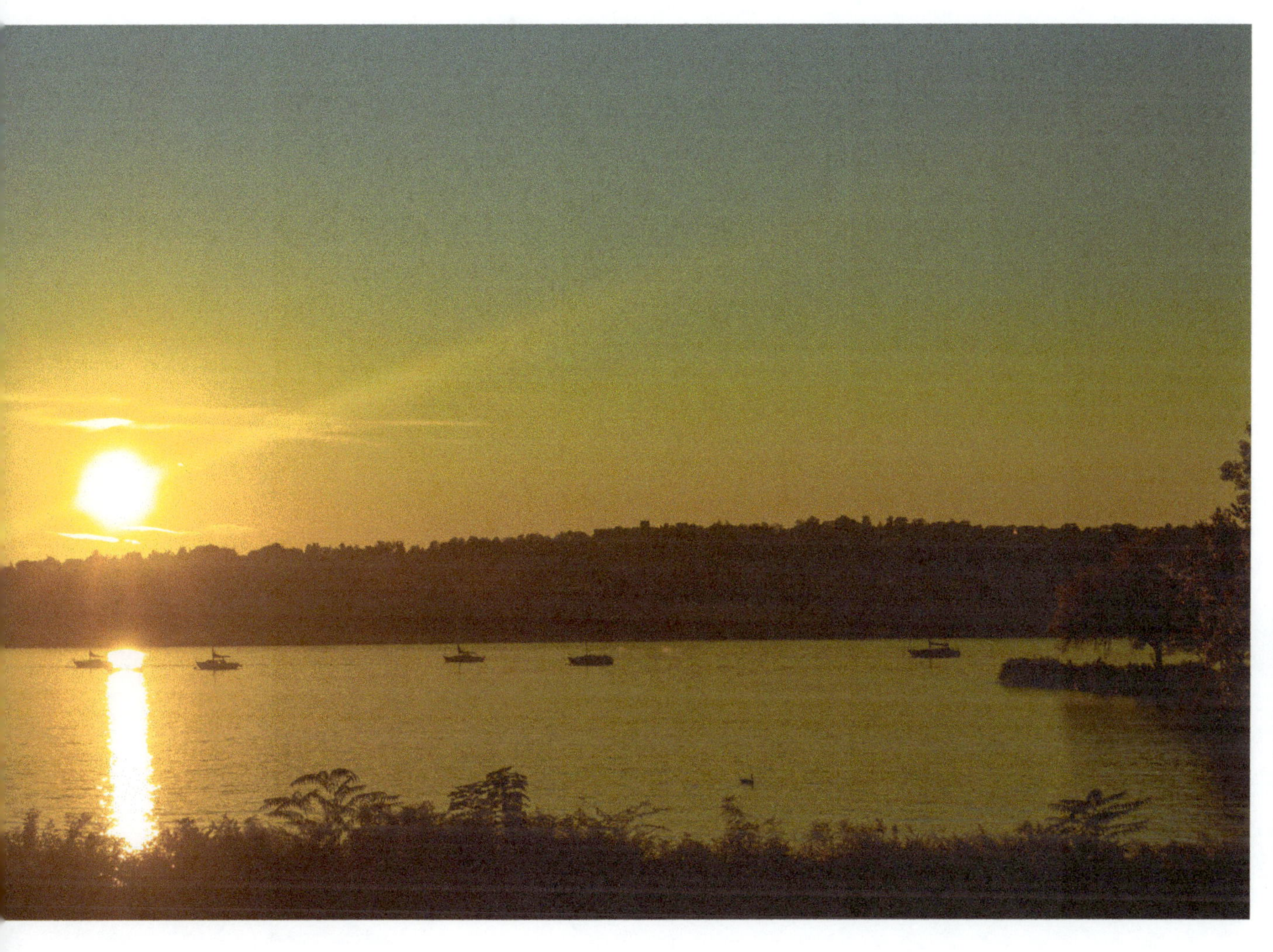

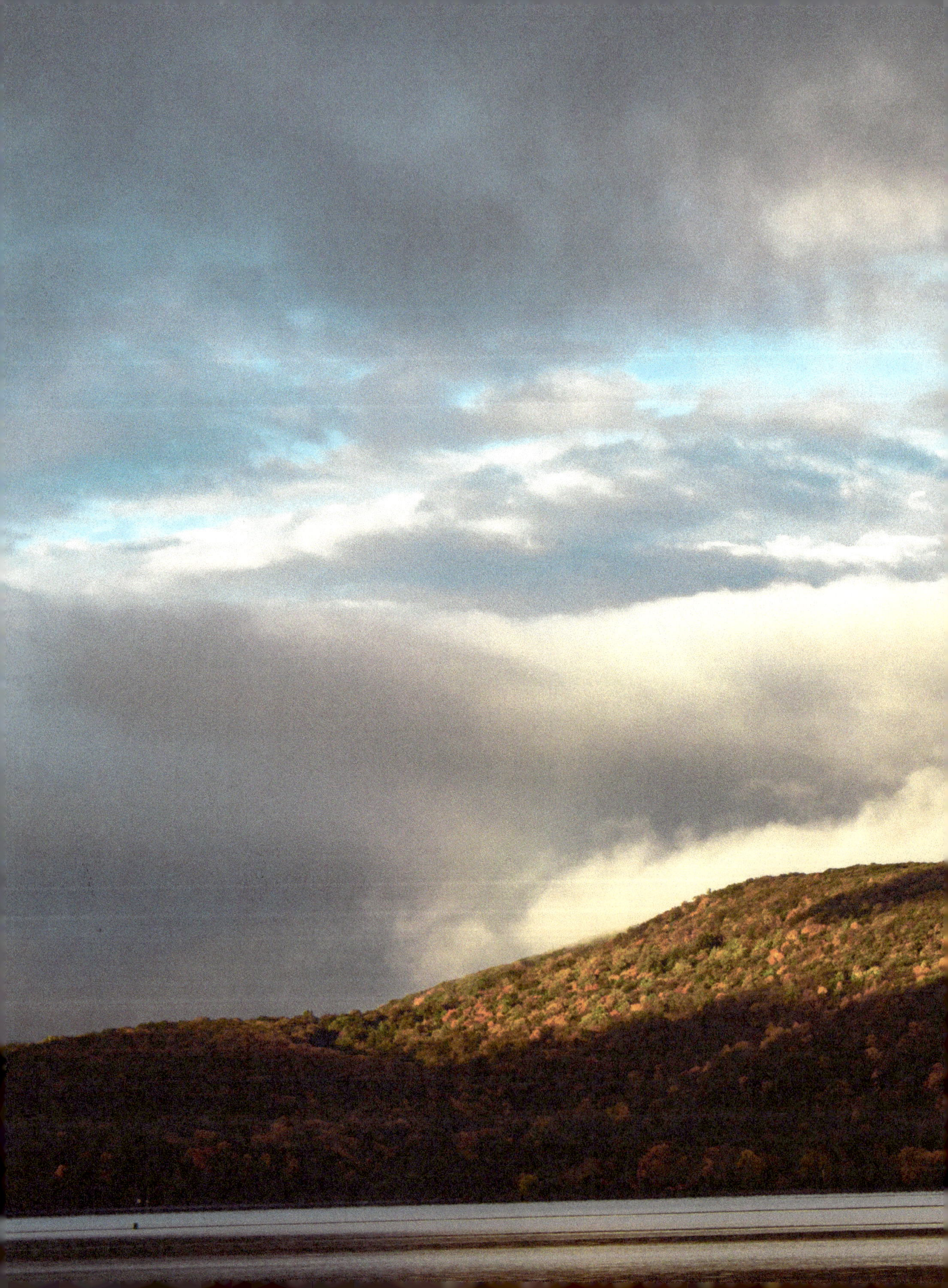

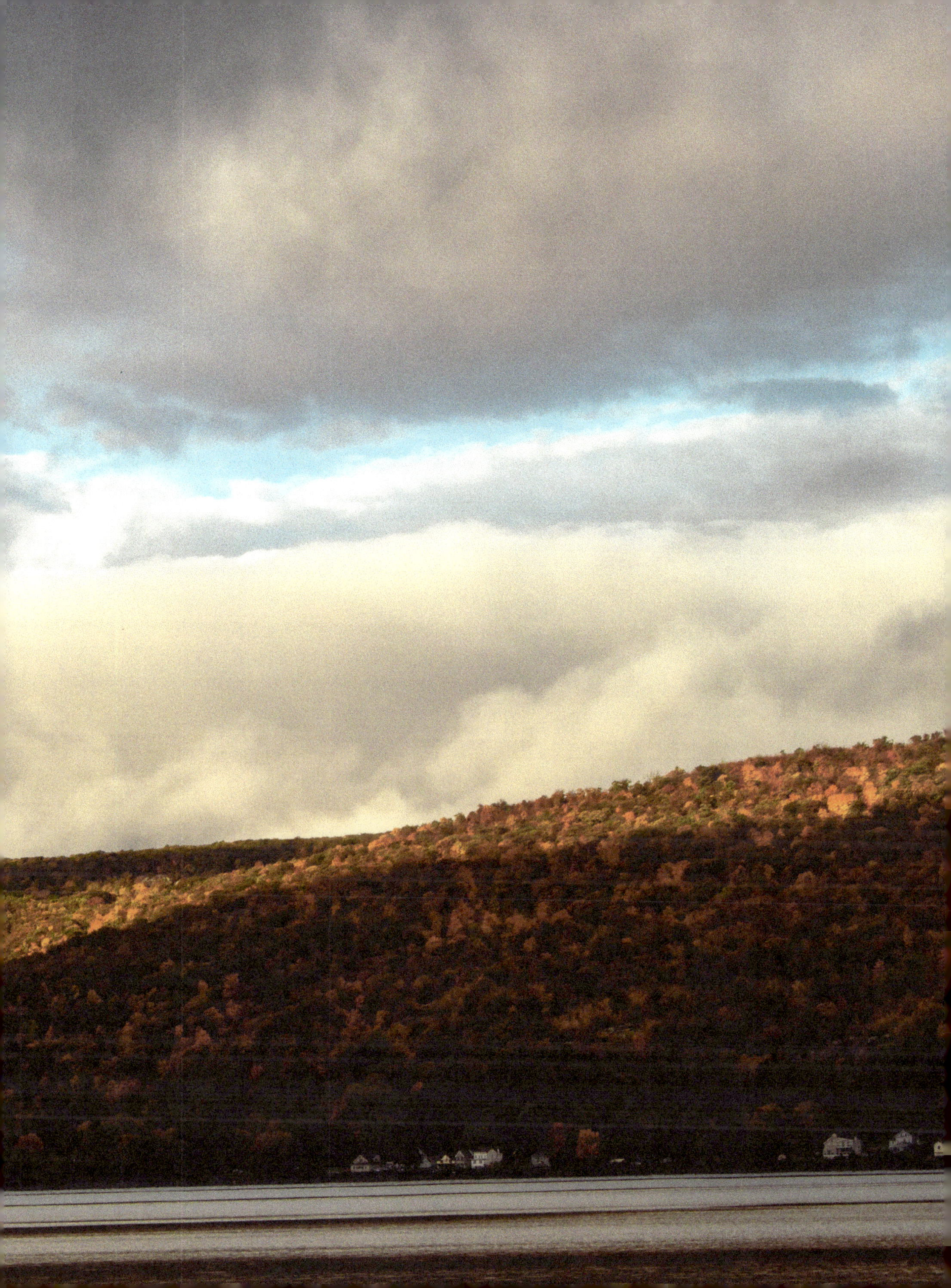

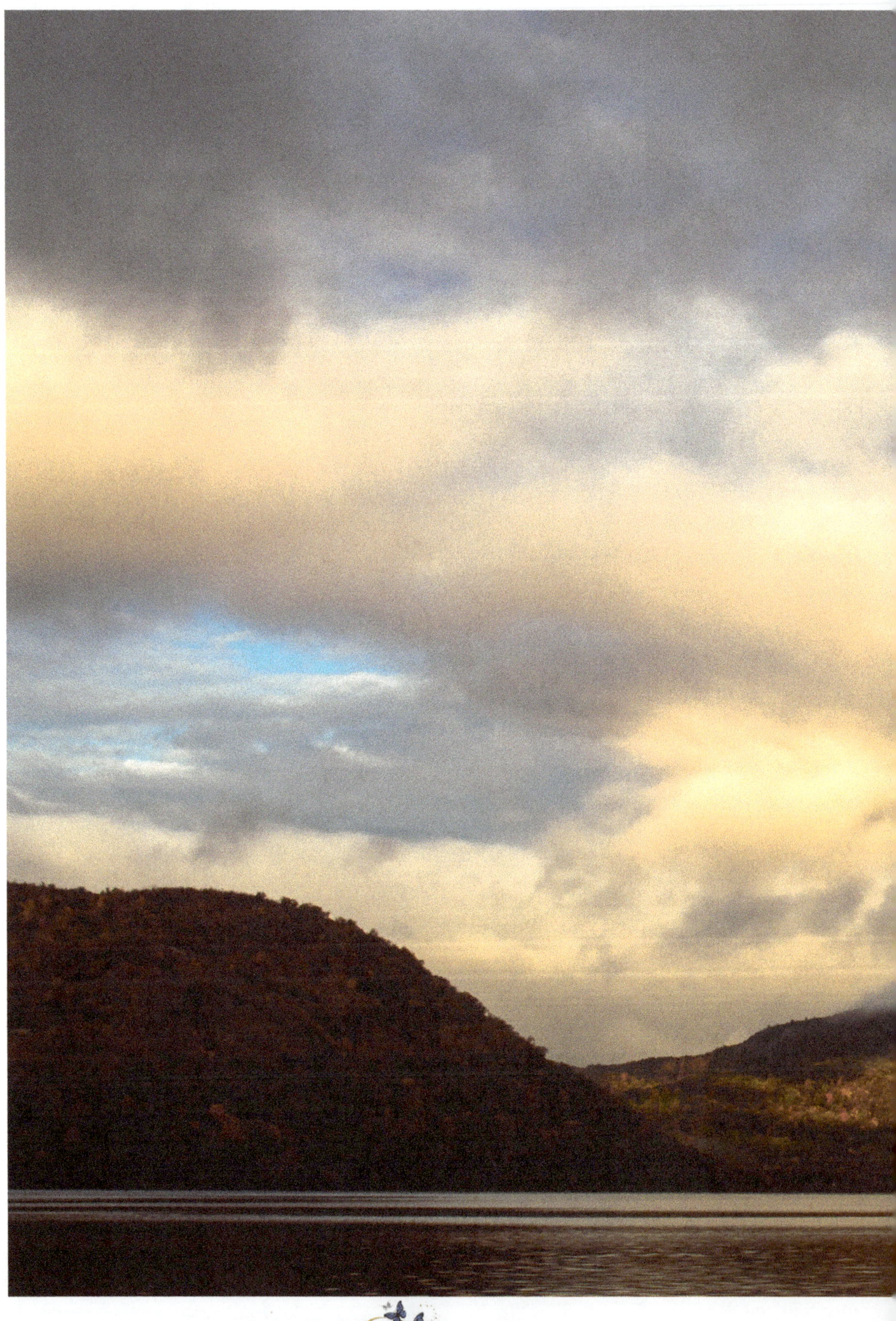

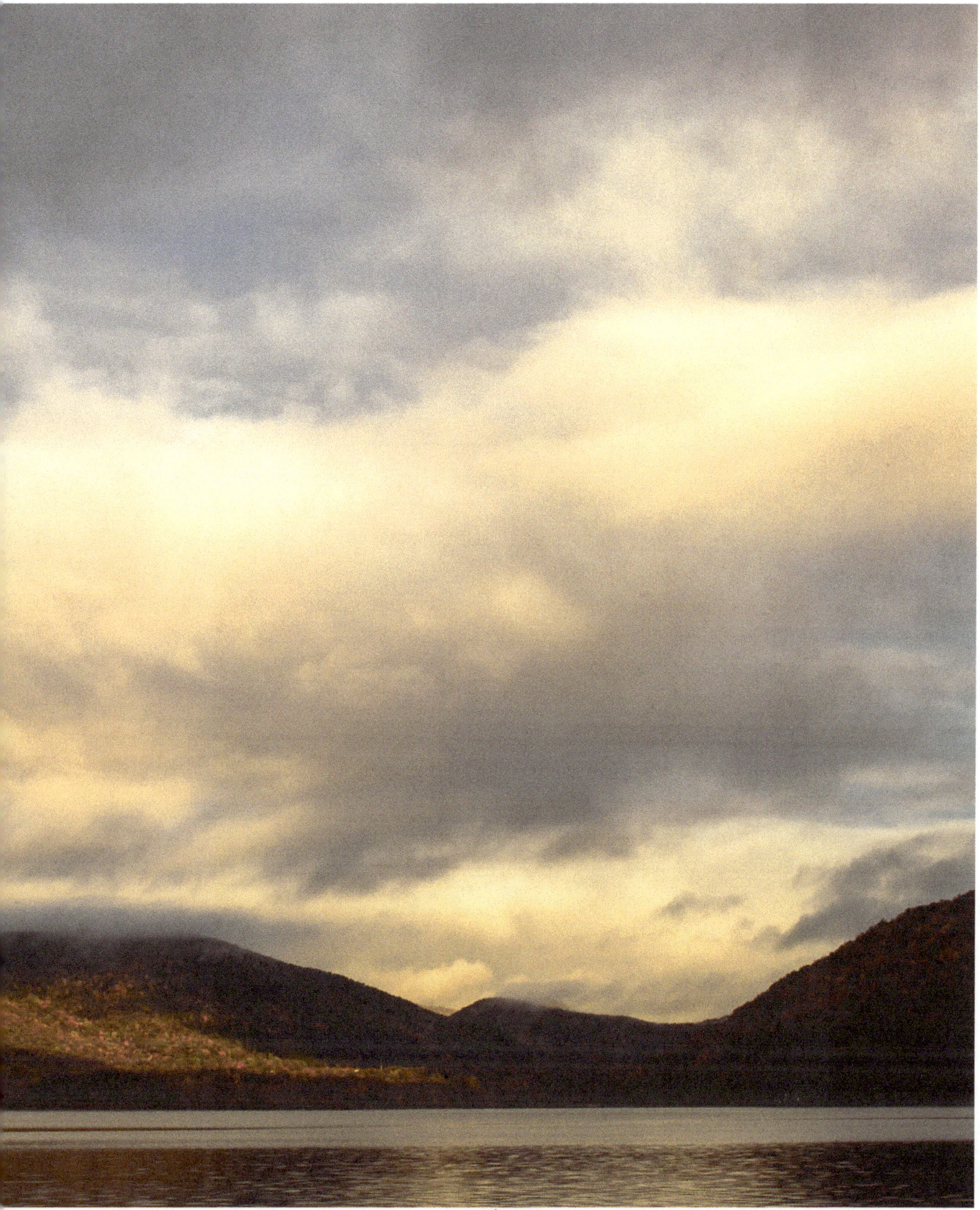

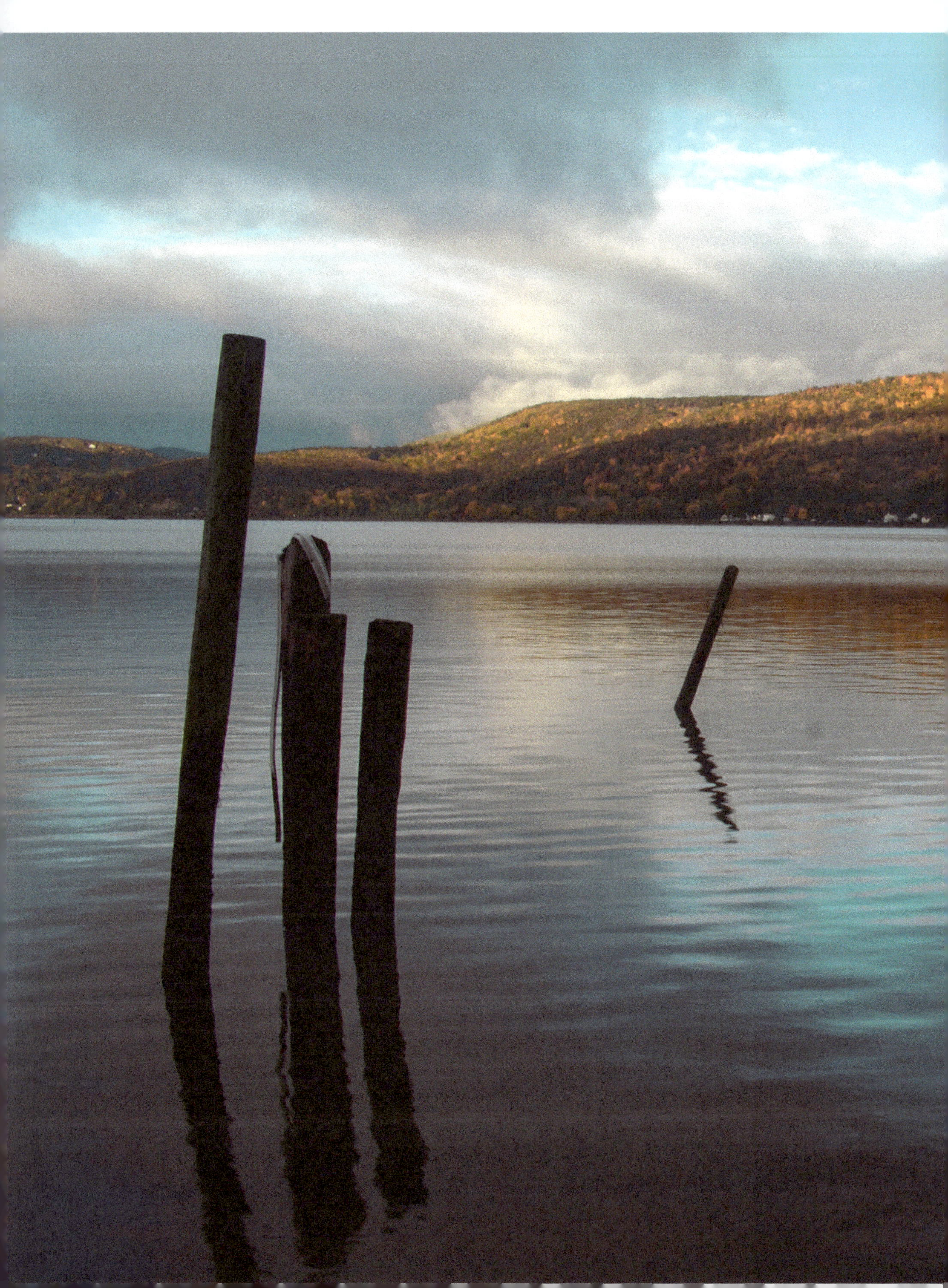

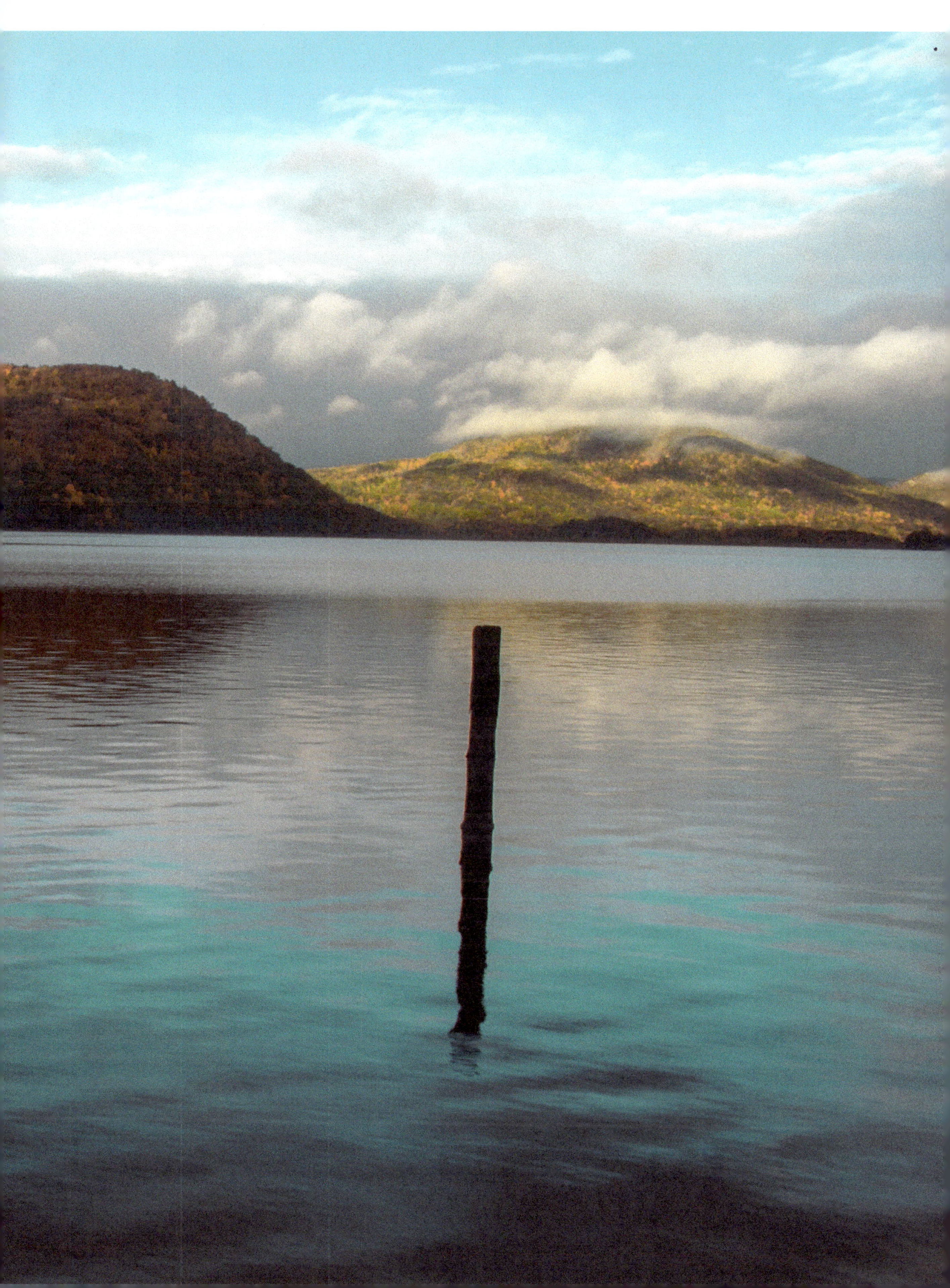

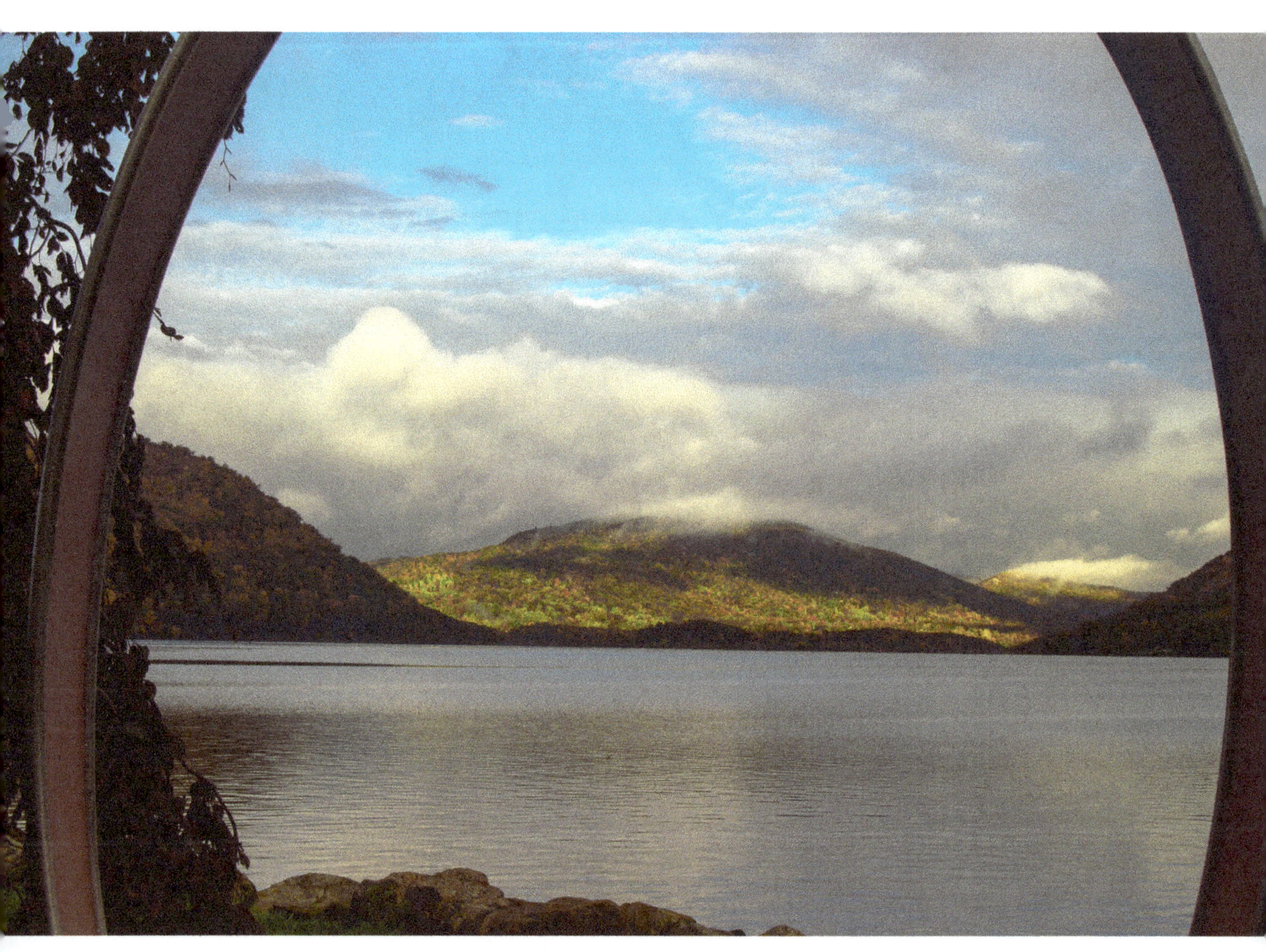

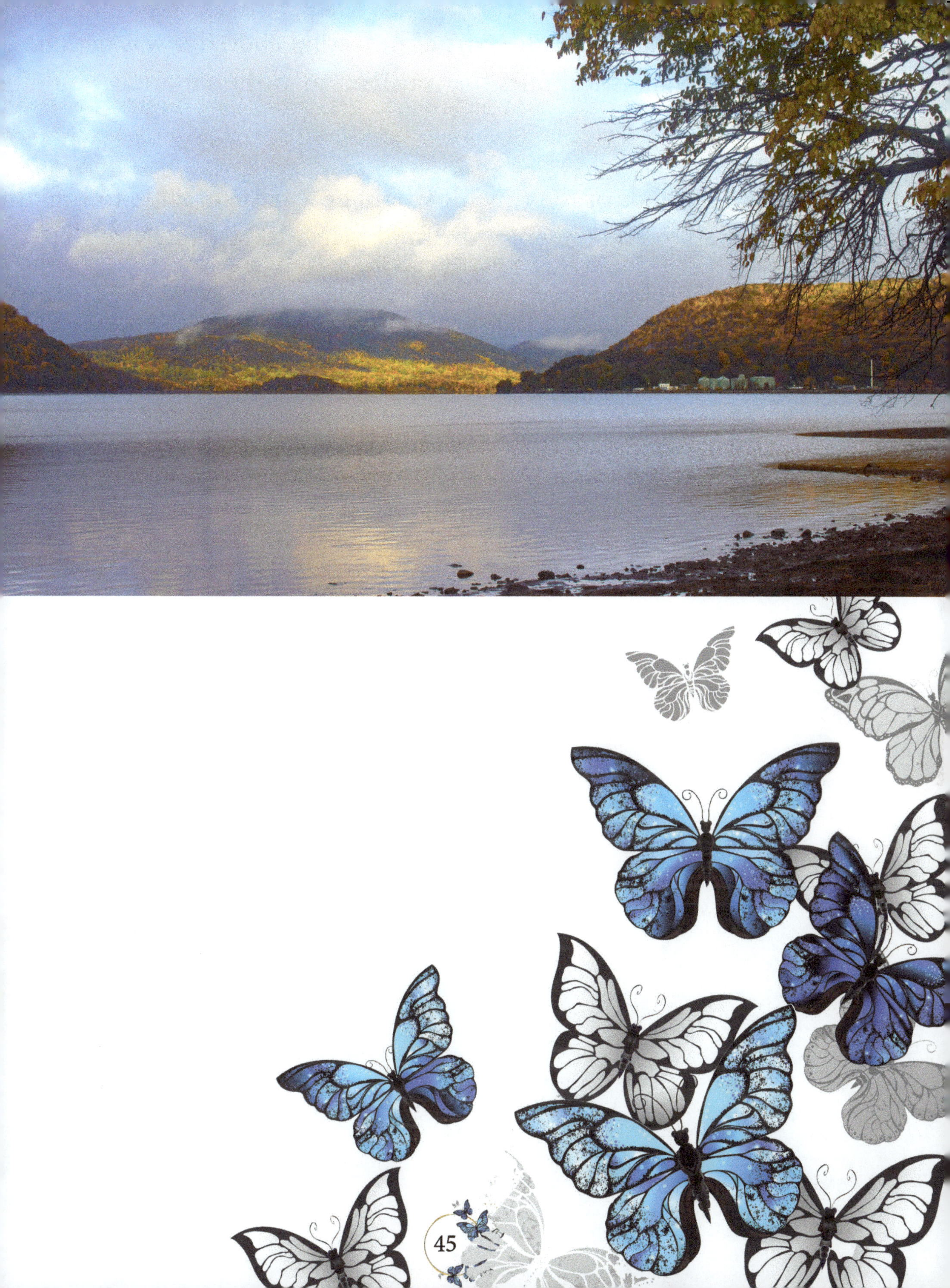

Even as he stared at the rising sun, part of him still believed it was fiction.
But, to chase those fantastical tales the way he chased the sun, that would be
living the dream.

He didn't have the funds or the time. It would be a waste of a life to run after
this imagination. It would only be a dream. He had to be okay with that.

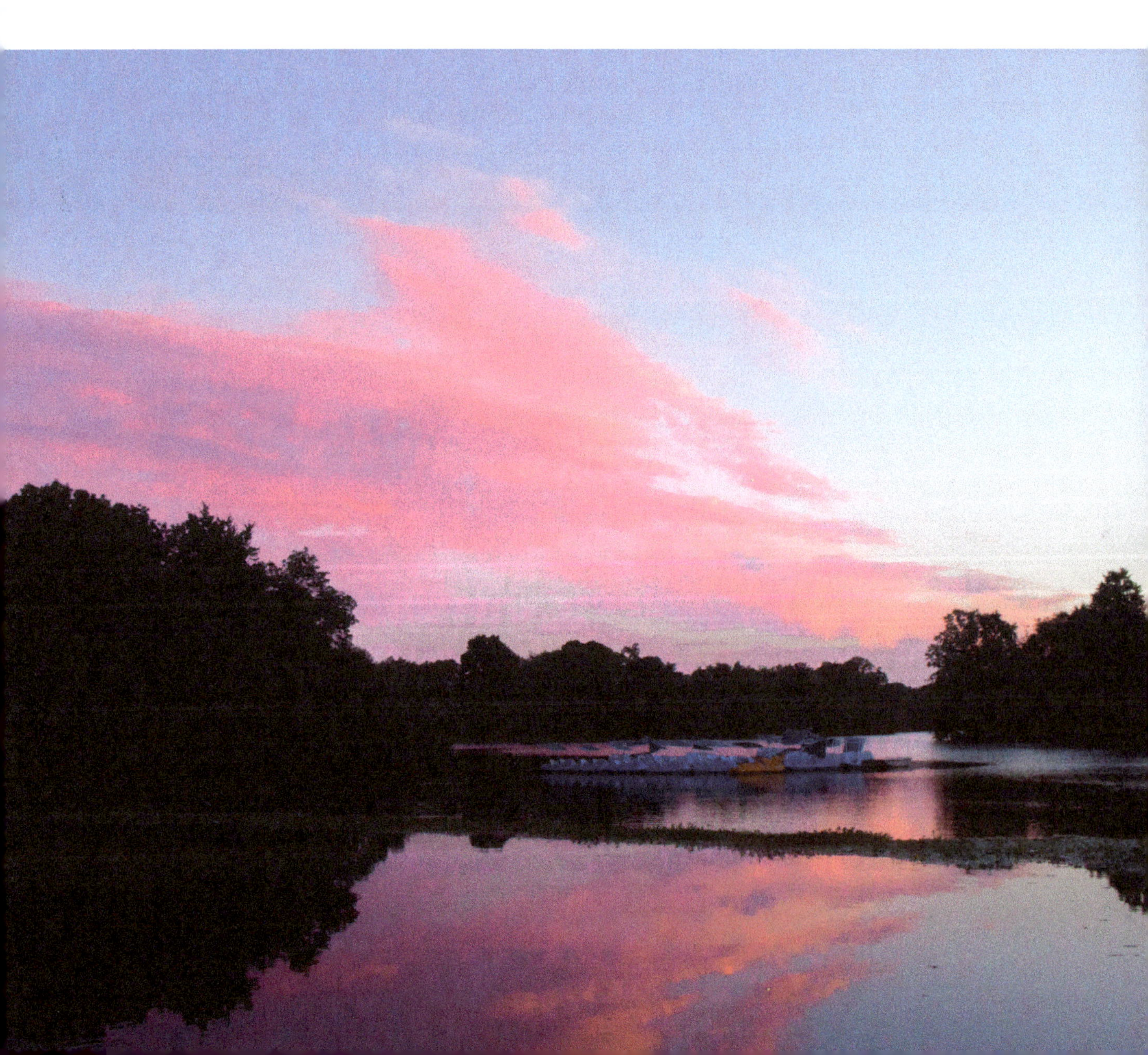

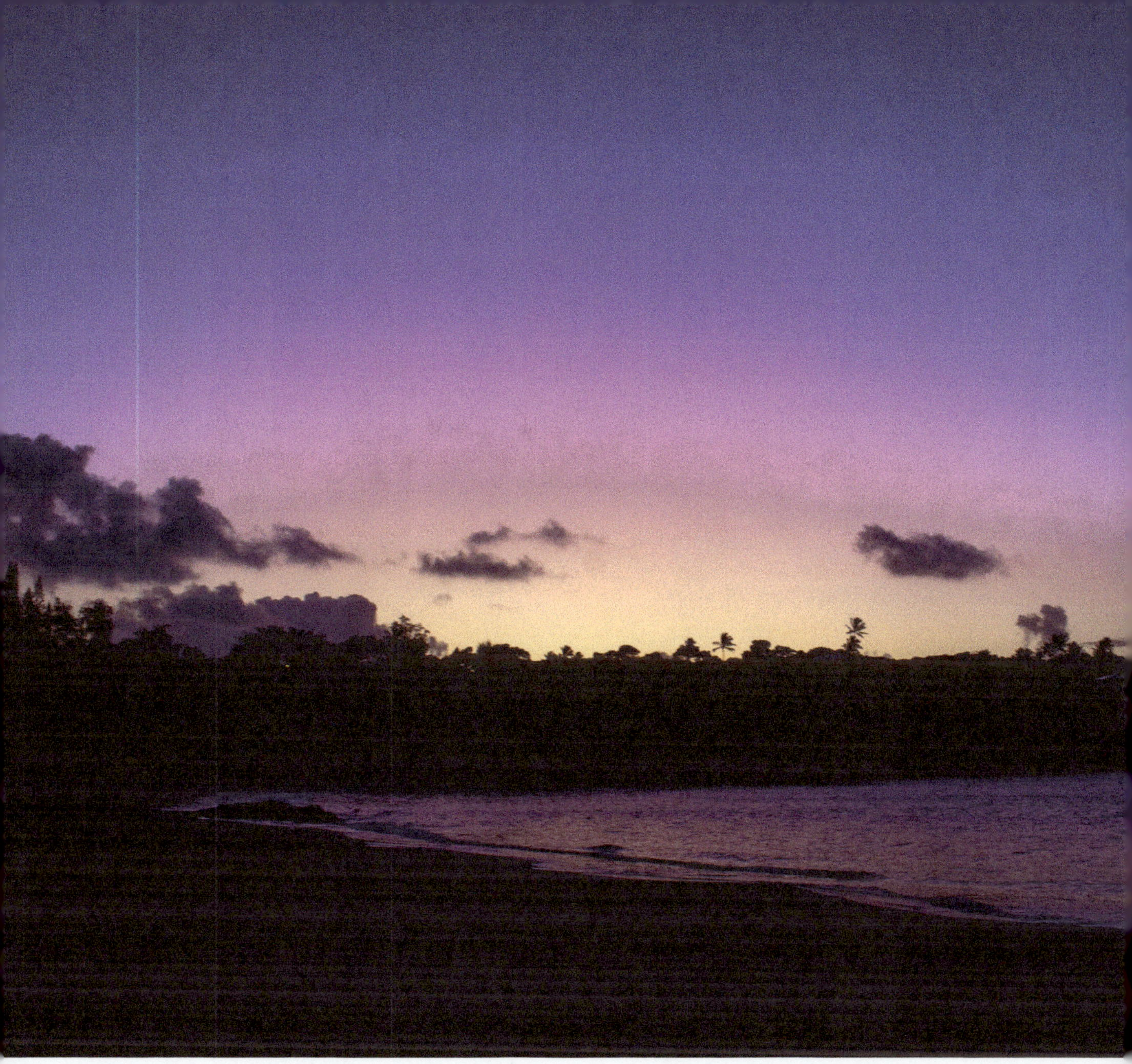

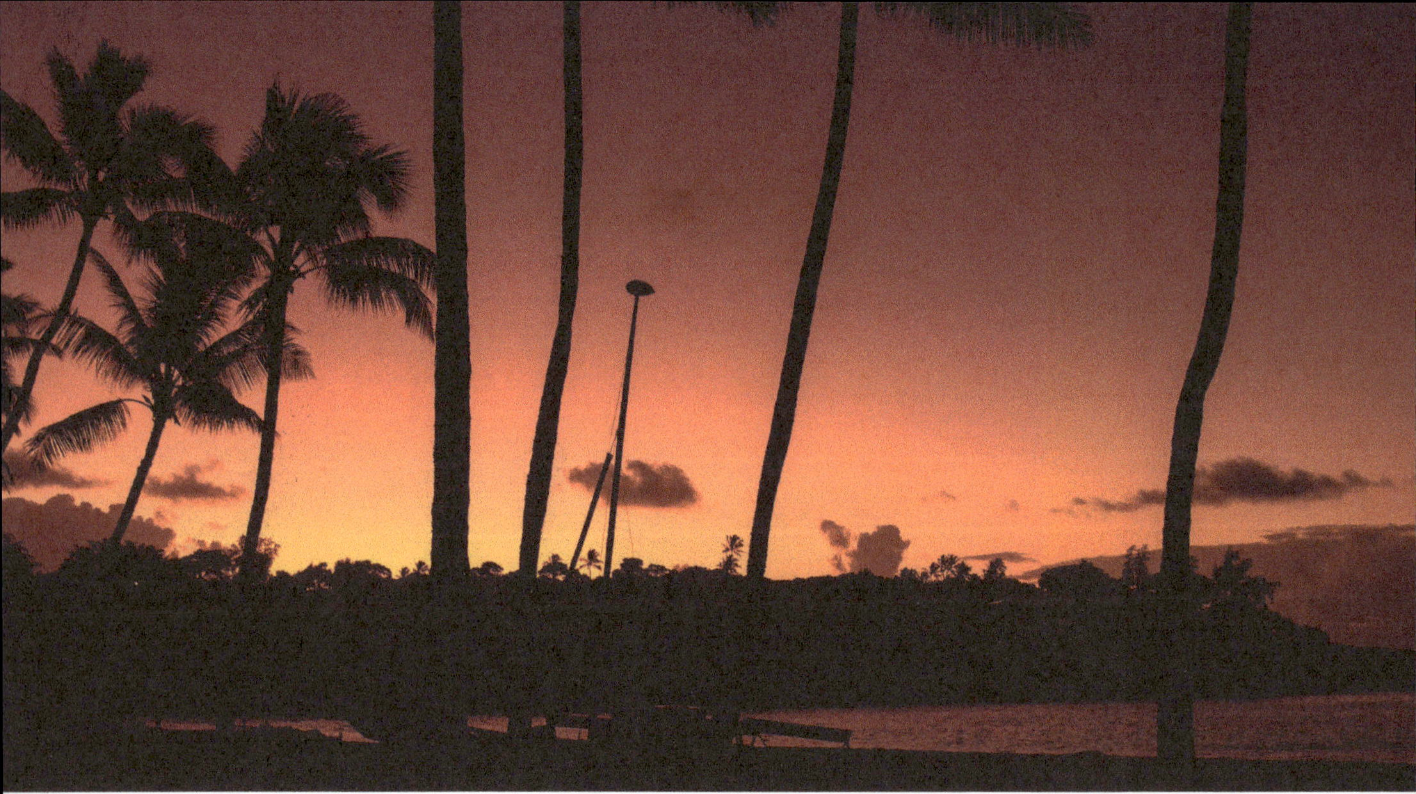

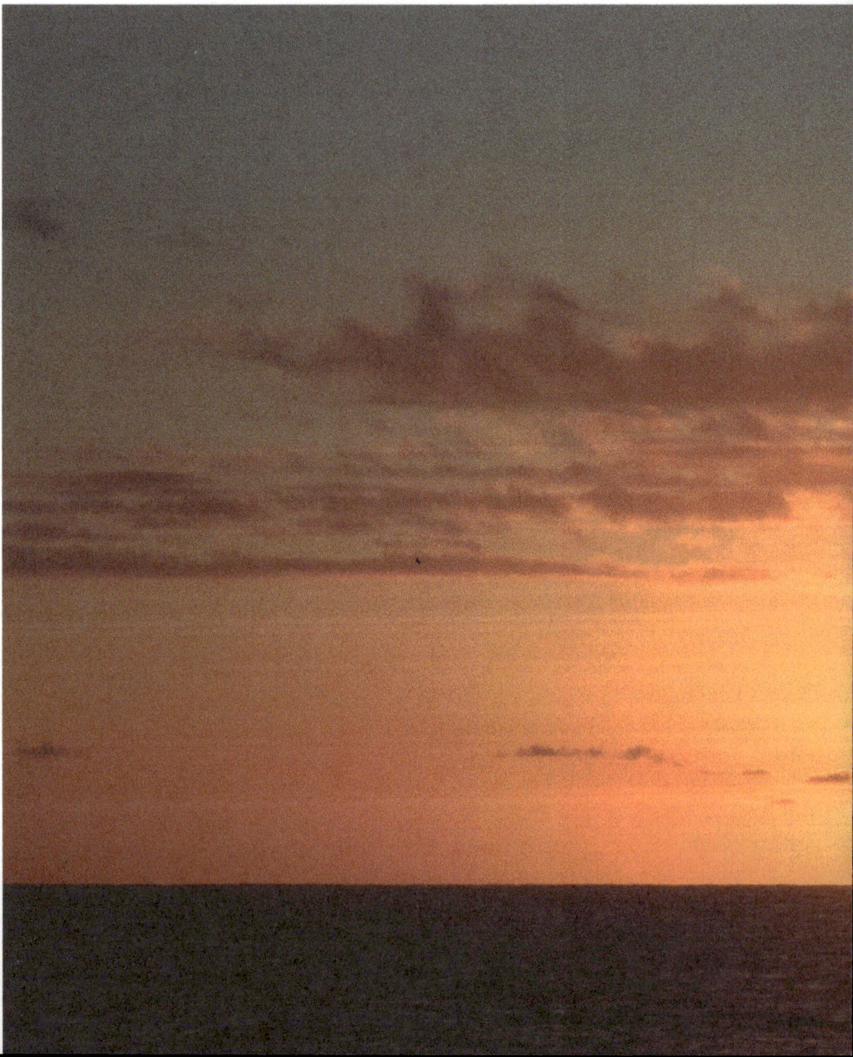

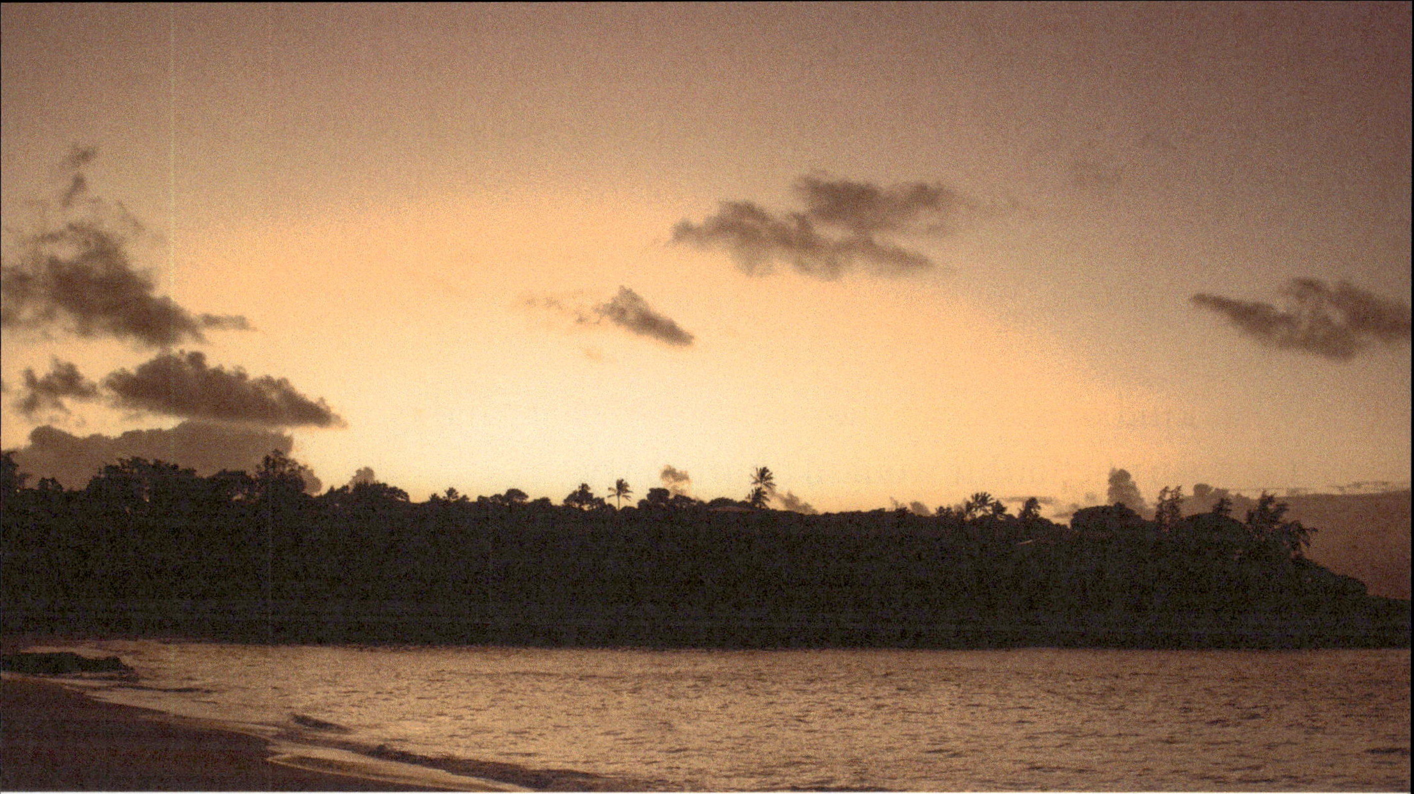

But, no matter how many logical reasons his mind threw in his way, the idea would not die. It grew stronger day-by-day, devouring both his waking and sleeping life.

It was madness.

What kind of stories would he create? What kind of things he'd see? What if it wasn't fiction? It wouldn't hurt to try.

He kept the plan to himself, knowing those closest to him would object. This would not stay a dream.

It took years and hard work. So many nights of little sleep. Many hours working jobs he thoroughly despised, dealing with people who were rude because they thought it was their right.

The dream kept him going. Planning was his daylight.

Then one day, he began his journey.

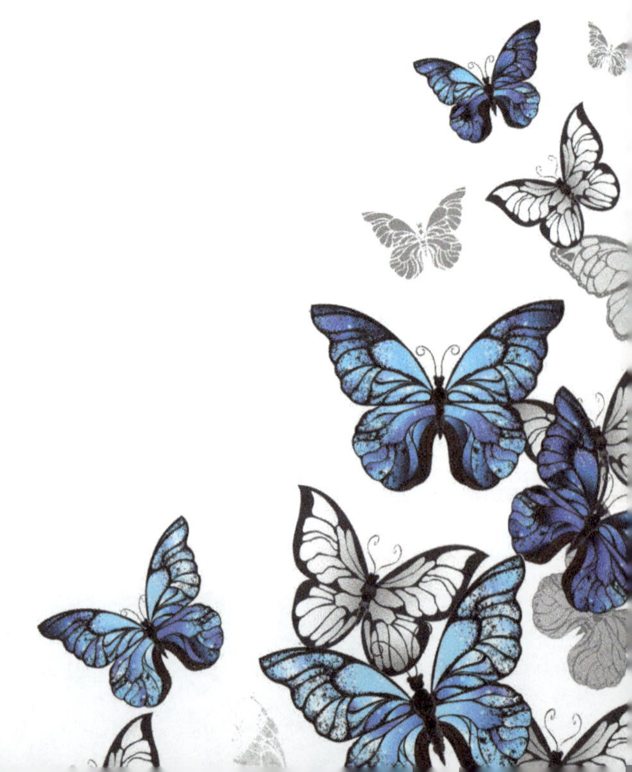

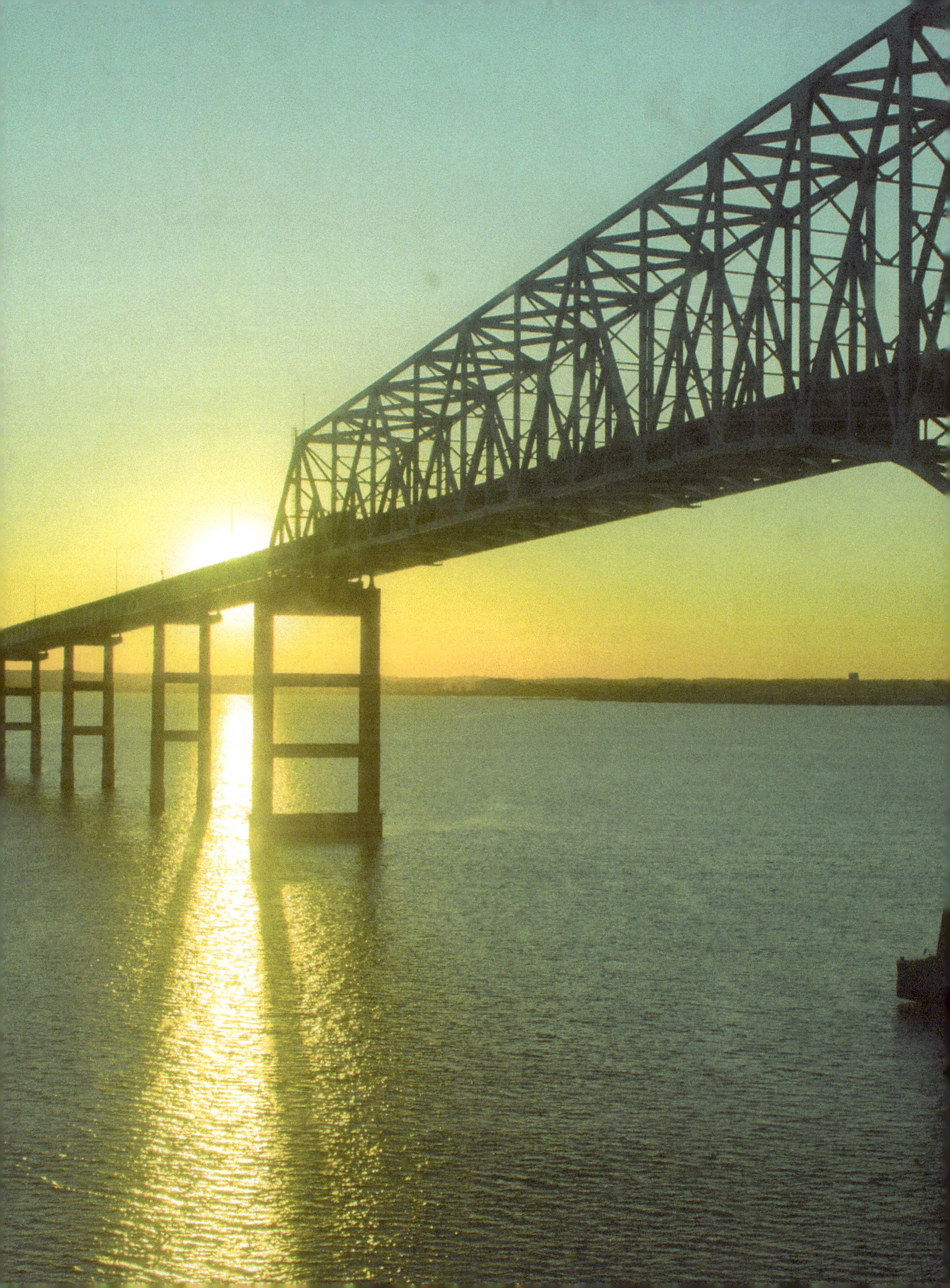

THE JOURNEY

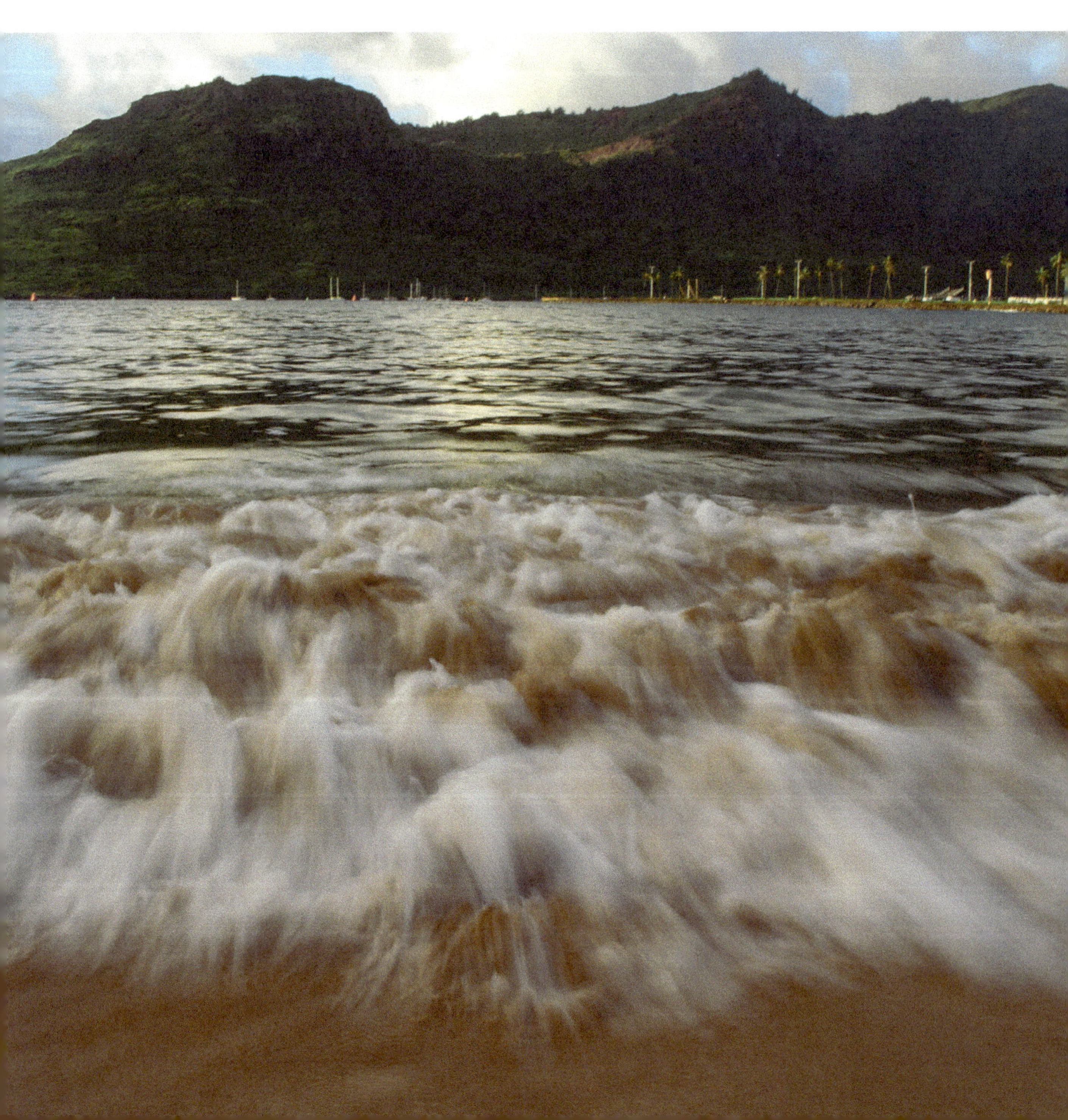

e never expected the journey to be easy but the hardships that rose nearly
ade him quit. Getting food and supplies when he needed them became a
xury. His dark skin helped him blended in but still, something about him
reamed outsider, which made him a target.

e trained beforehand but that didn't fully prepare him for the kind of ter-
in he had to traverse for research. Several times, he thought he'd die alone
the middle of the forest.

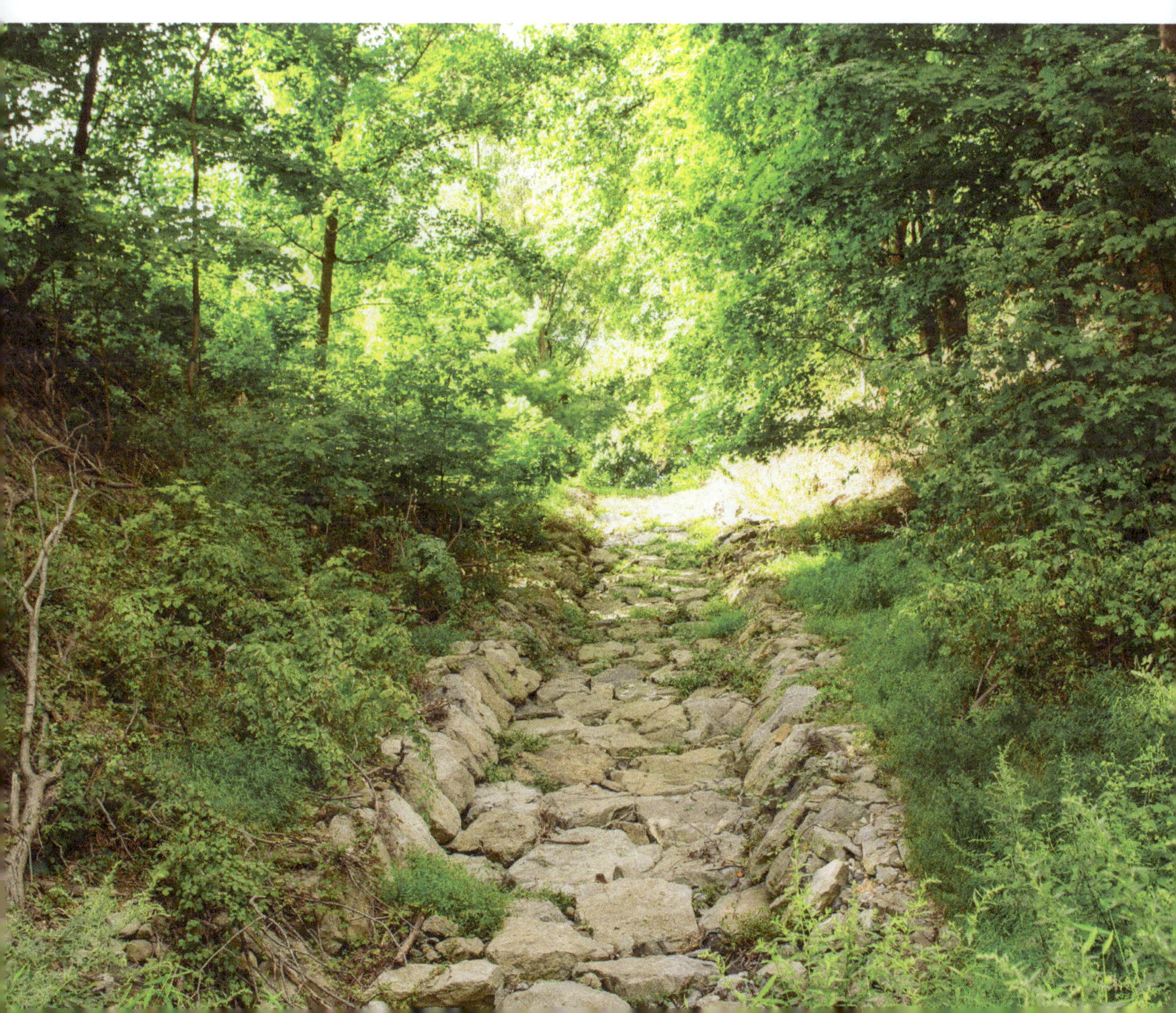

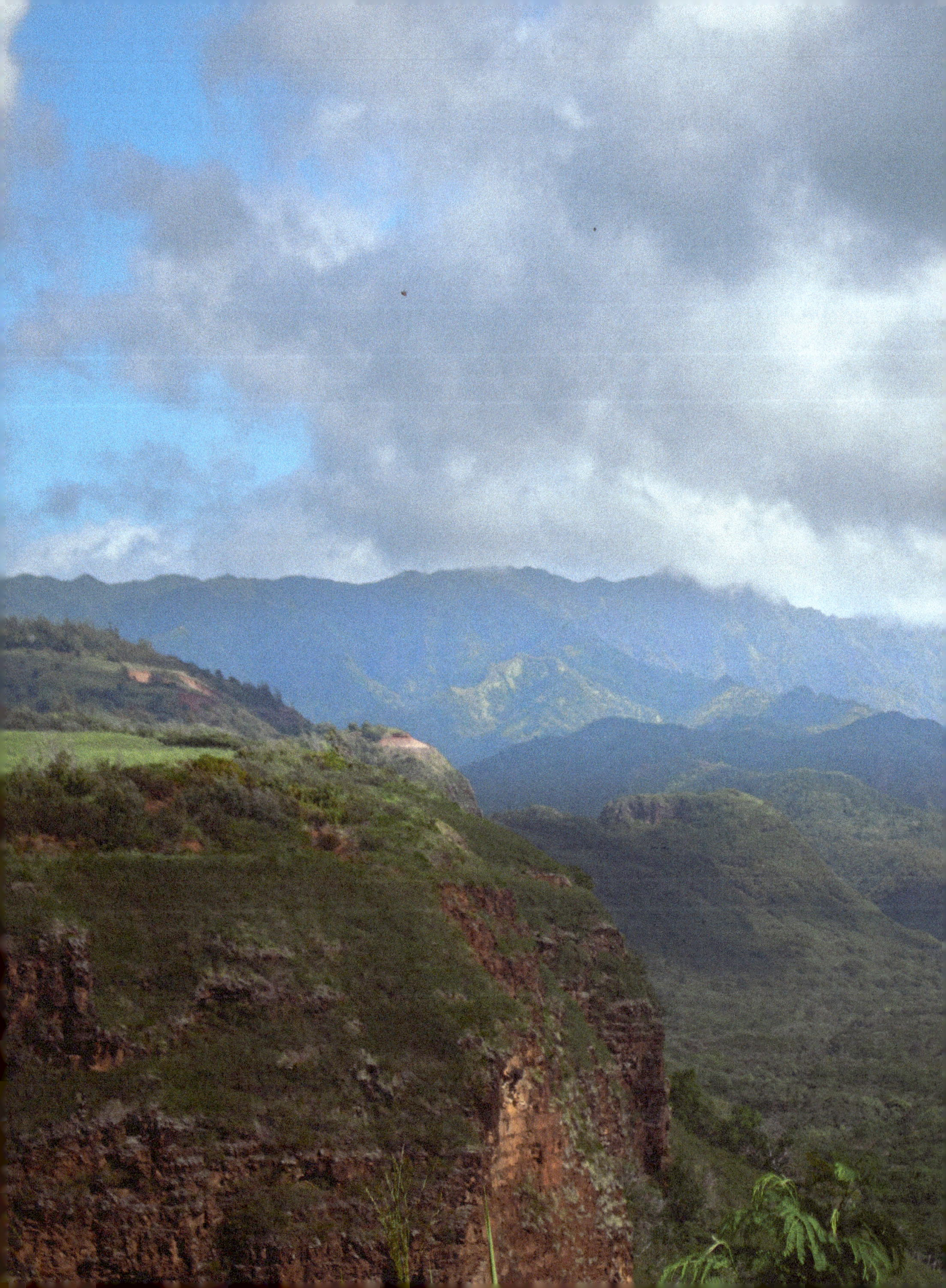

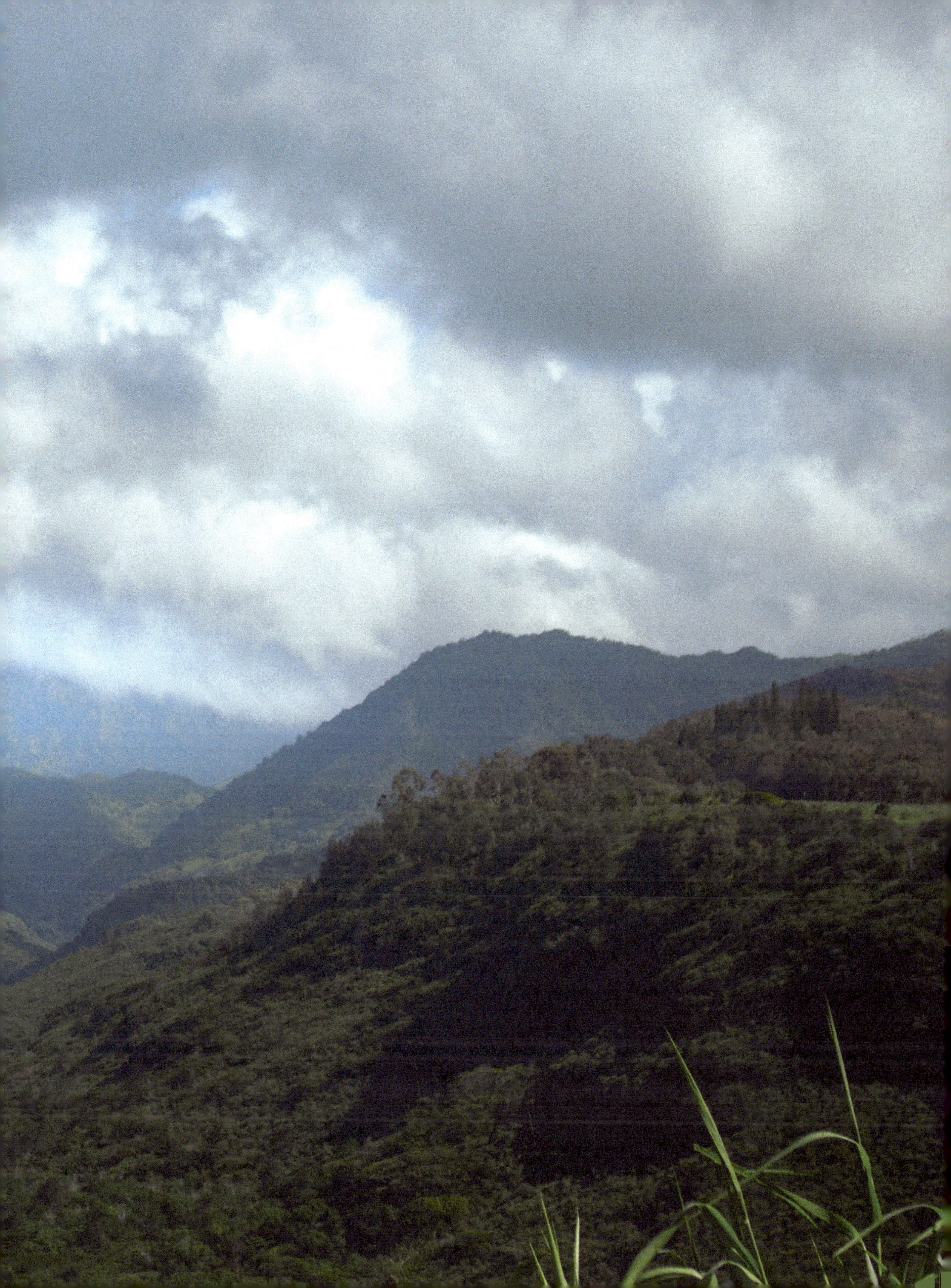

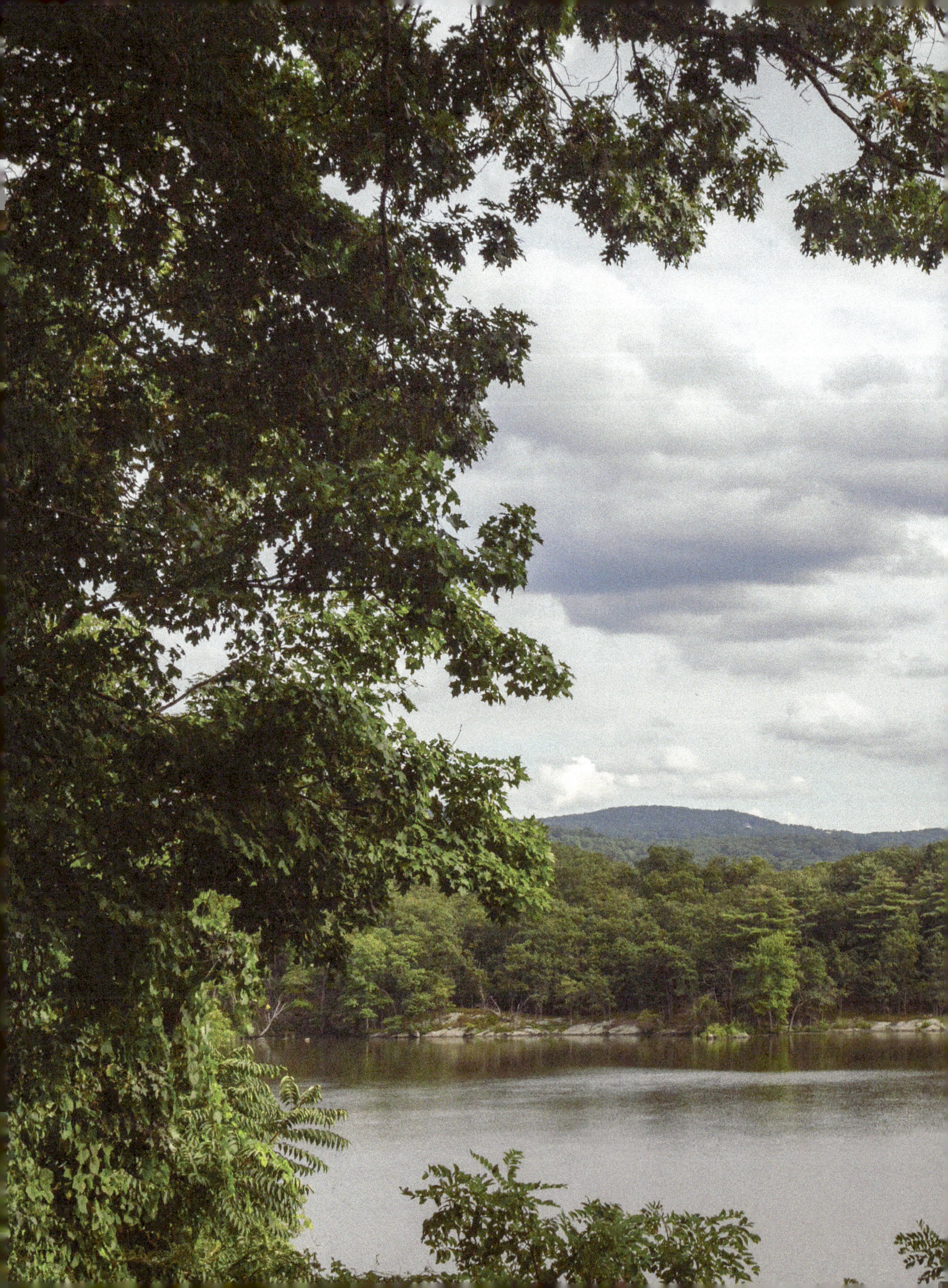

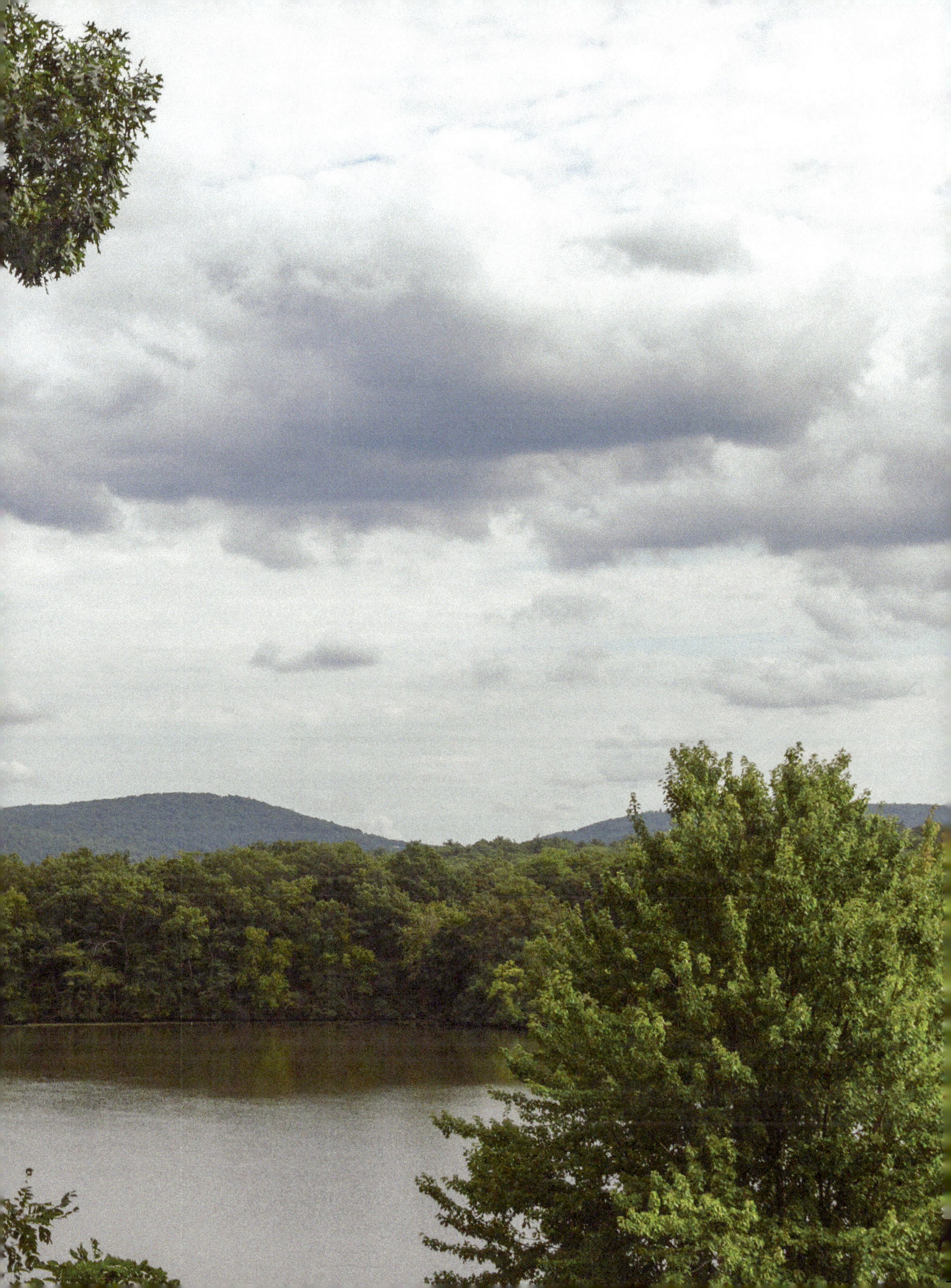

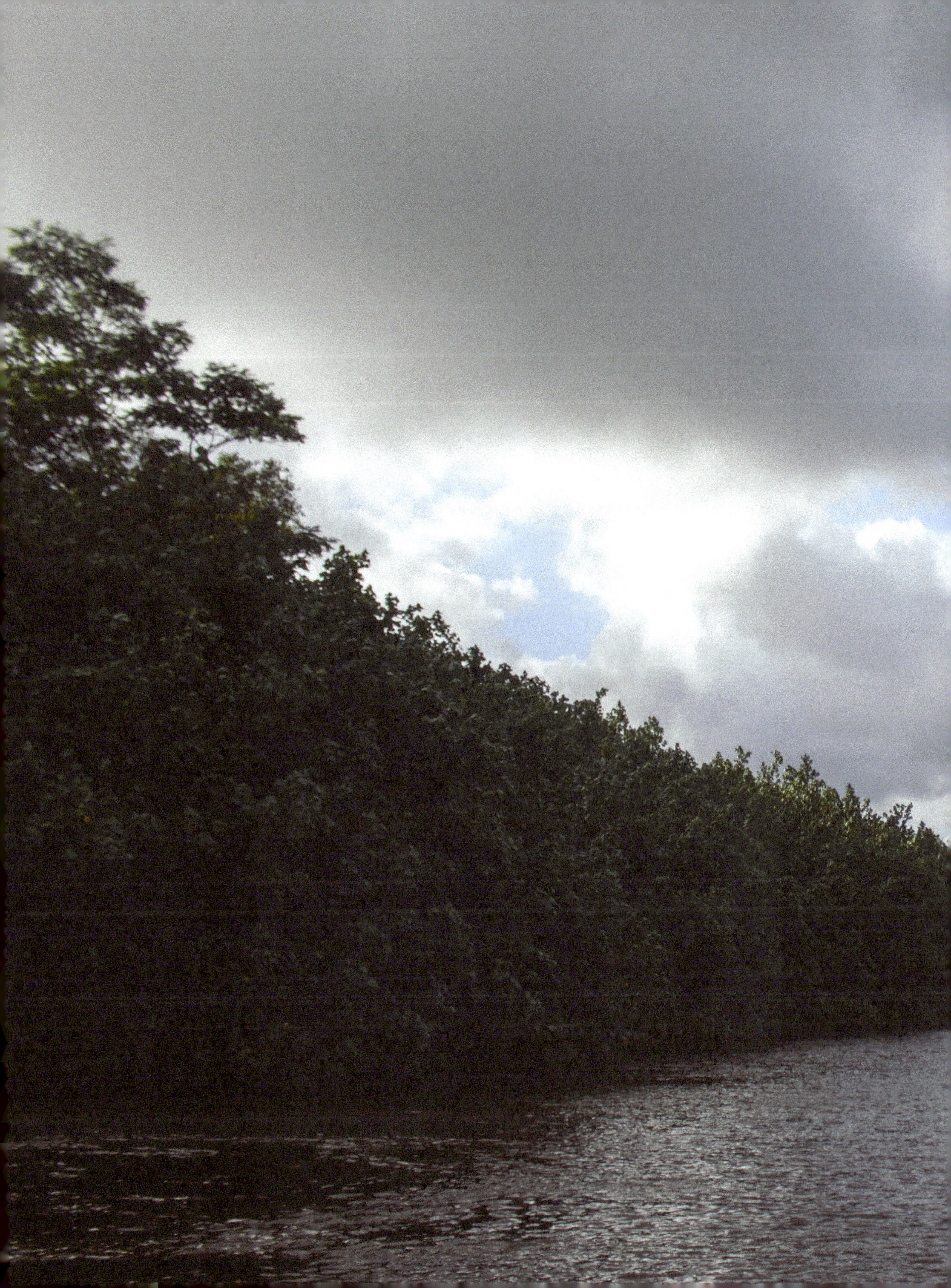

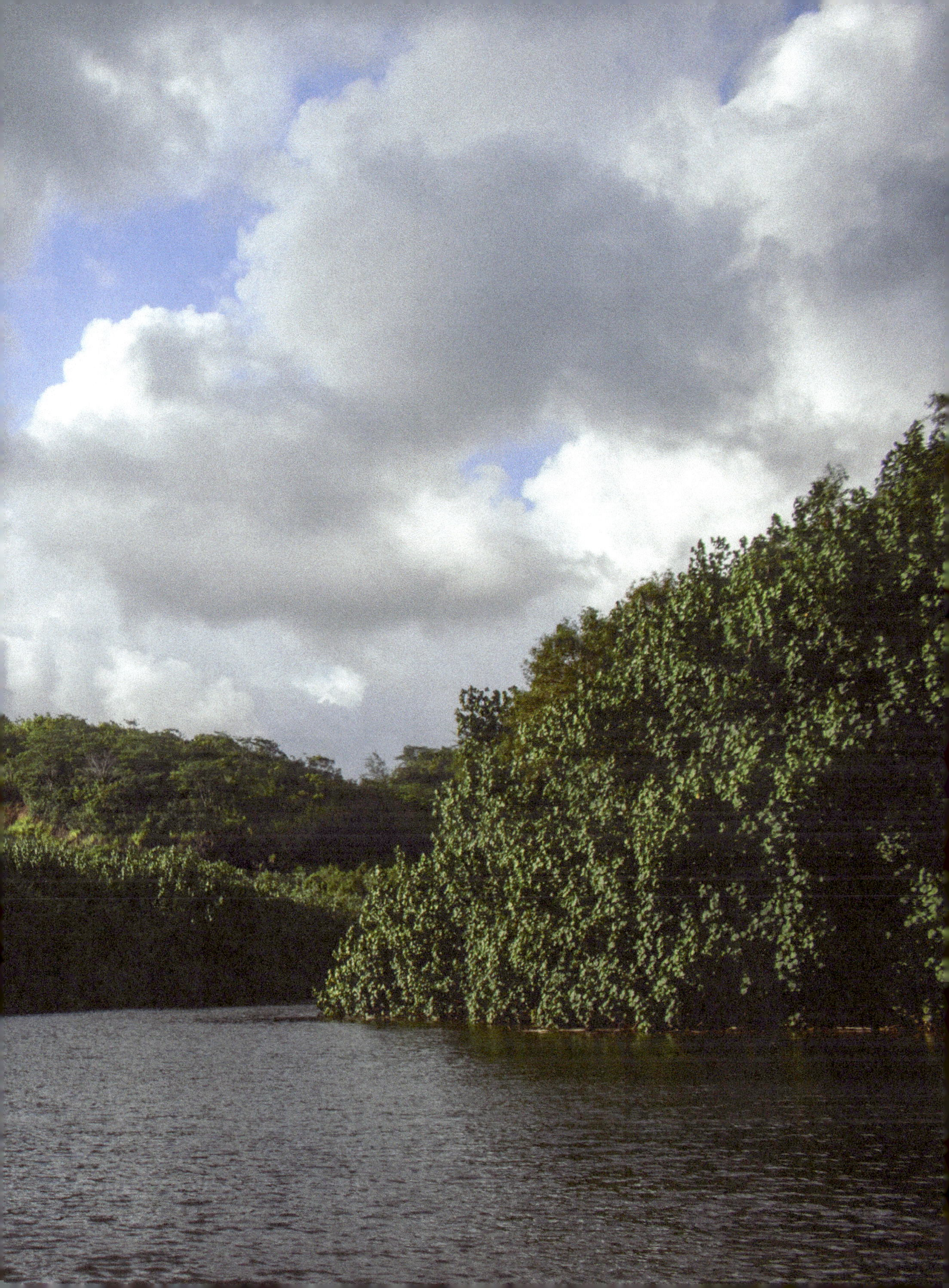

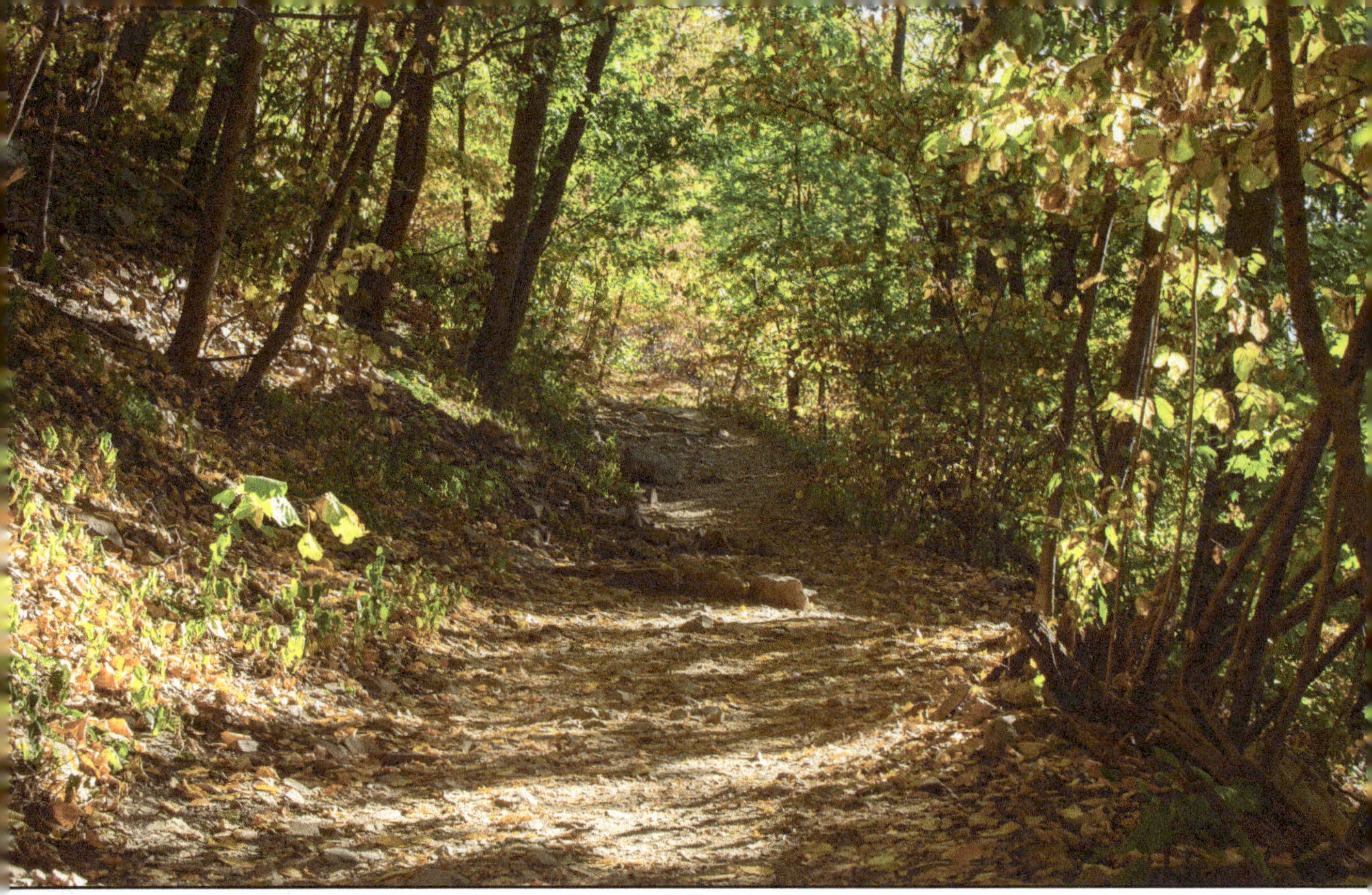

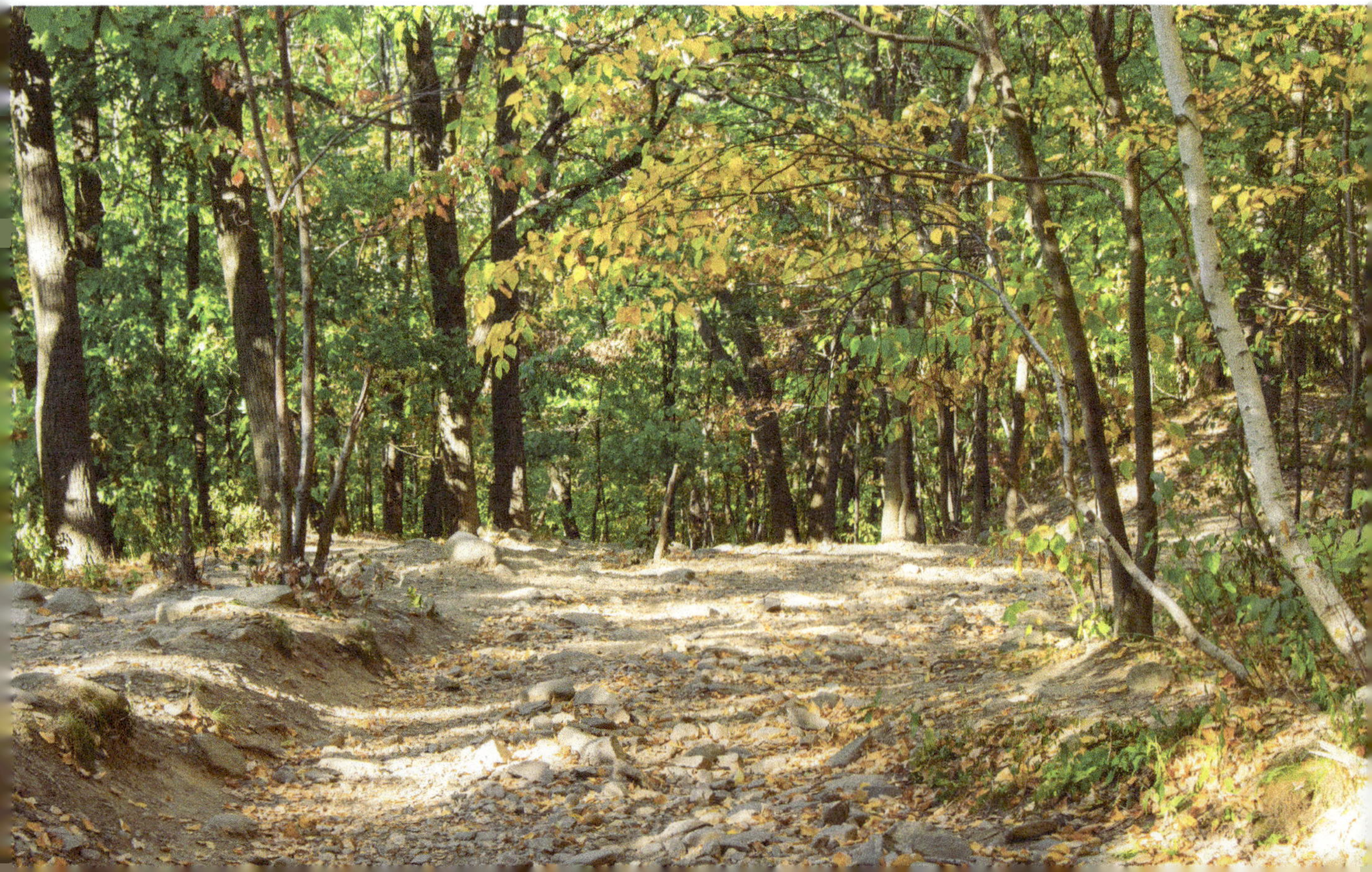

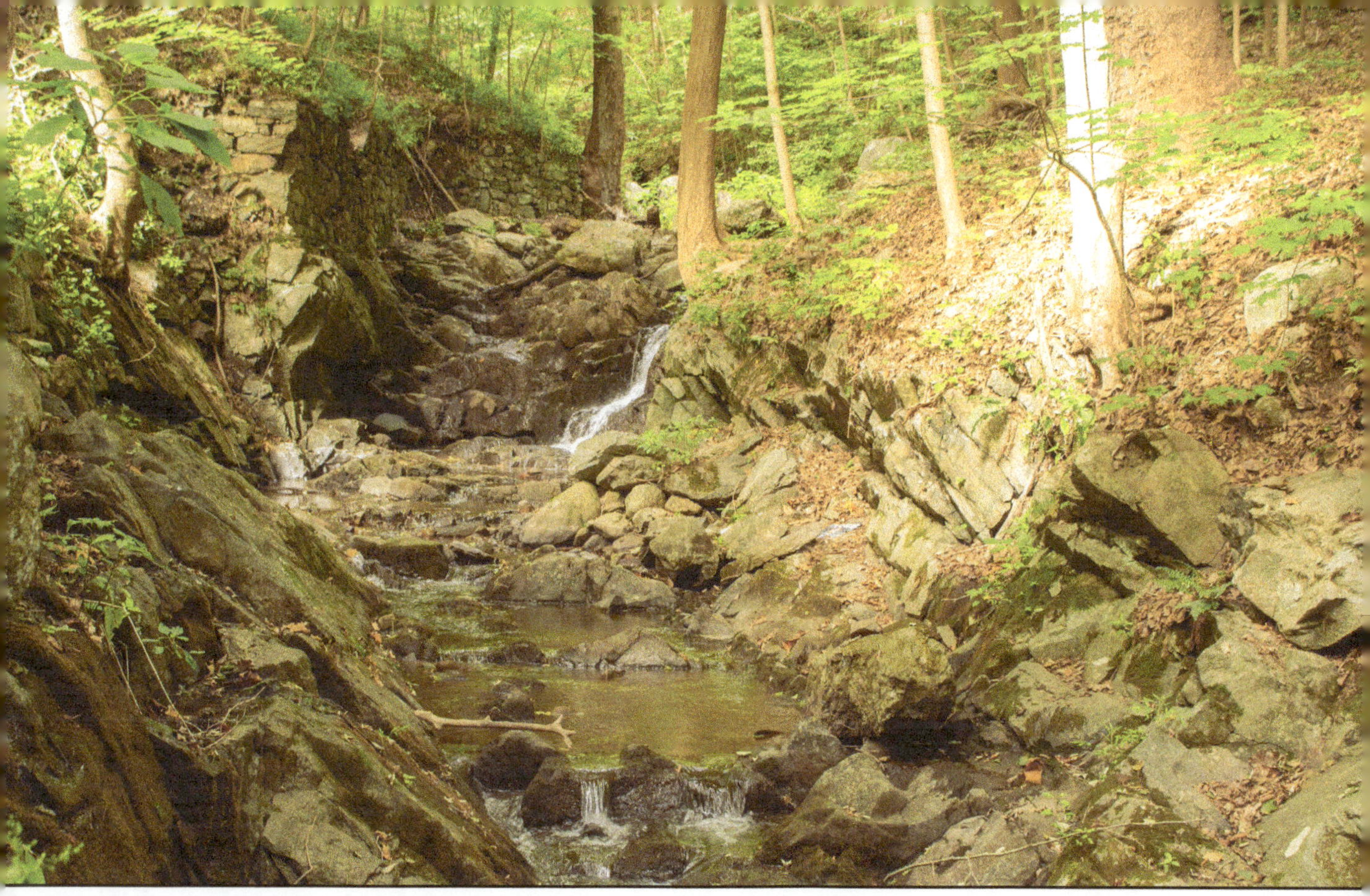

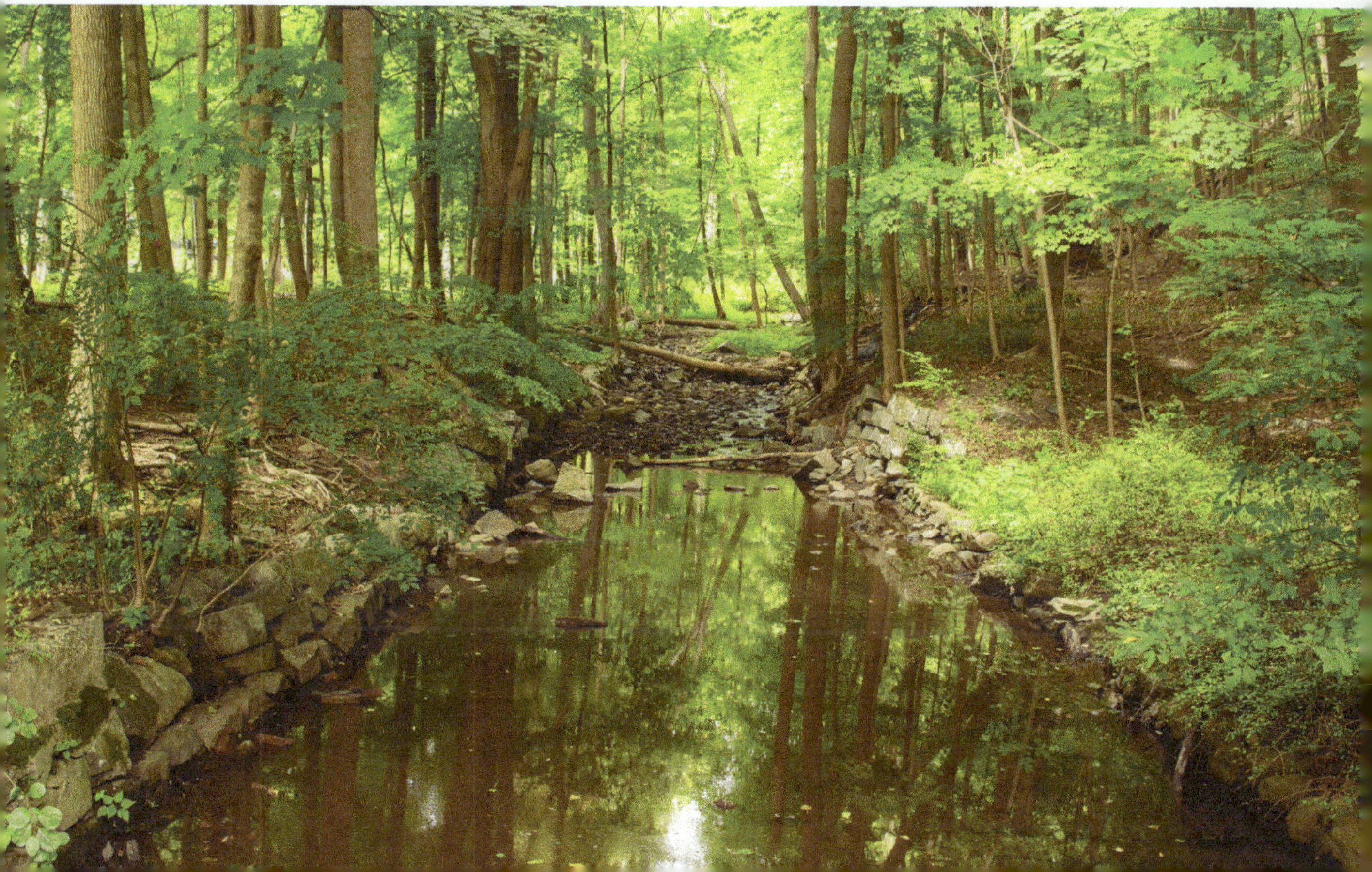

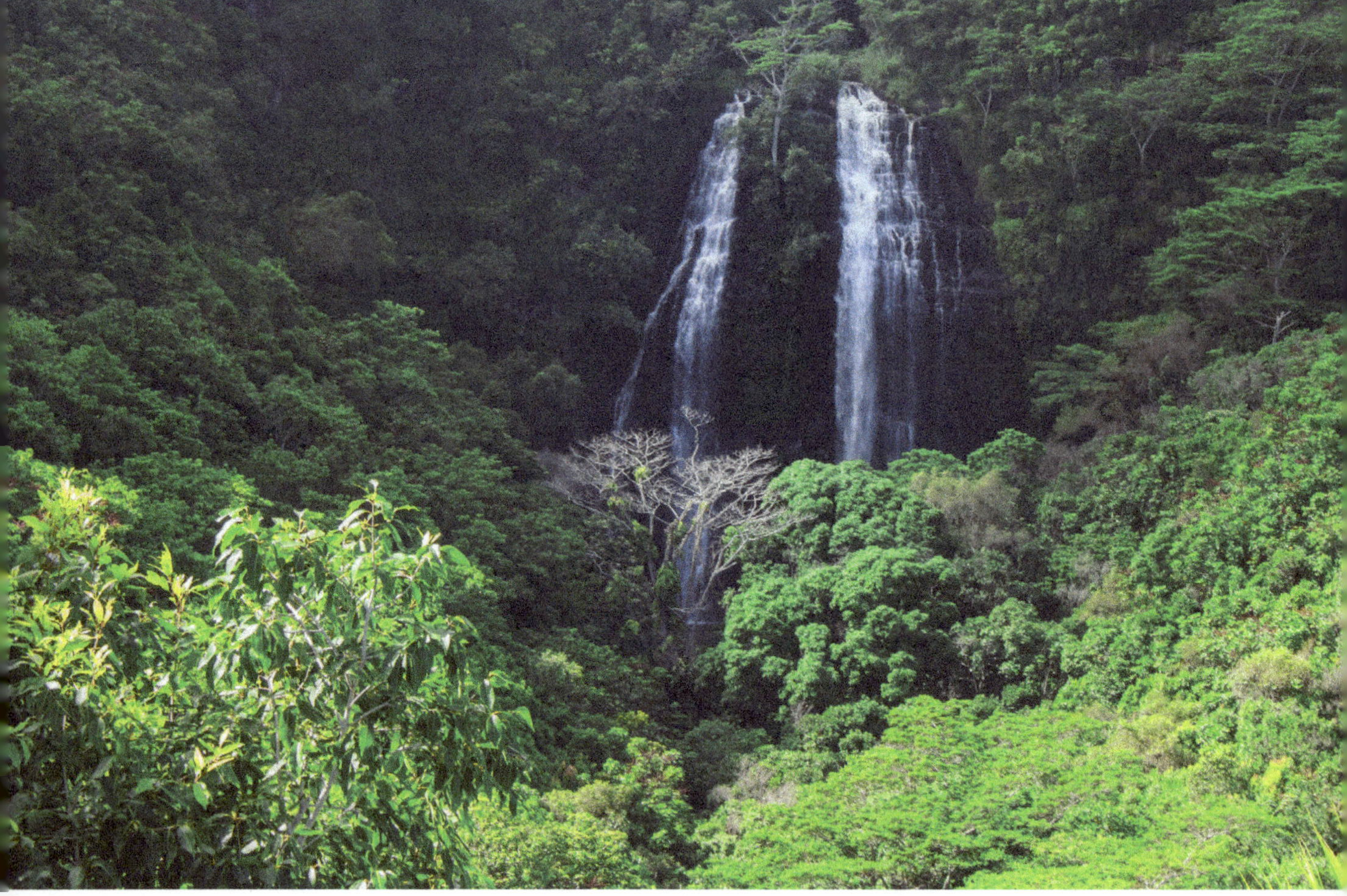

e pushed through each time and was rewarded. He traveled across oceans
nd found stories come to life. Legends in the flesh. He found hidden towns
rgotten by most books. Long abandoned fortresses on islands at the end of
e world.

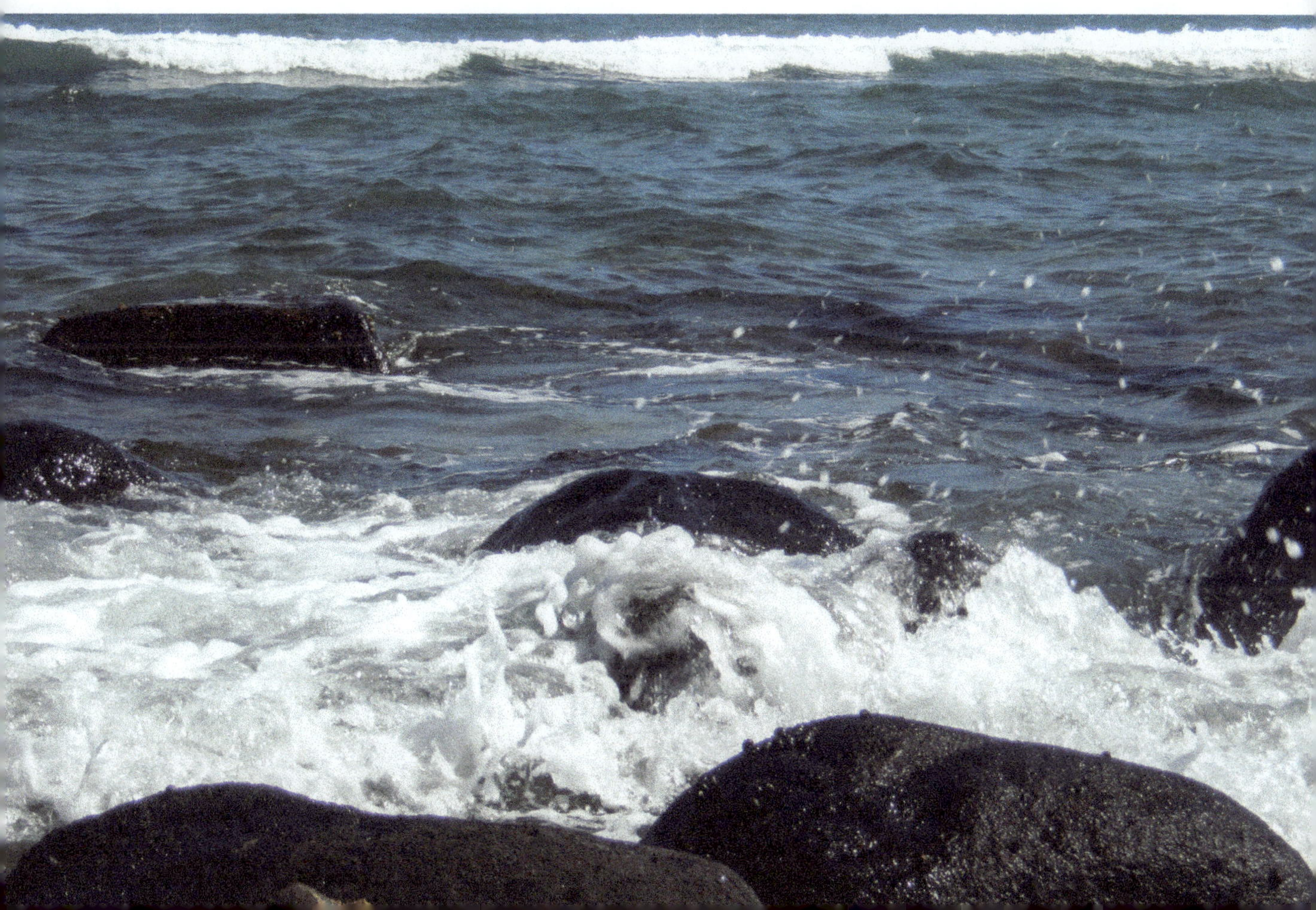

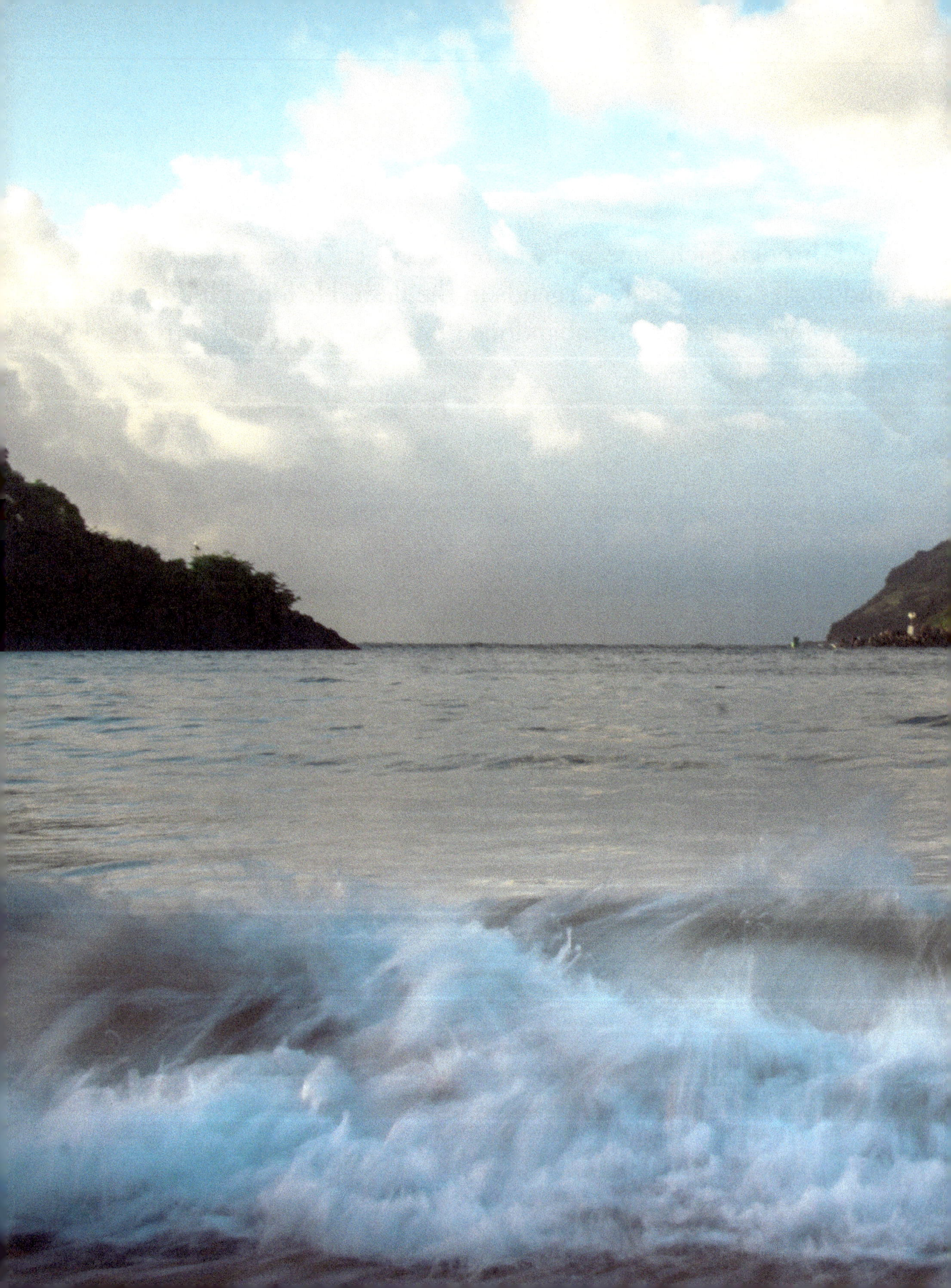

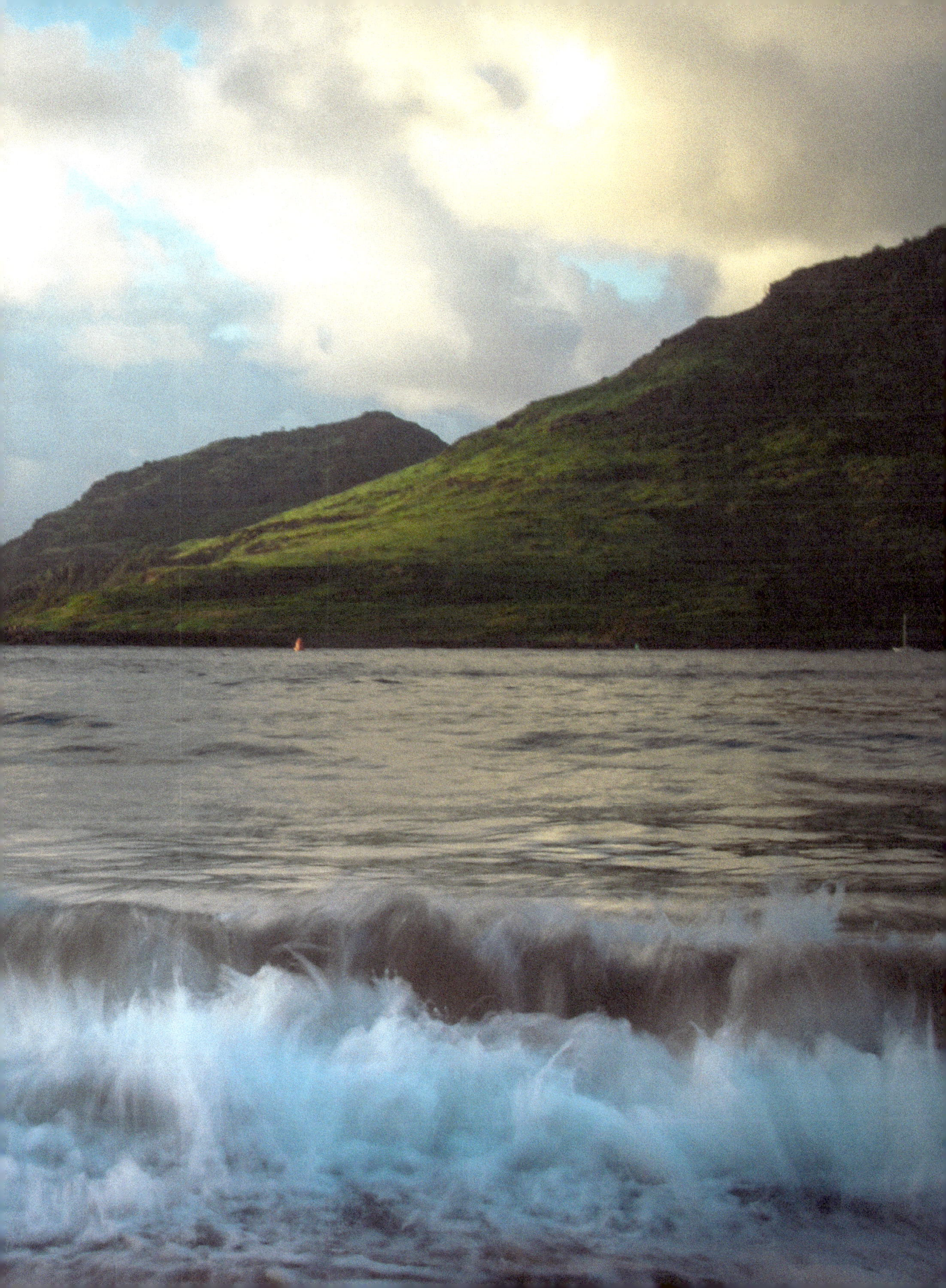

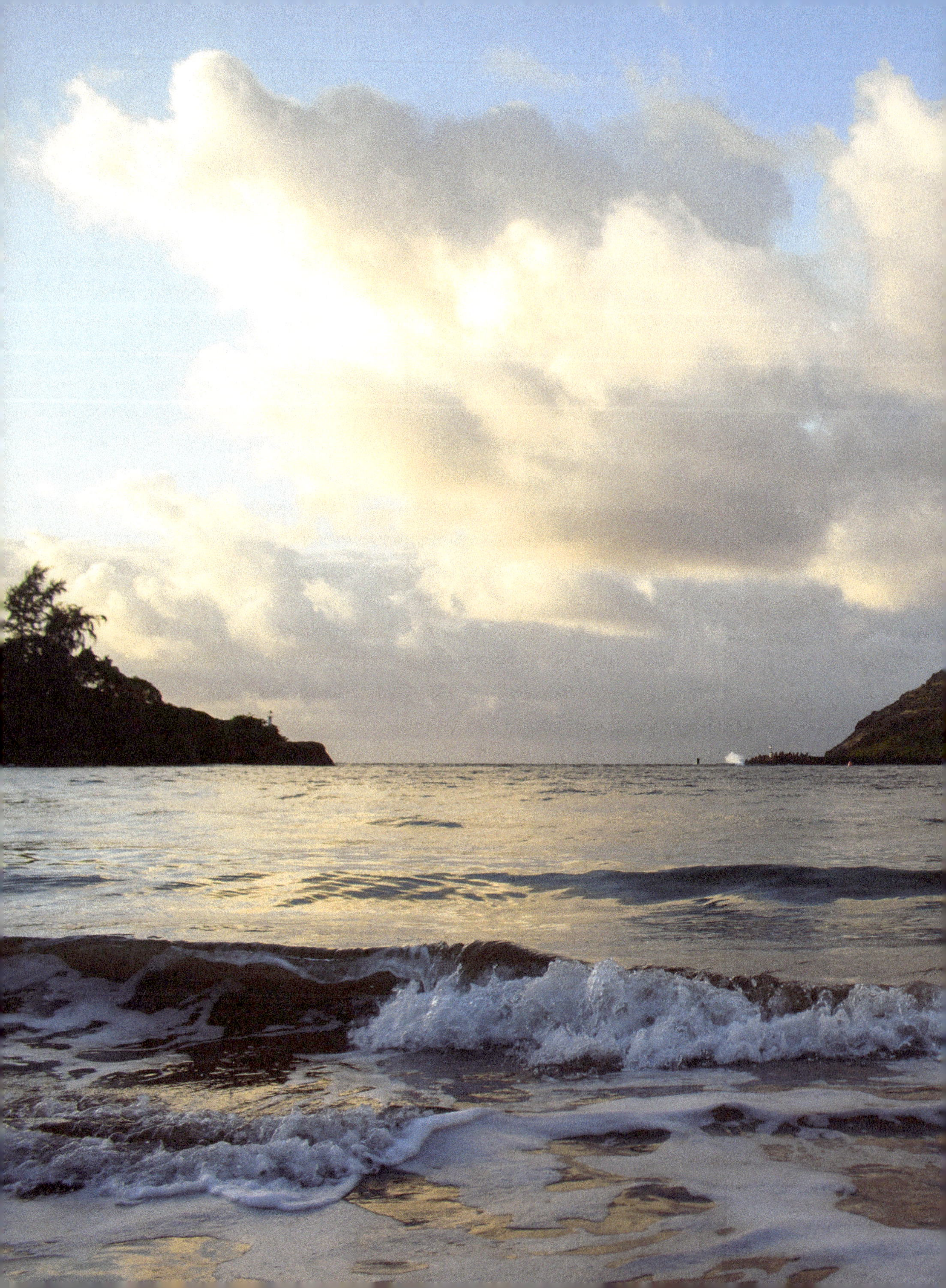

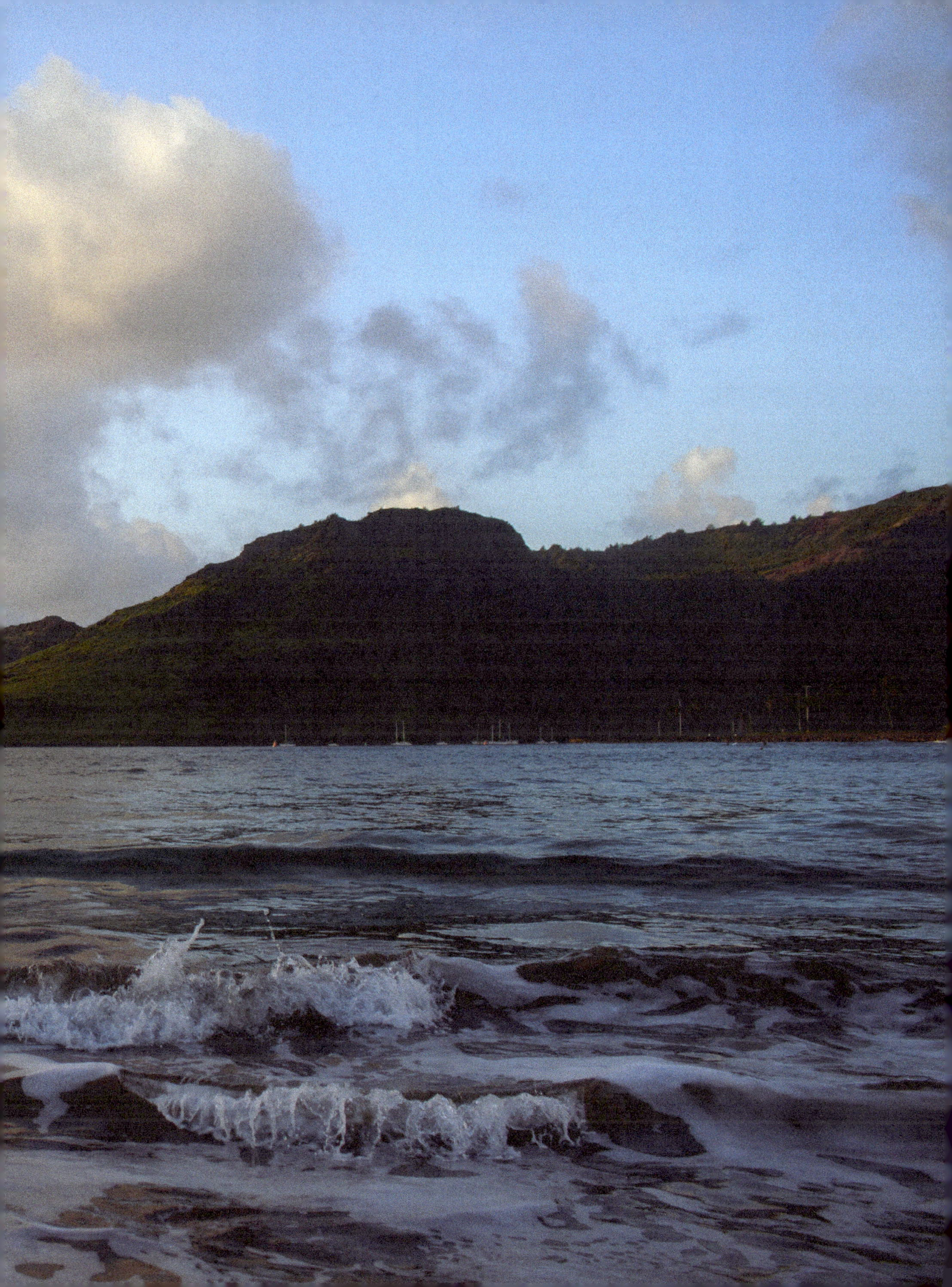

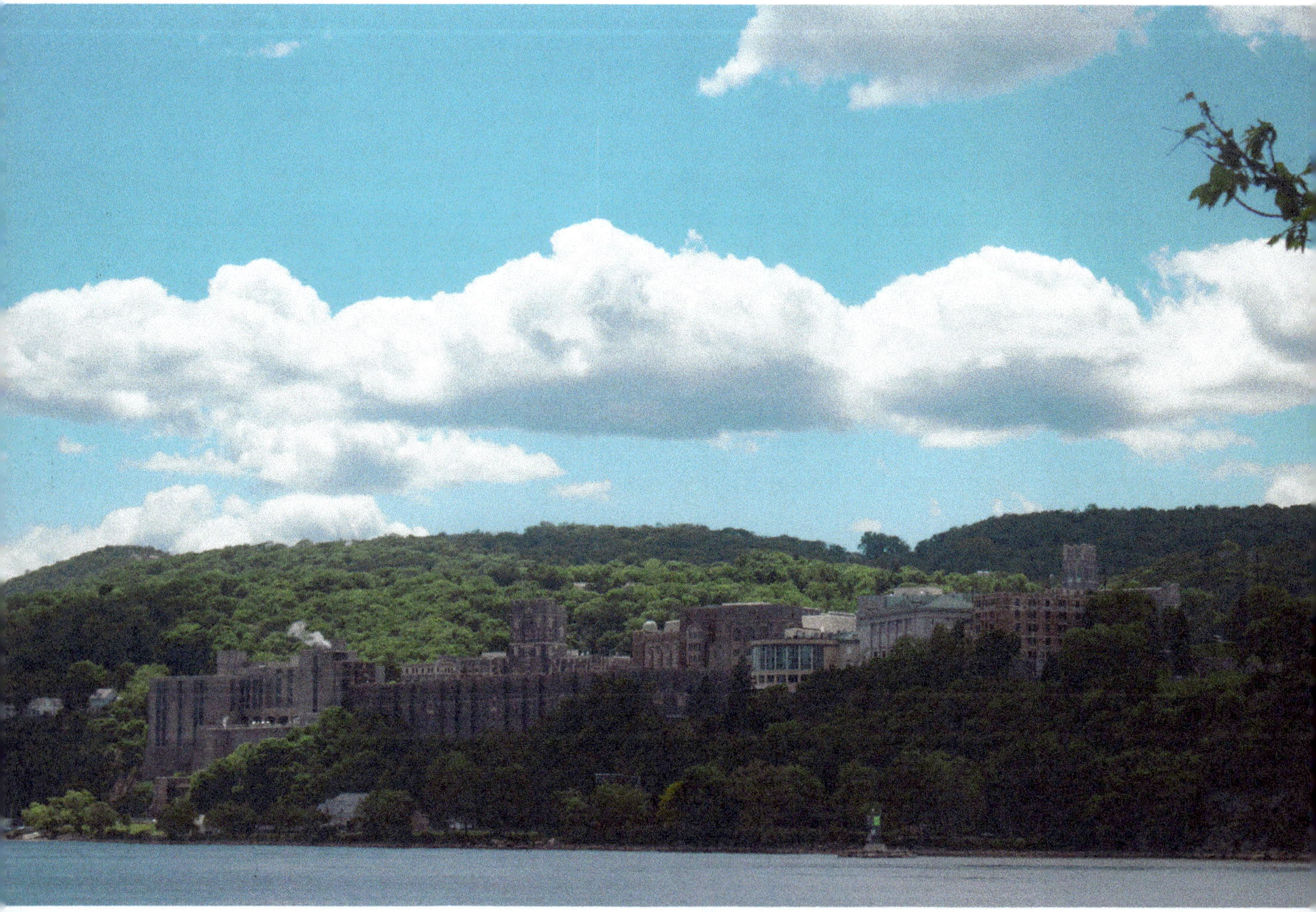

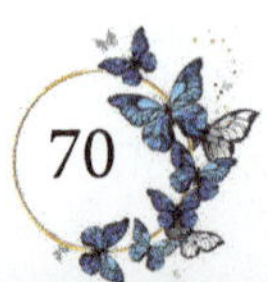

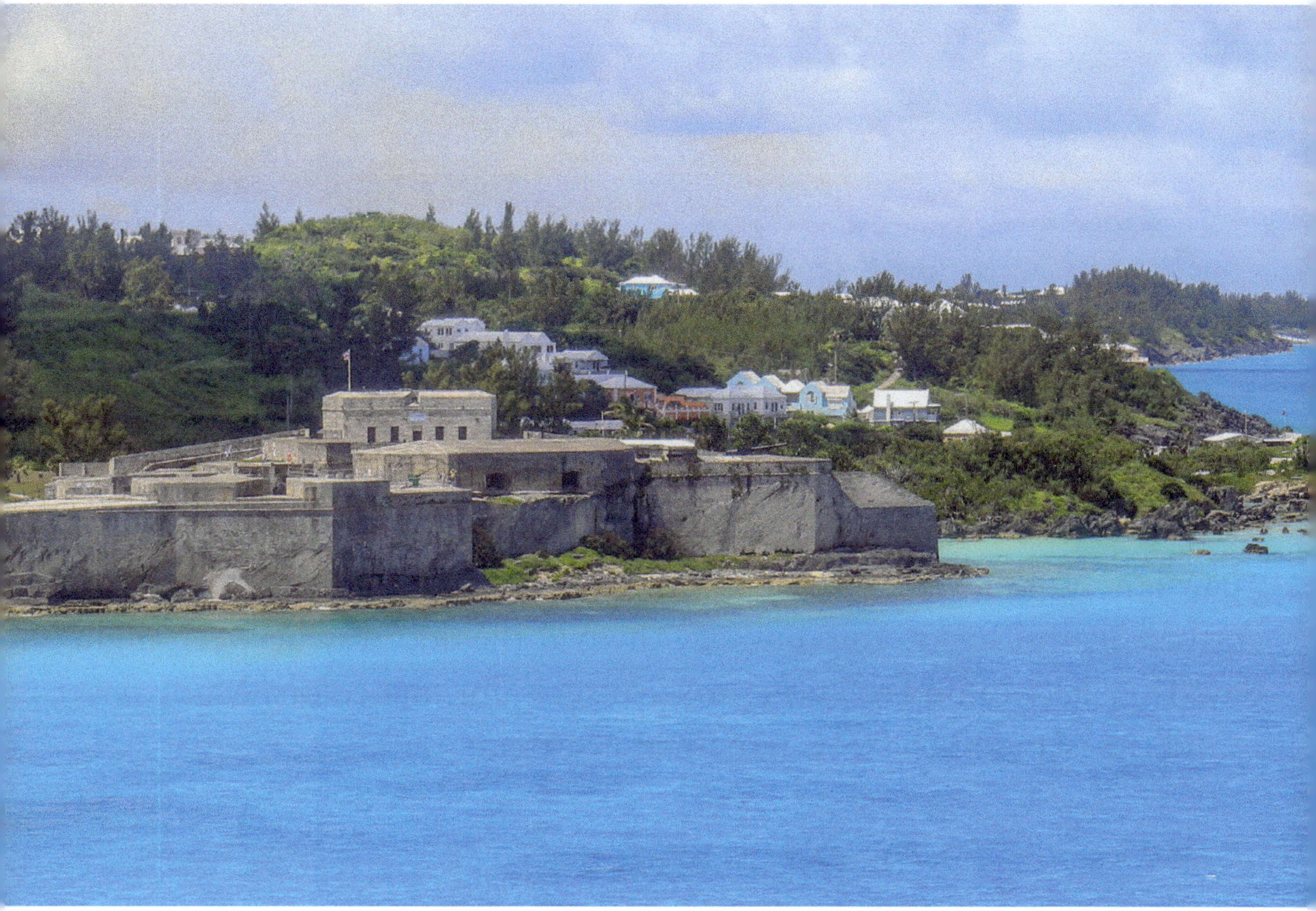

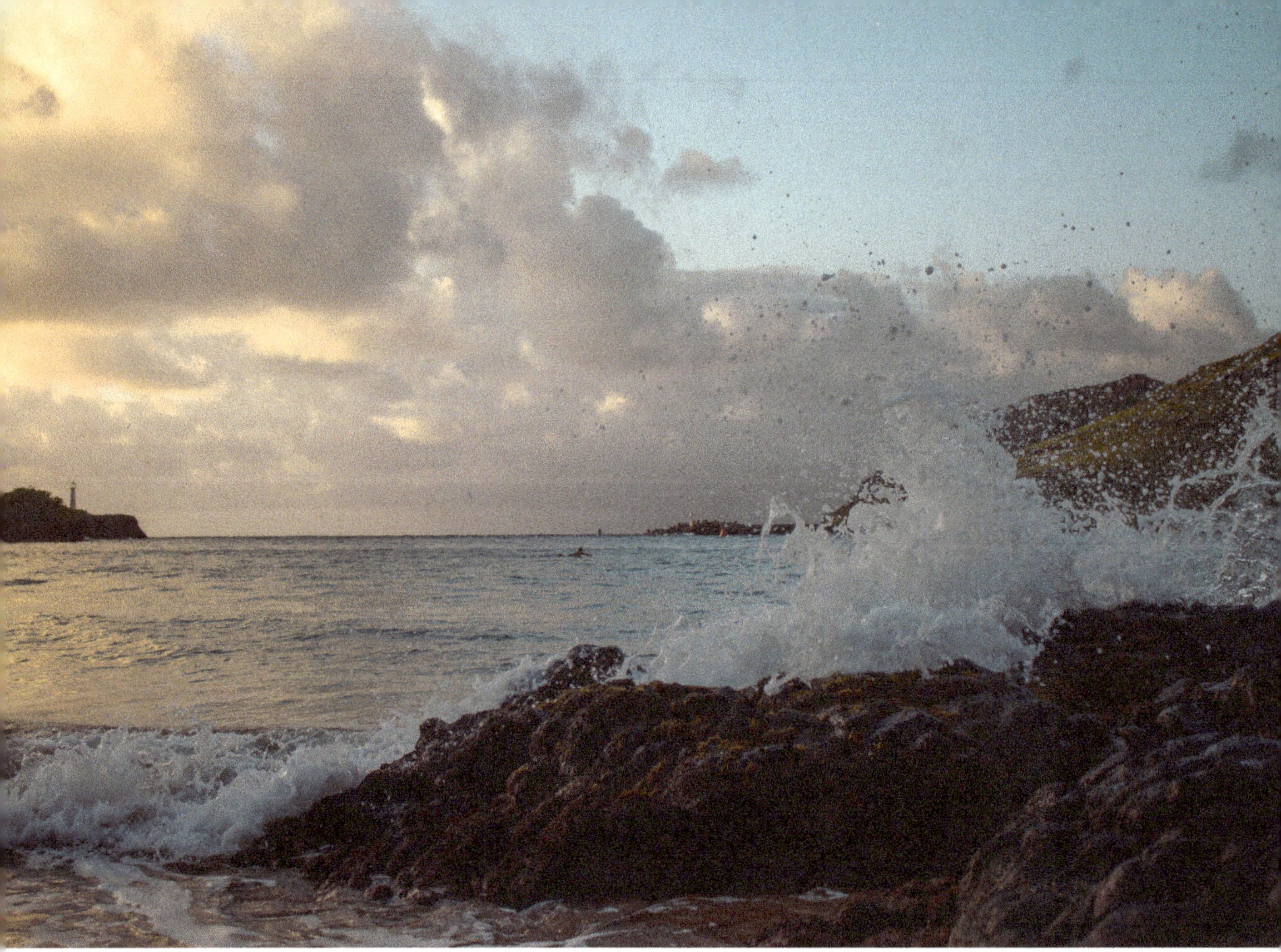

He read stories of an island with vibrant colored waters protected by an ocea
guardian. Stories went, you caught the guardian's full form in waves as they
crashed against rocks. You only saw them at the doorway between night and
day. This deity caused the water to turn such unusual colors. Many never
found the island so the tales remained just that.

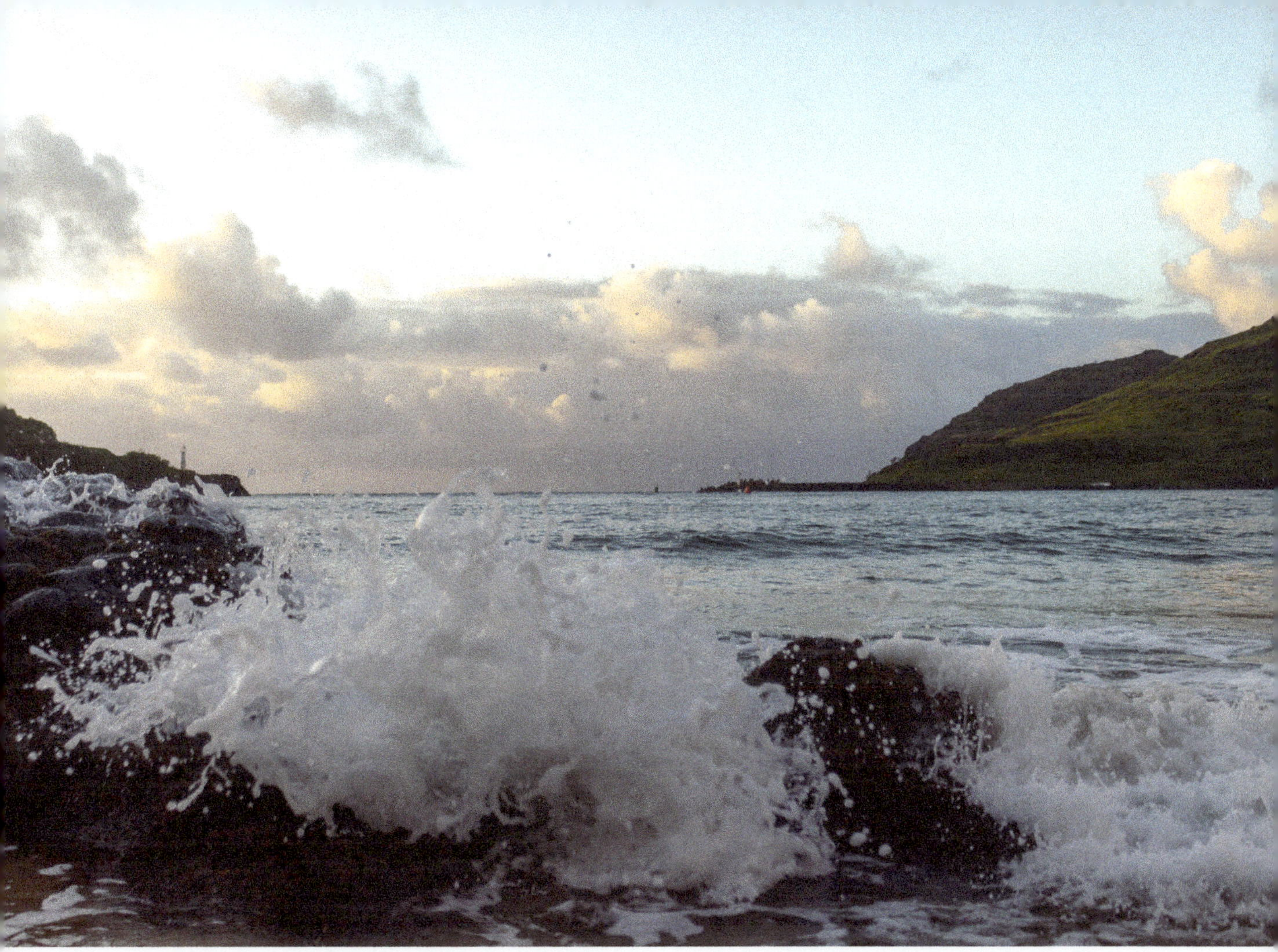

e had researched before starting the journey. He had an idea of where
at island was located. It wasn't exact and it took him days to find it but he
id. He saw the purple water. He saw waves take the shape of a person as it
ashed into rocks.

he searched hard enough, he could probably find a logical explanation for
l of this. But, this journey was about magic. He wanted to see these stories.
o, he did.

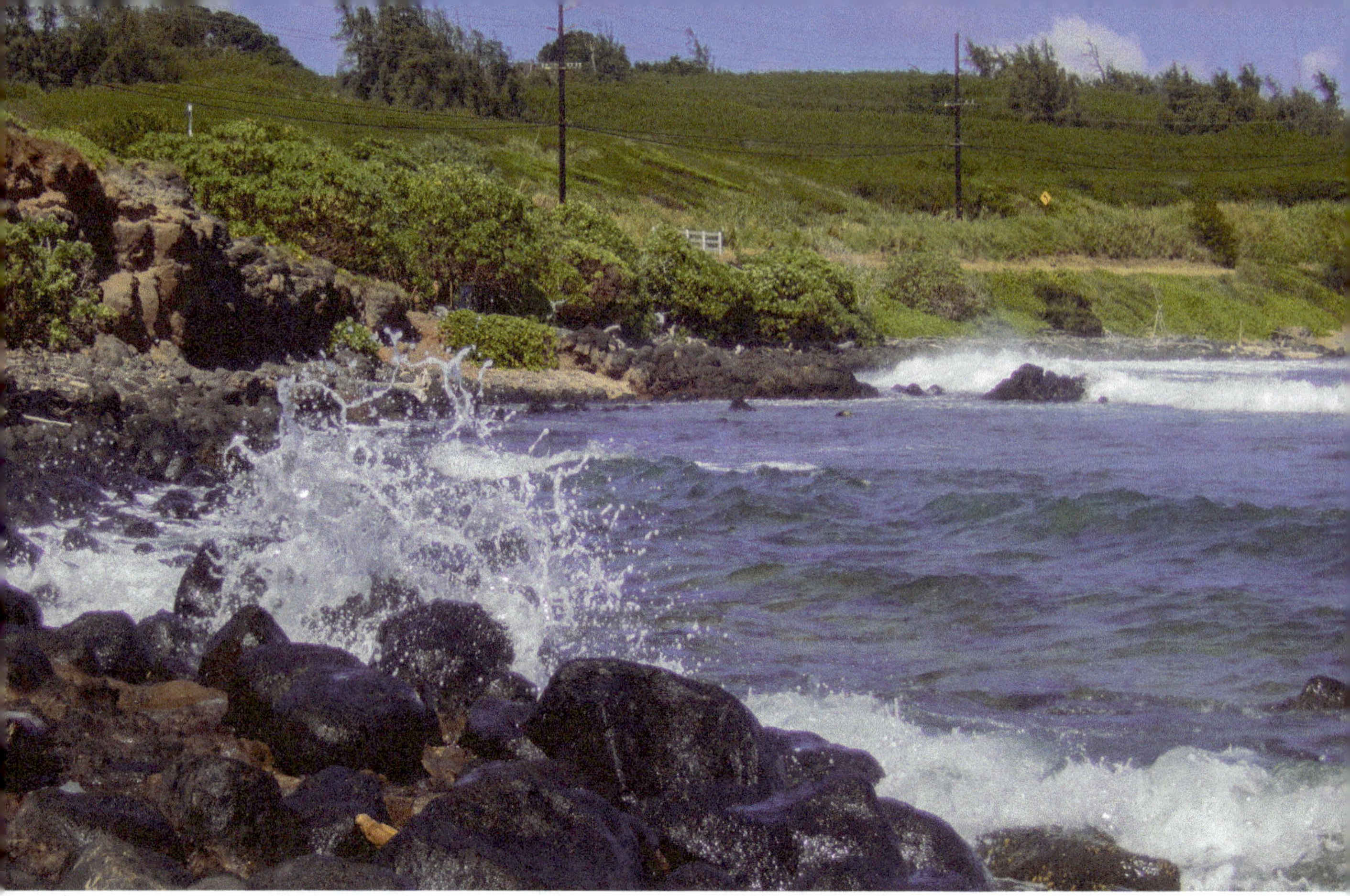

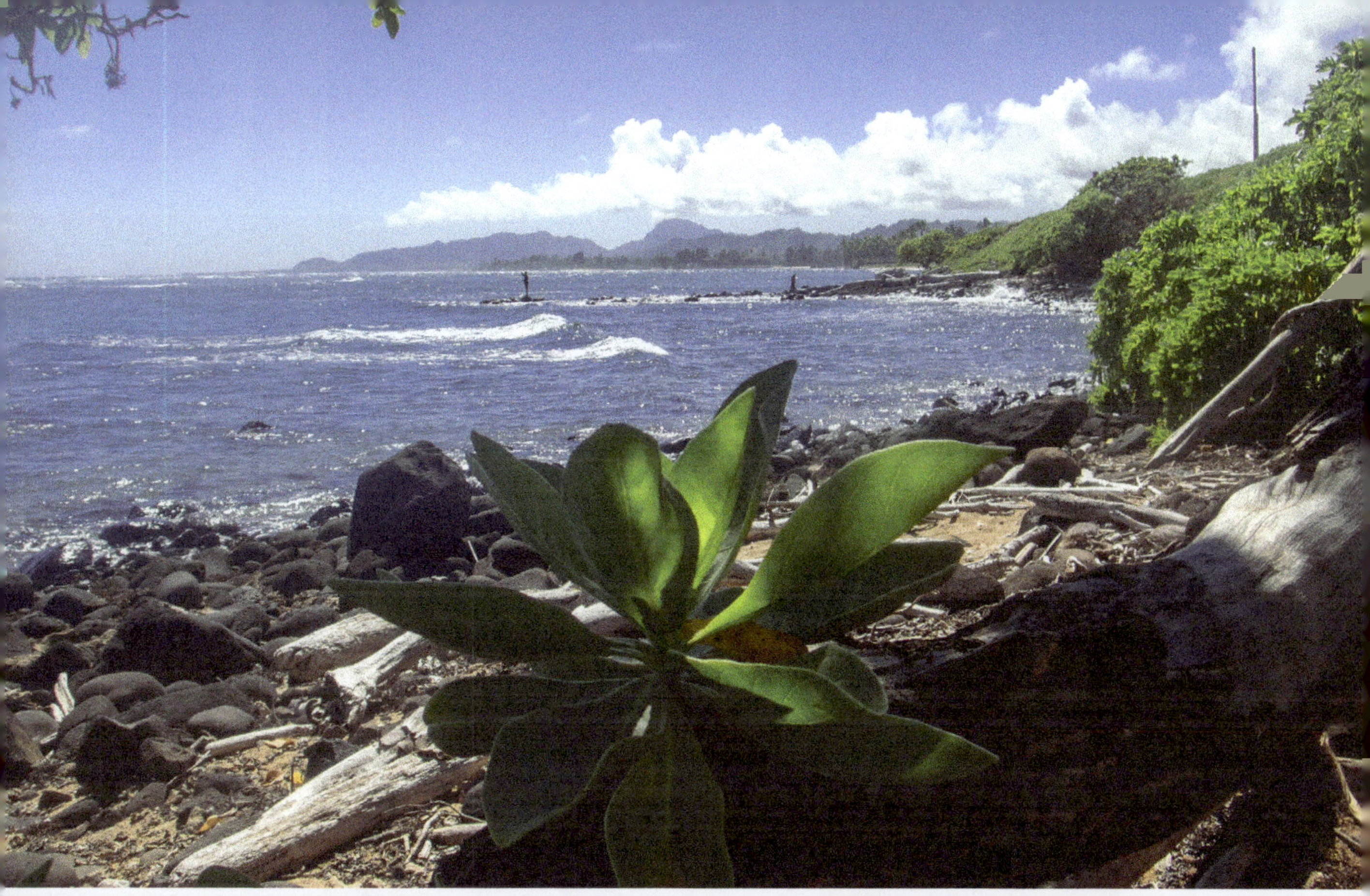

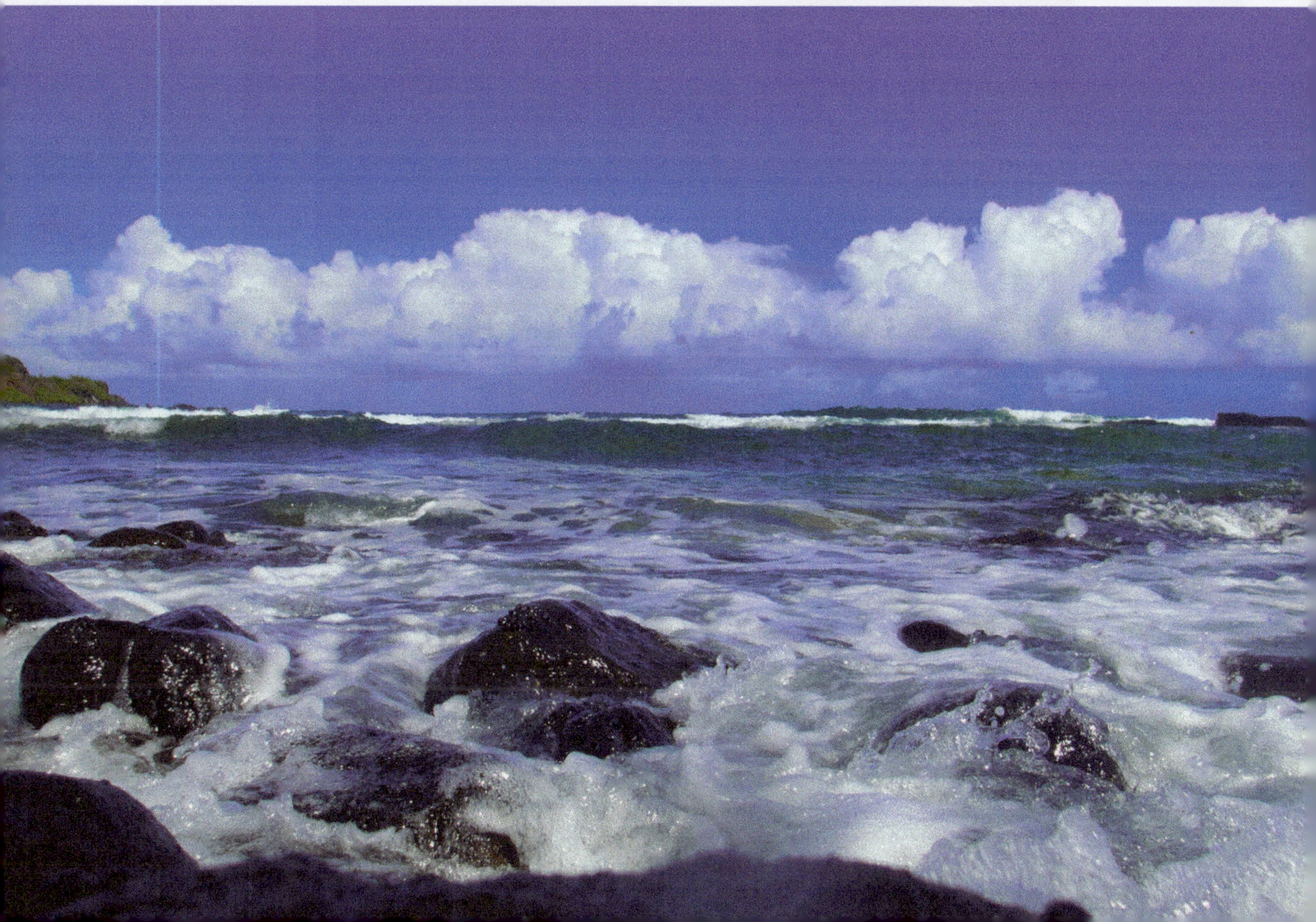

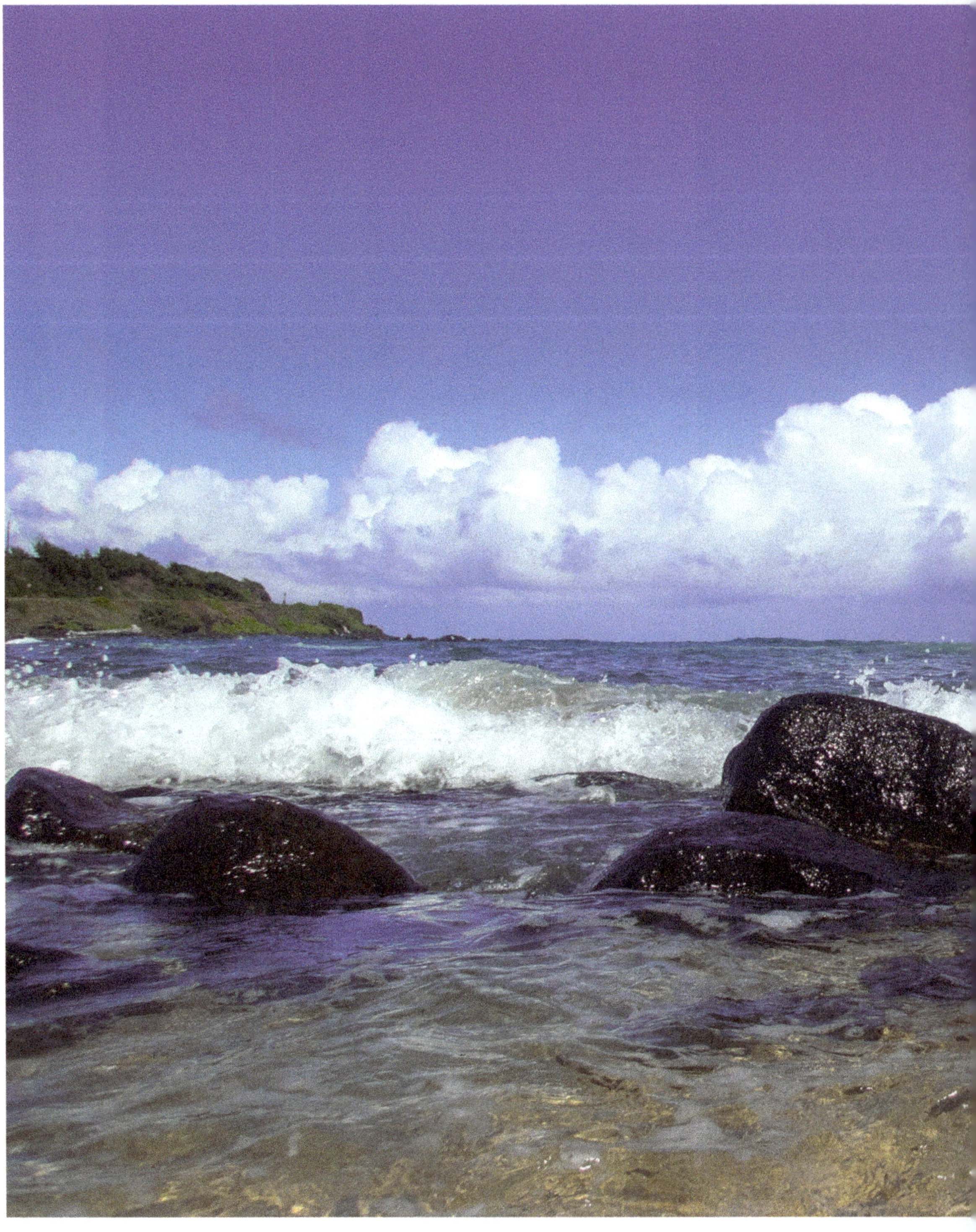

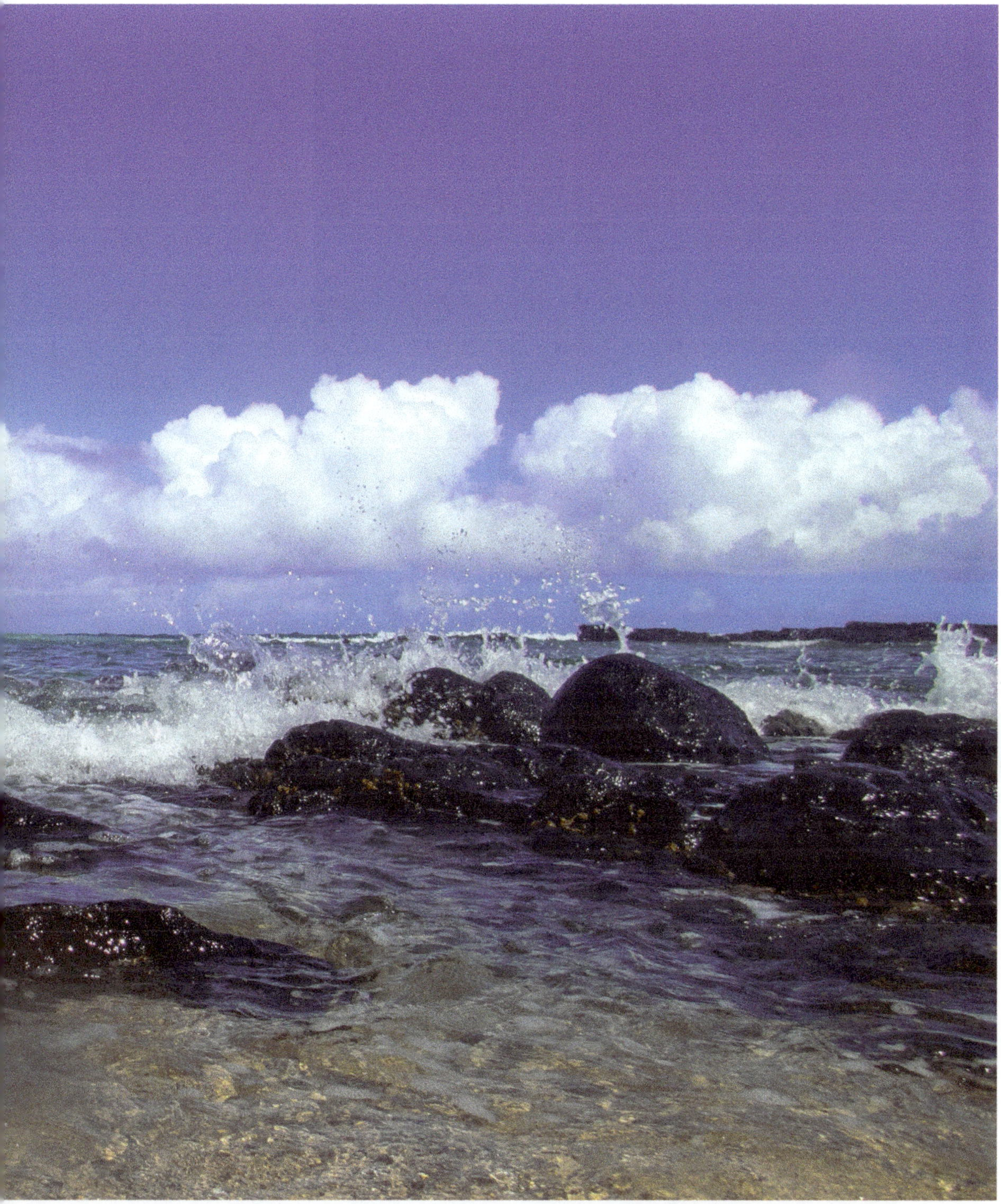

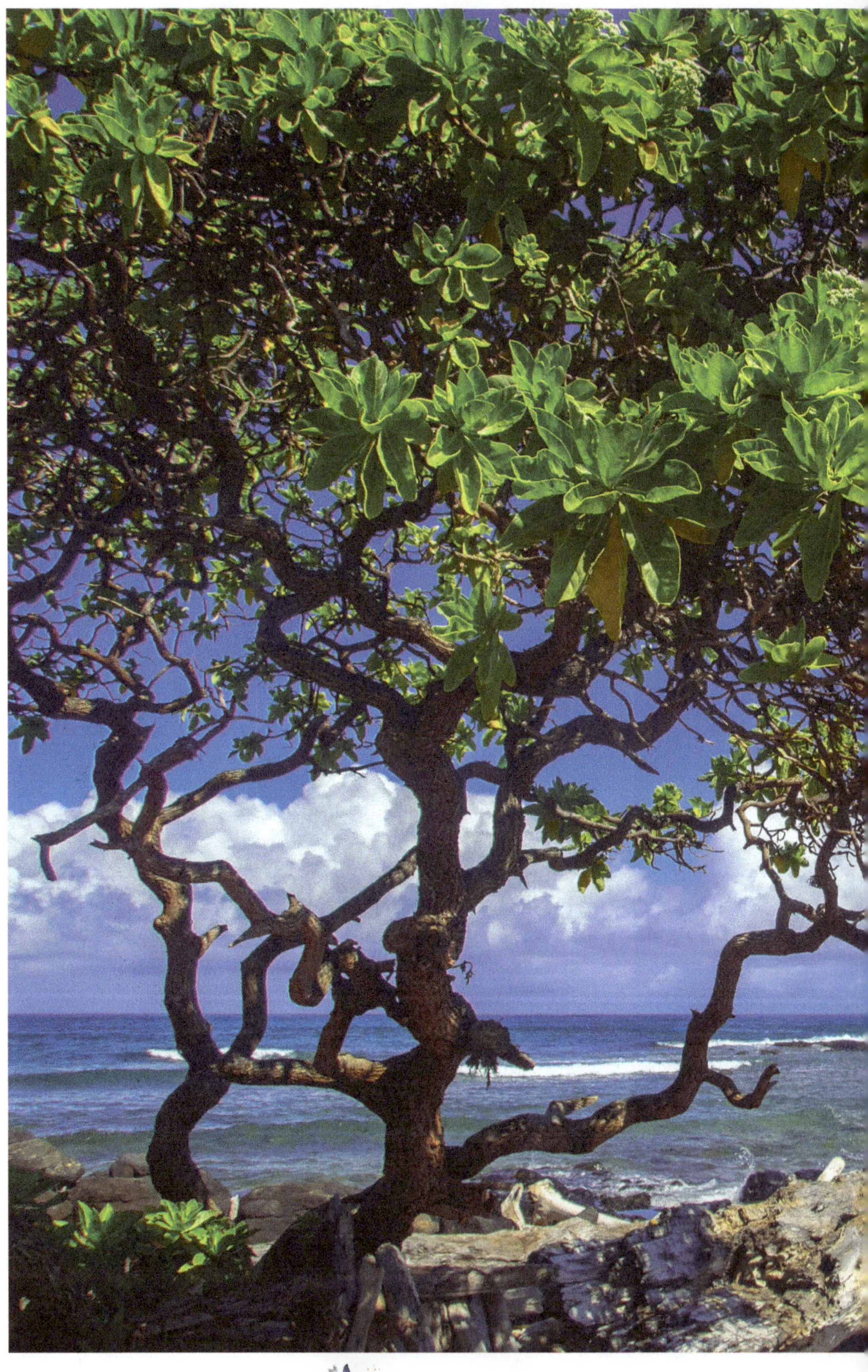

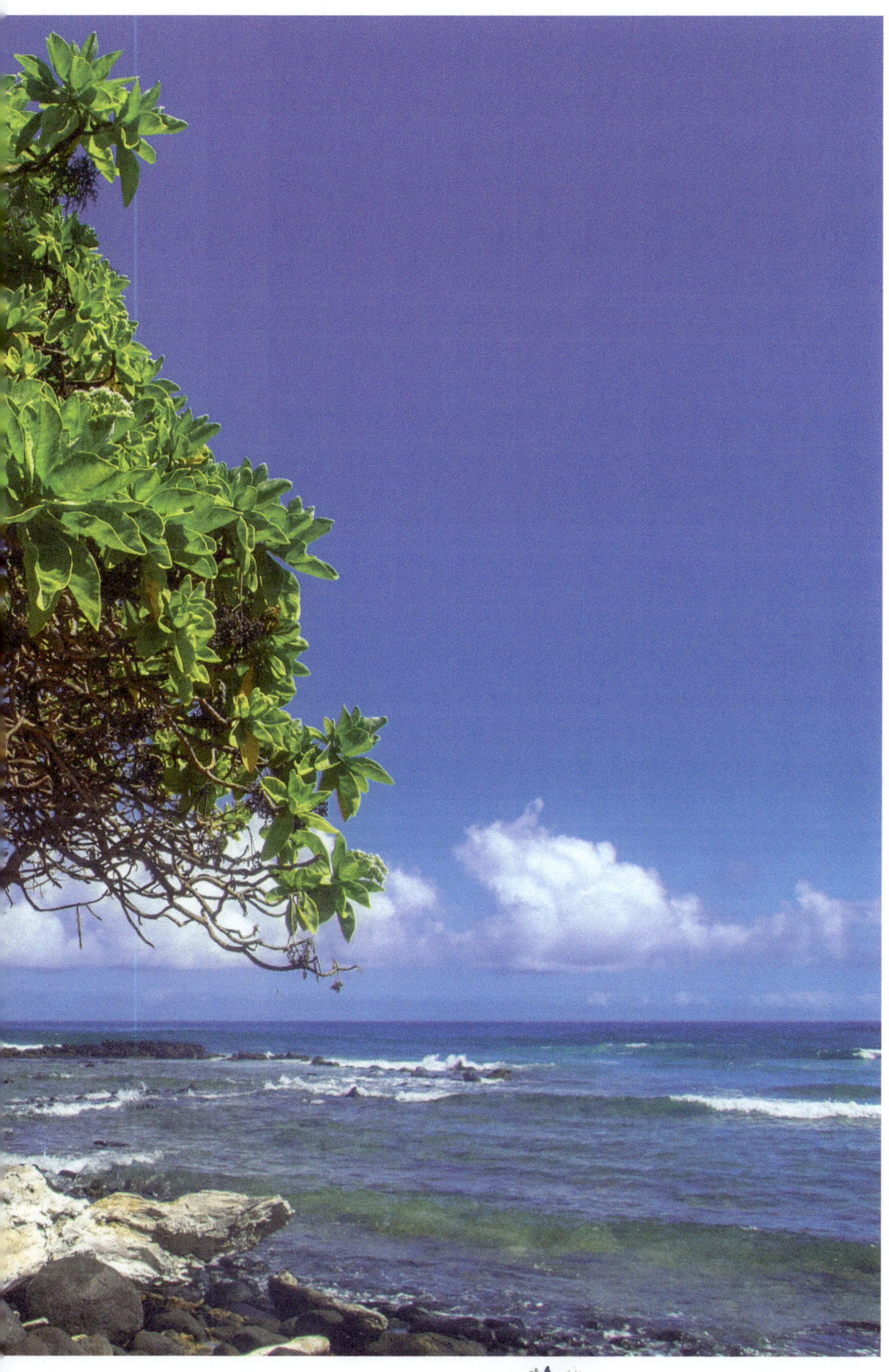

He worked alongside the residents to earn money and supplies for the rest of his trip. In doing so, he heard more tales about the guardian. He sat by the ocean for hours as the ocean-figure rose each time. He thought he heard its voice in the wind but maybe it was his imagination.

The residents spoke of its resting place and gave him permission to seek it.

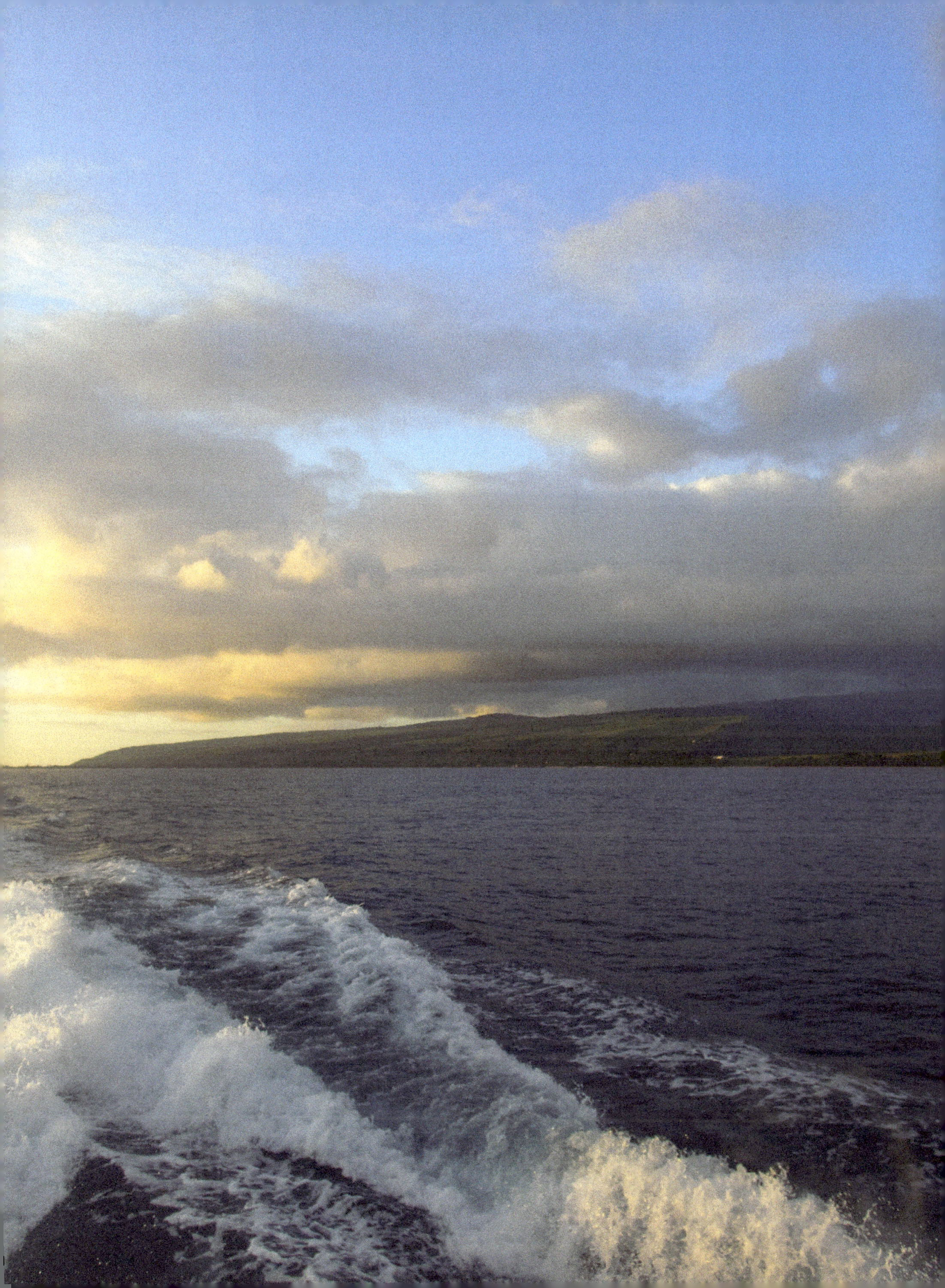

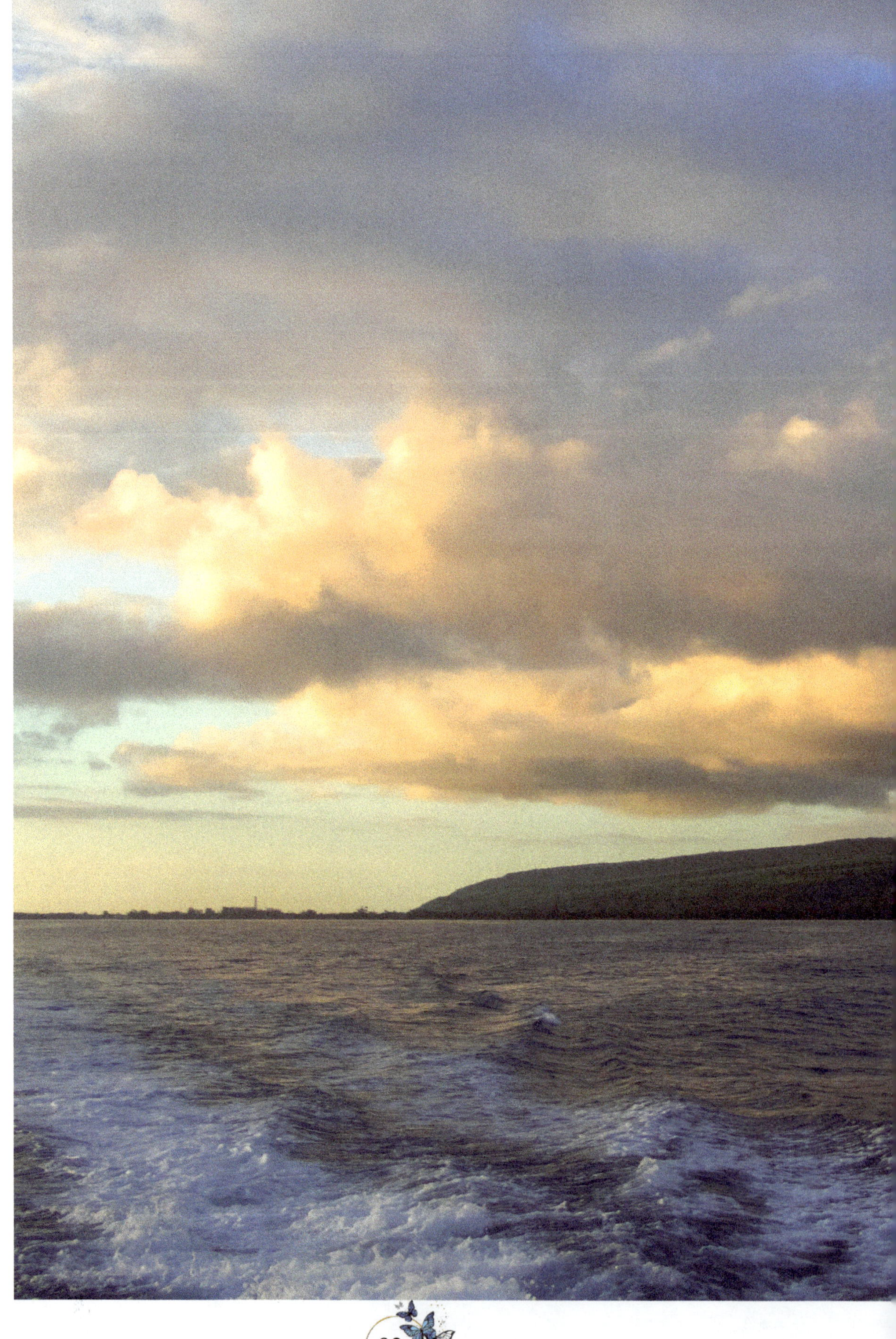

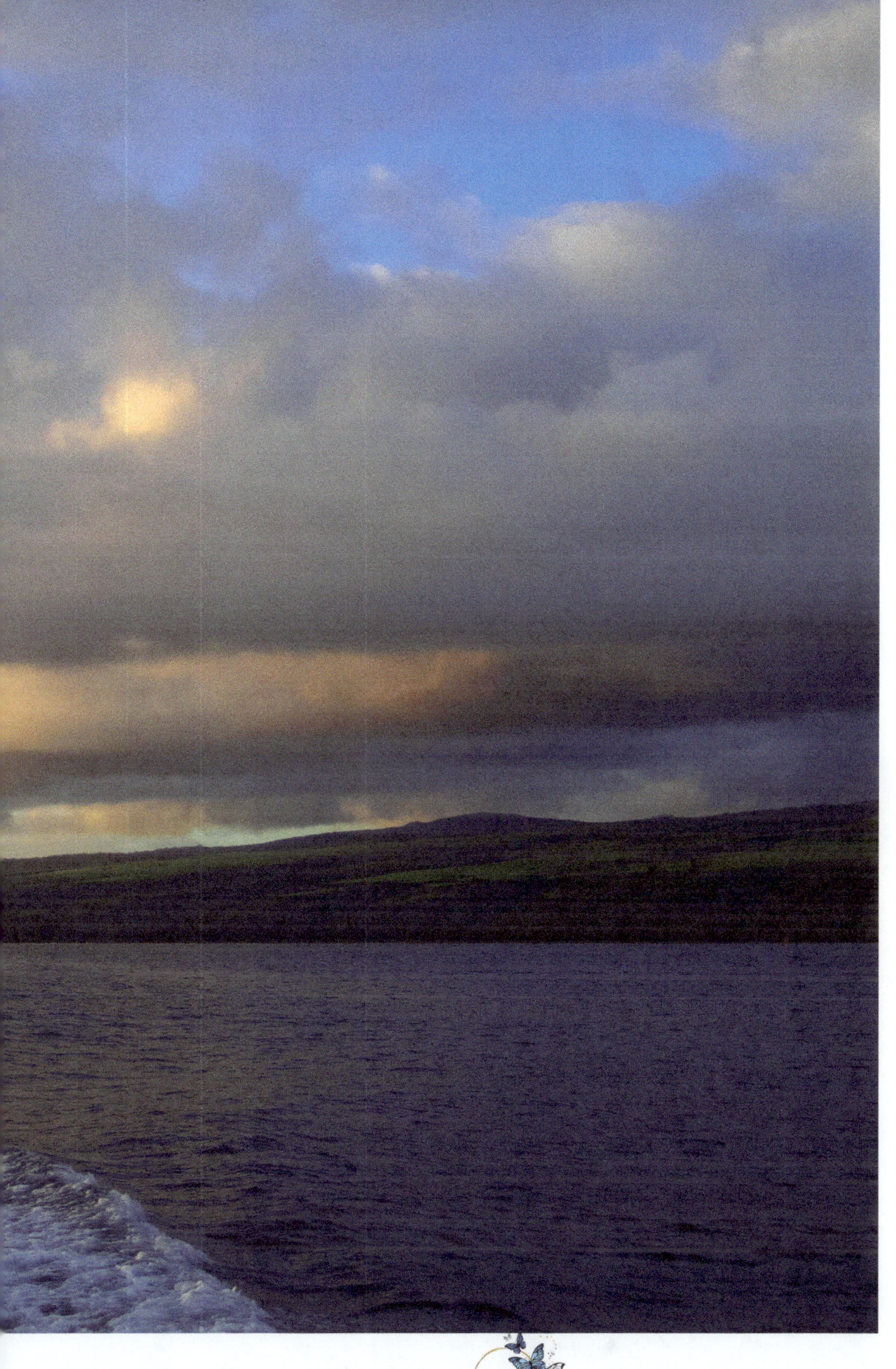

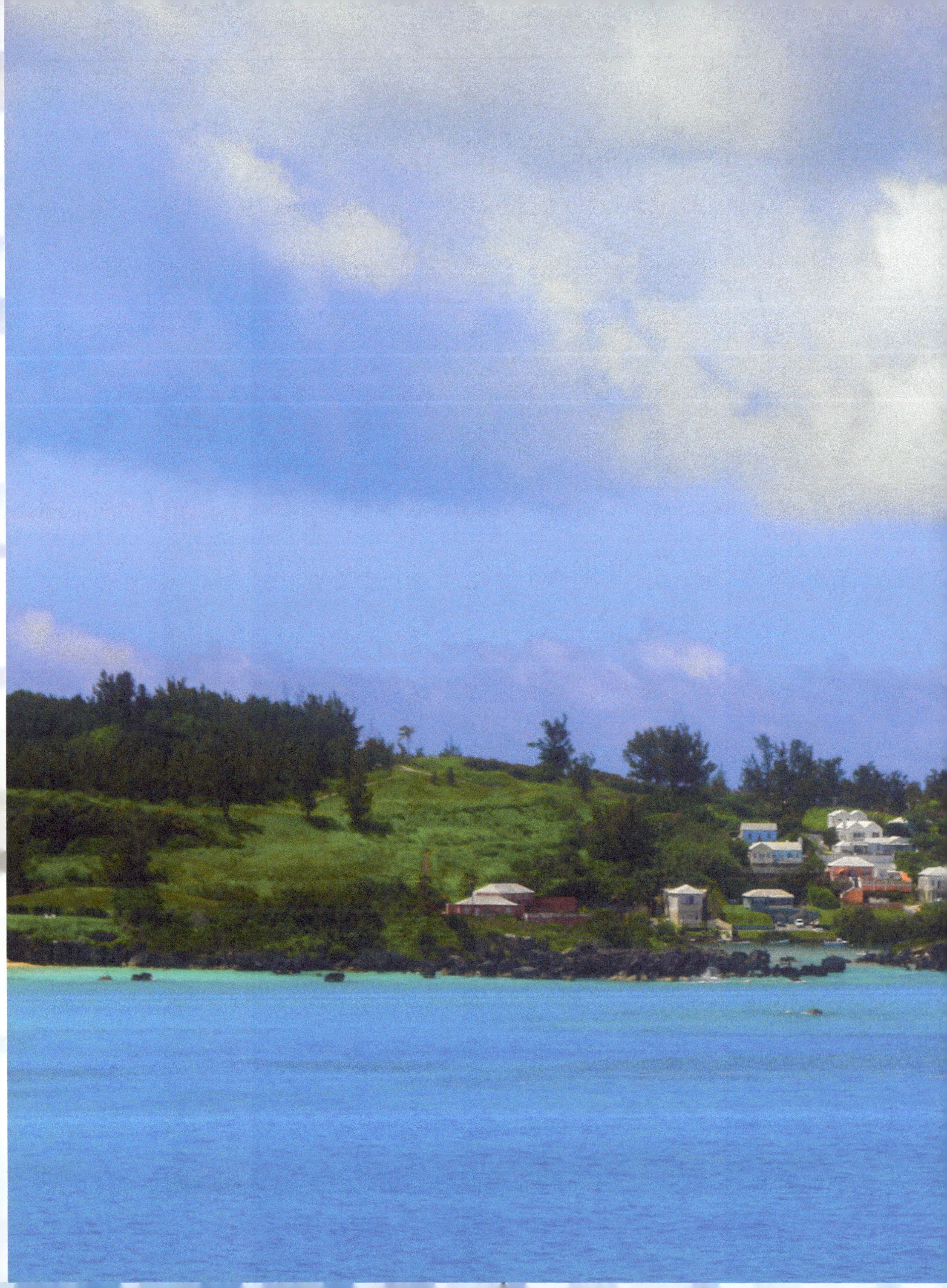

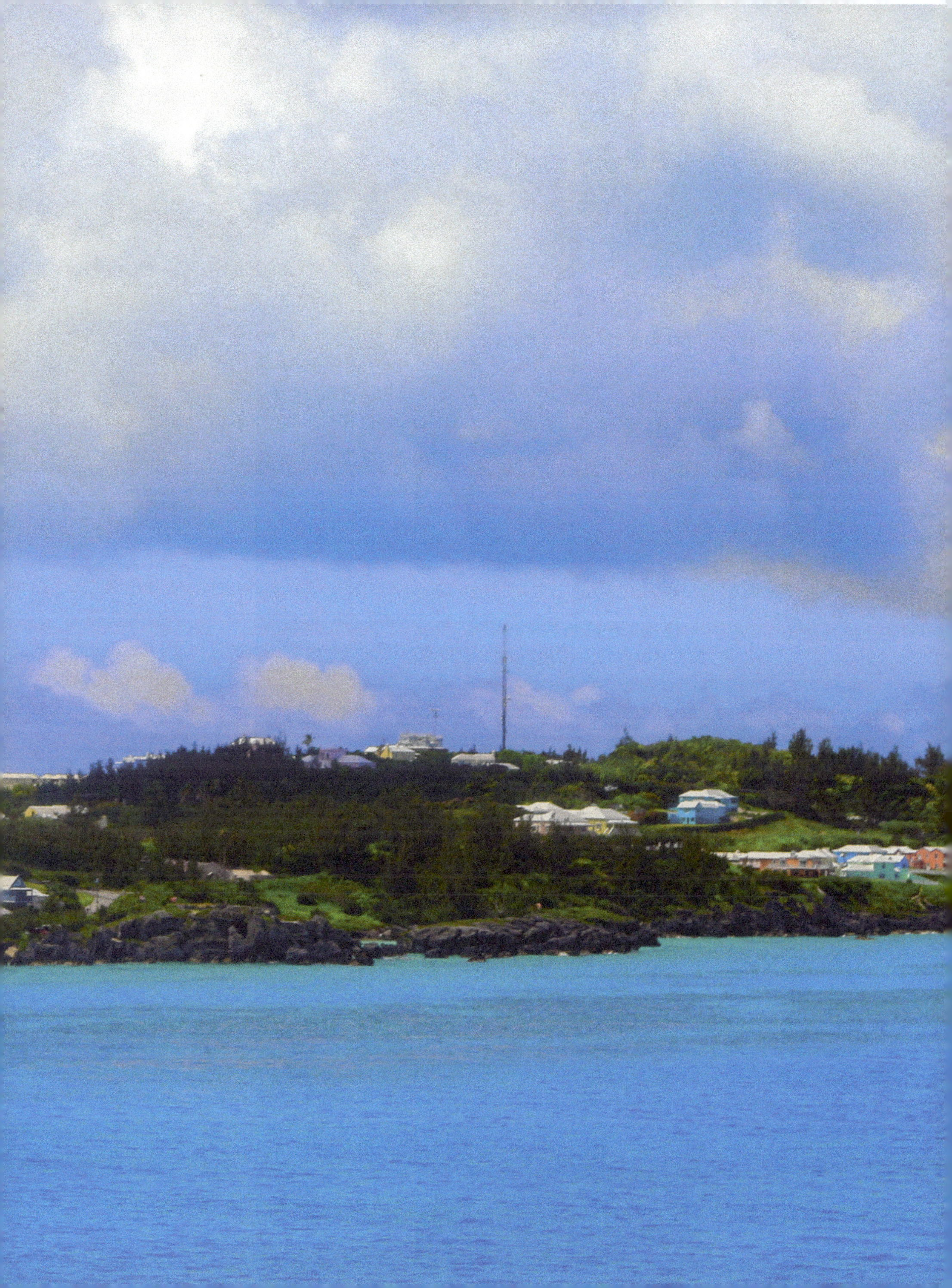

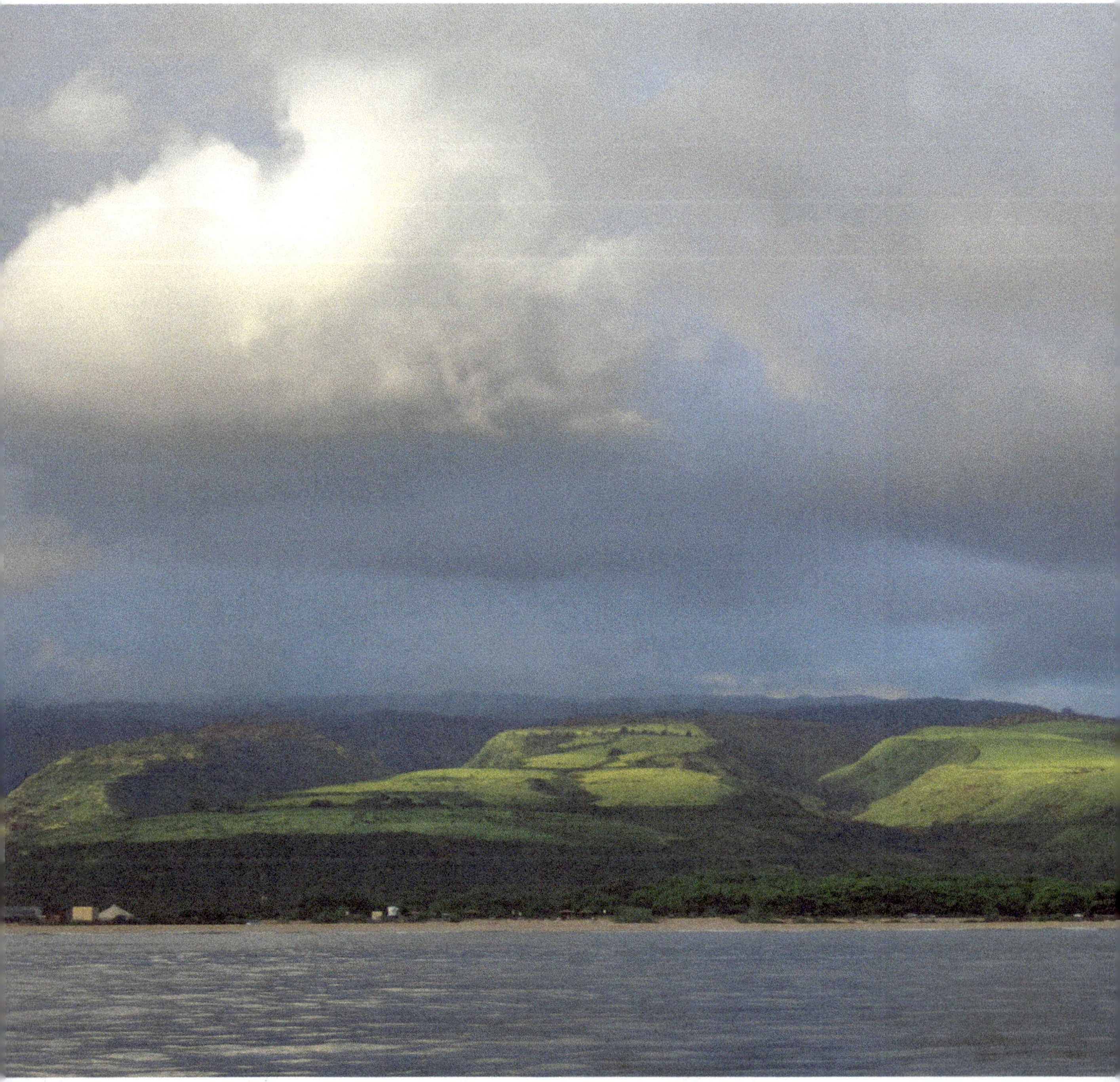

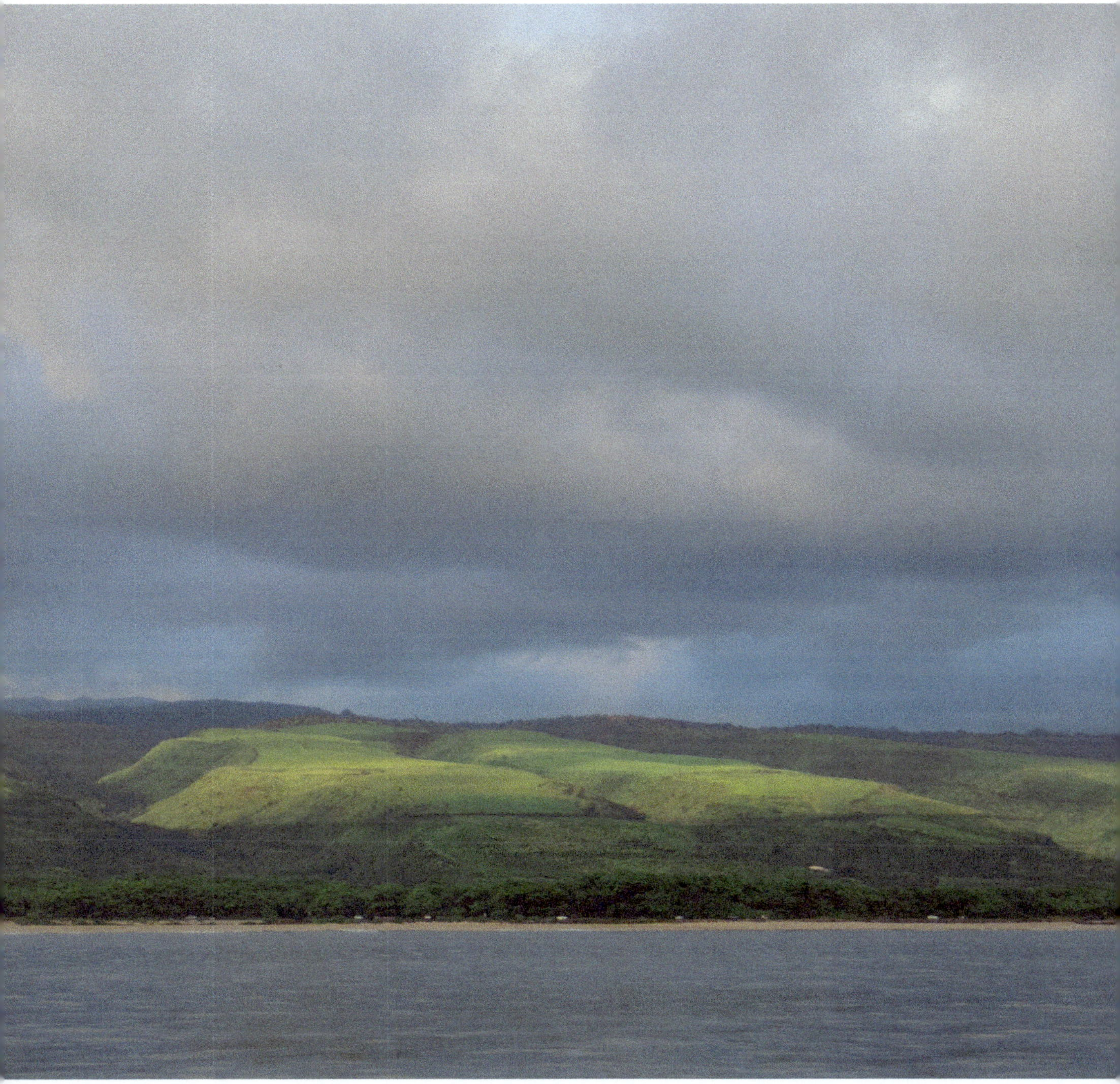

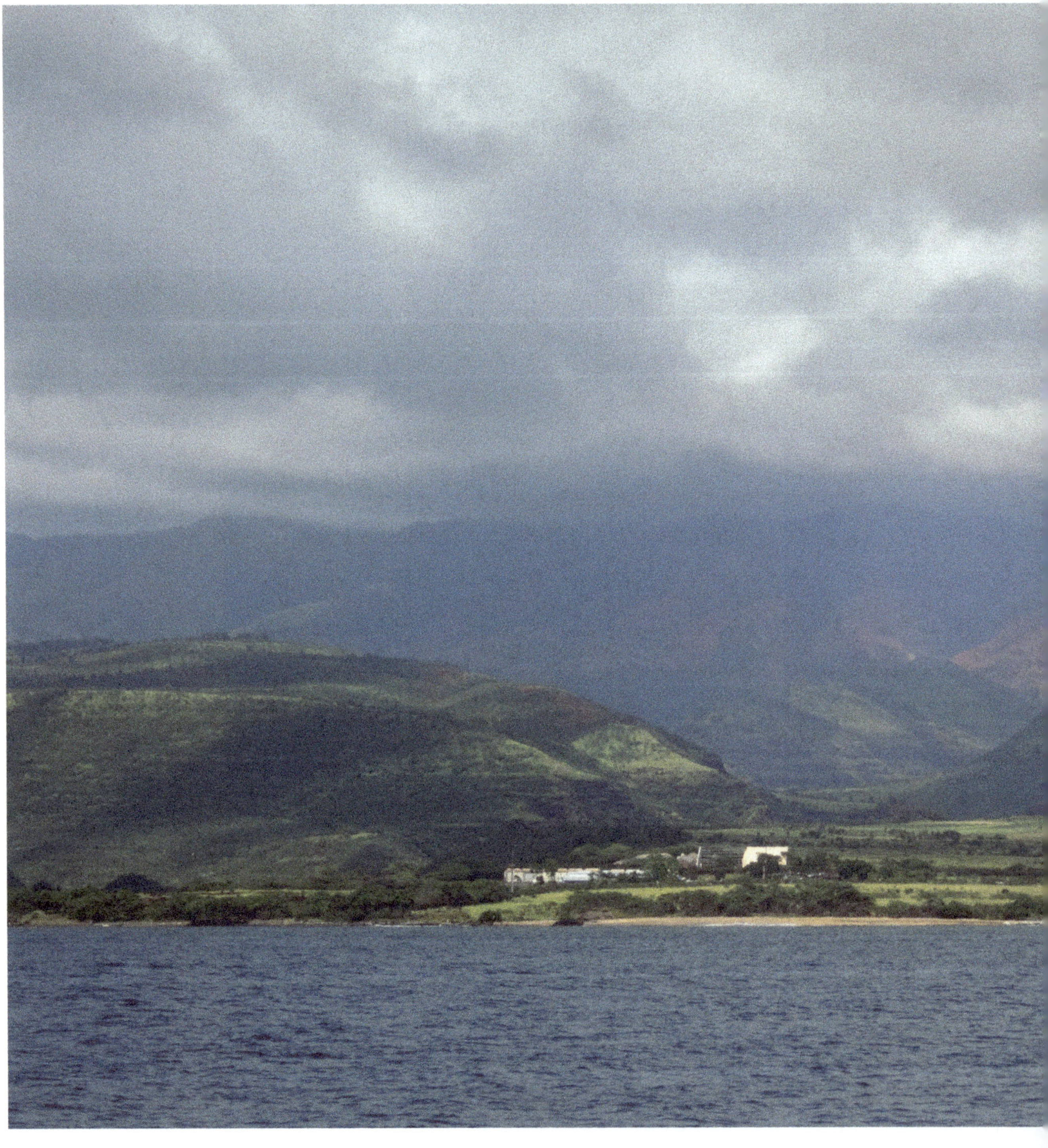

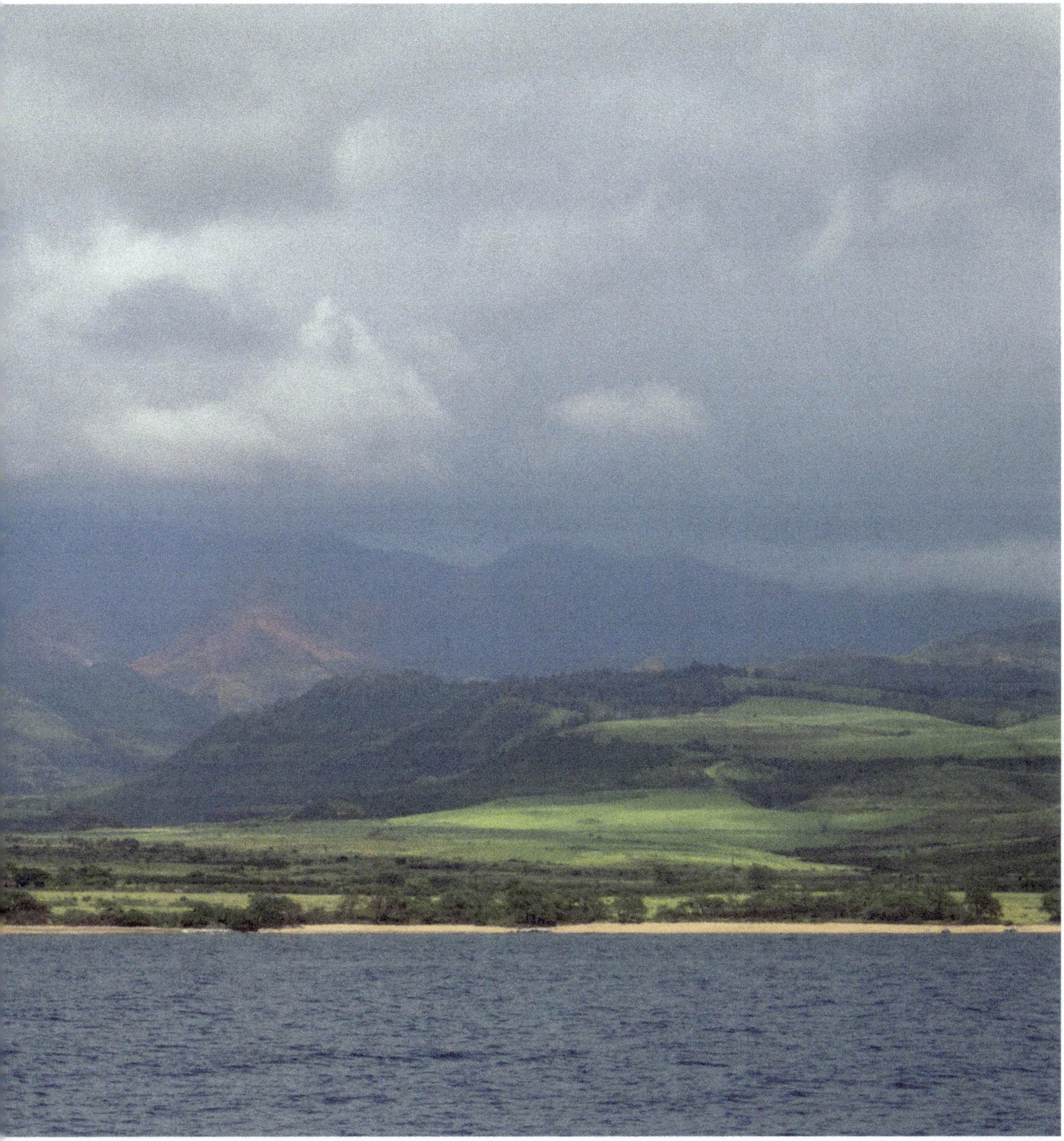

THE ISLAND'S GUARDIAN

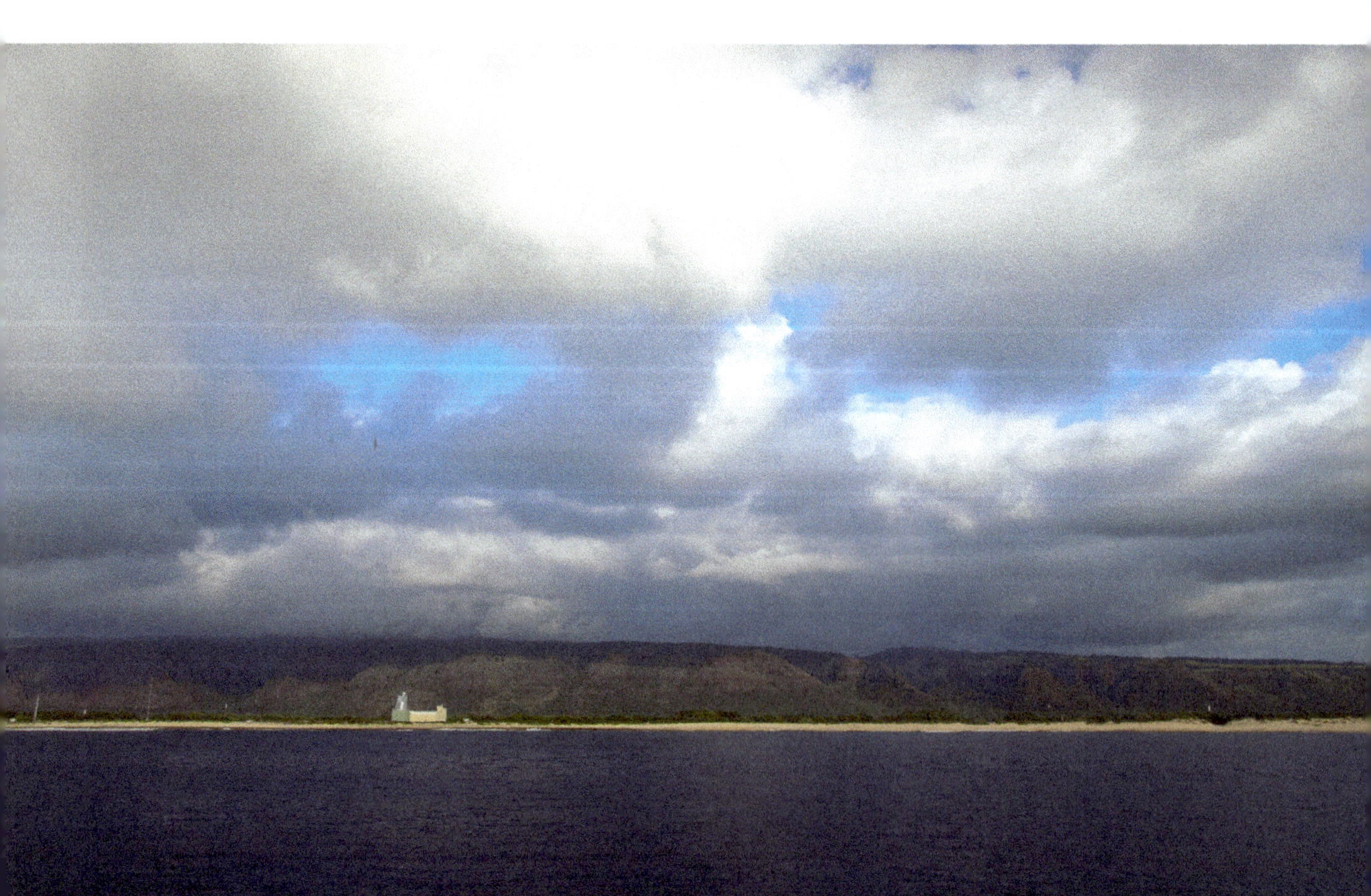

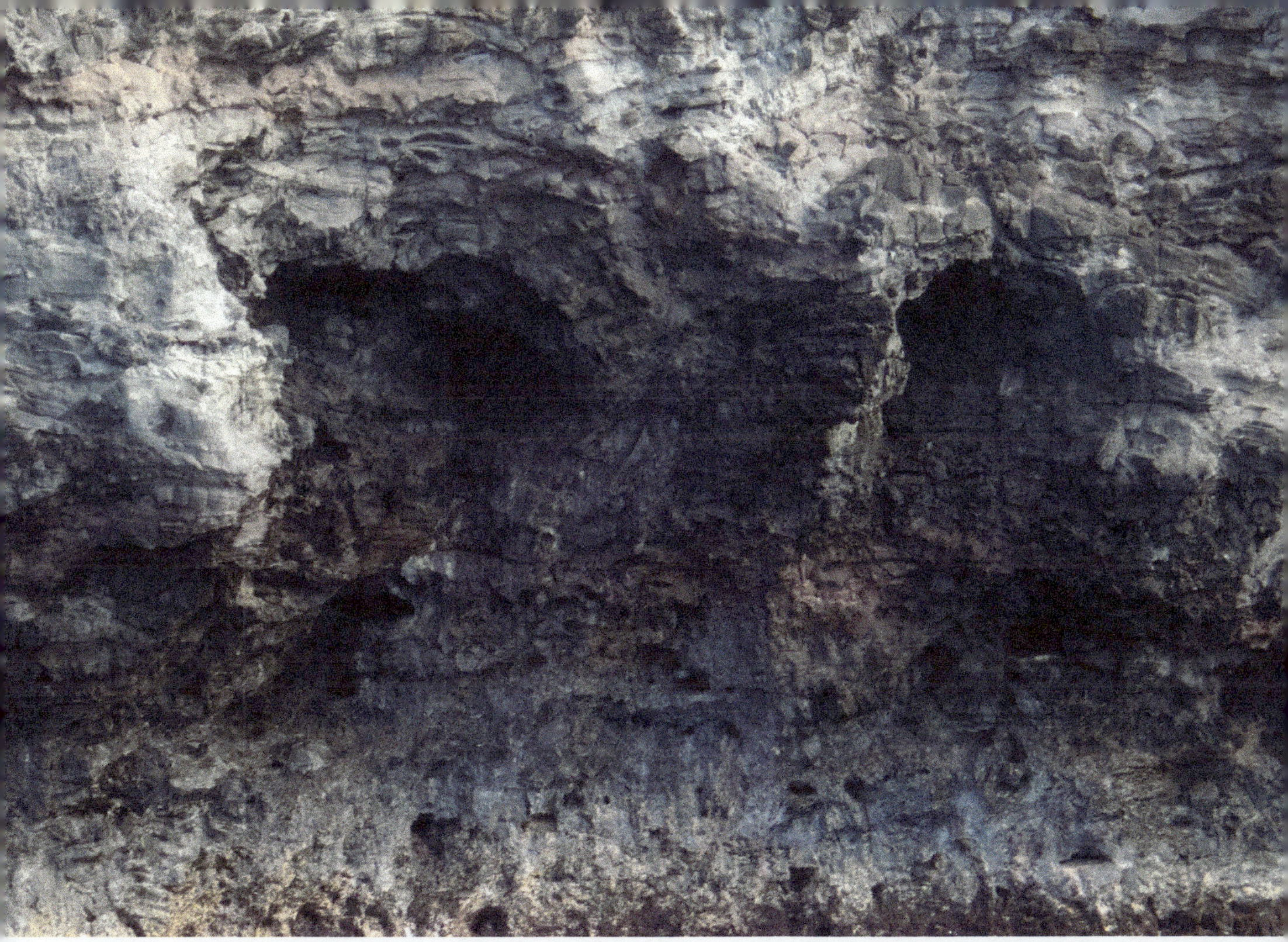

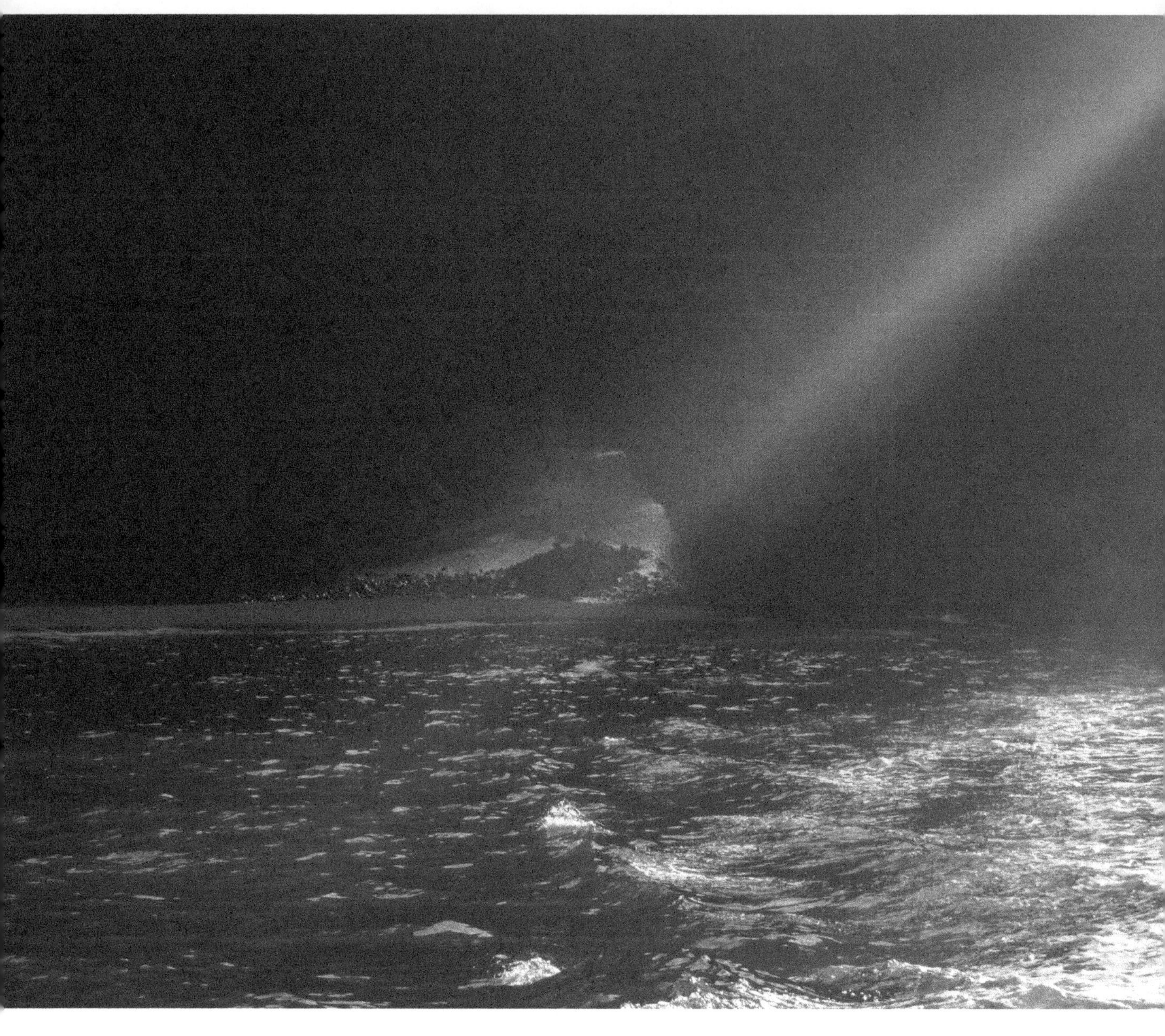

He took photos and wrote down the residents' stories. No one at home would believe him. His well-meaning family and friends would try to kill the magic. Once he returned home, if he ever returned, he'd share the stories and photos. He wouldn't allow the words of doubters to muddle his memory, darken the experience. He'd keep the journey's true purpose to himself.

THE GUARDIAN'S THRONE

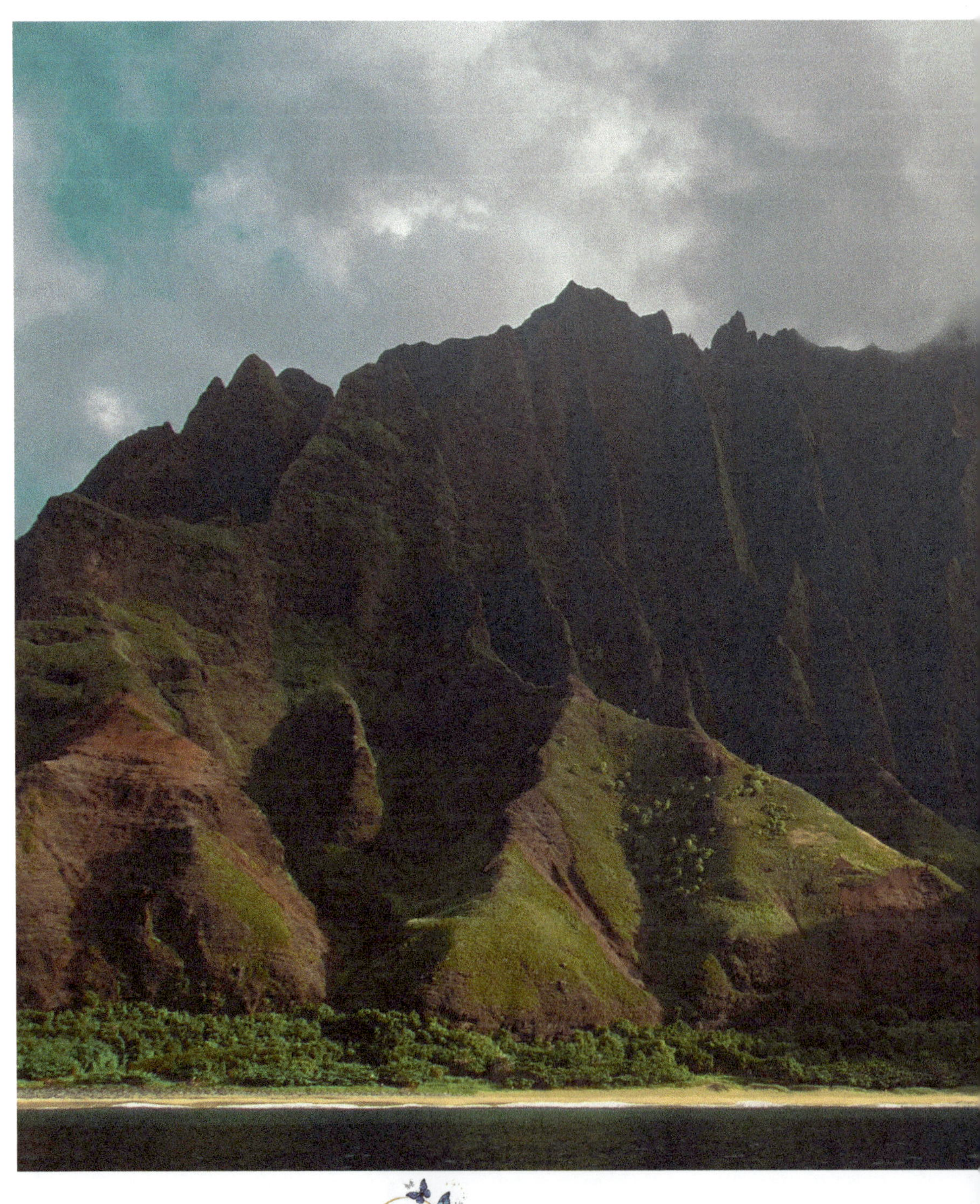

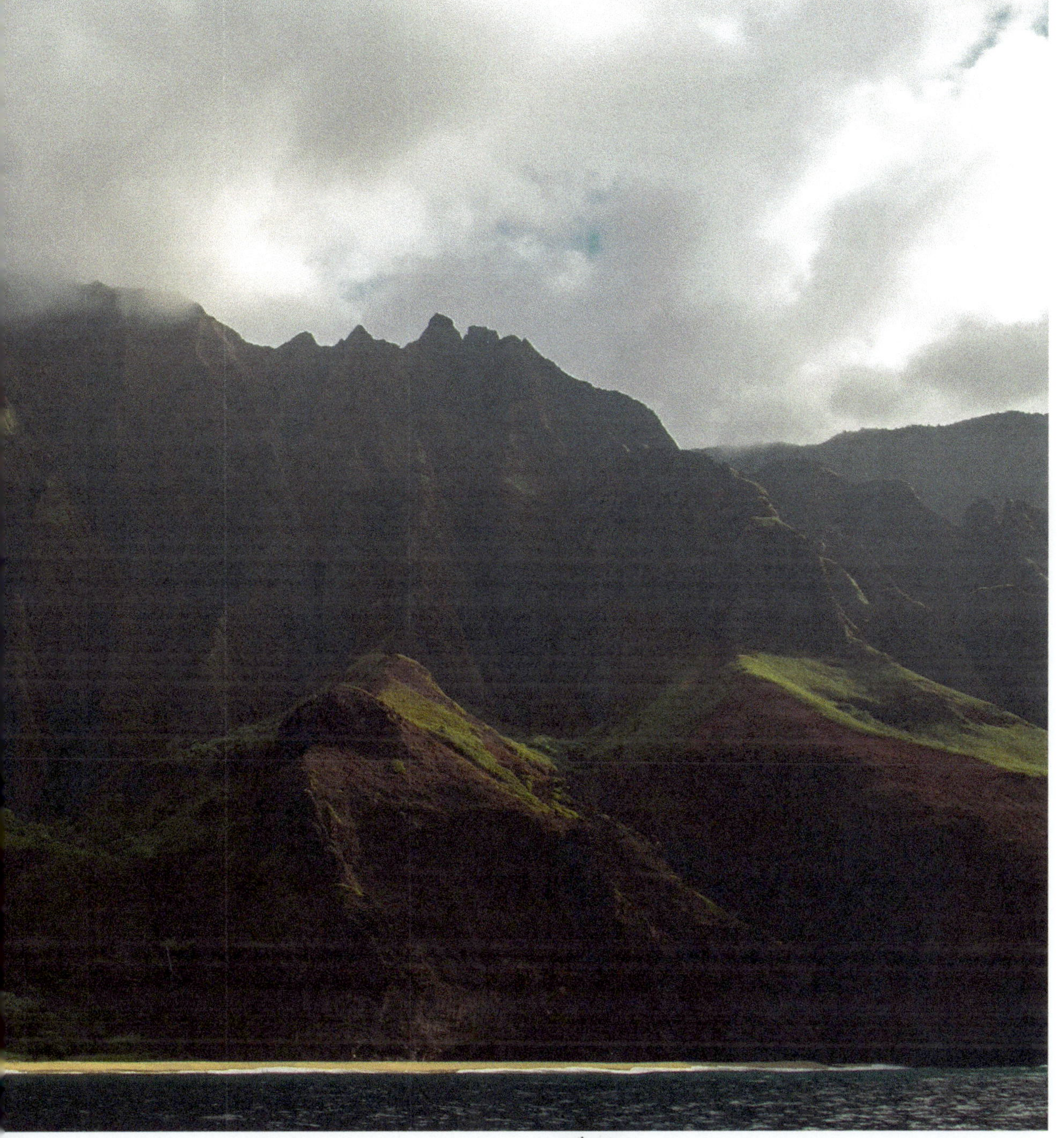

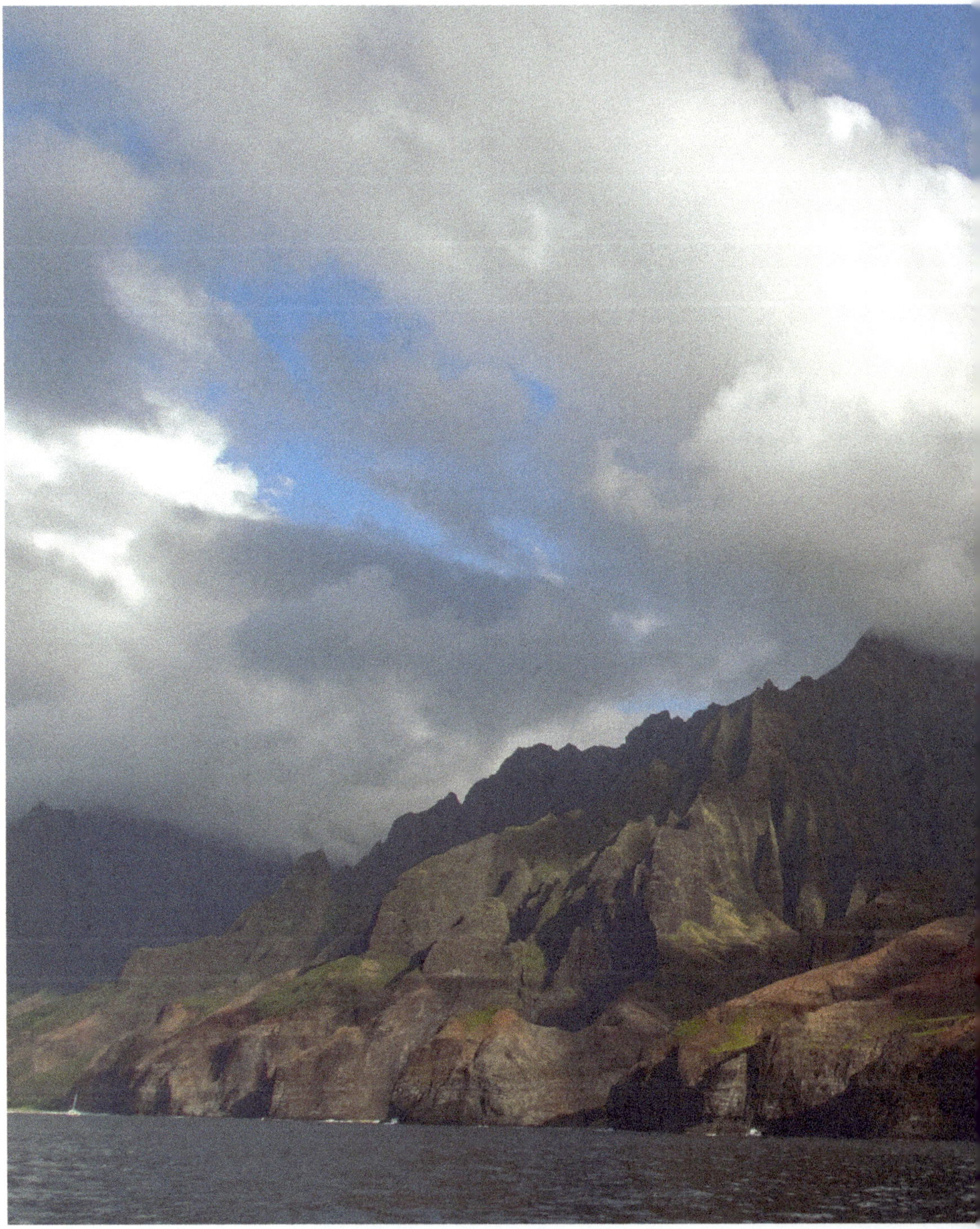

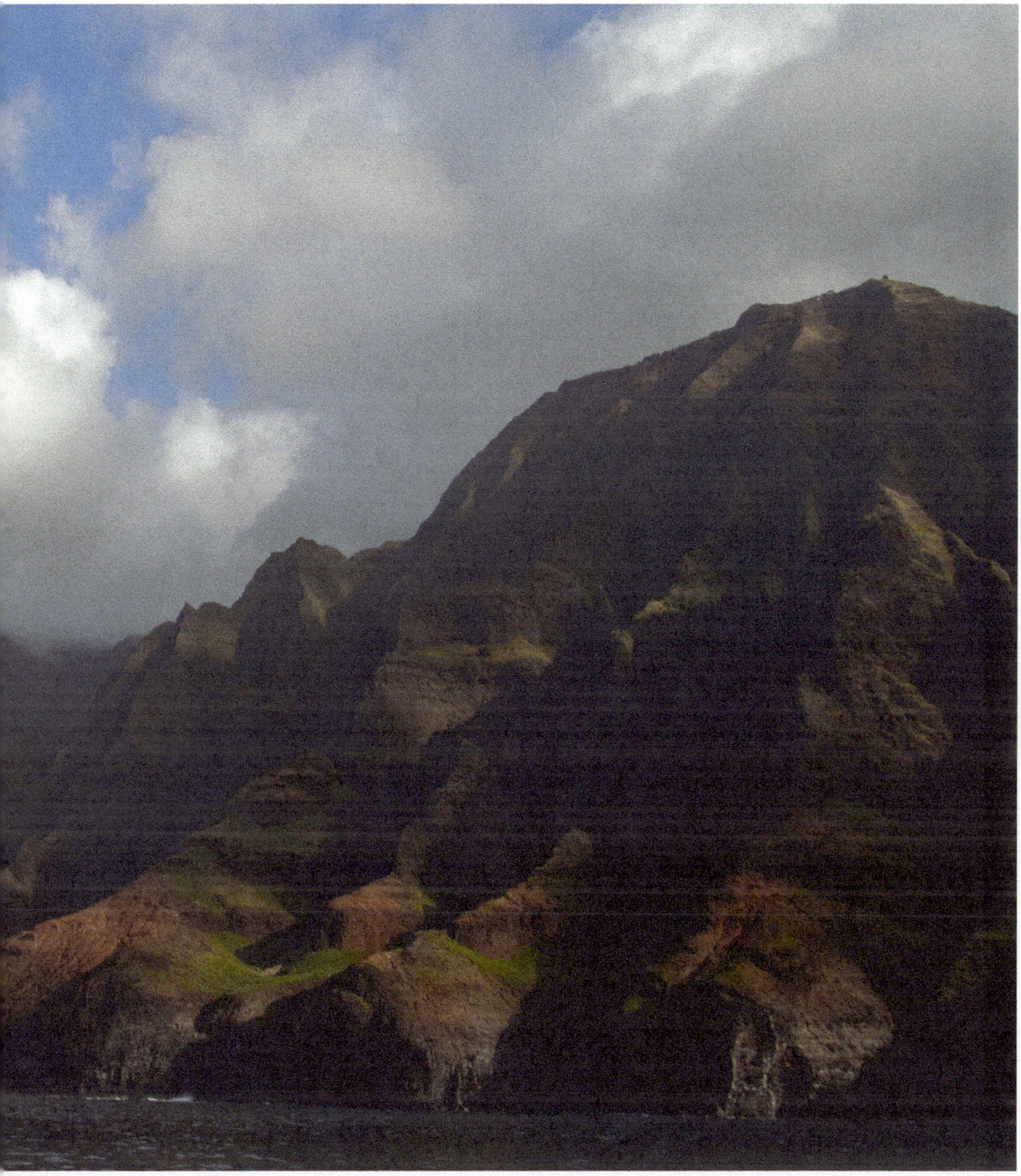

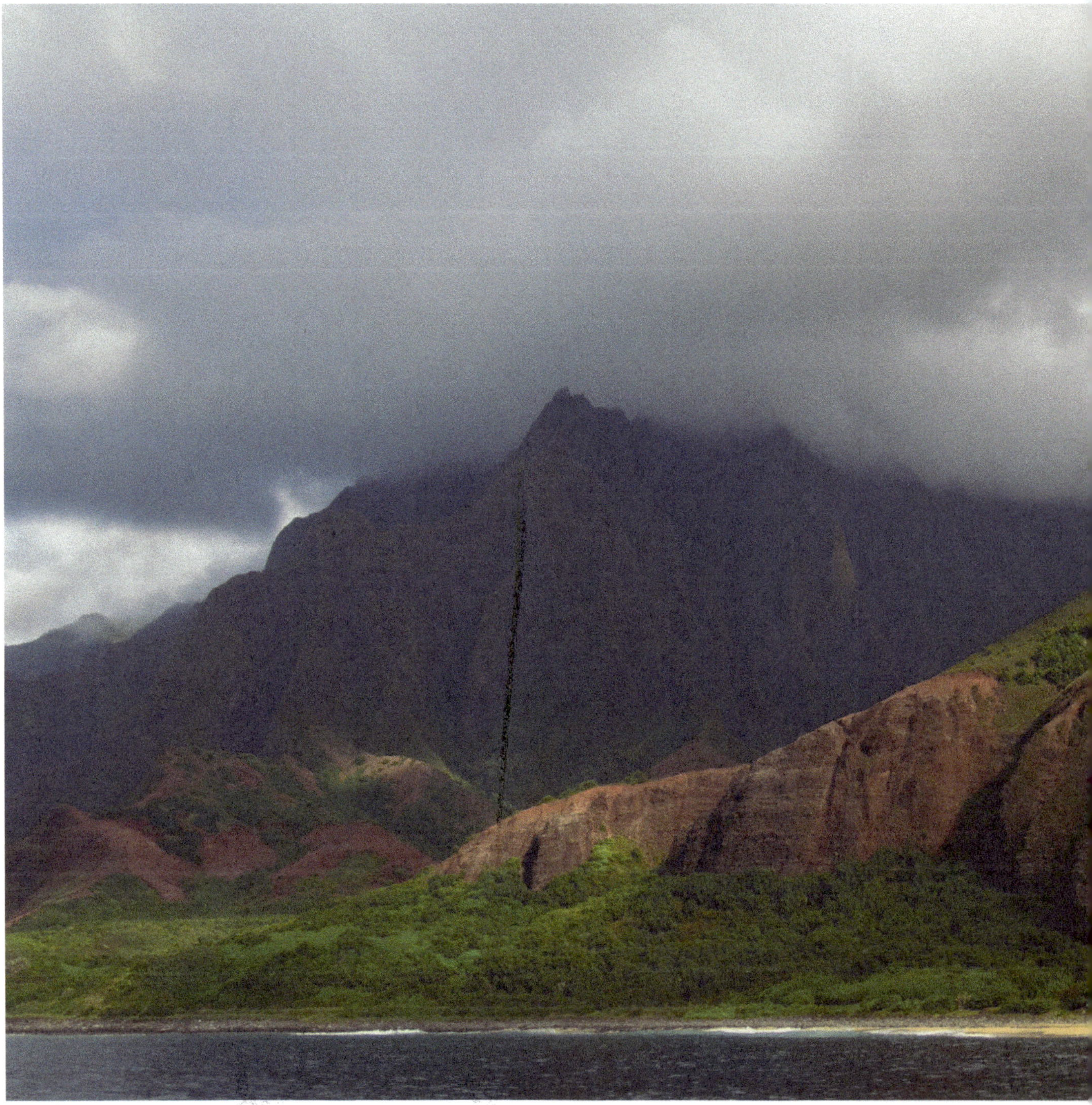

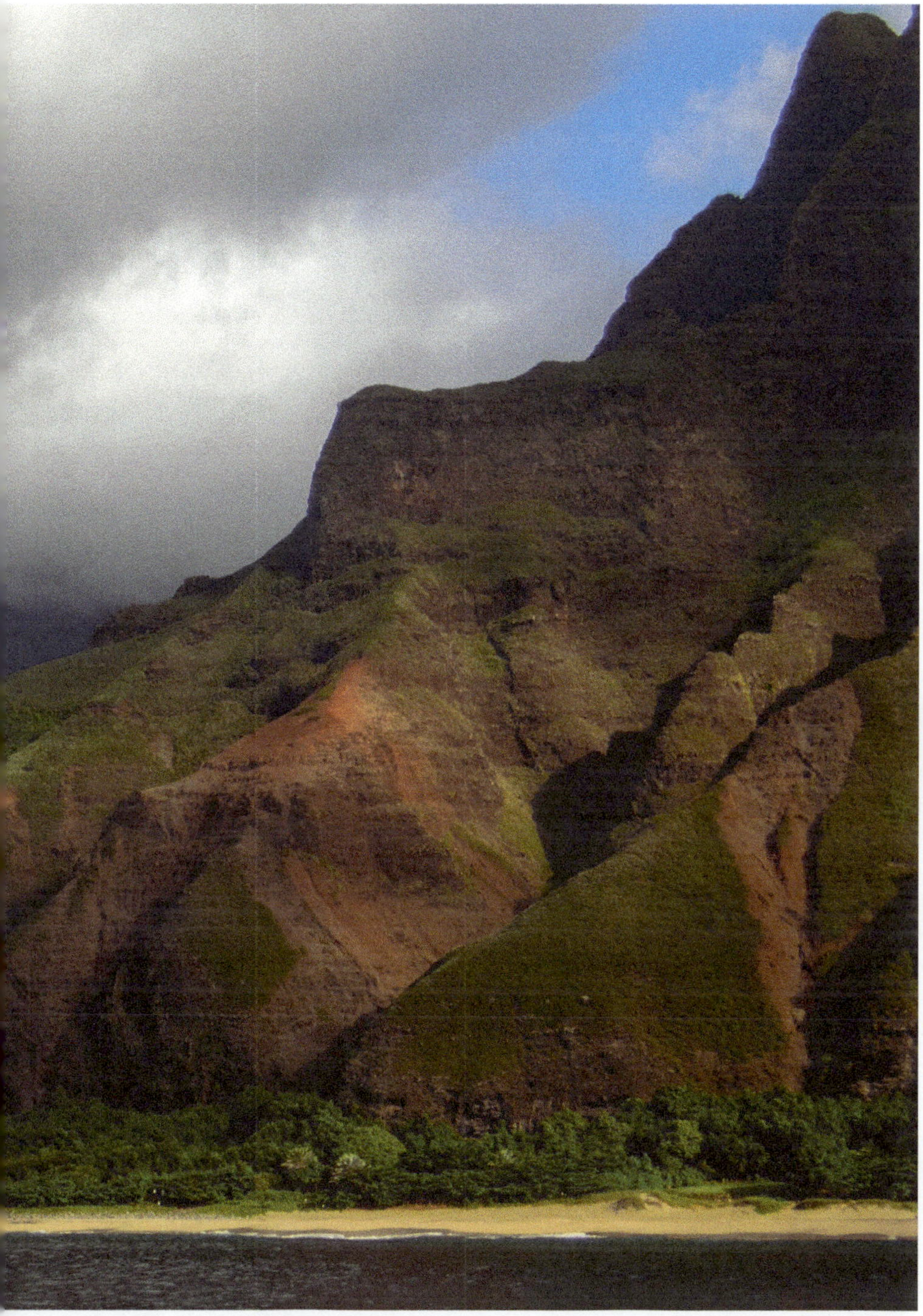

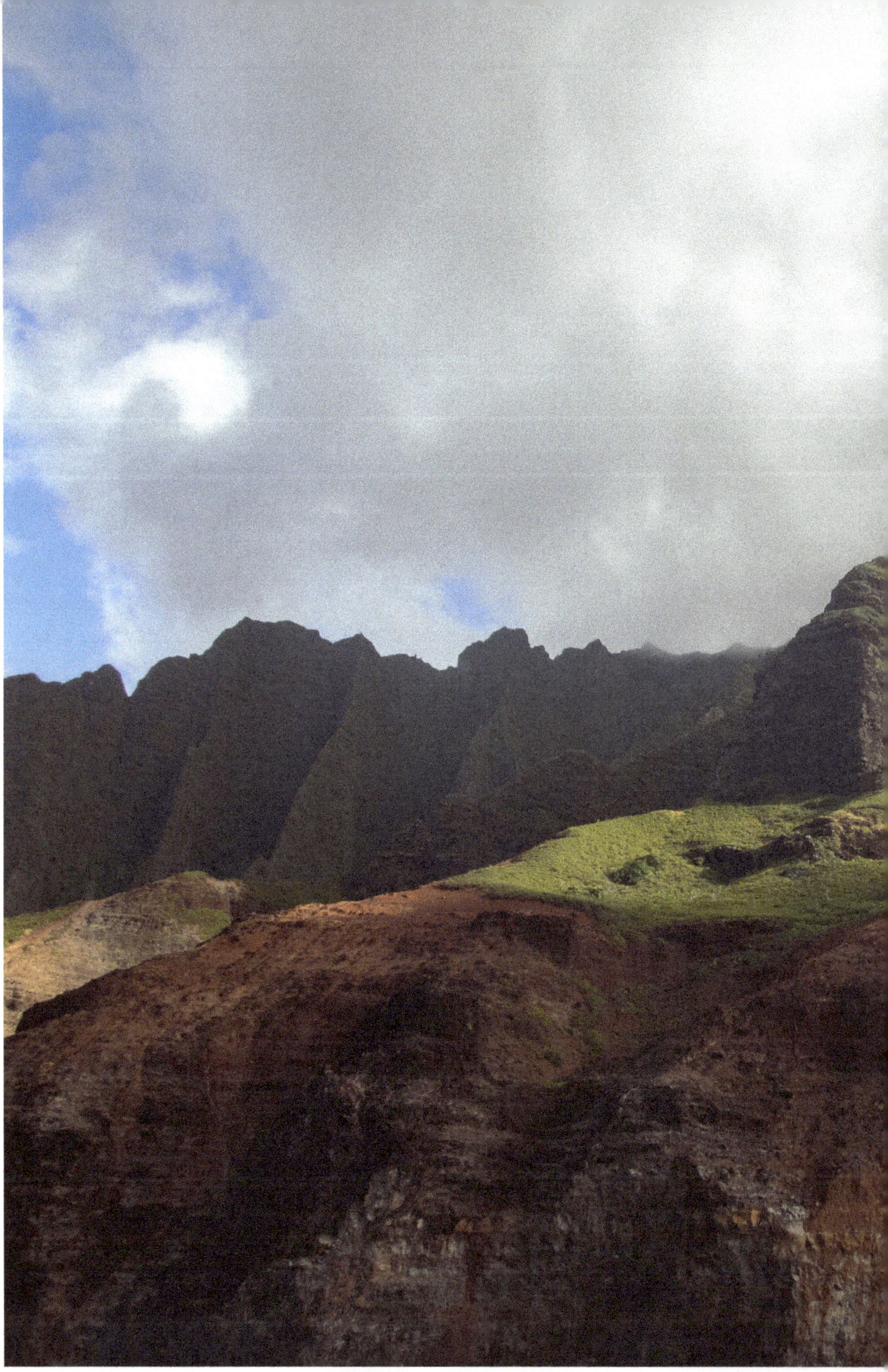

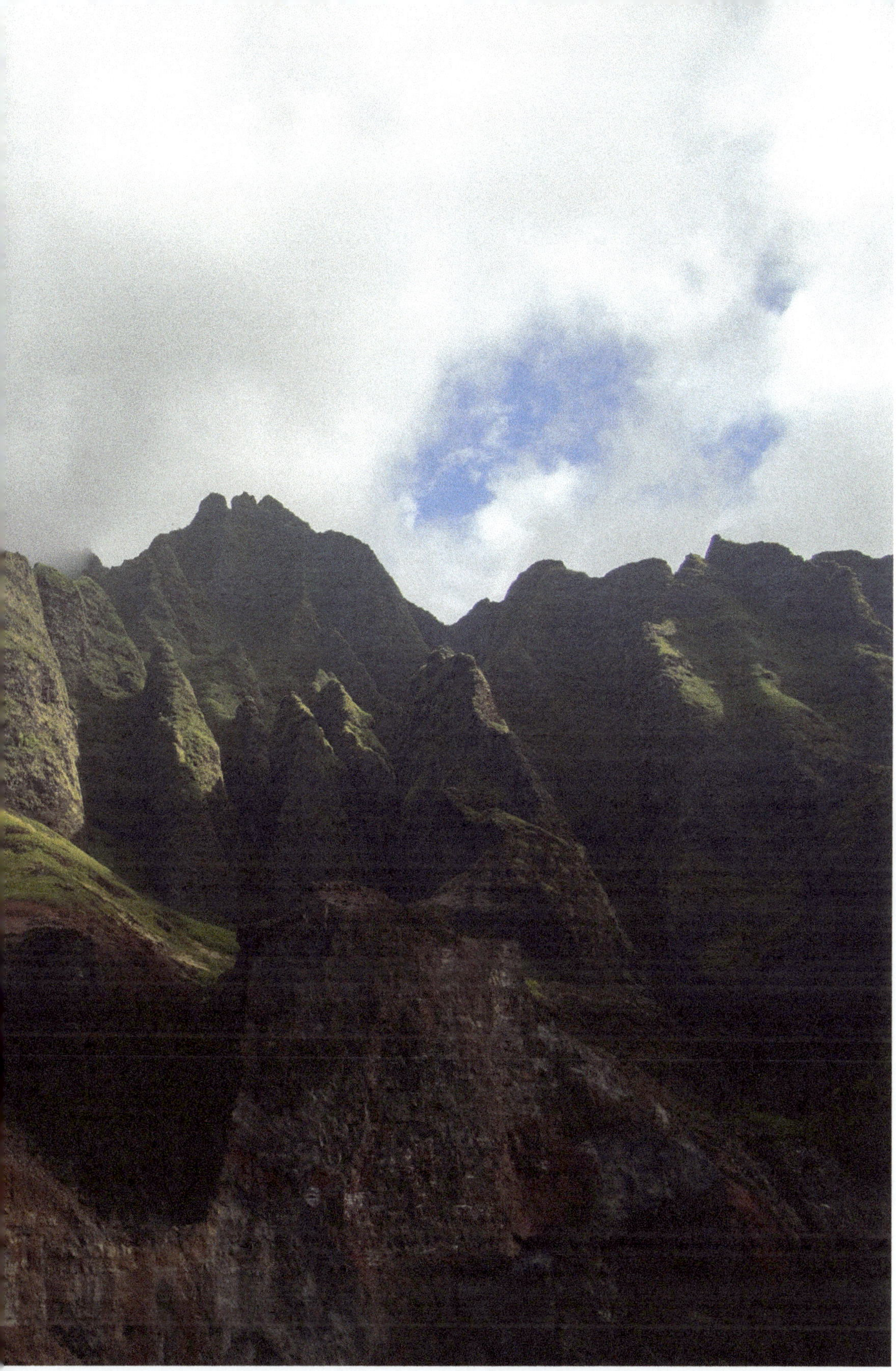

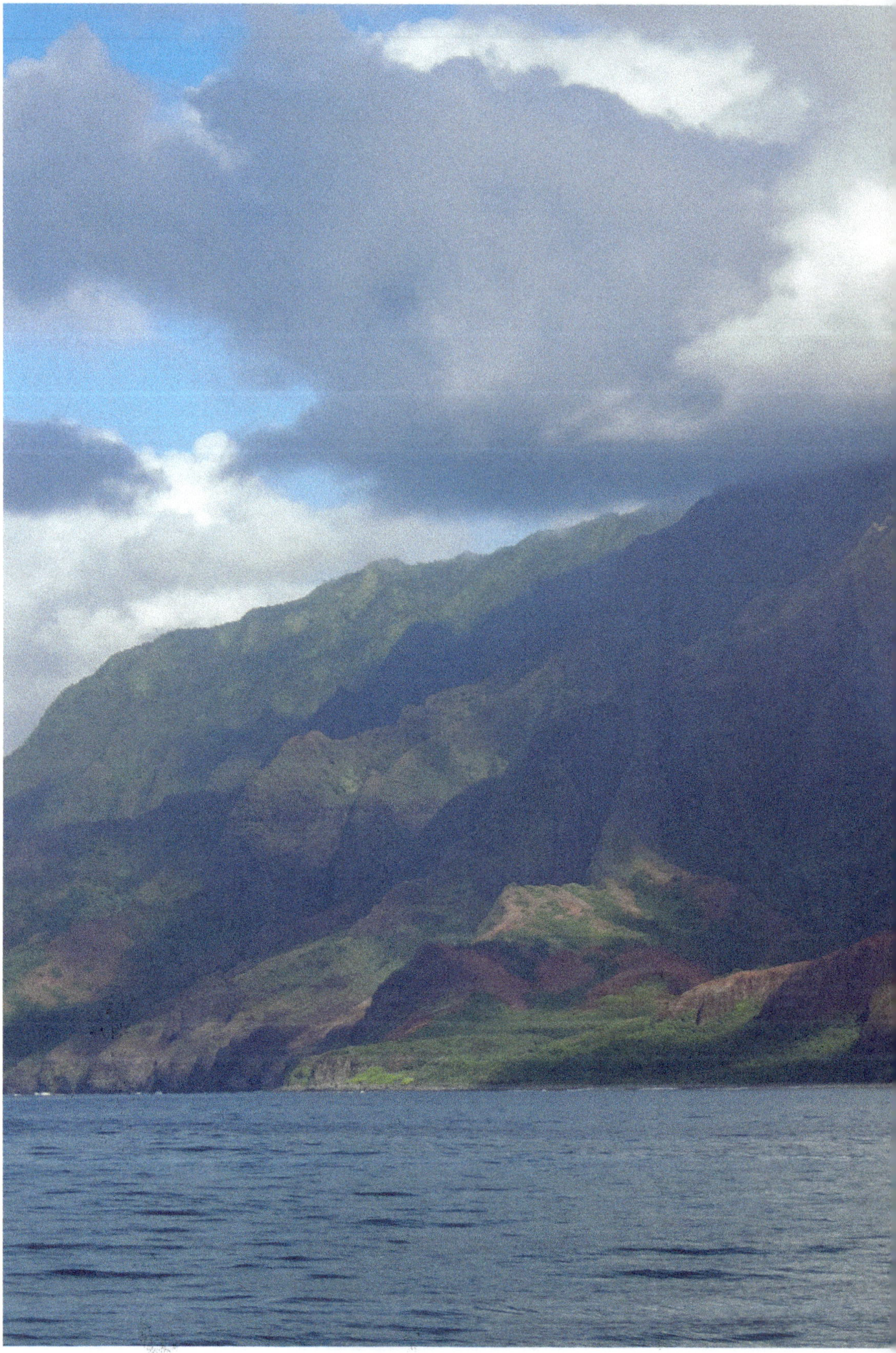

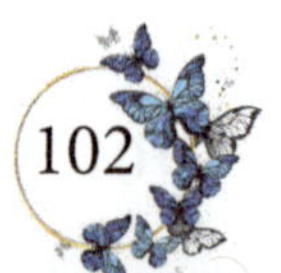

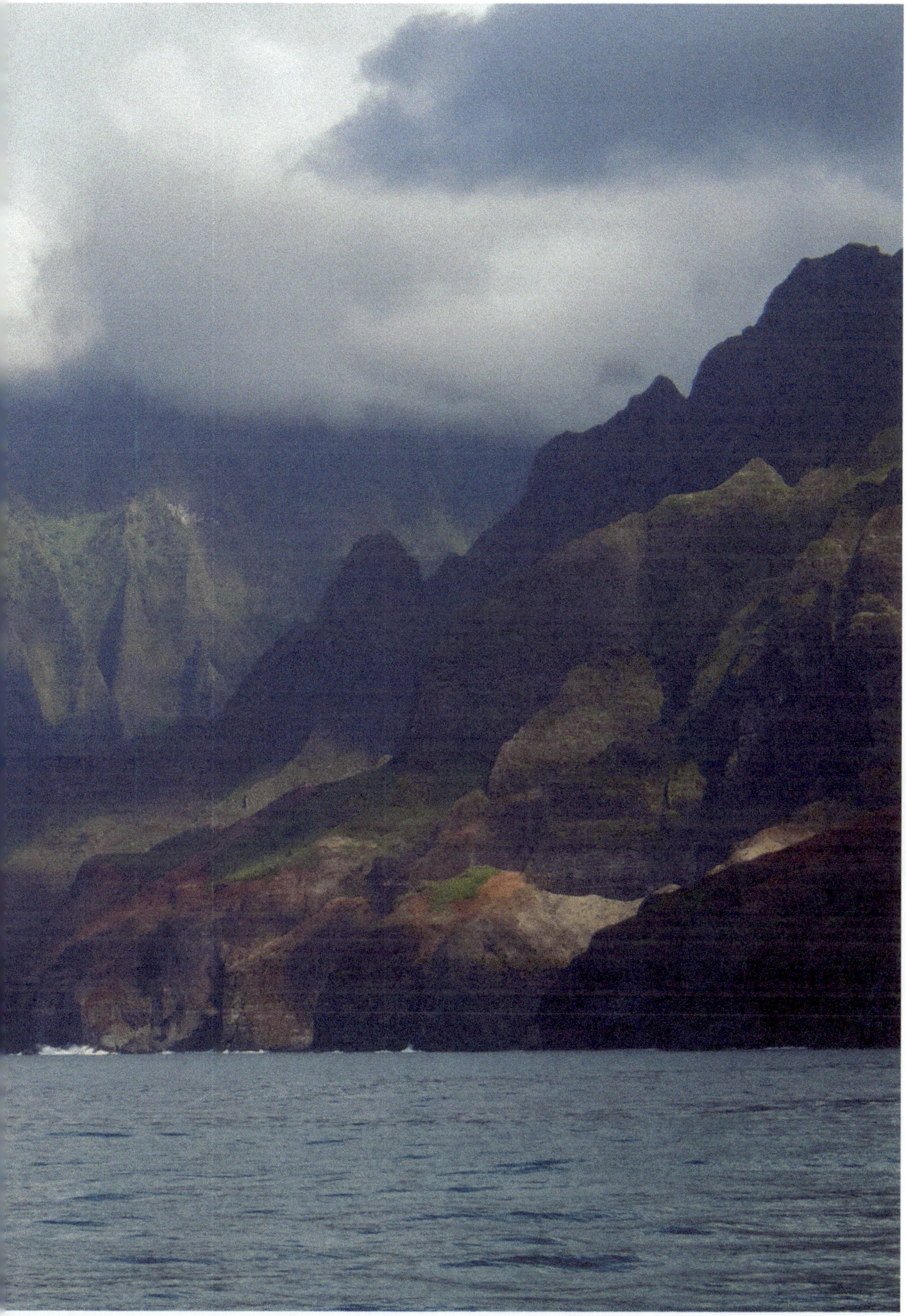

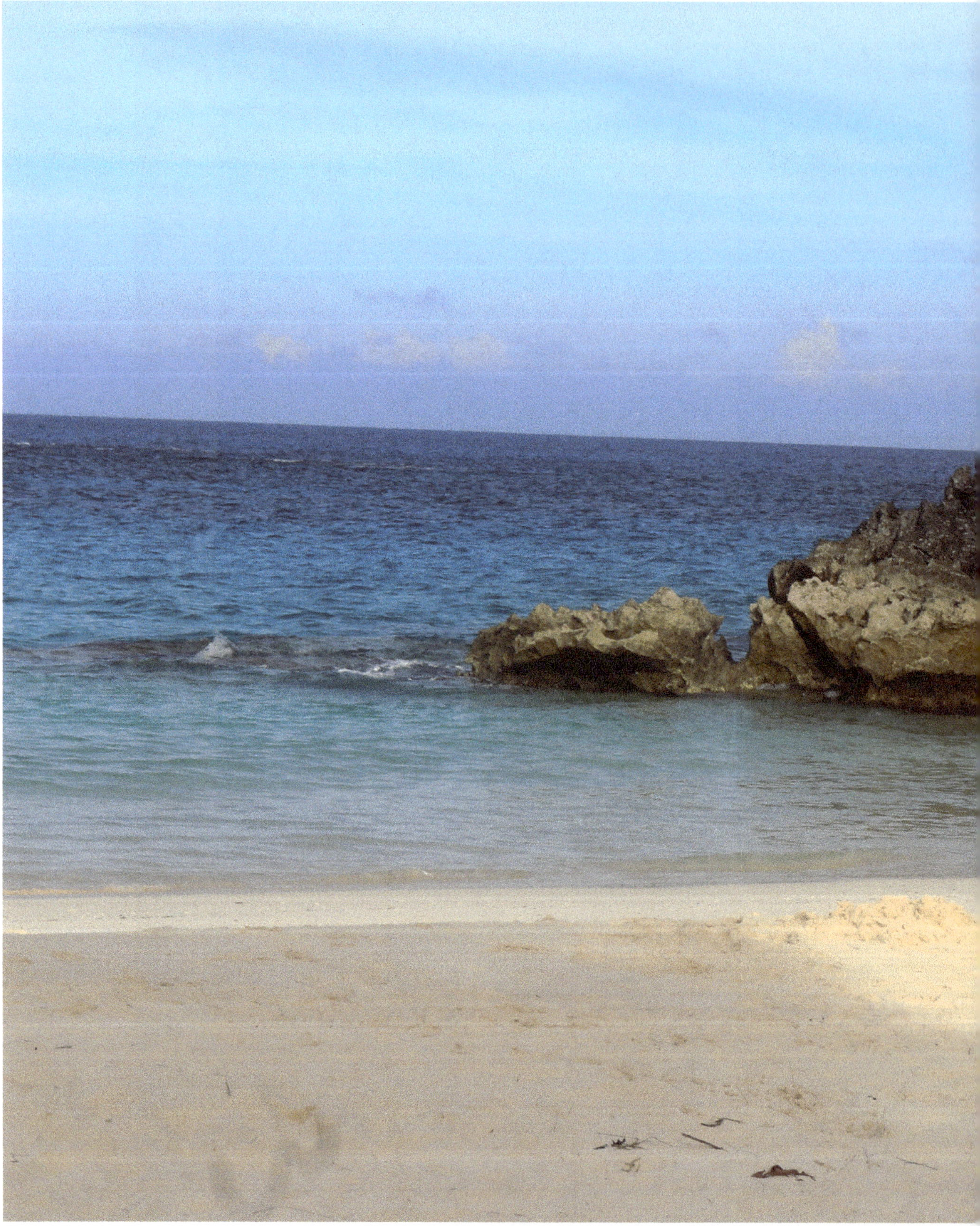

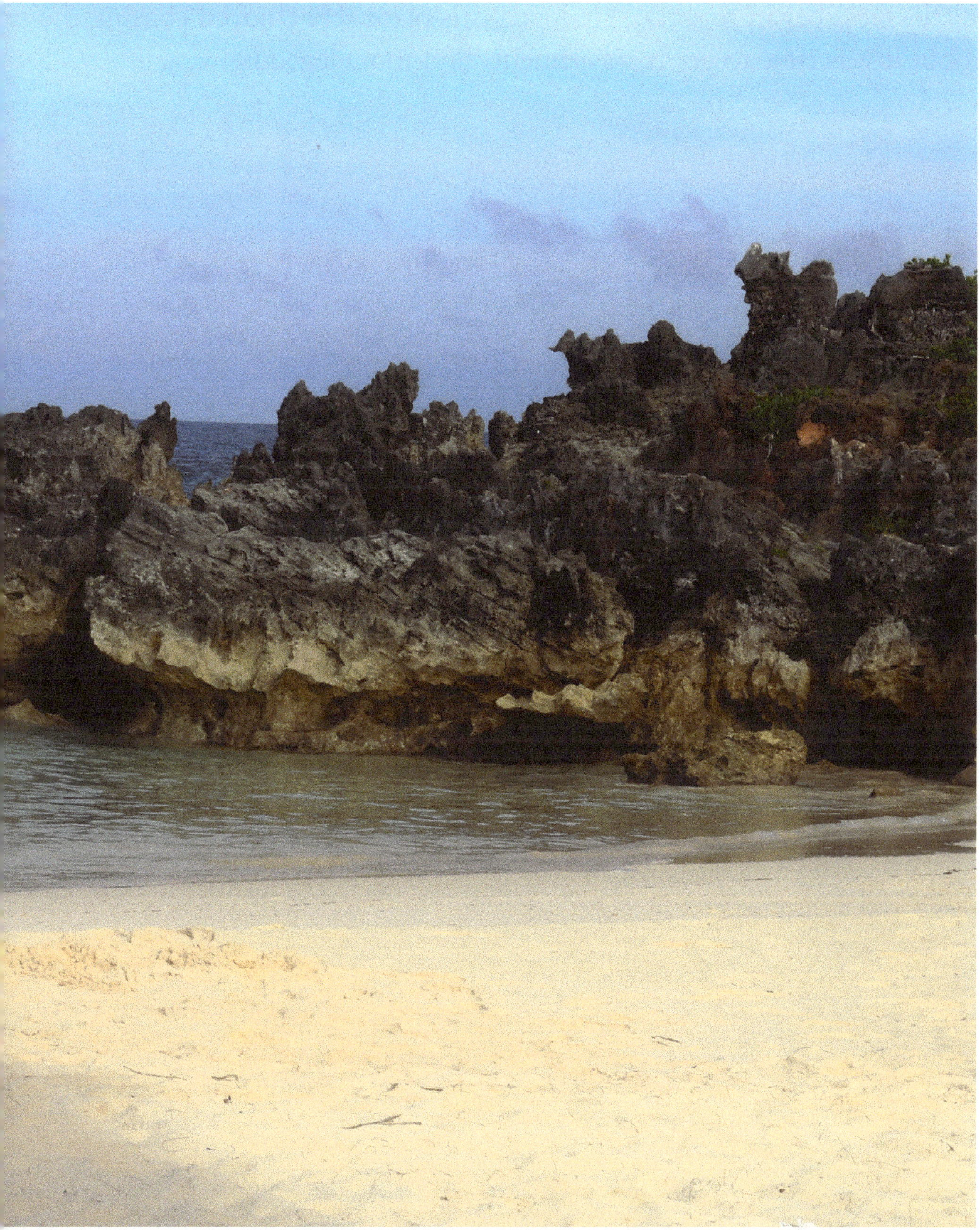

A restlessness began to settle. He loved this place. He enjoyed chasing the stories but it was time to go. It was time to find more legends.

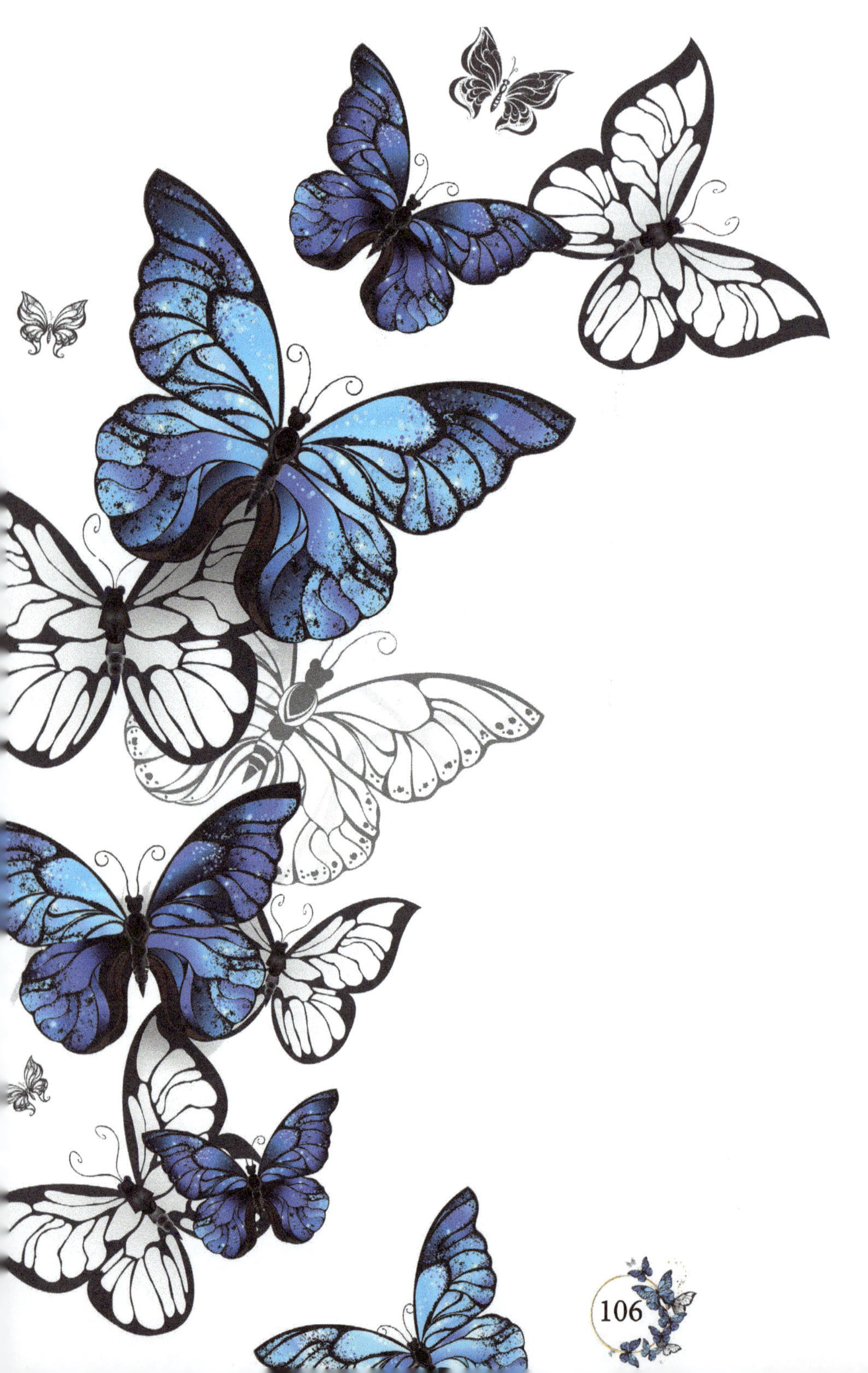

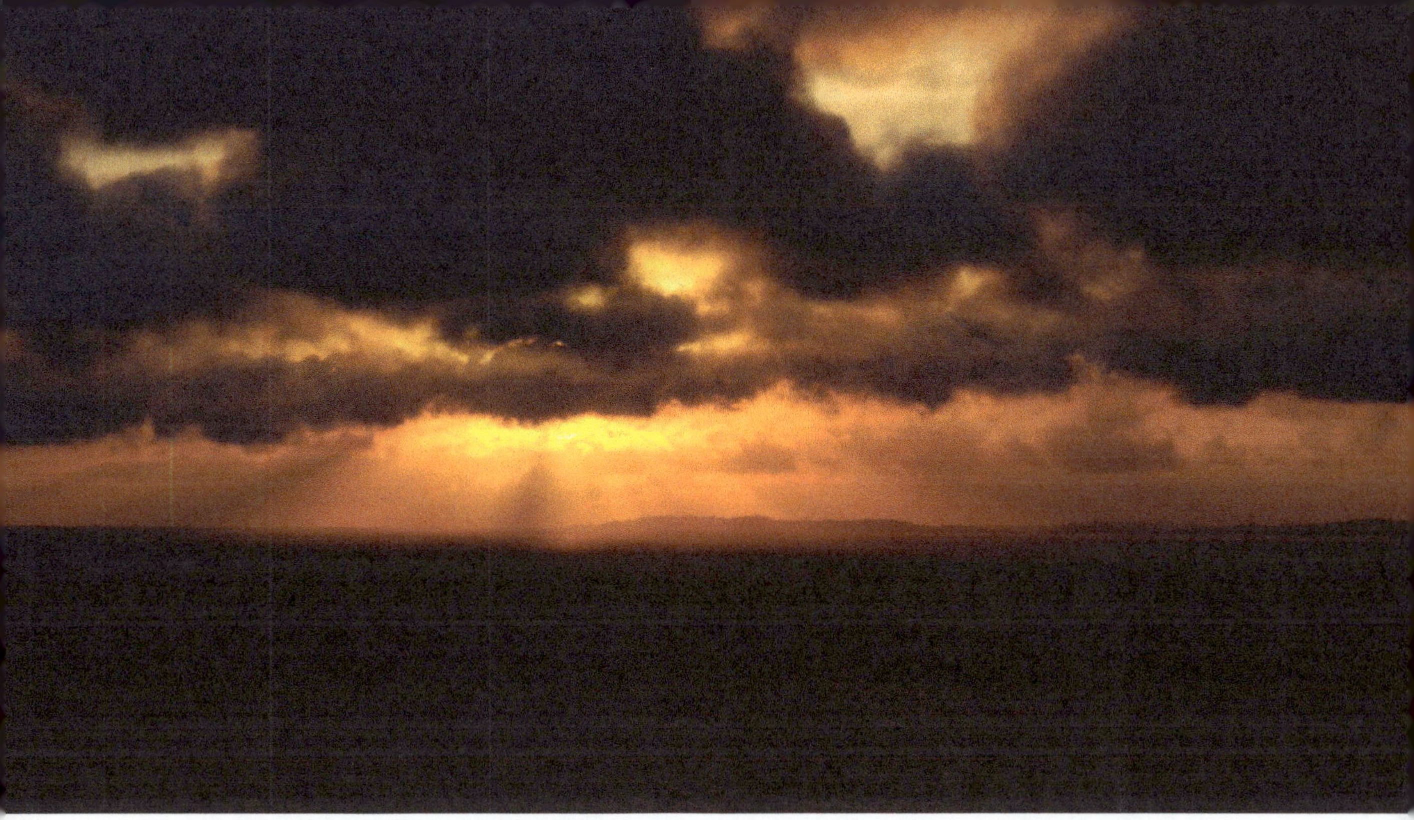

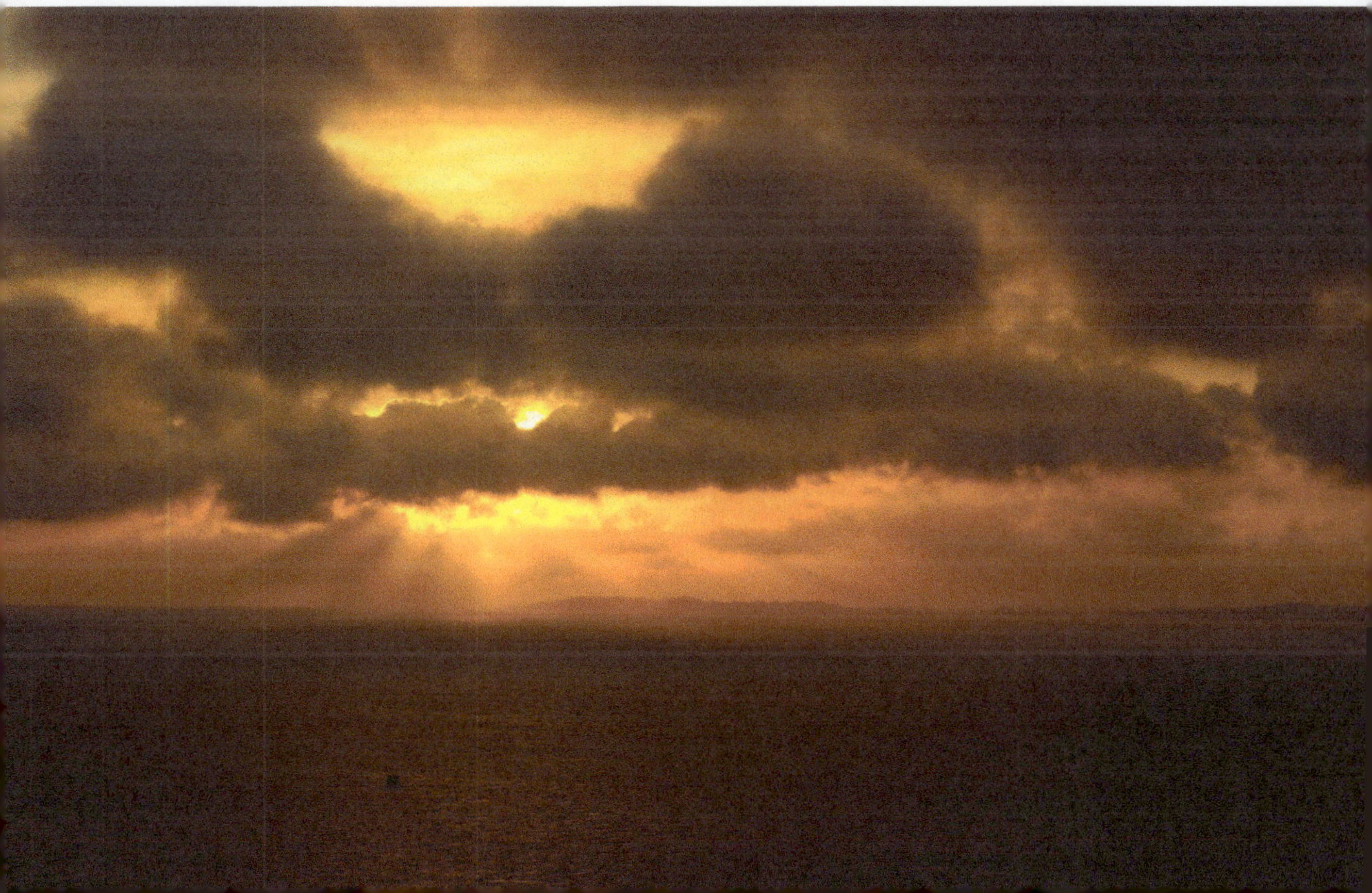

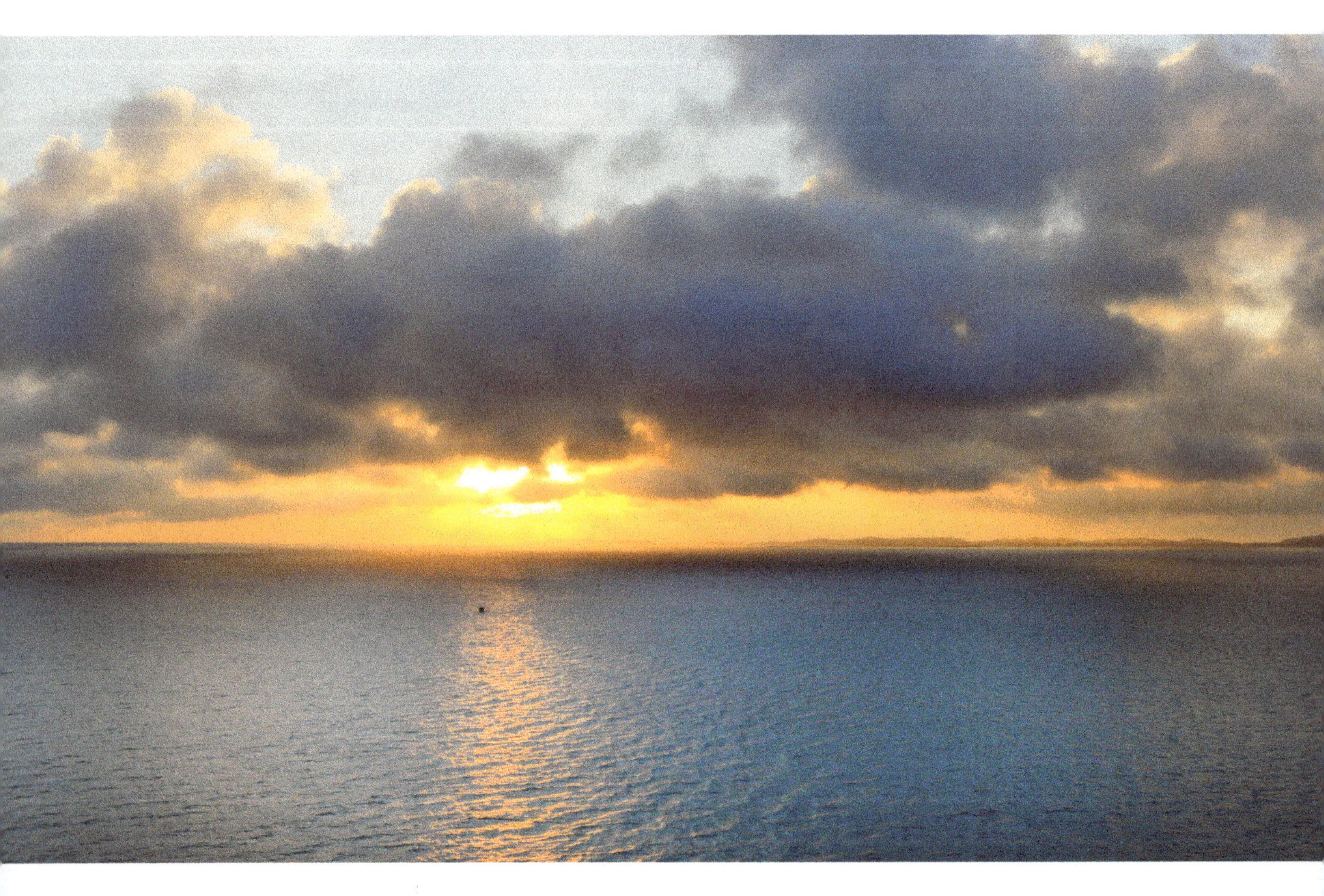

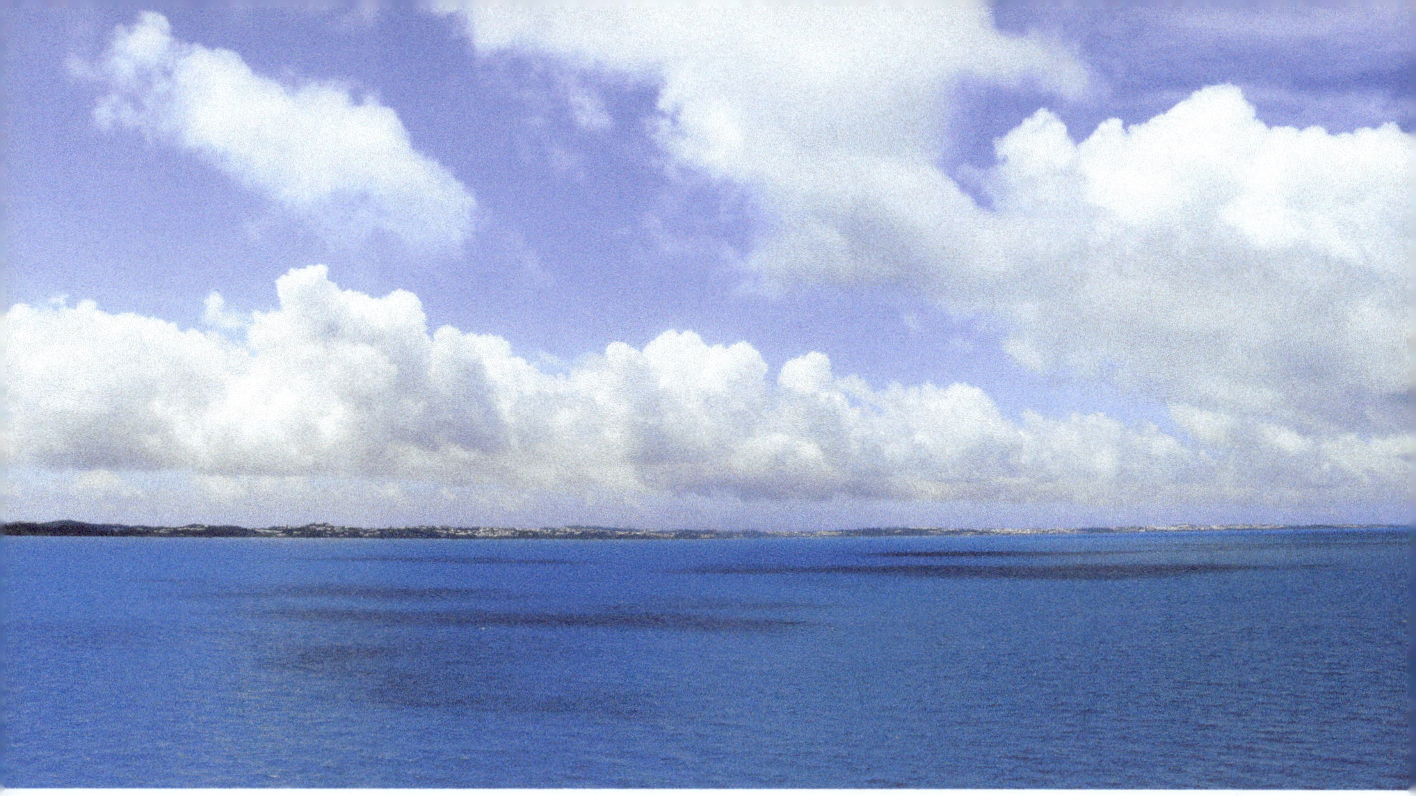

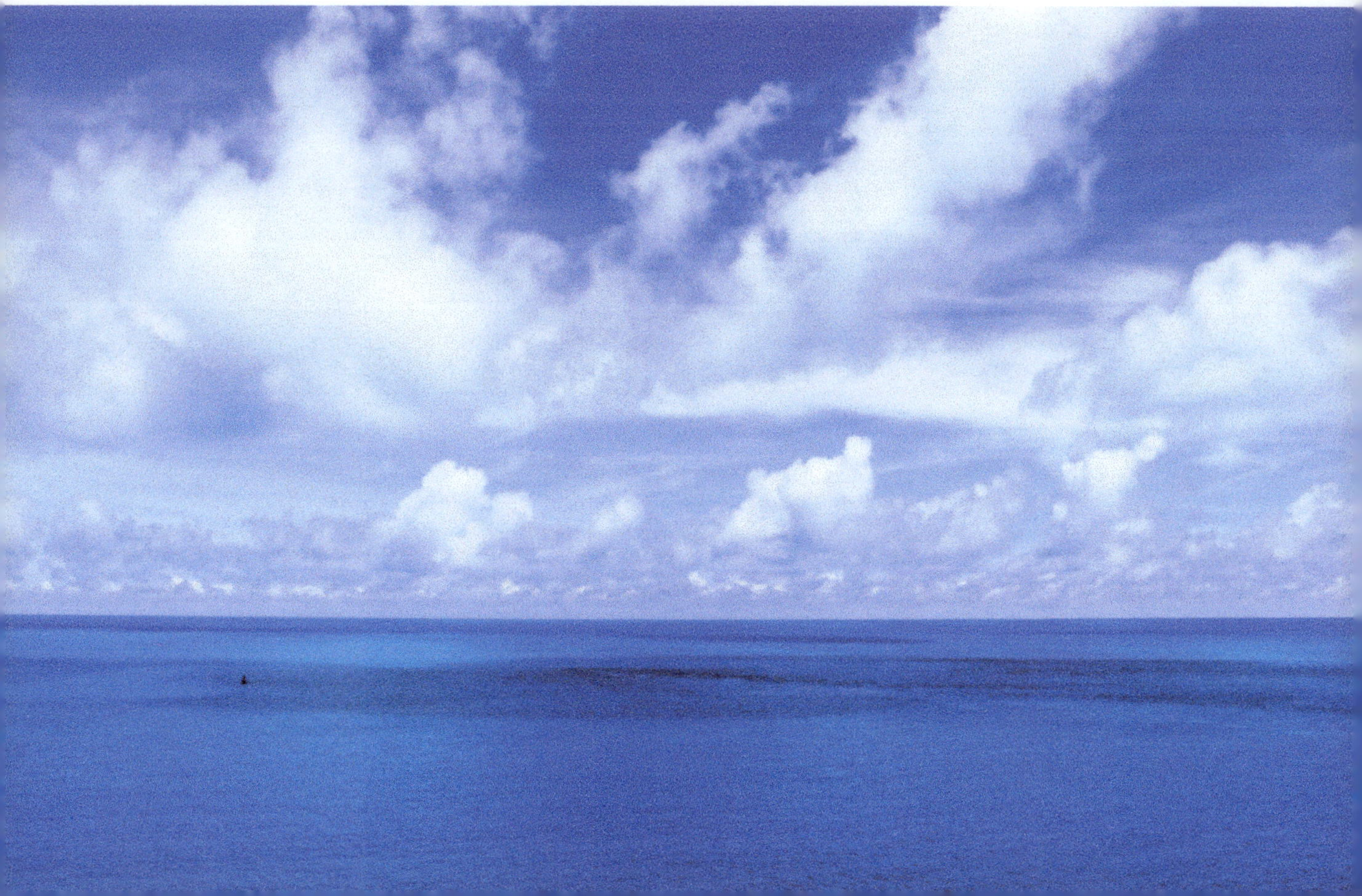

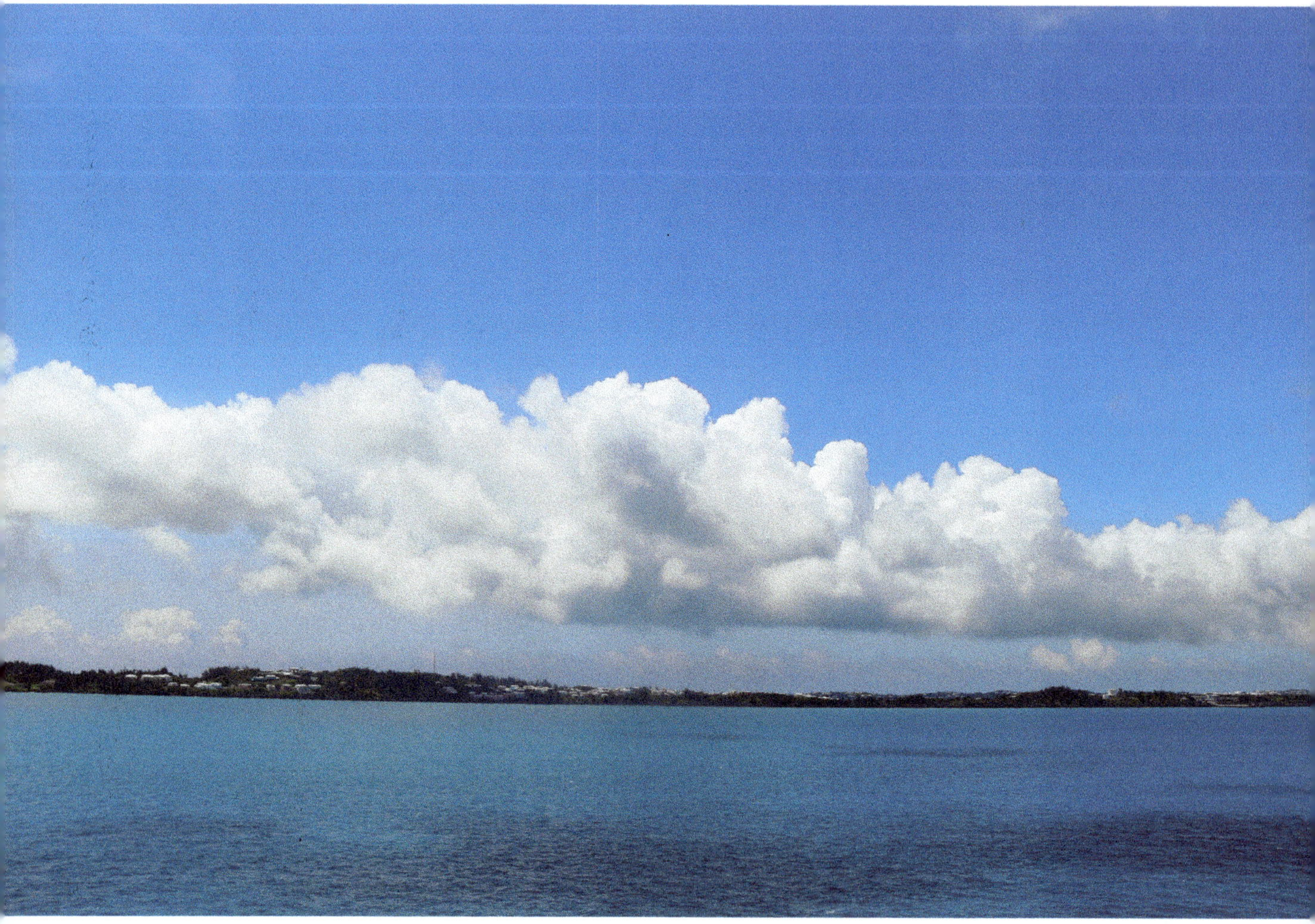

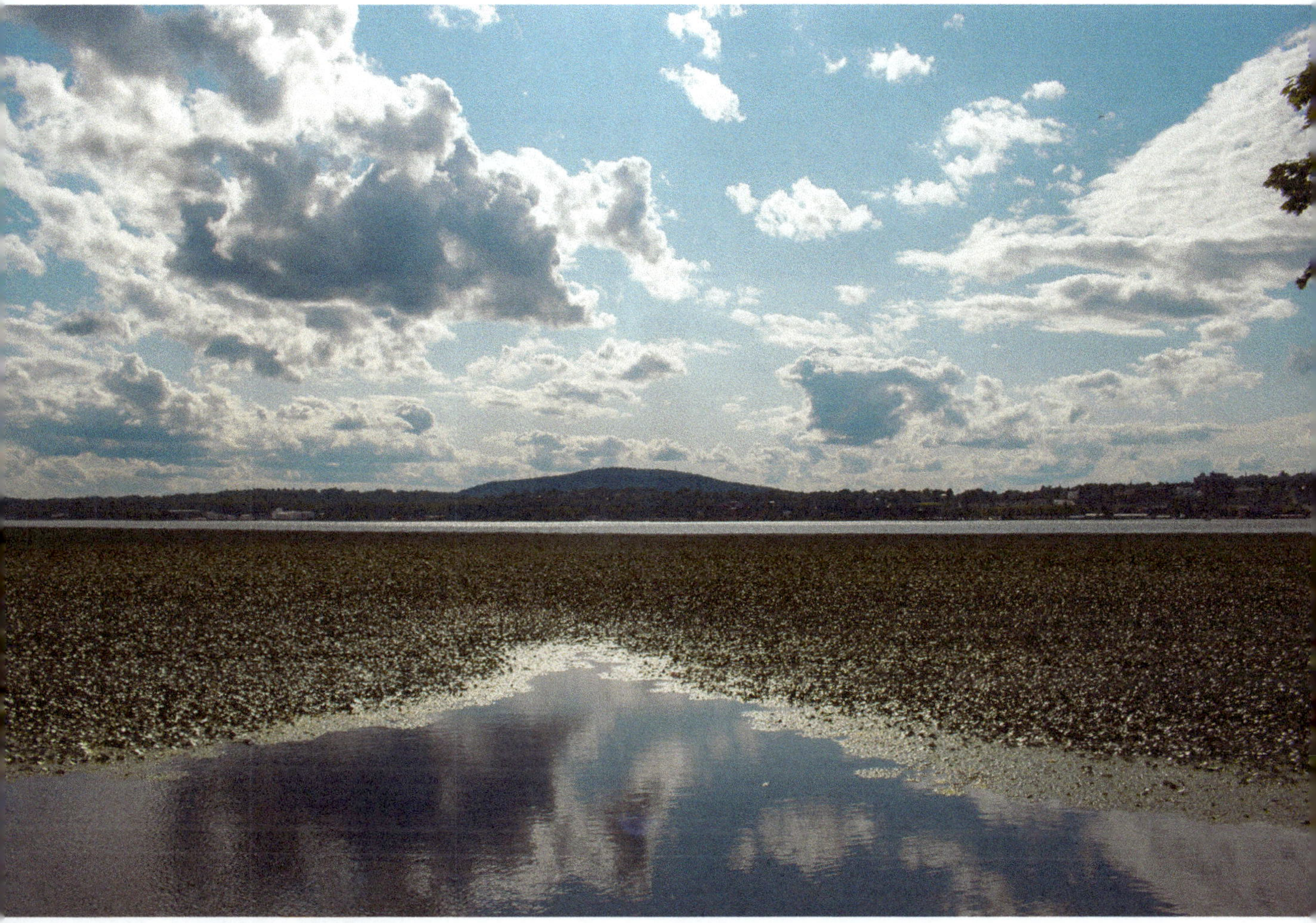

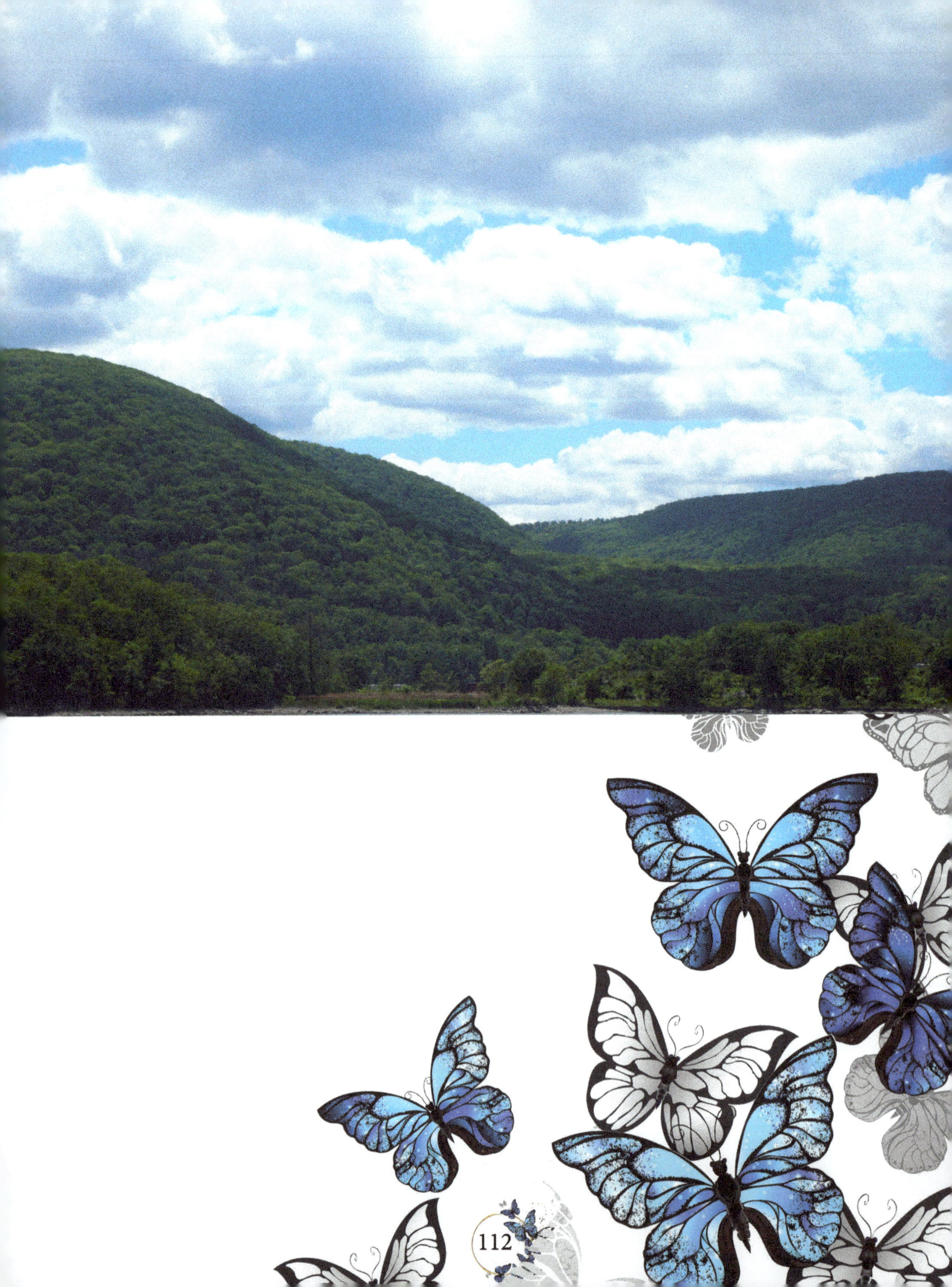

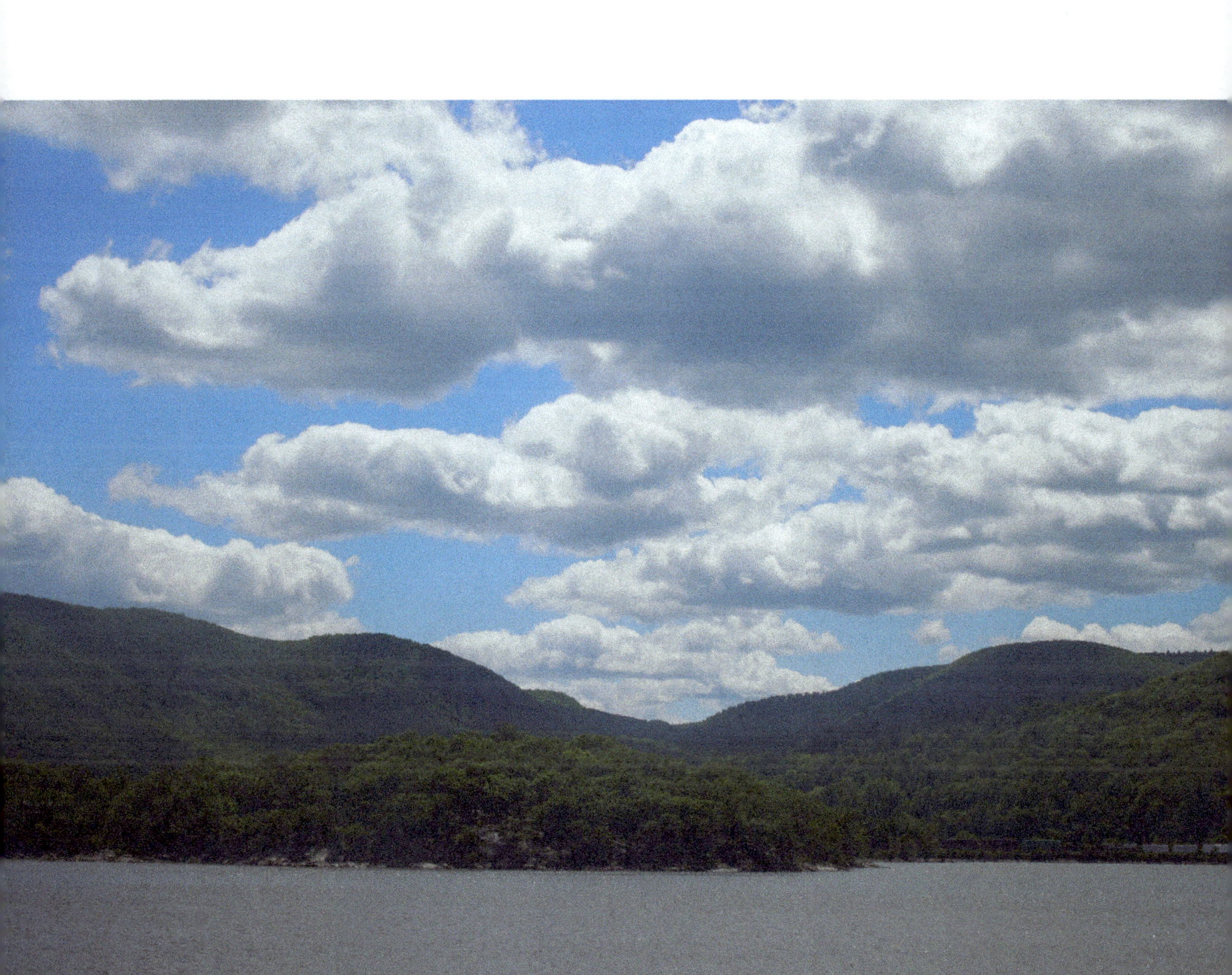

The land of colors was his favorite. It had beautiful sunrises, of course. But, he wasn't drawn to the city because of that.

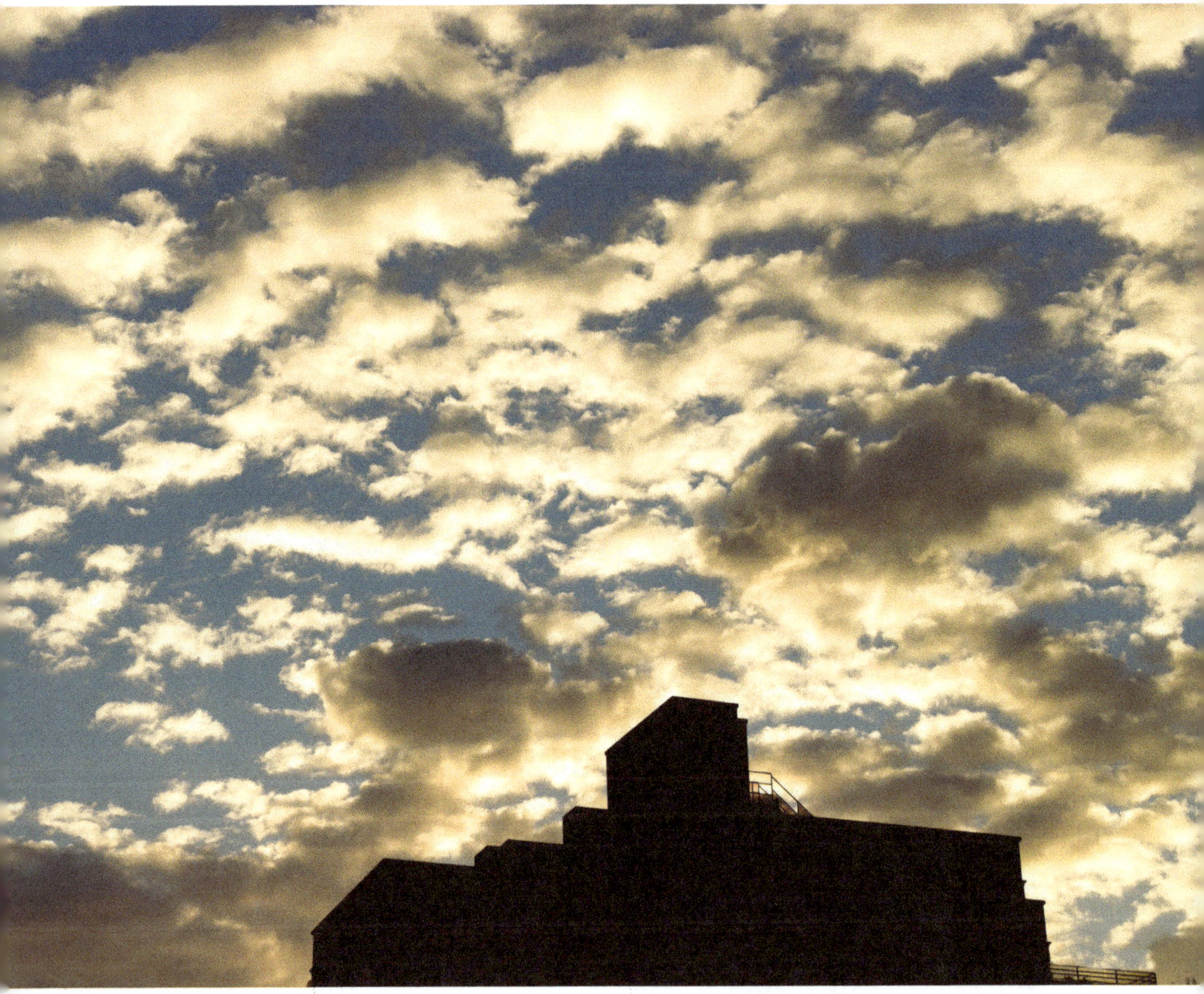

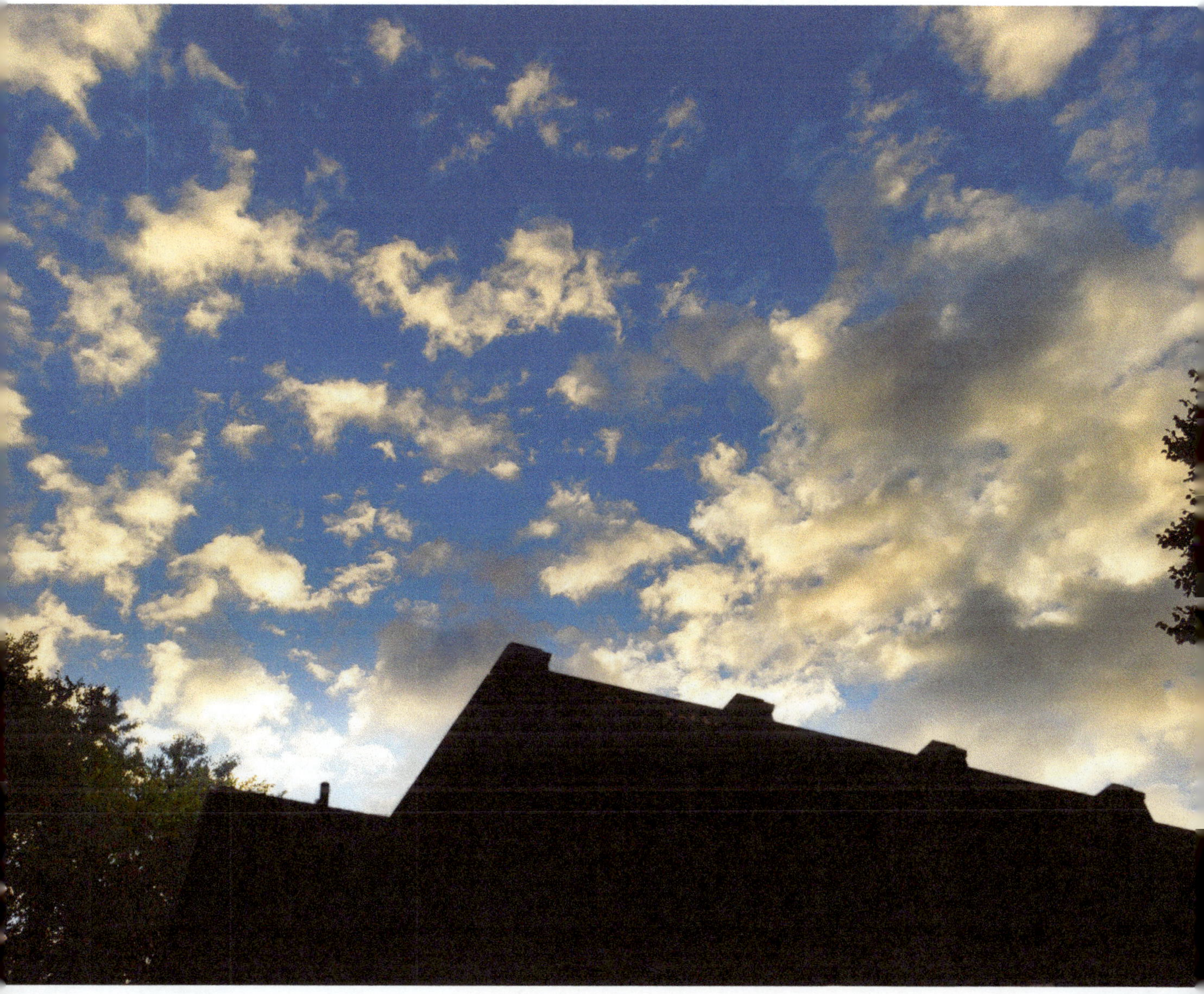

No matter the weather or month, the trees and flowers kept their exciting colors. It was as if he lived in a land made of jewels.

He stayed nearly a year, working several jobs to earn a living.

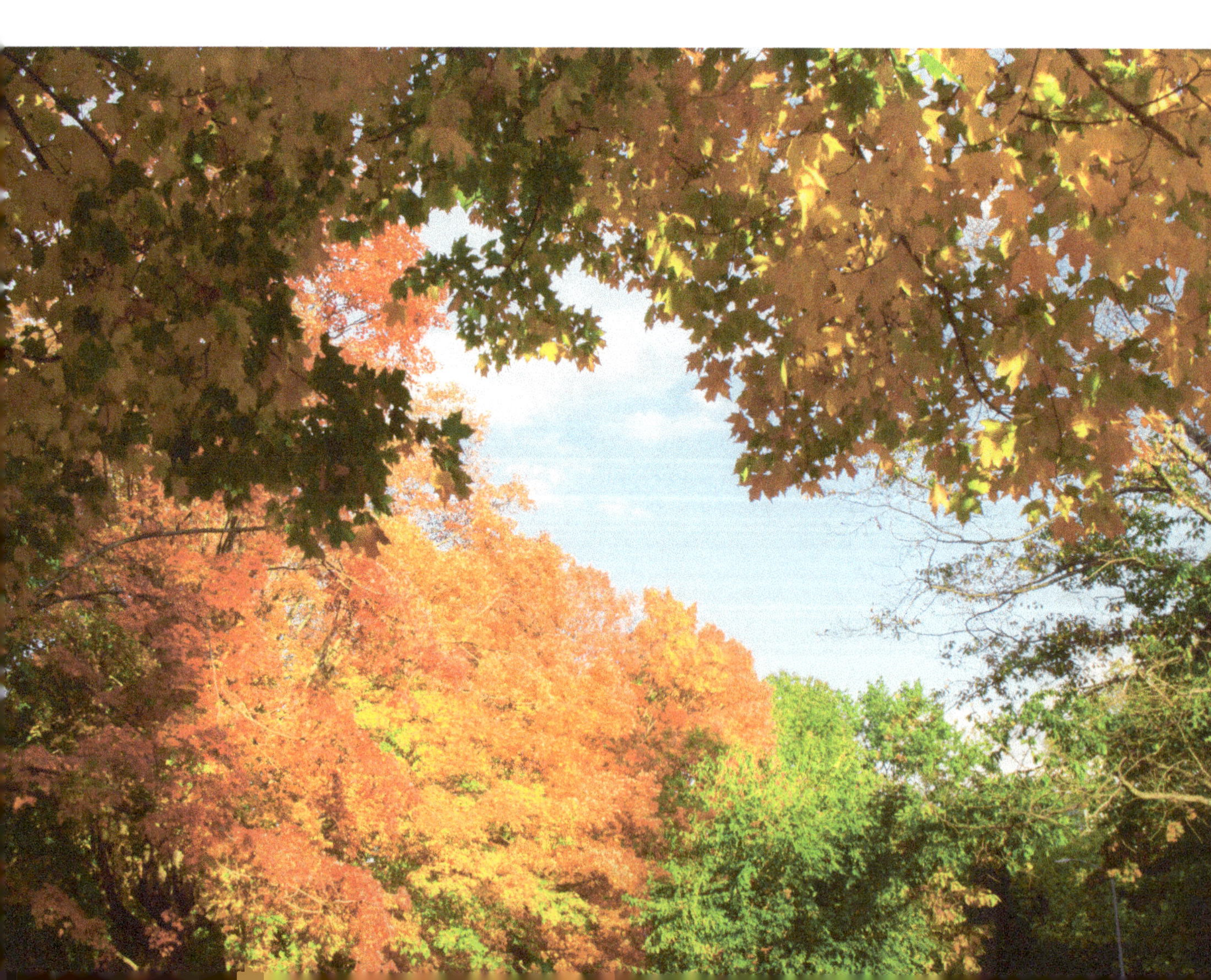

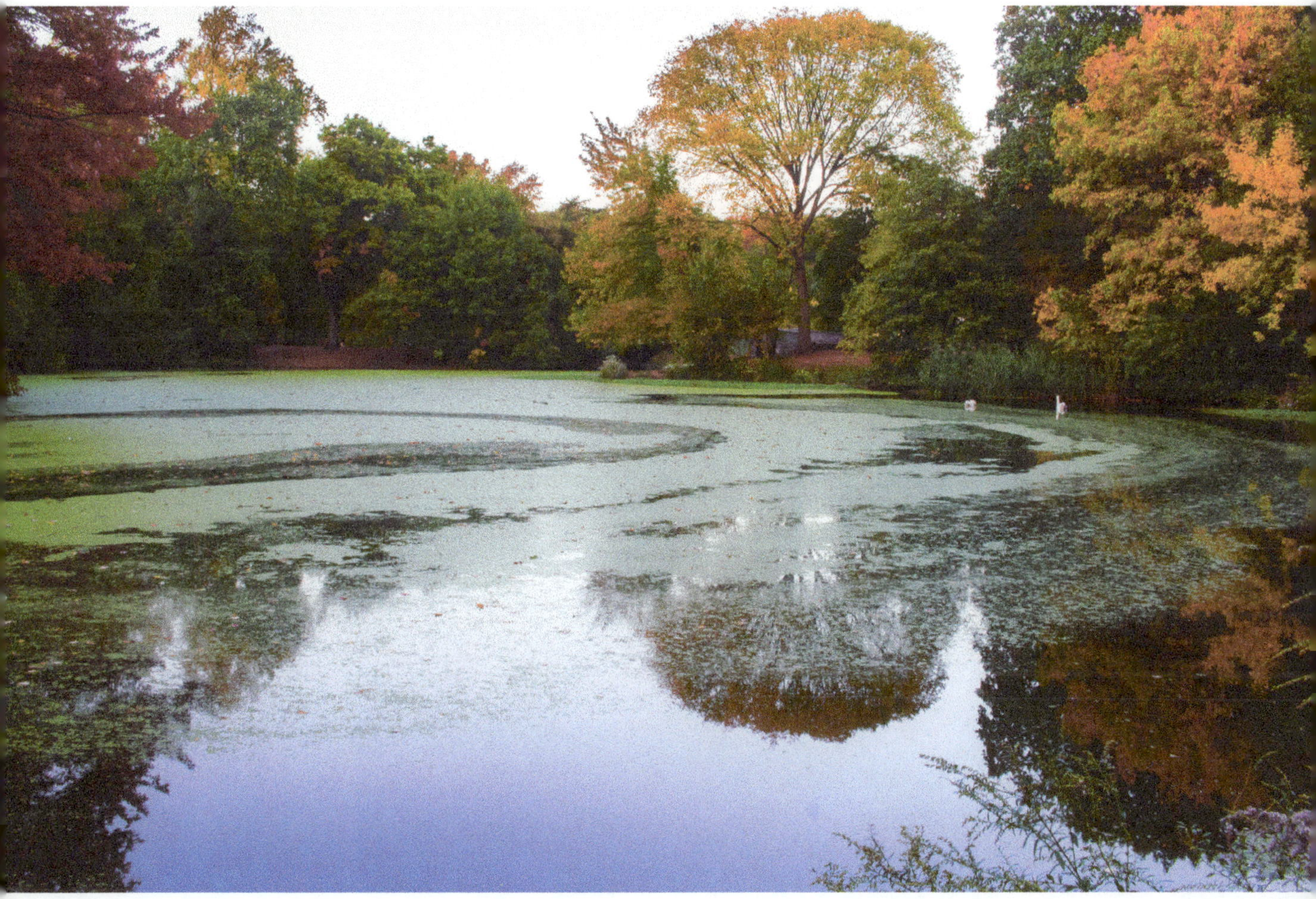

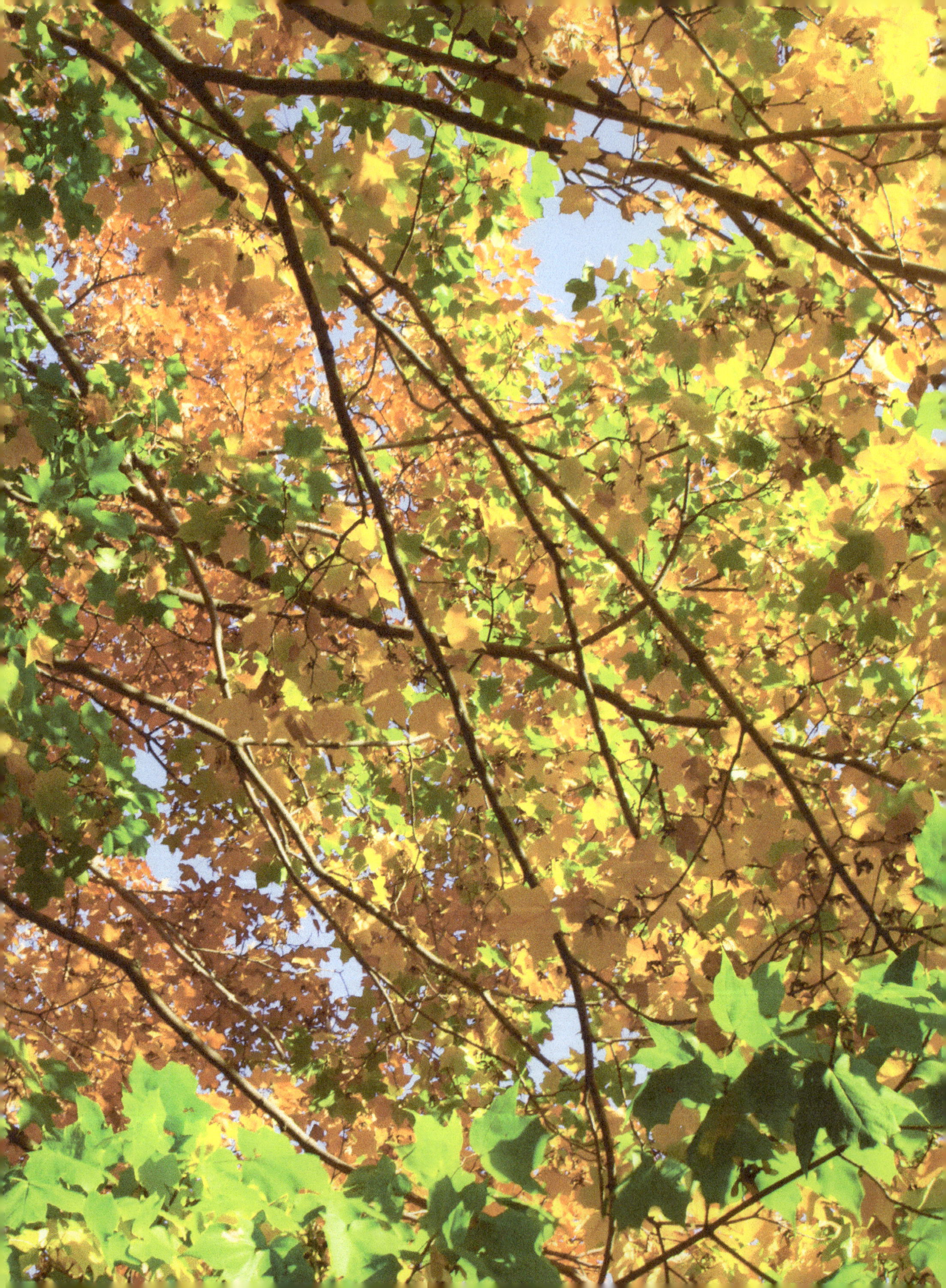

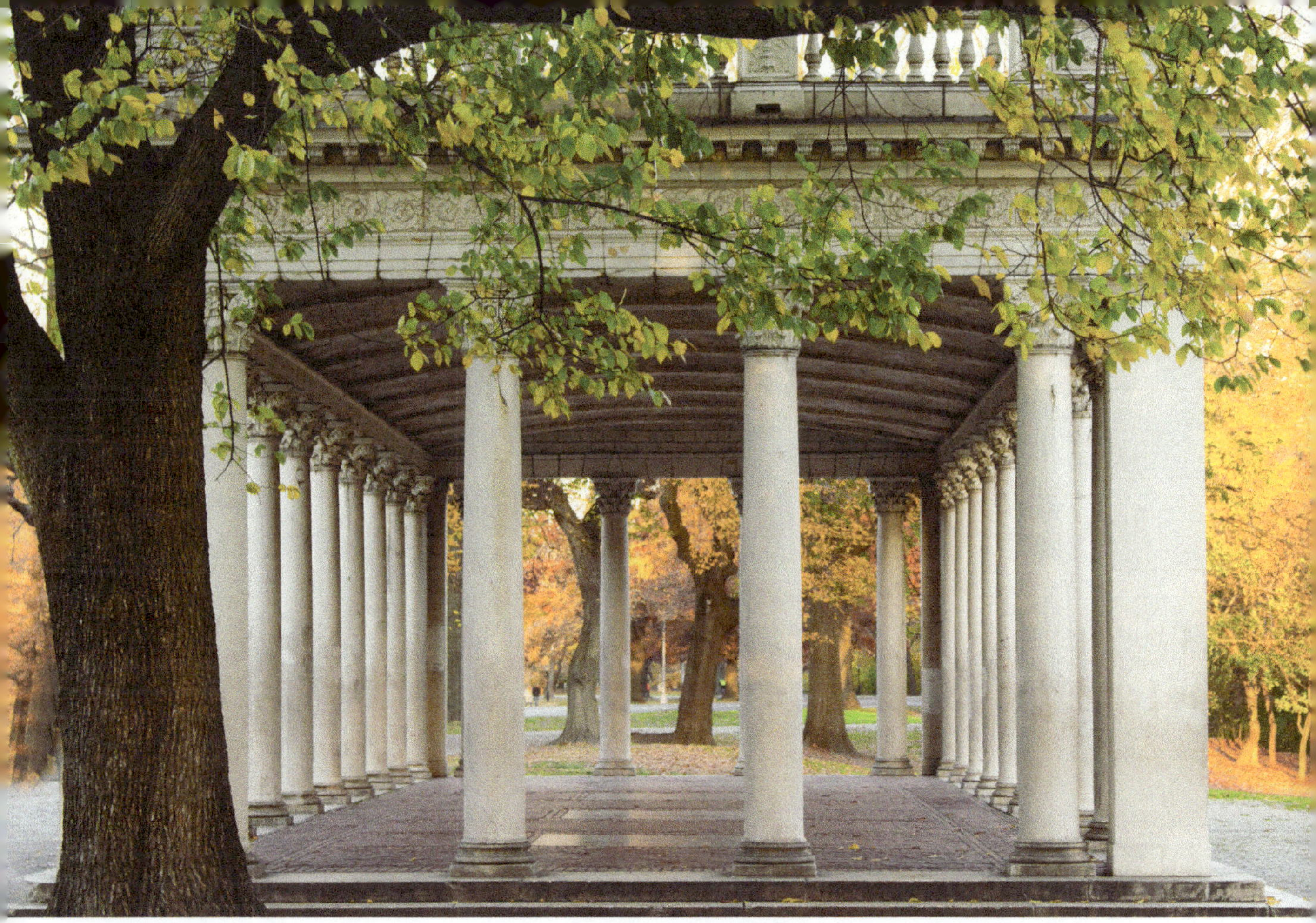

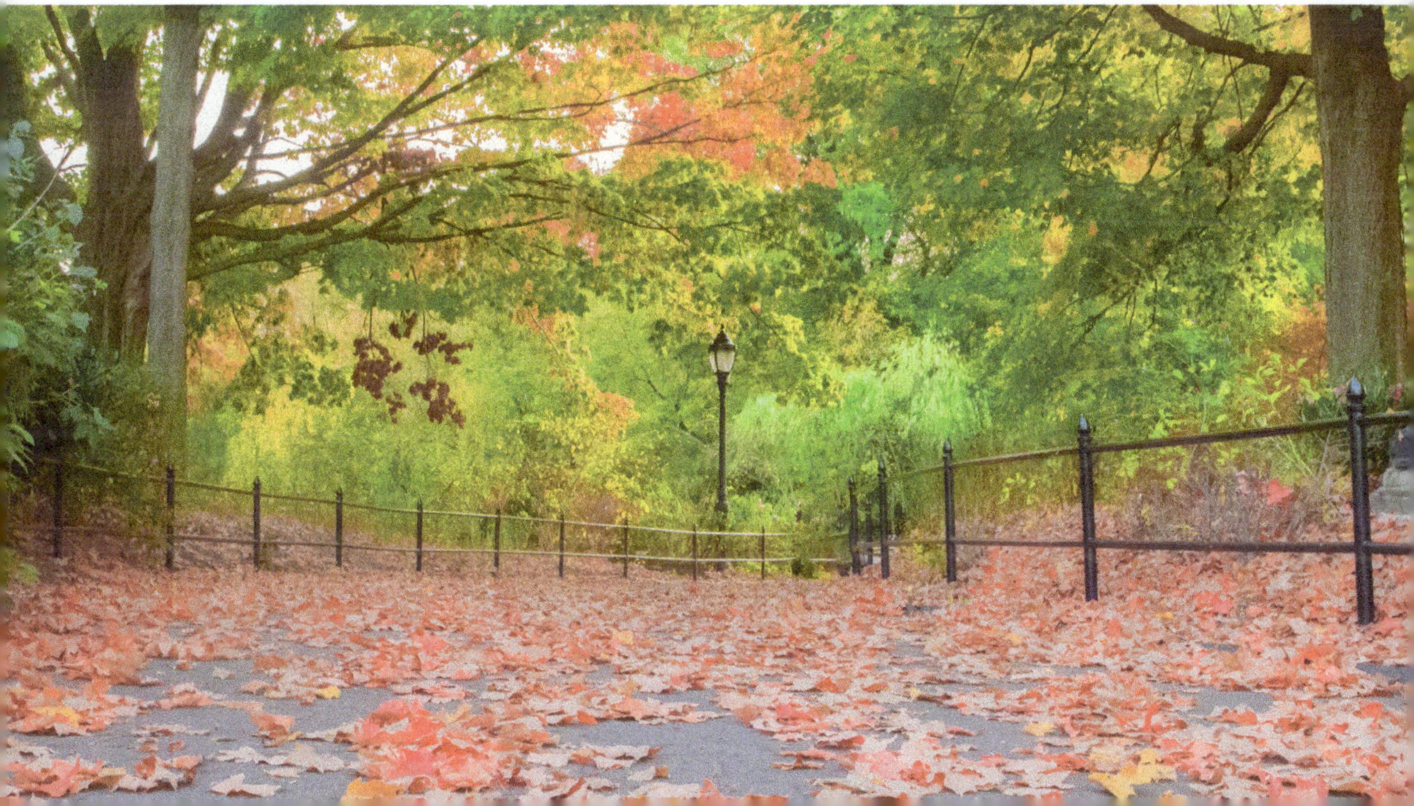

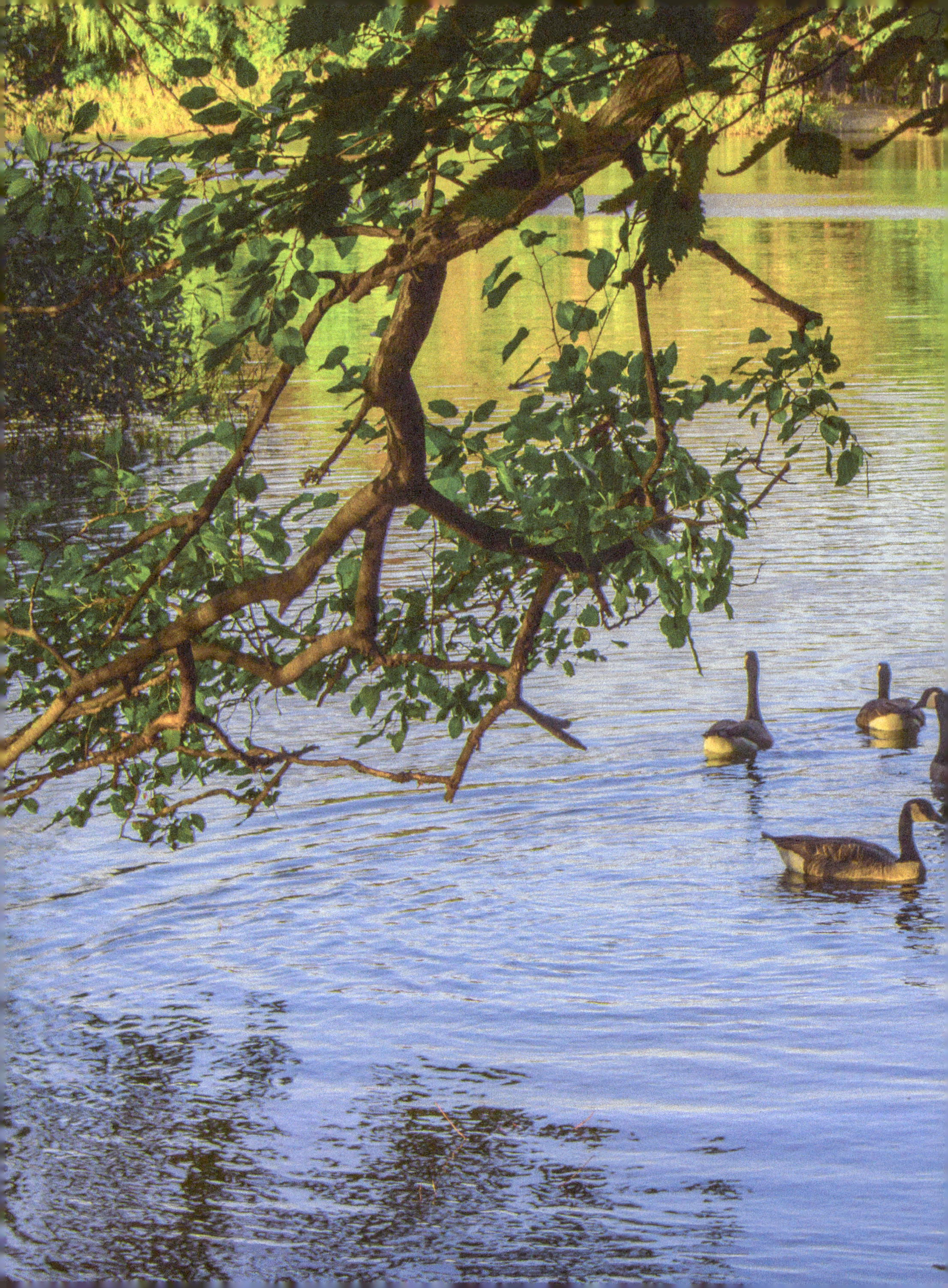

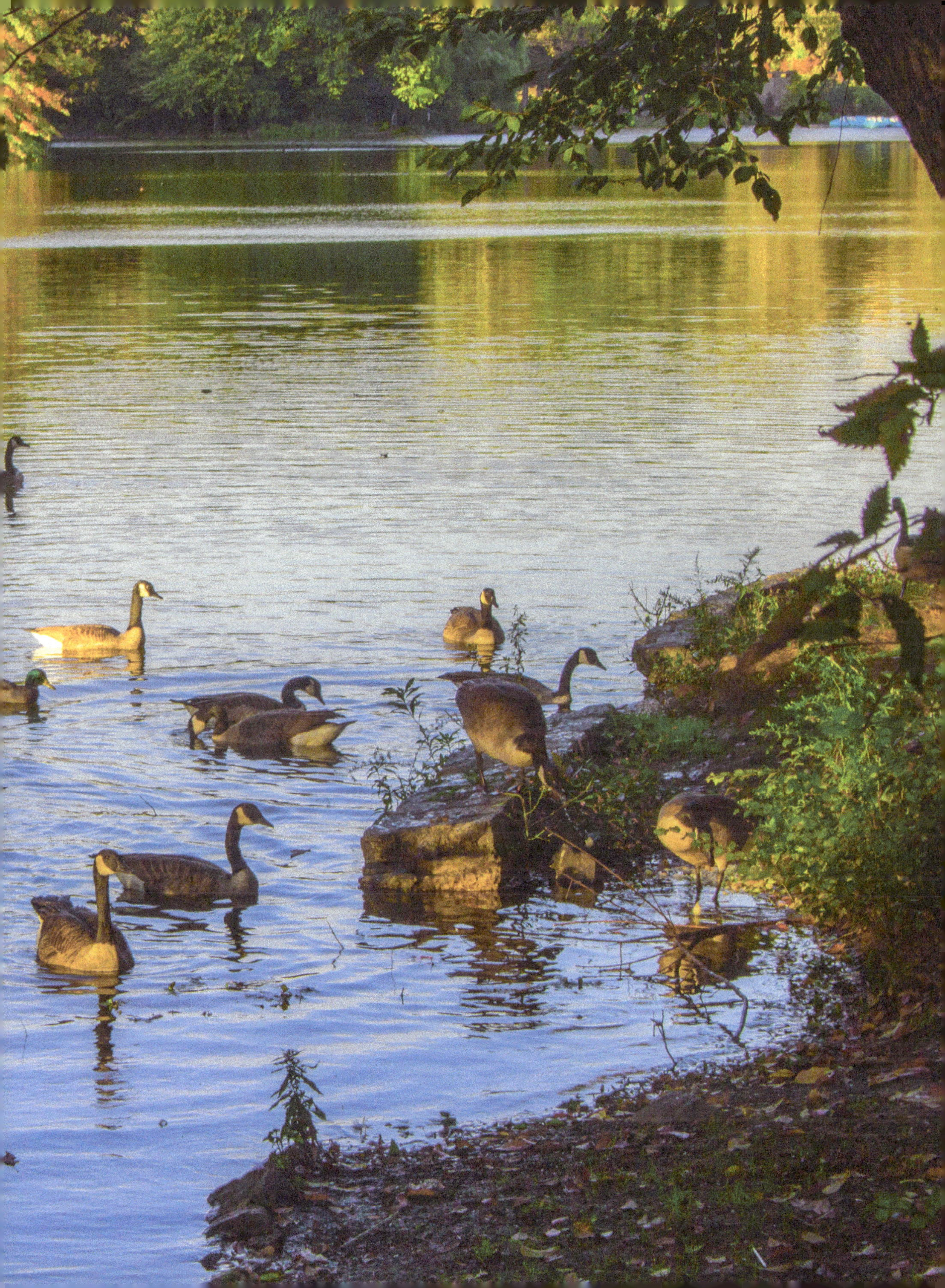

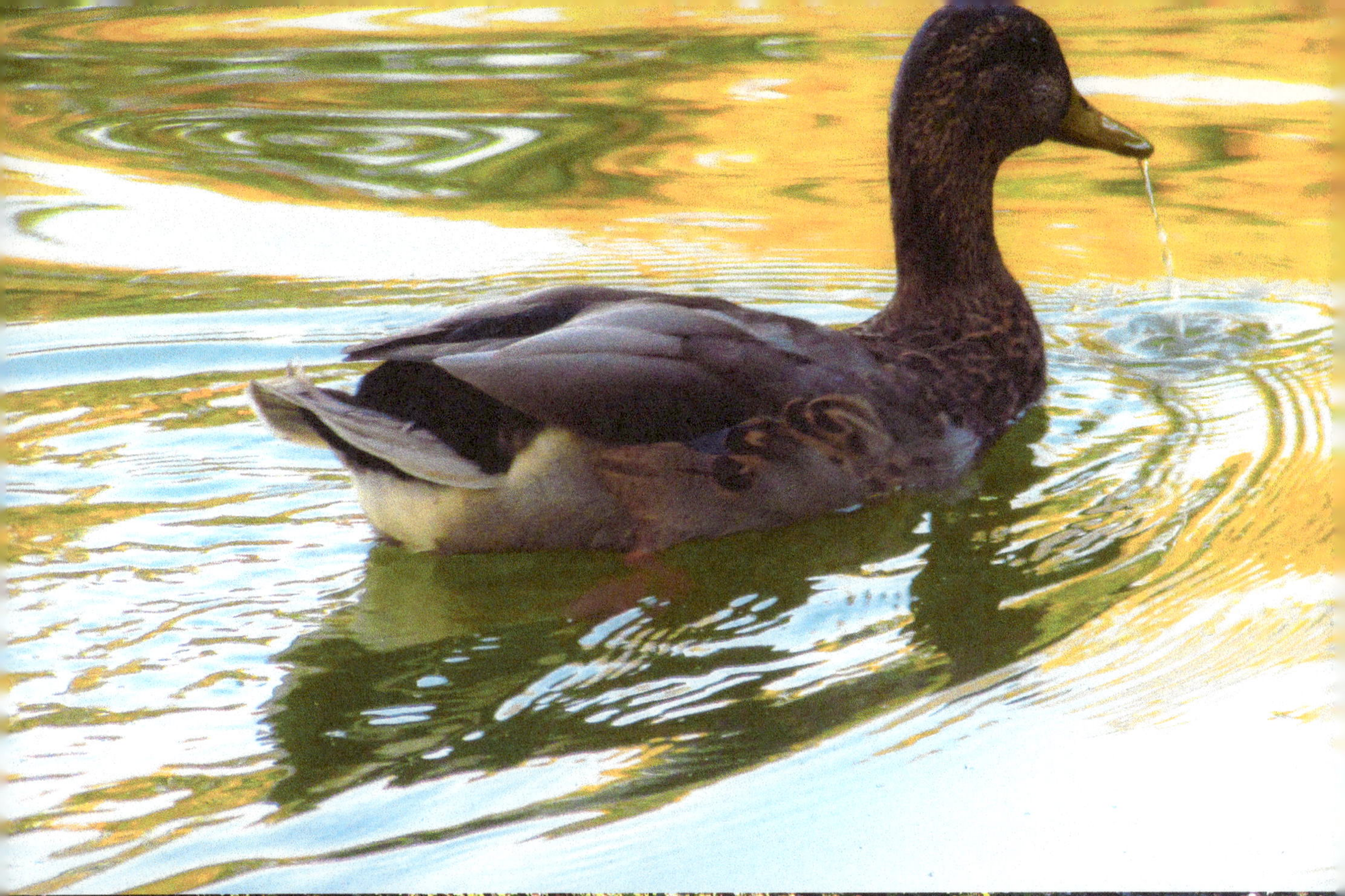

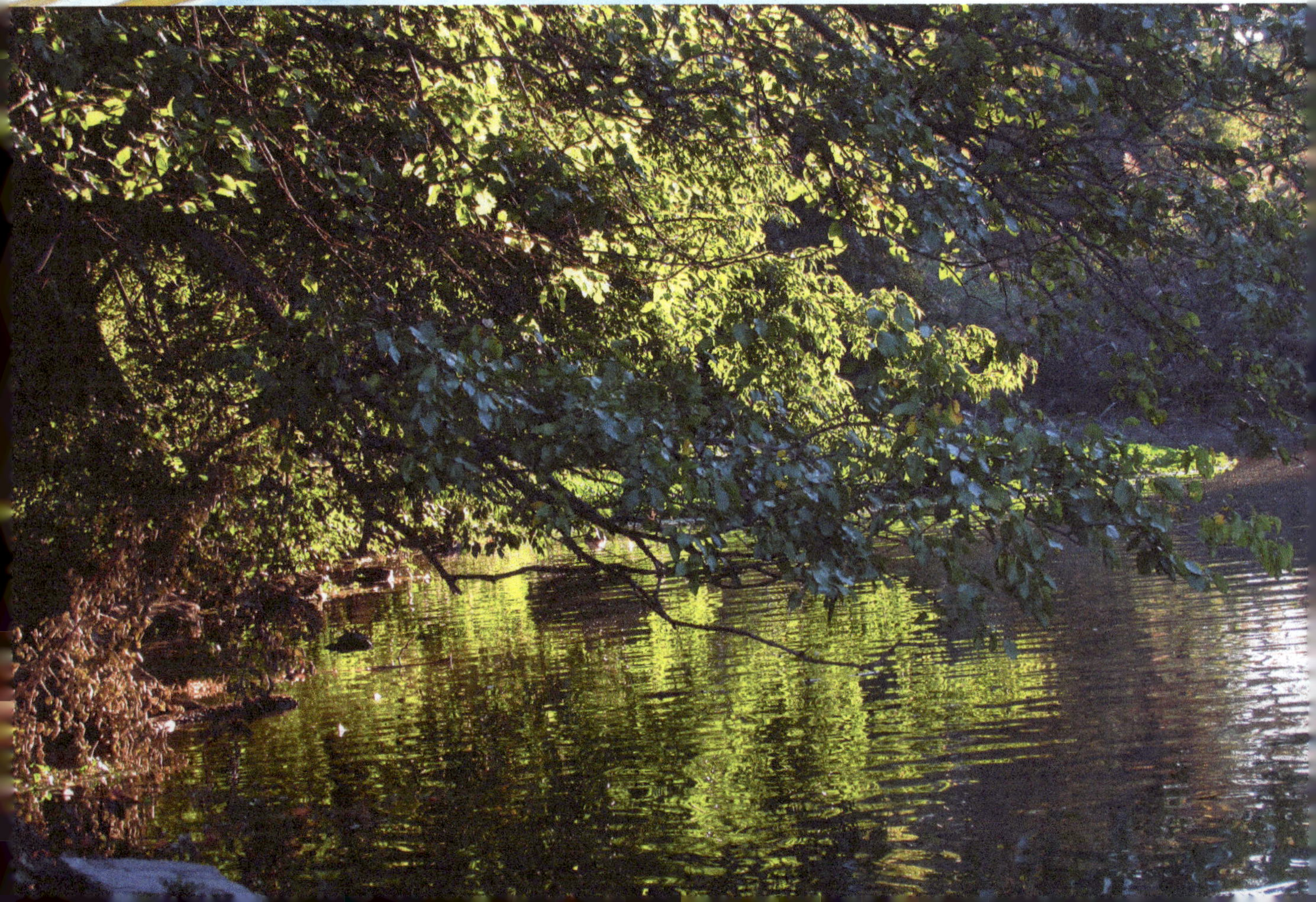

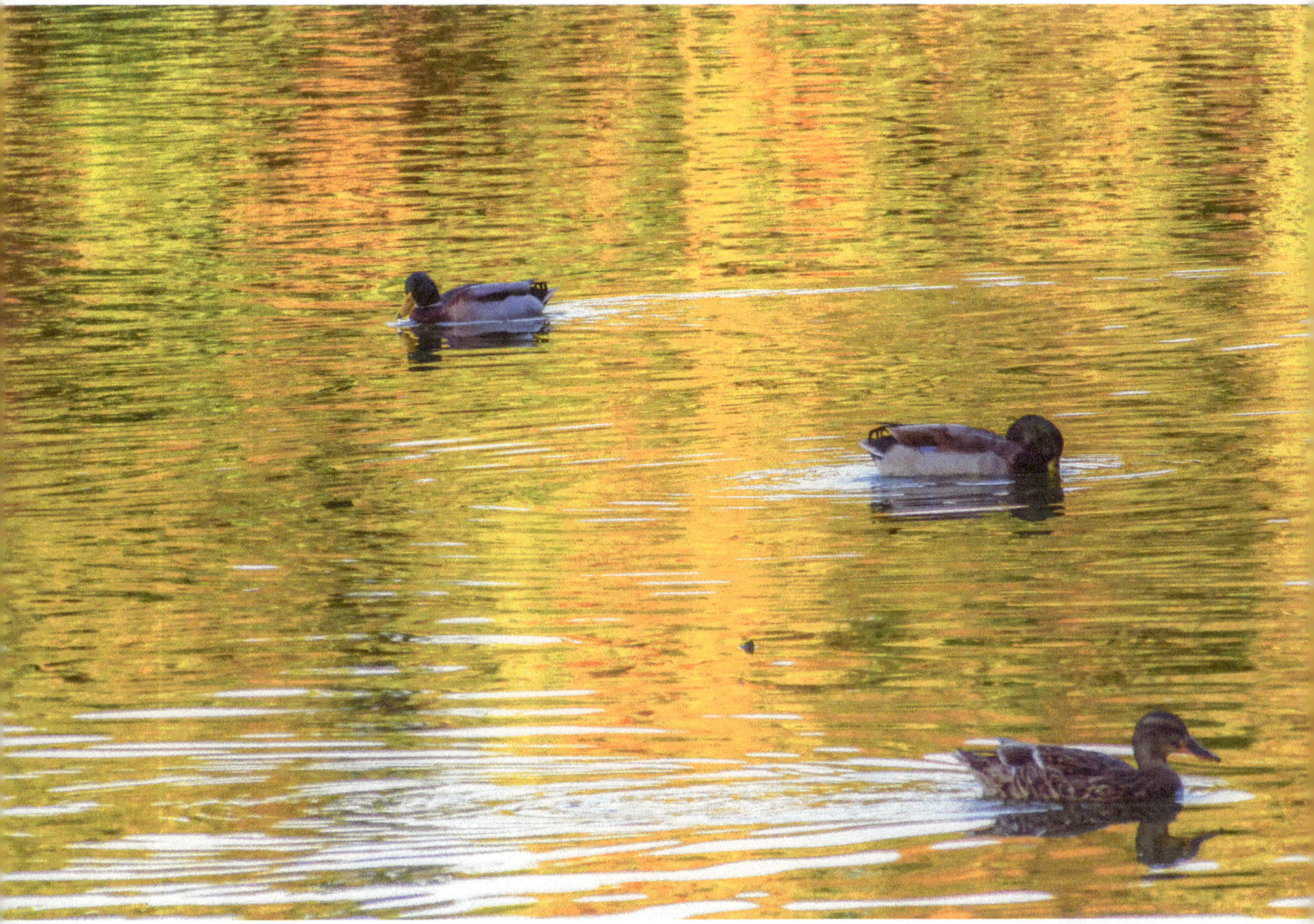

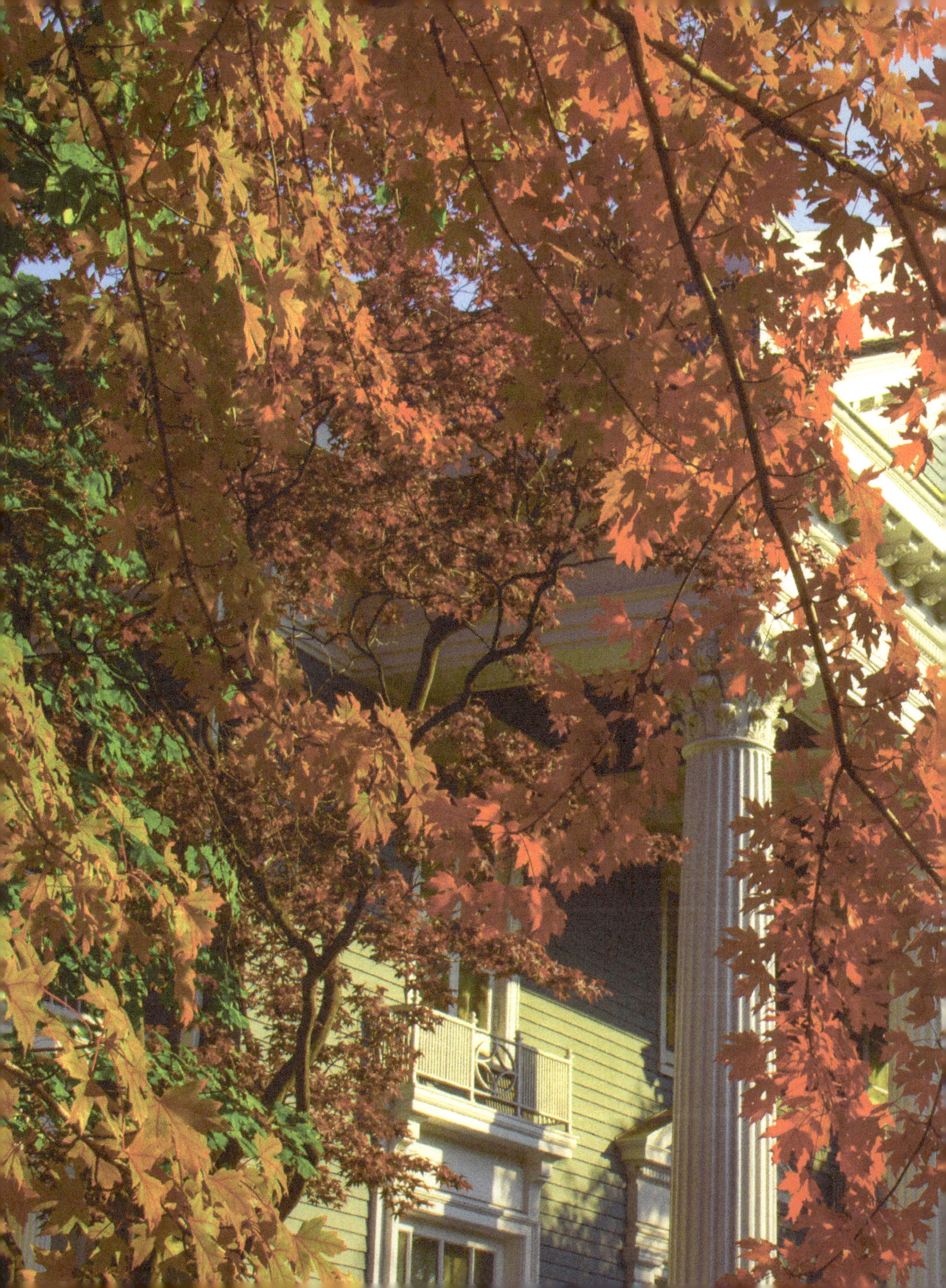

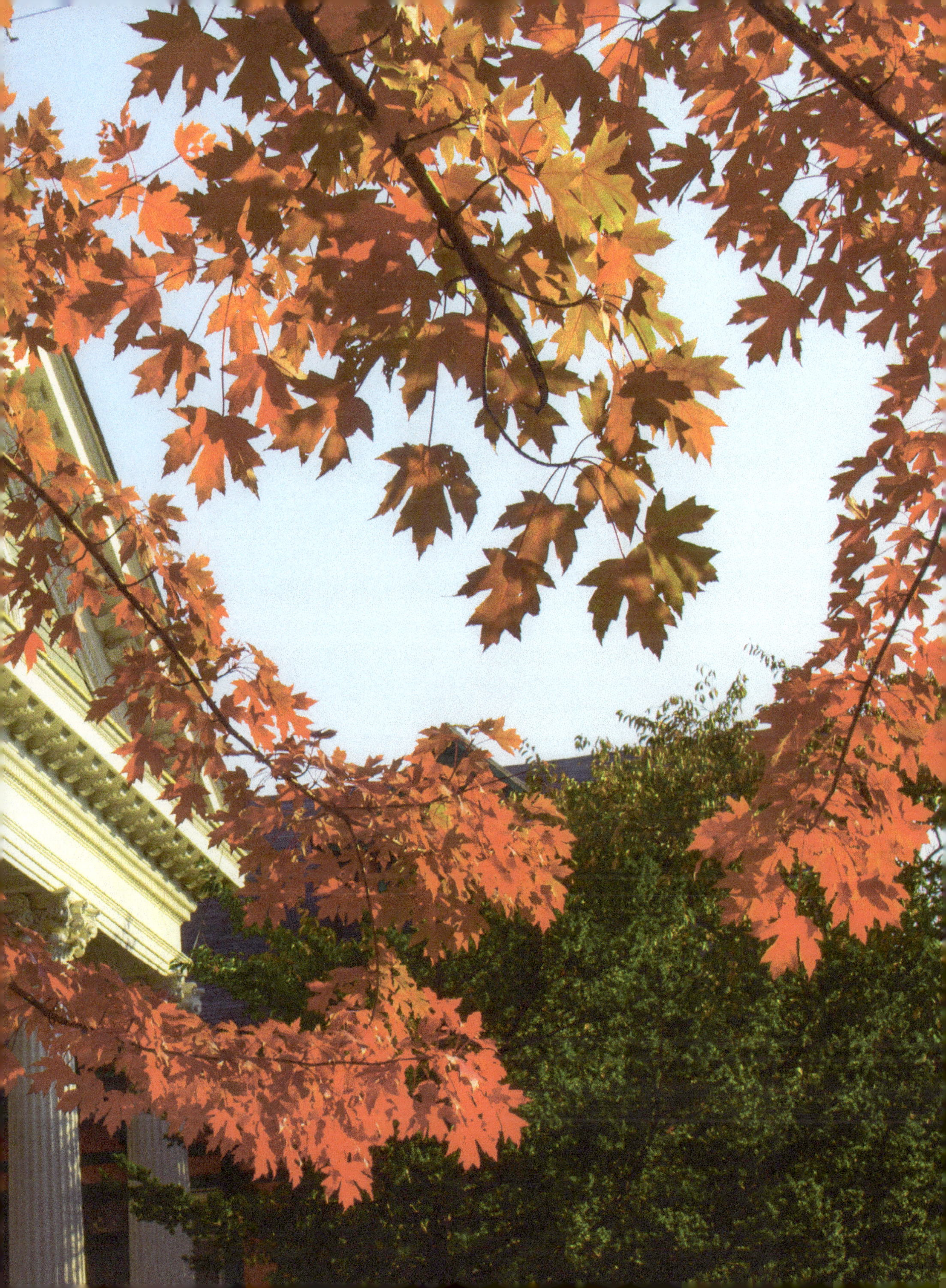

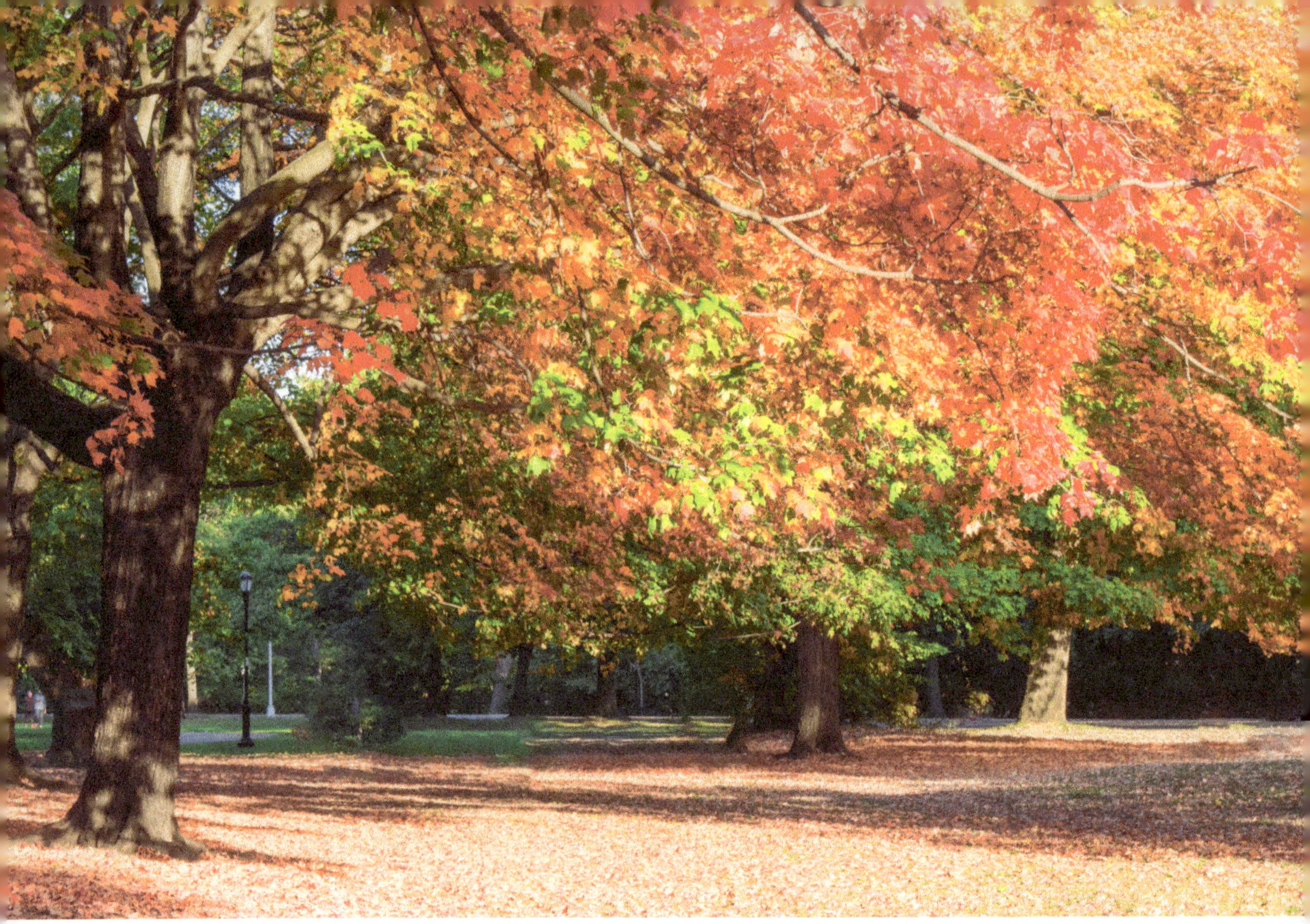

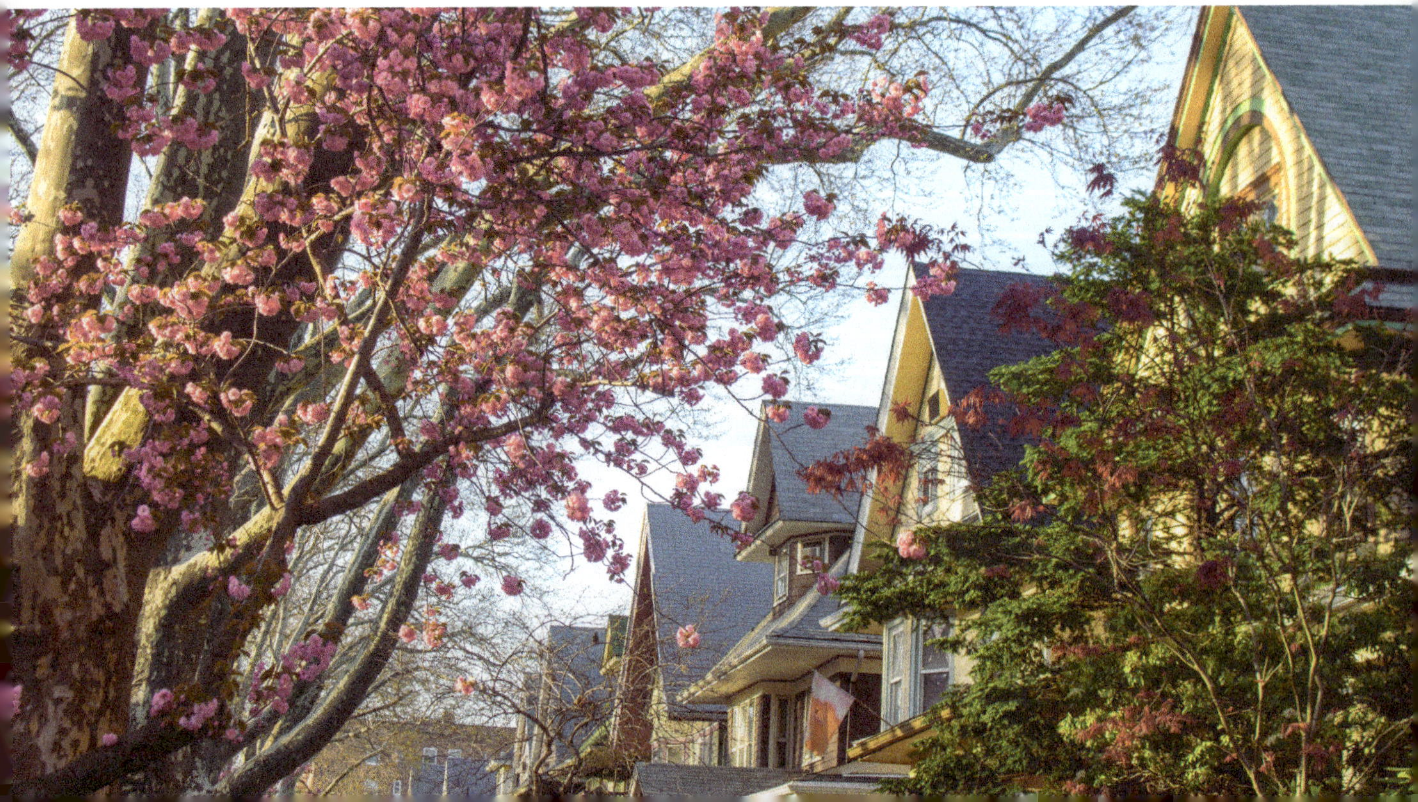

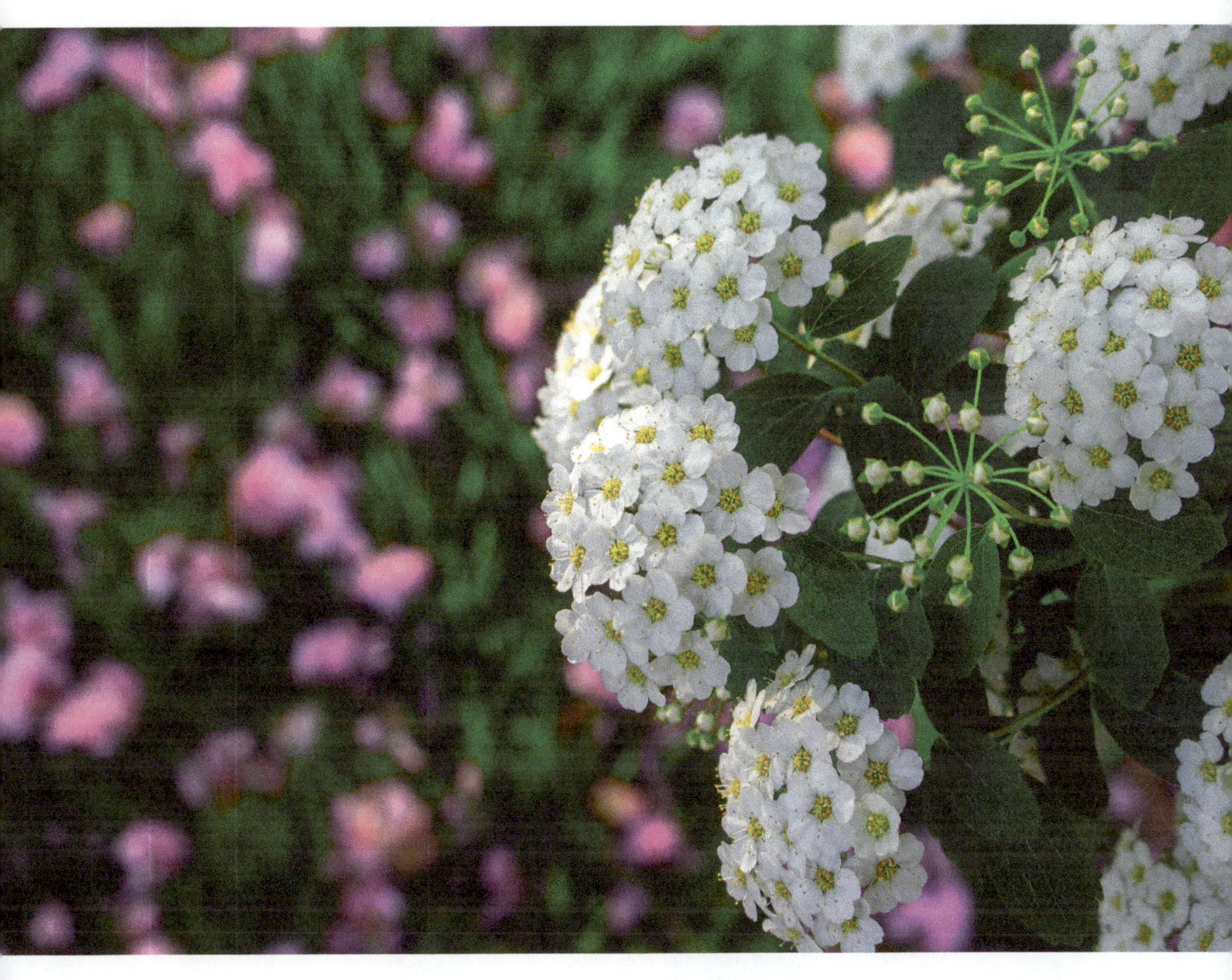

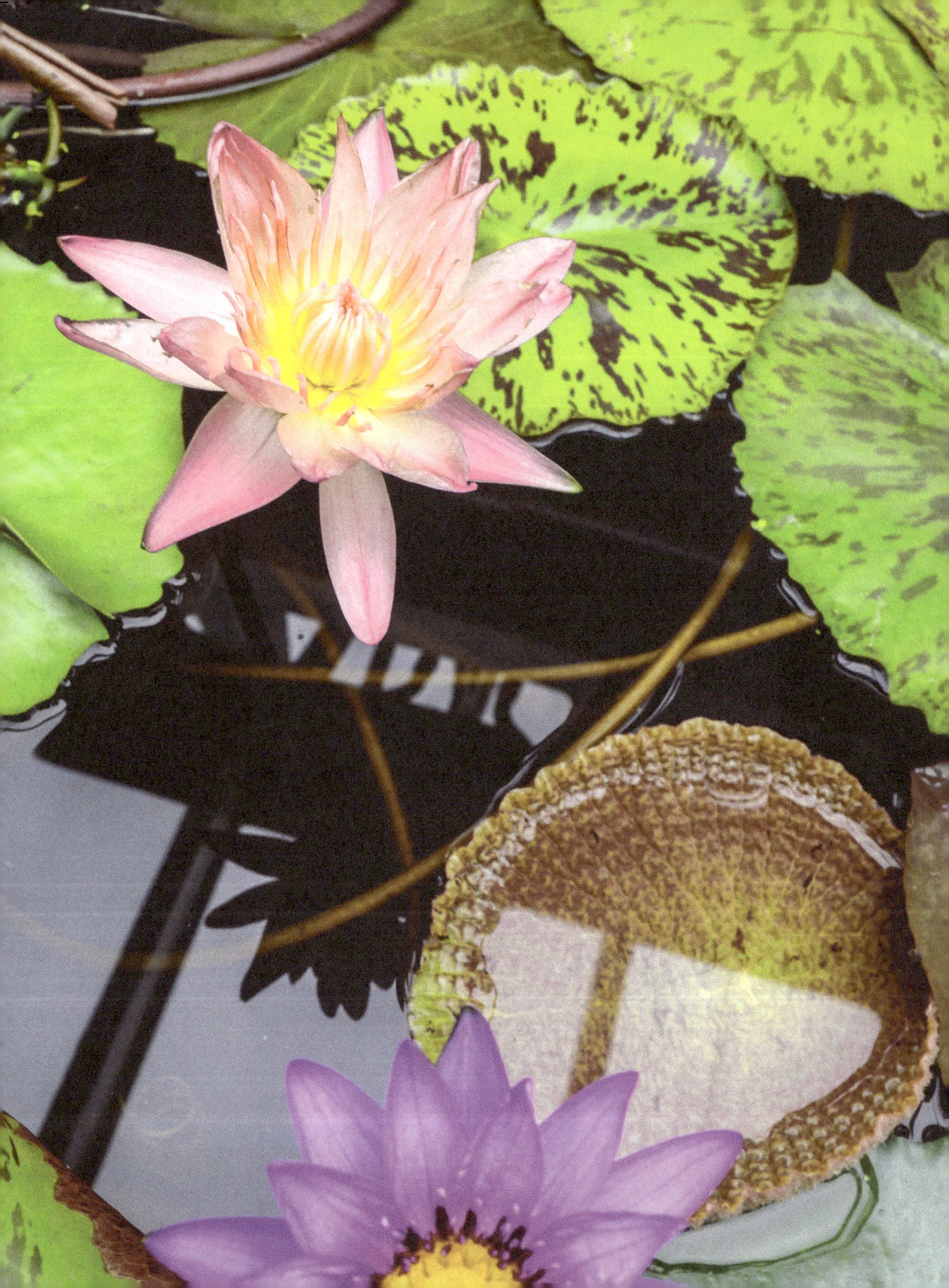

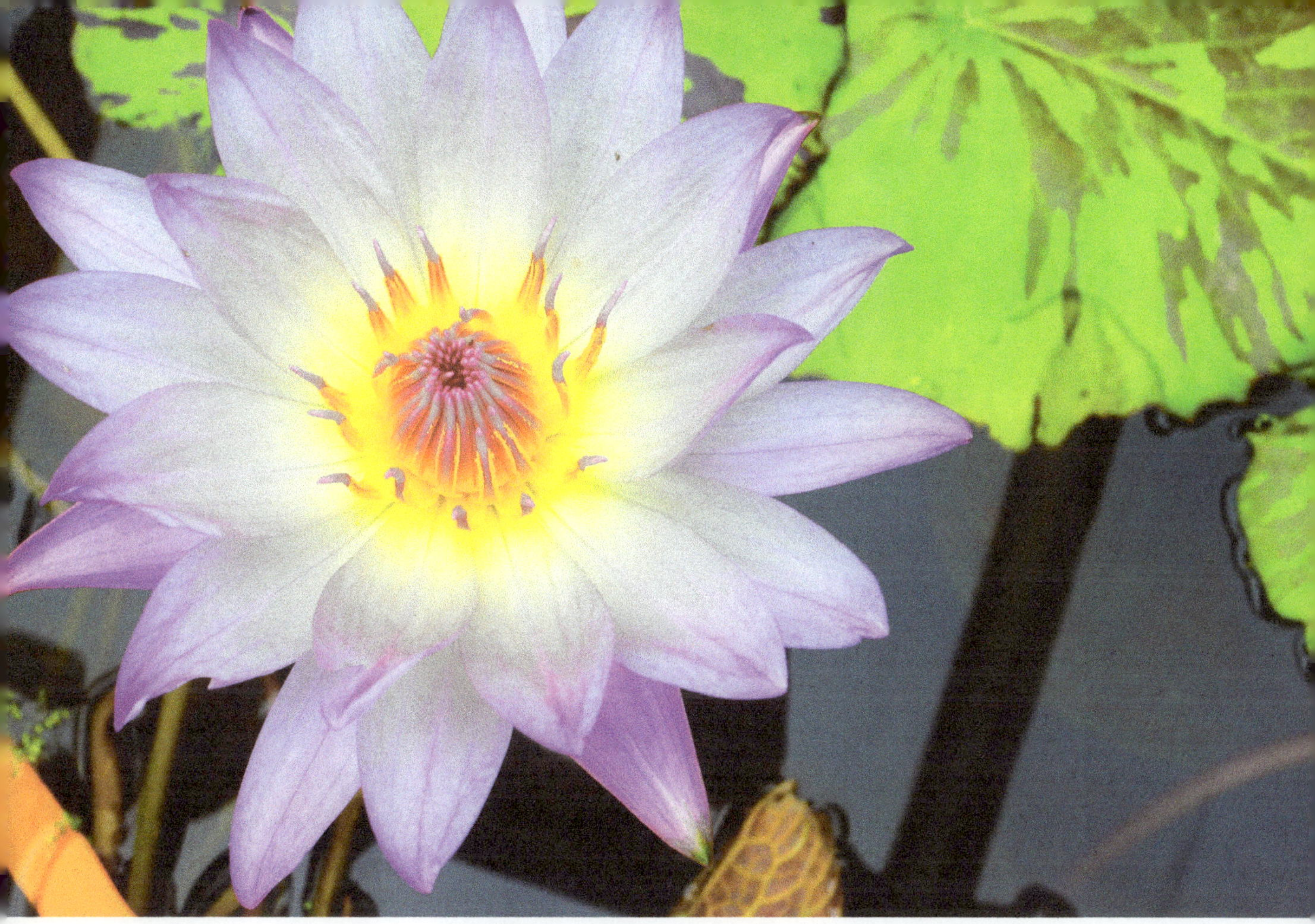

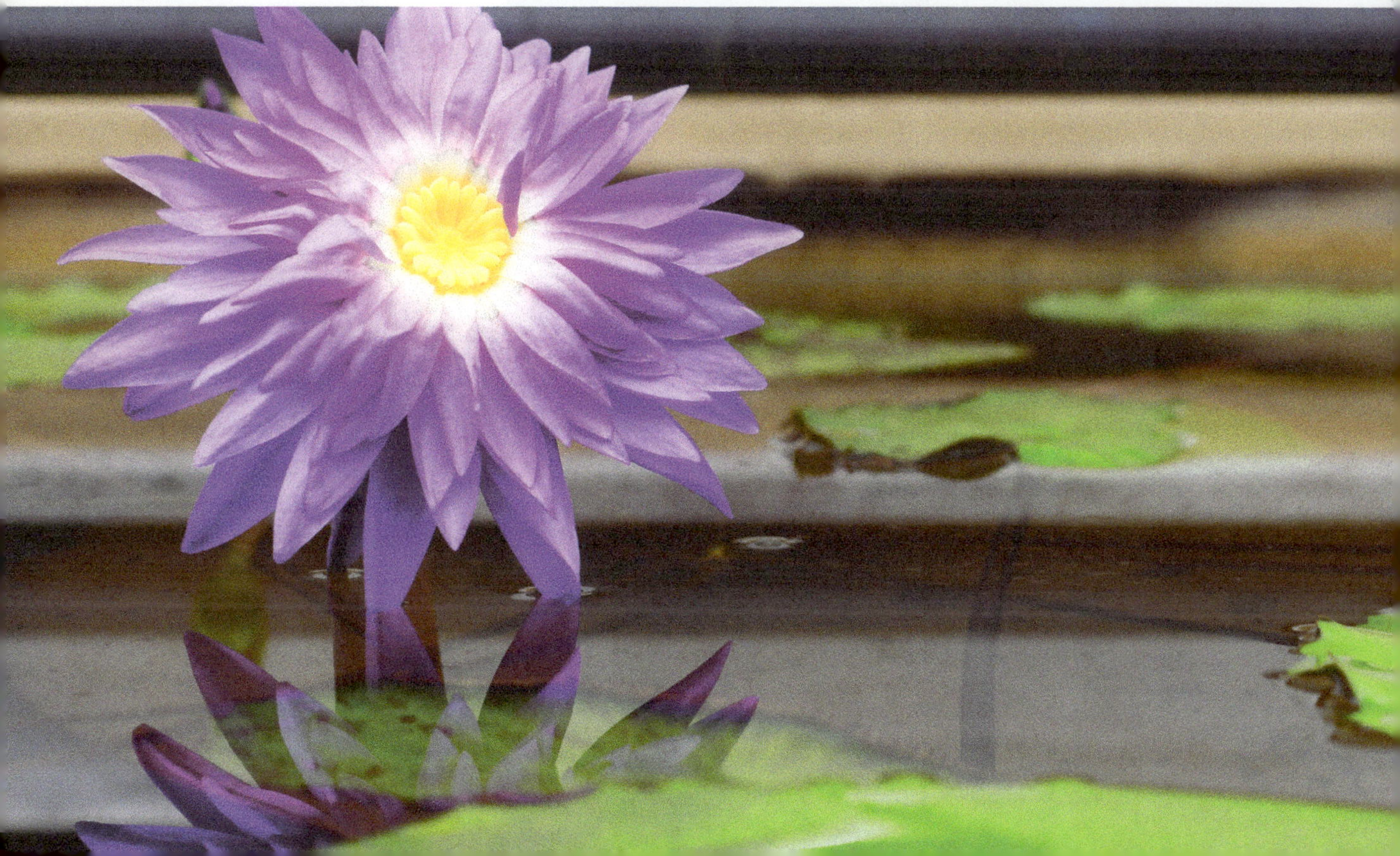

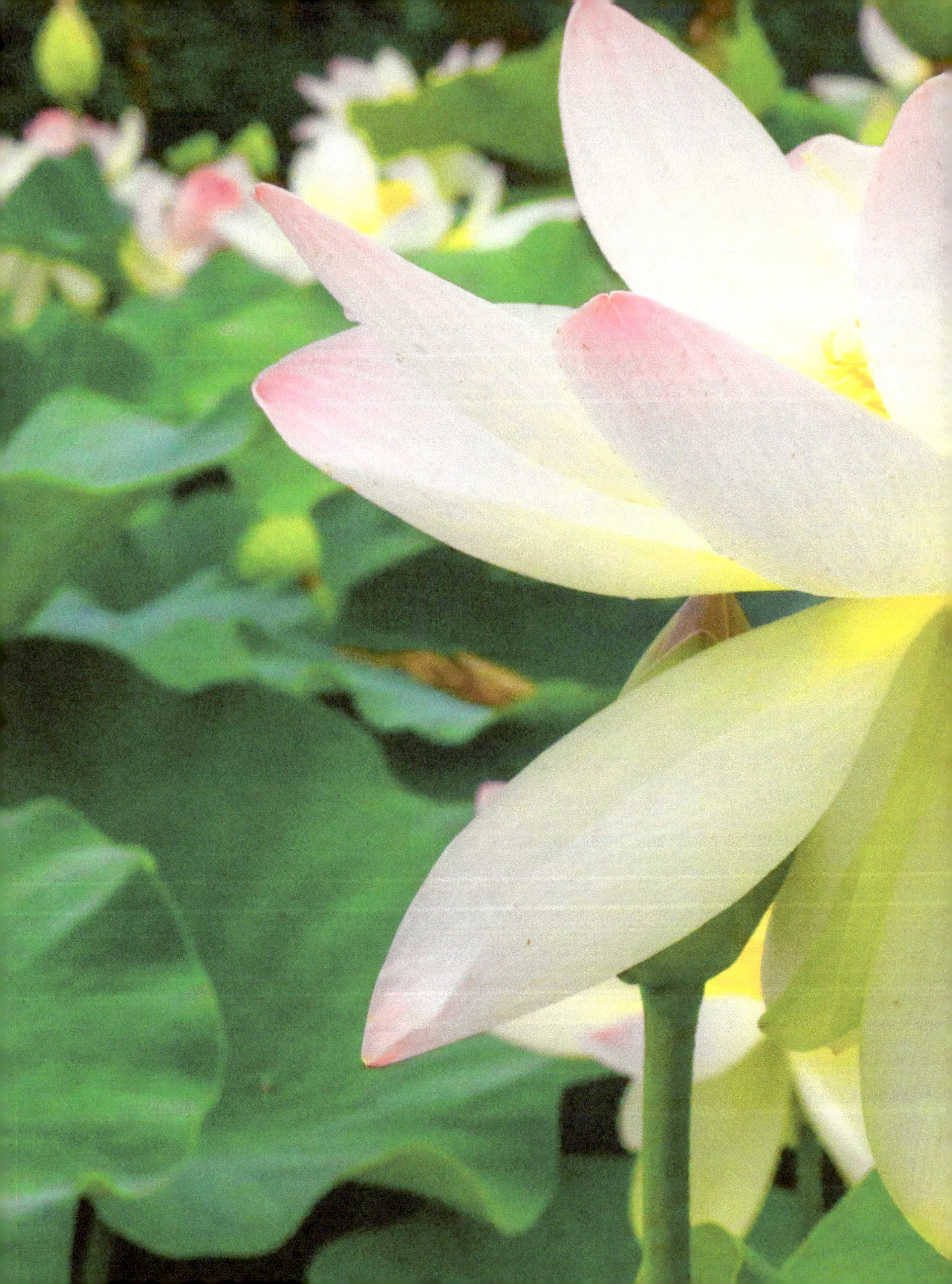

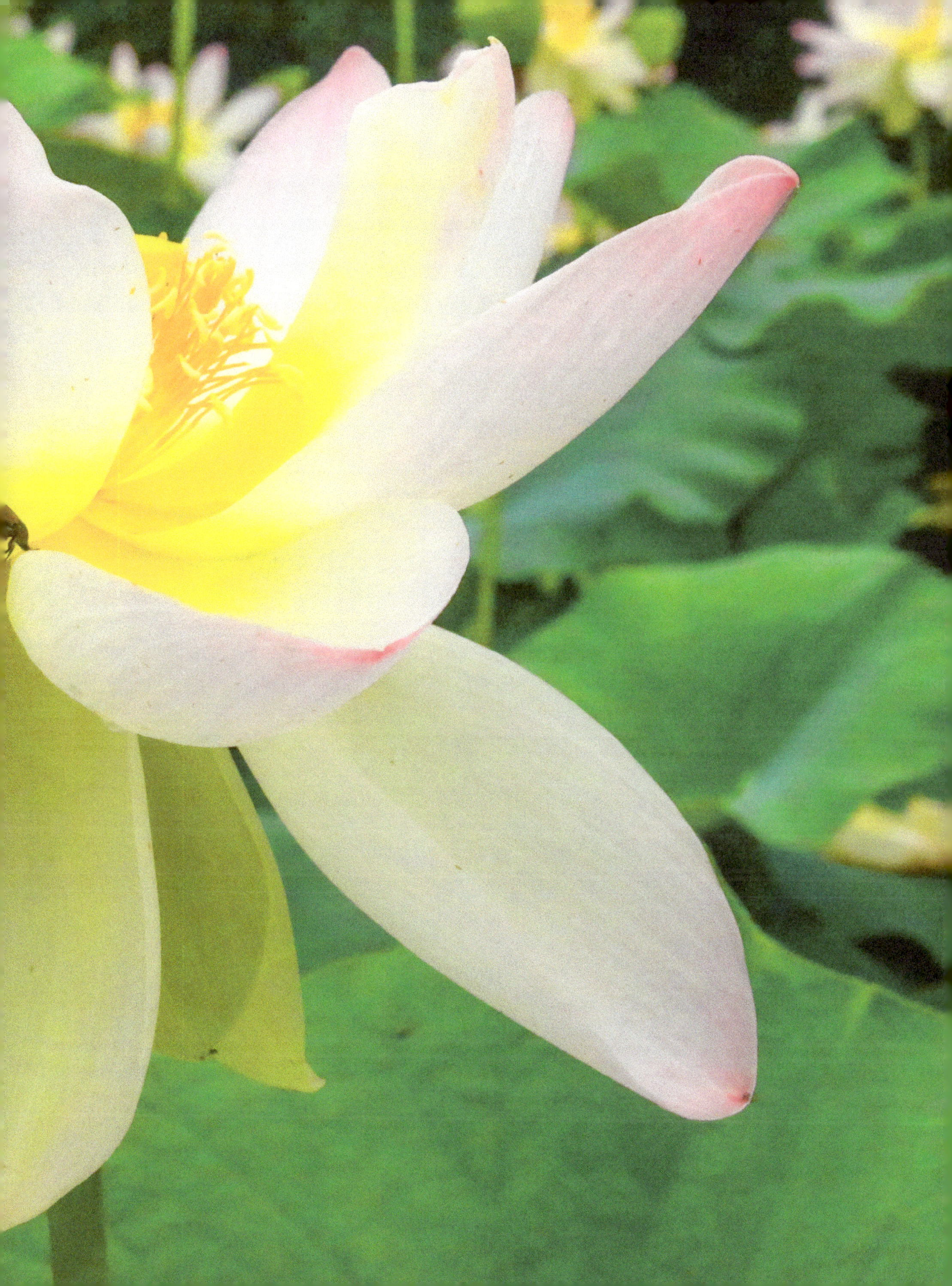

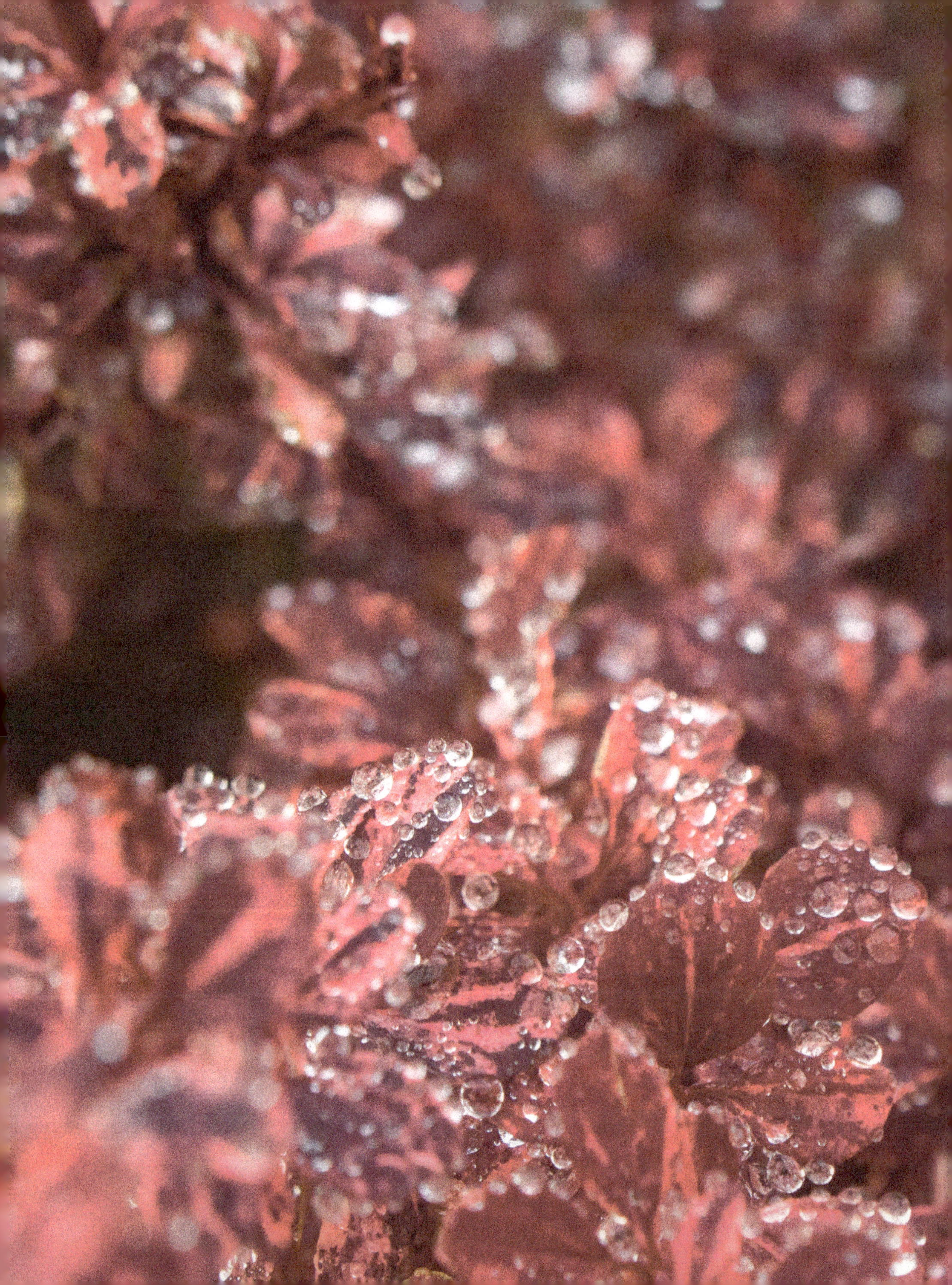

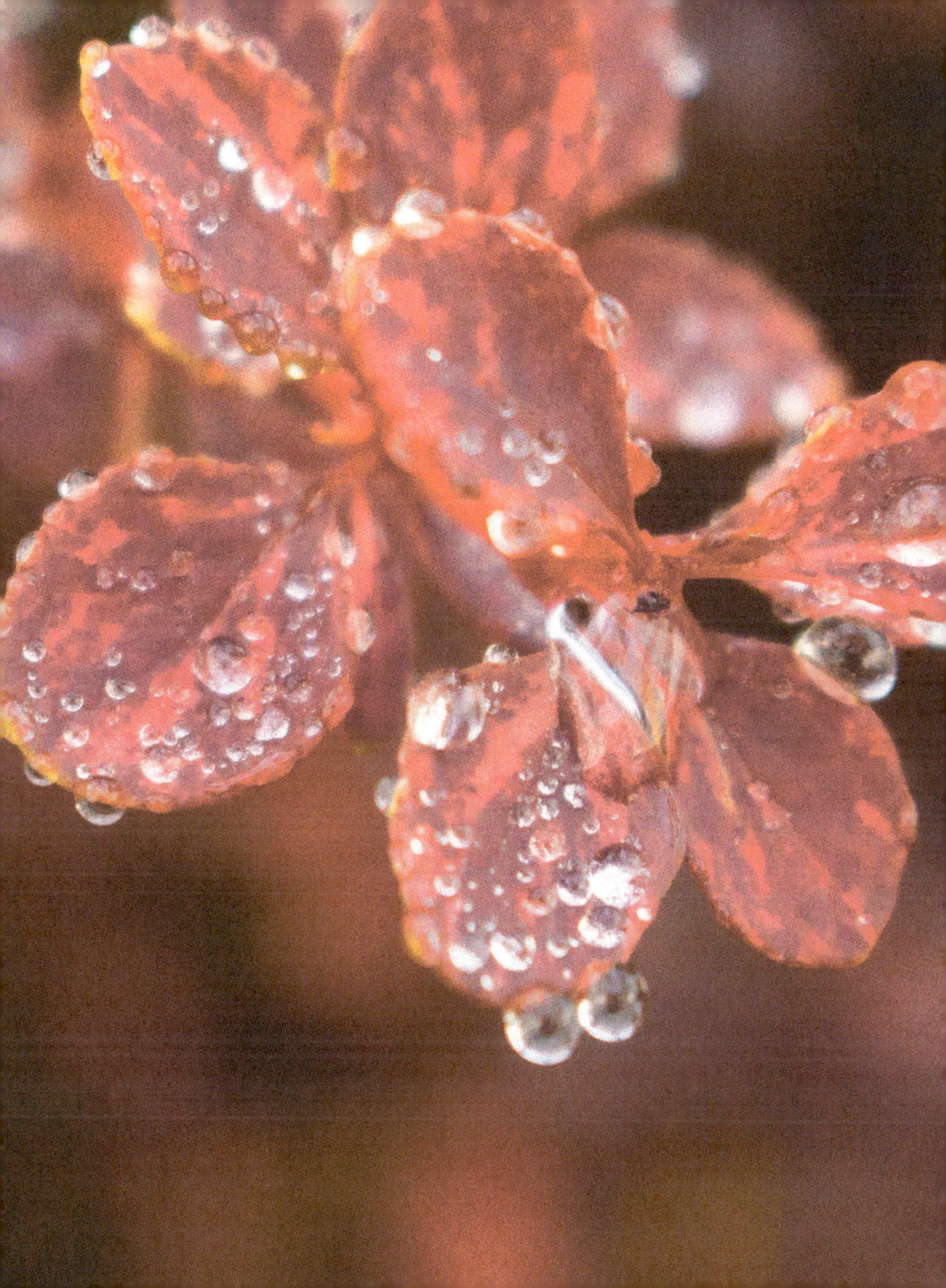

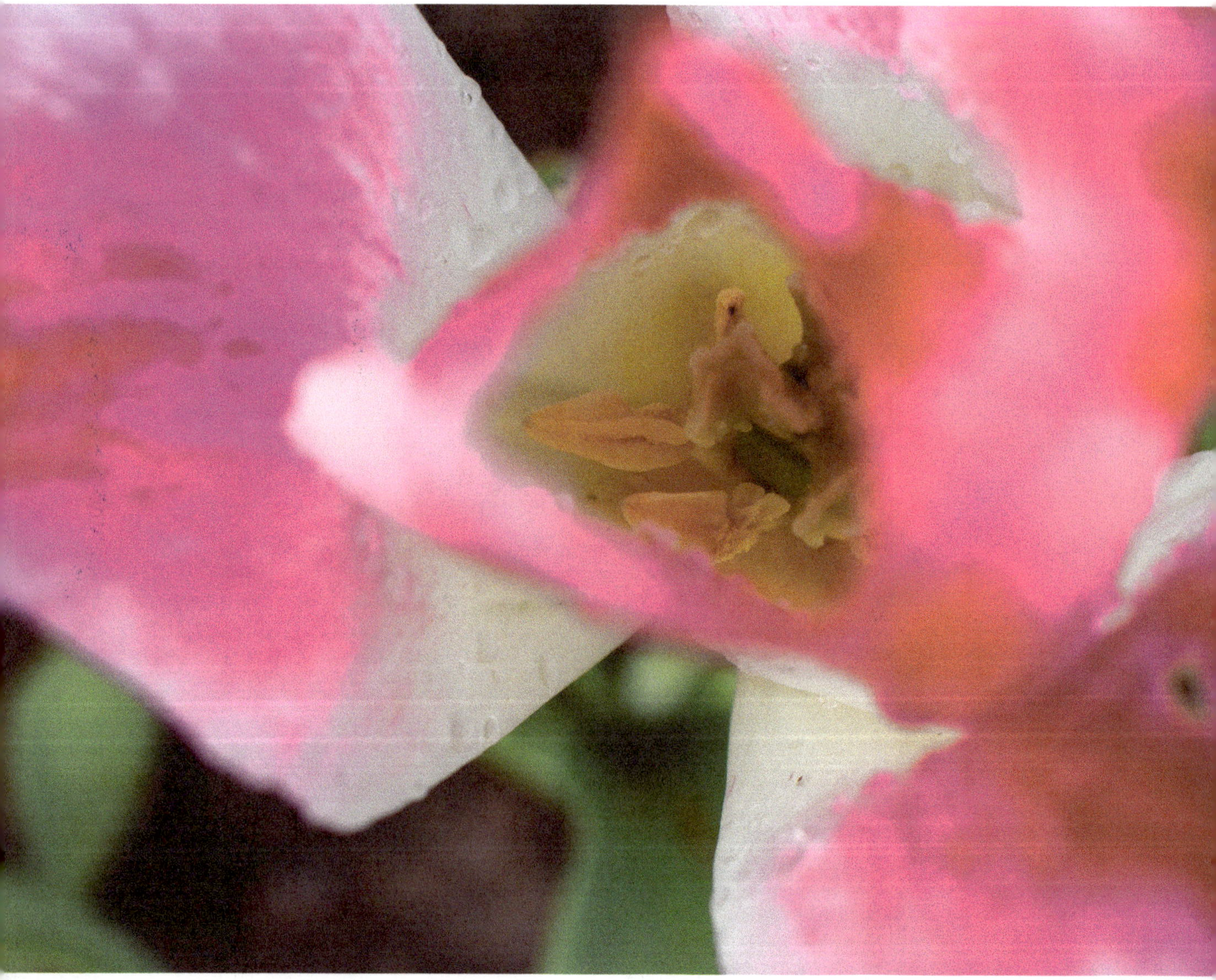

esidents believed their dragon deity preserved the land's color. They grew
special red flower in its honor. People trained for years to care for this rare
ant. Residents dedicated one week in the middle of the year to celebrate
e deity. During that time, they picked the flowers and carried them to
eir god's home. The residents allowed him to attend the celebration but he
uldn't touch any flowers.

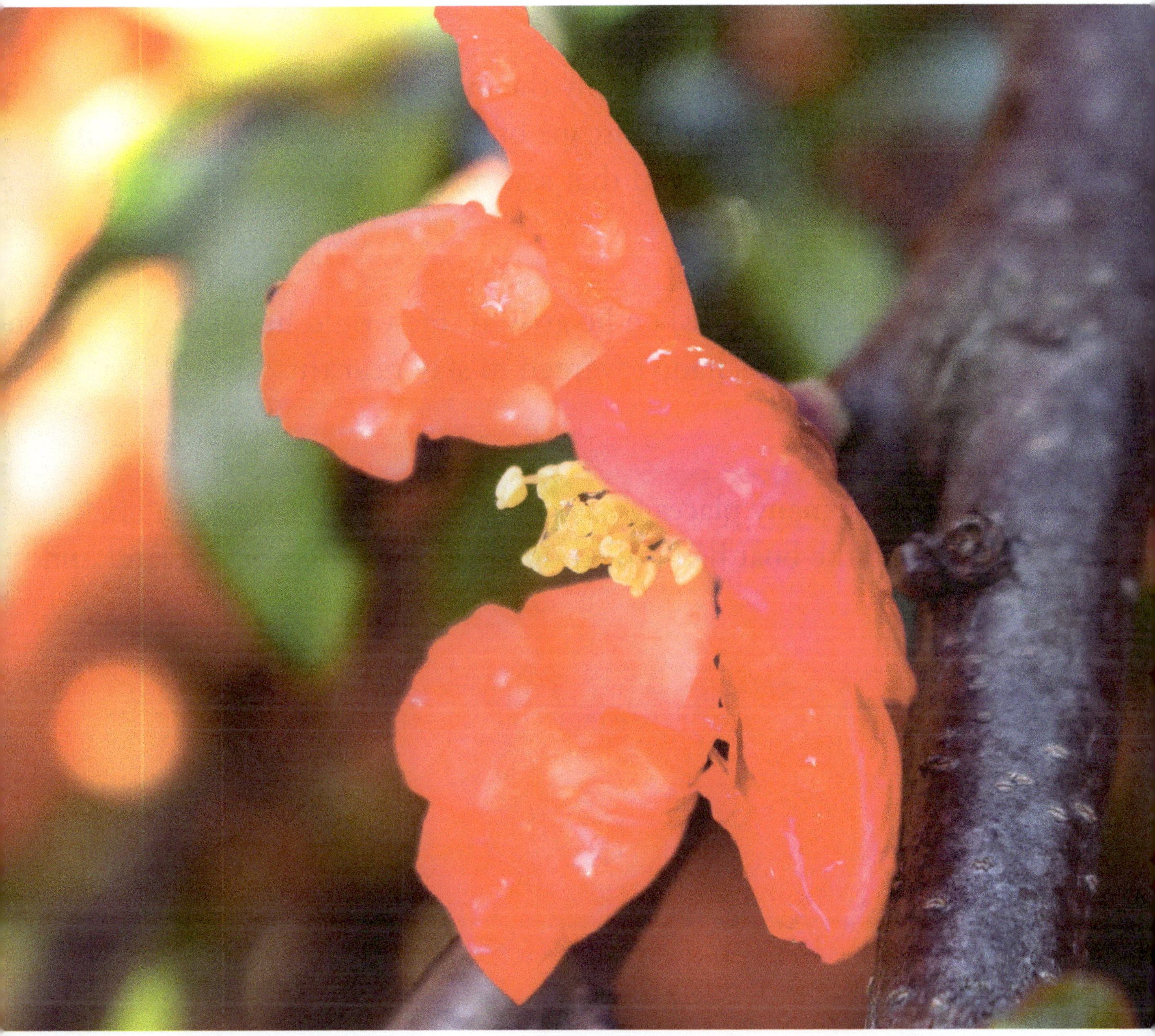

The world without color was probably the most unnerving. Perpetual fall and cold seasons had stripped the landscape of any vibrant colors he had grown used to. He heard about the land that saw no sun and it had sparked his curiosity.

It had been unusually quiet when he arrived. He would have ran back on the ship except the passengers hadn't wanted to stay near this island longer than necessary.

He had traveled to many places at this point and had never seen a dock so empty. It seemed the boat had pulled up to the closest stretch of land and threw him off.

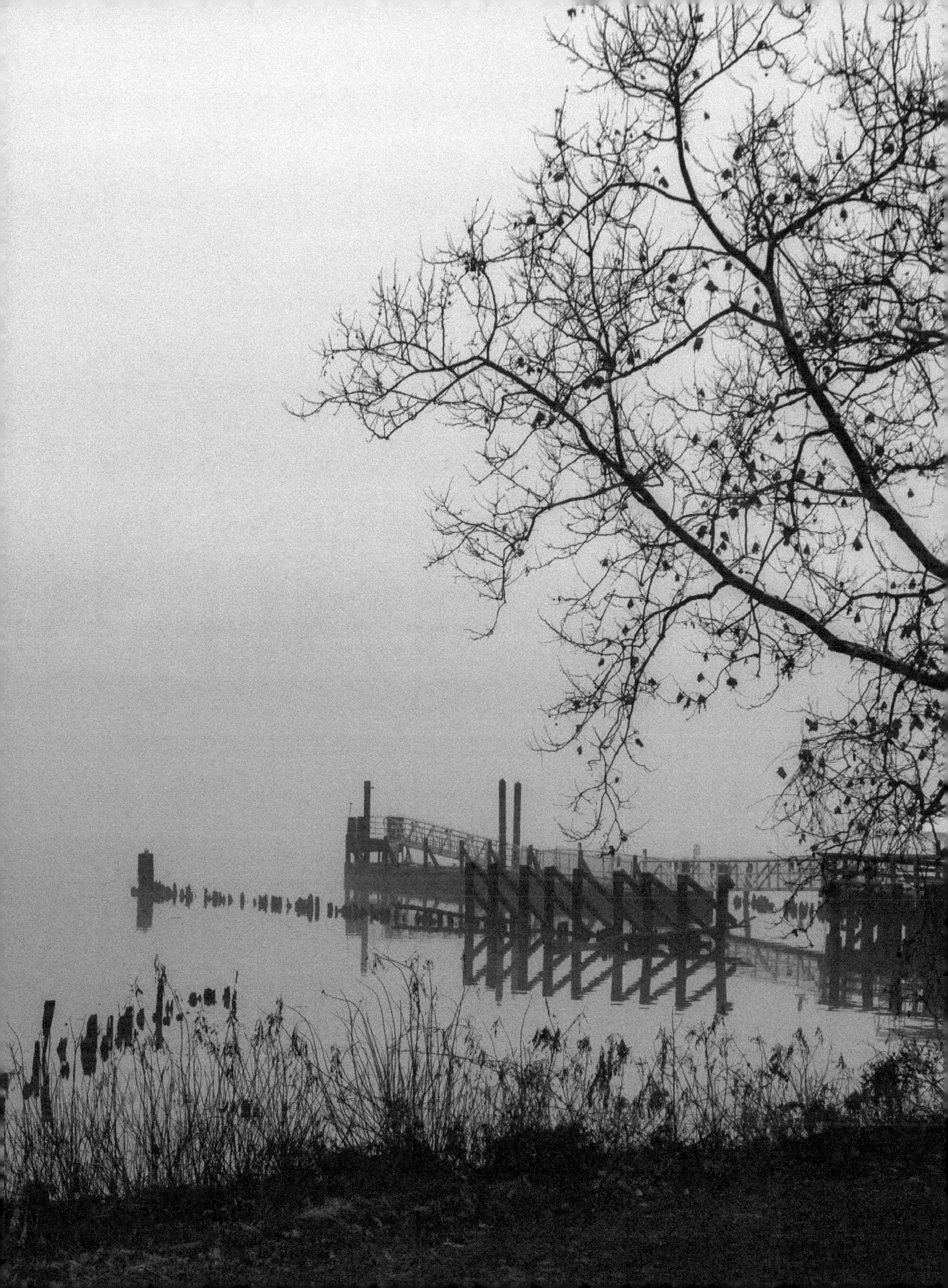

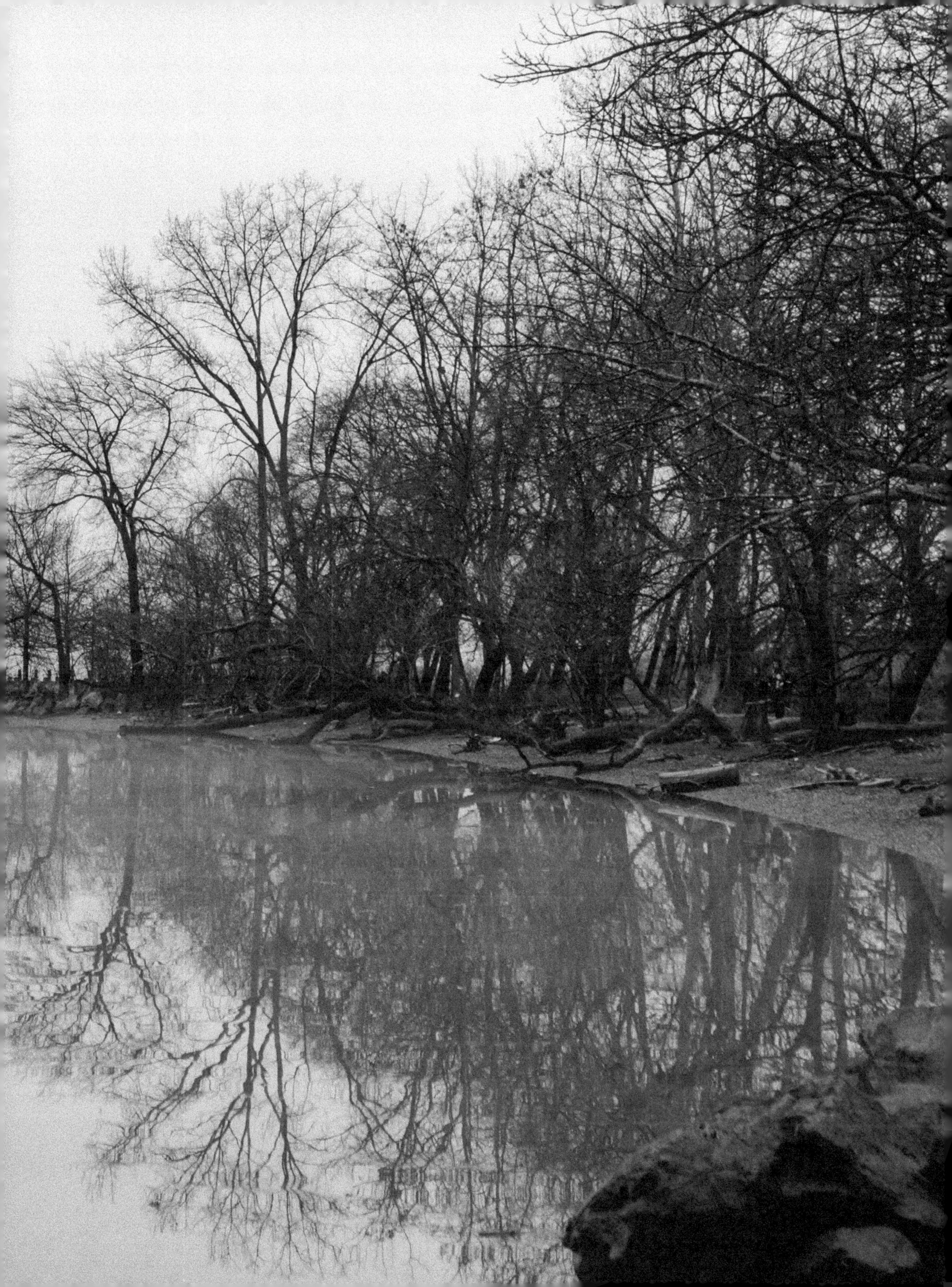

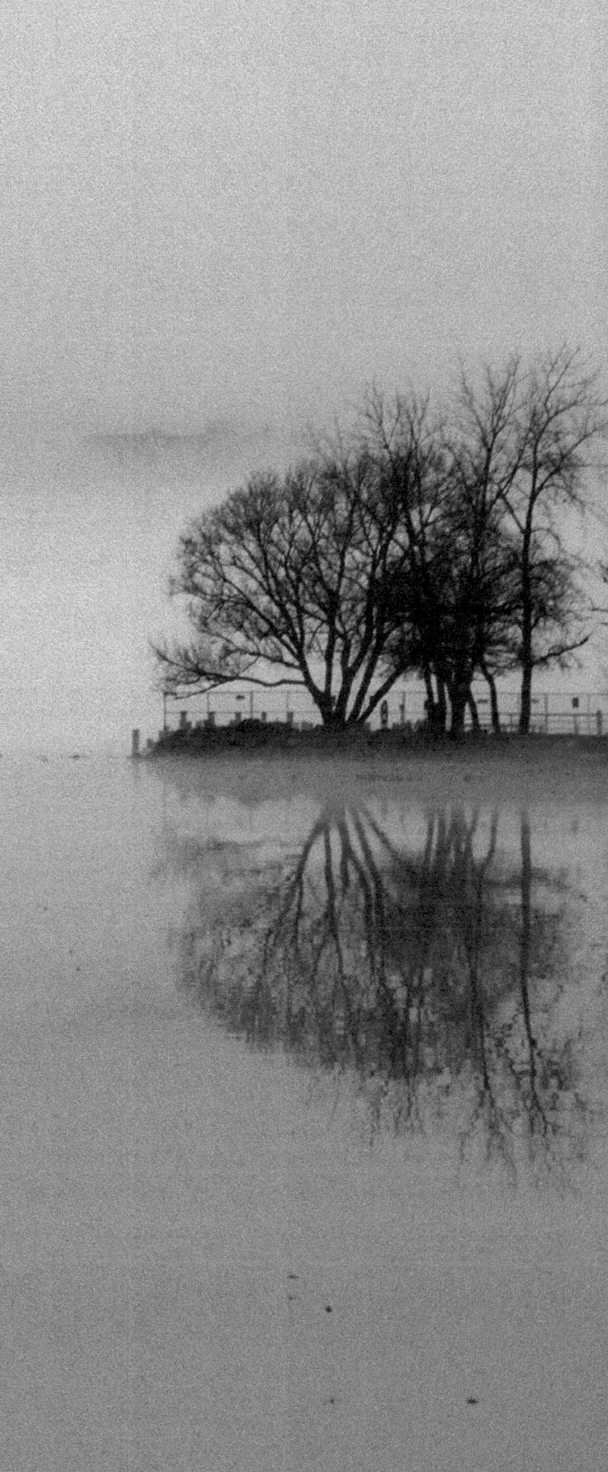

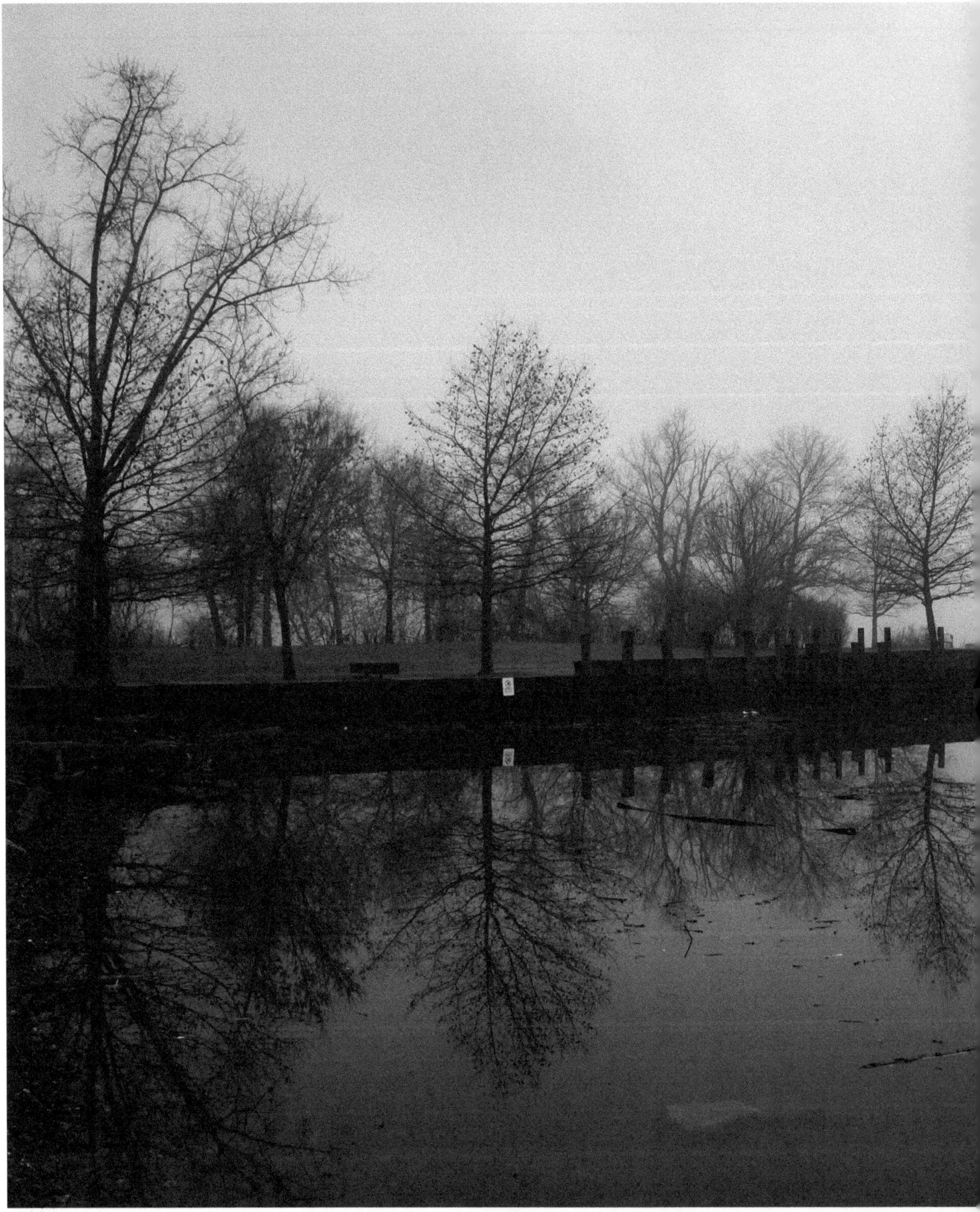

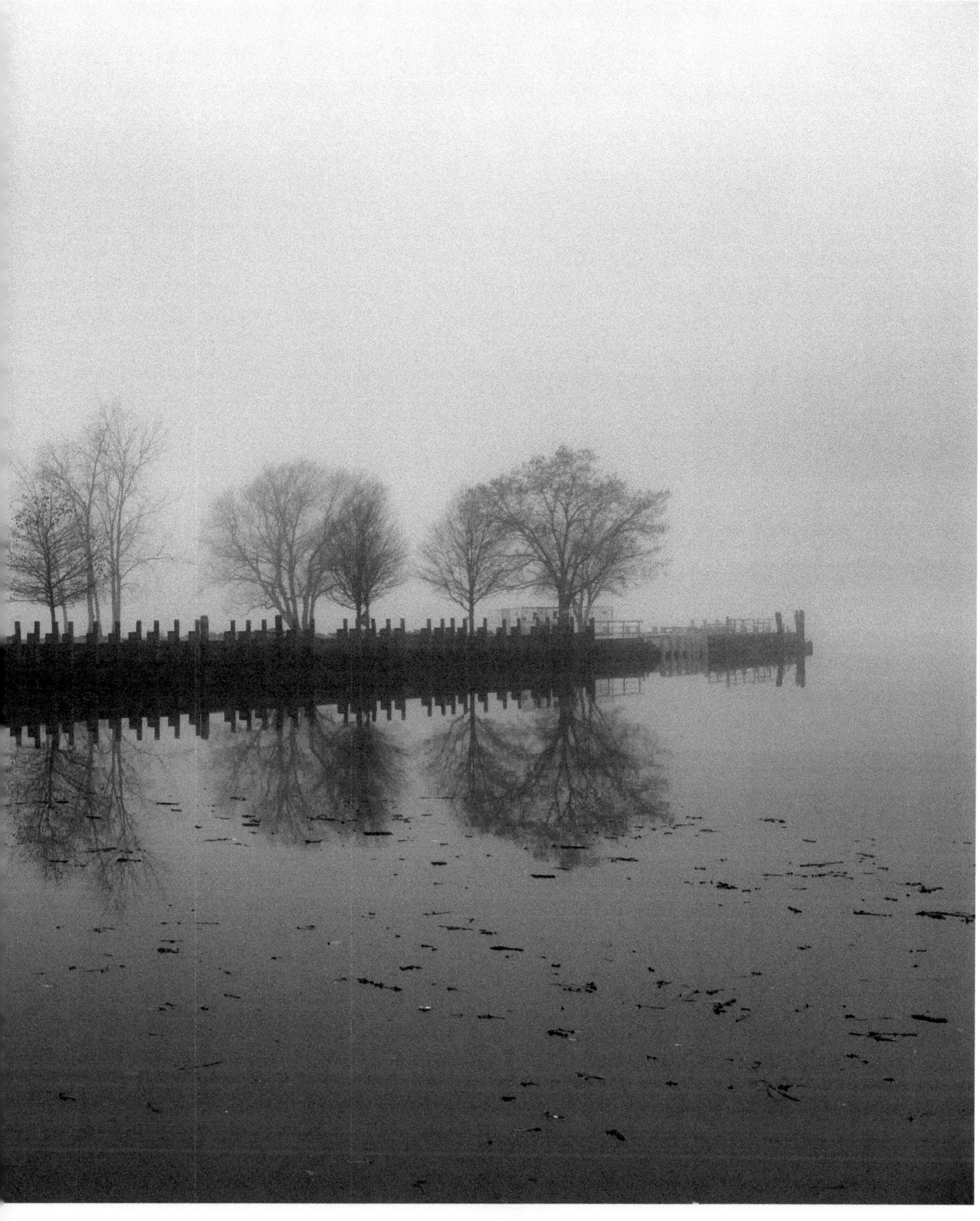

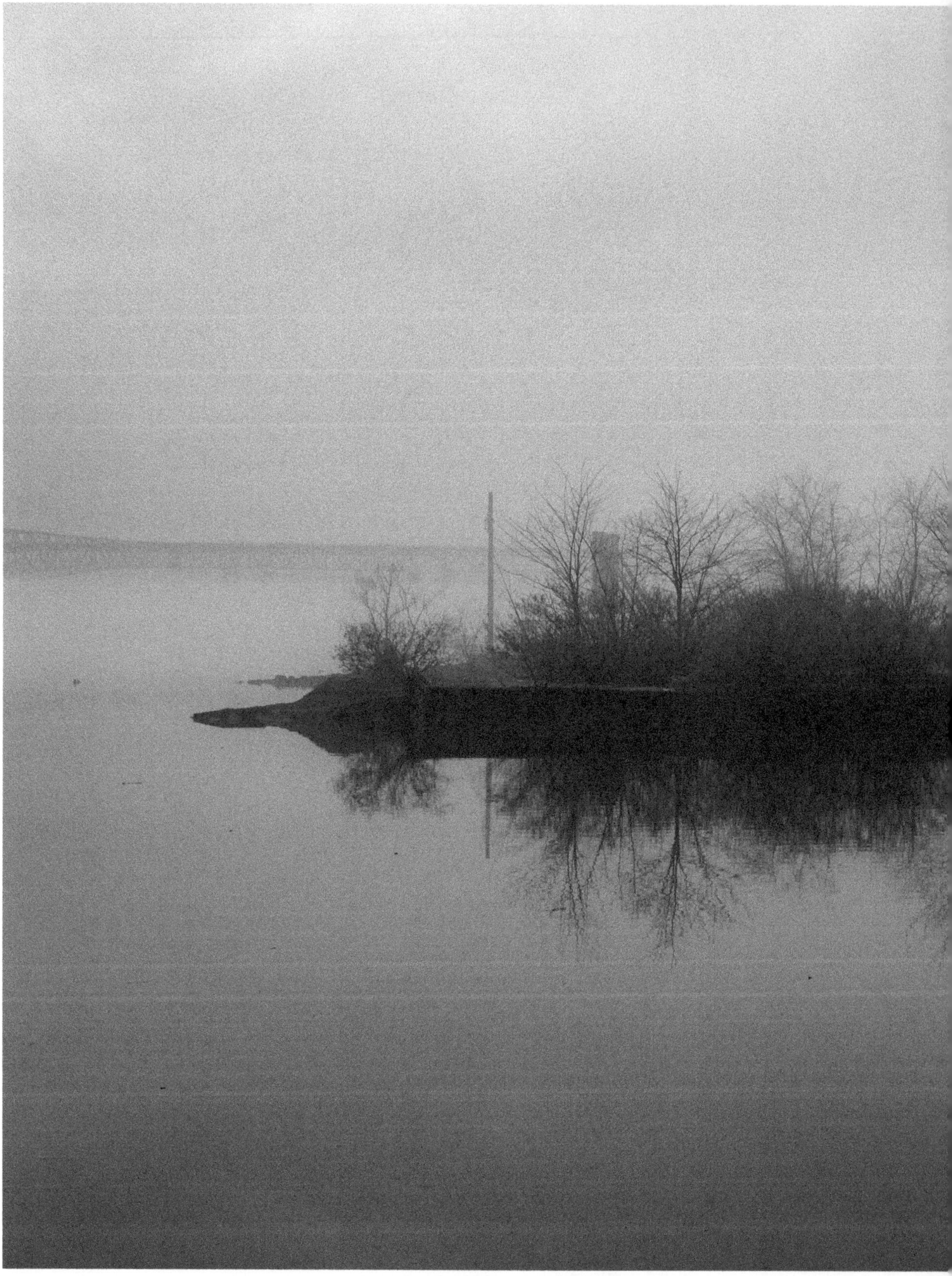

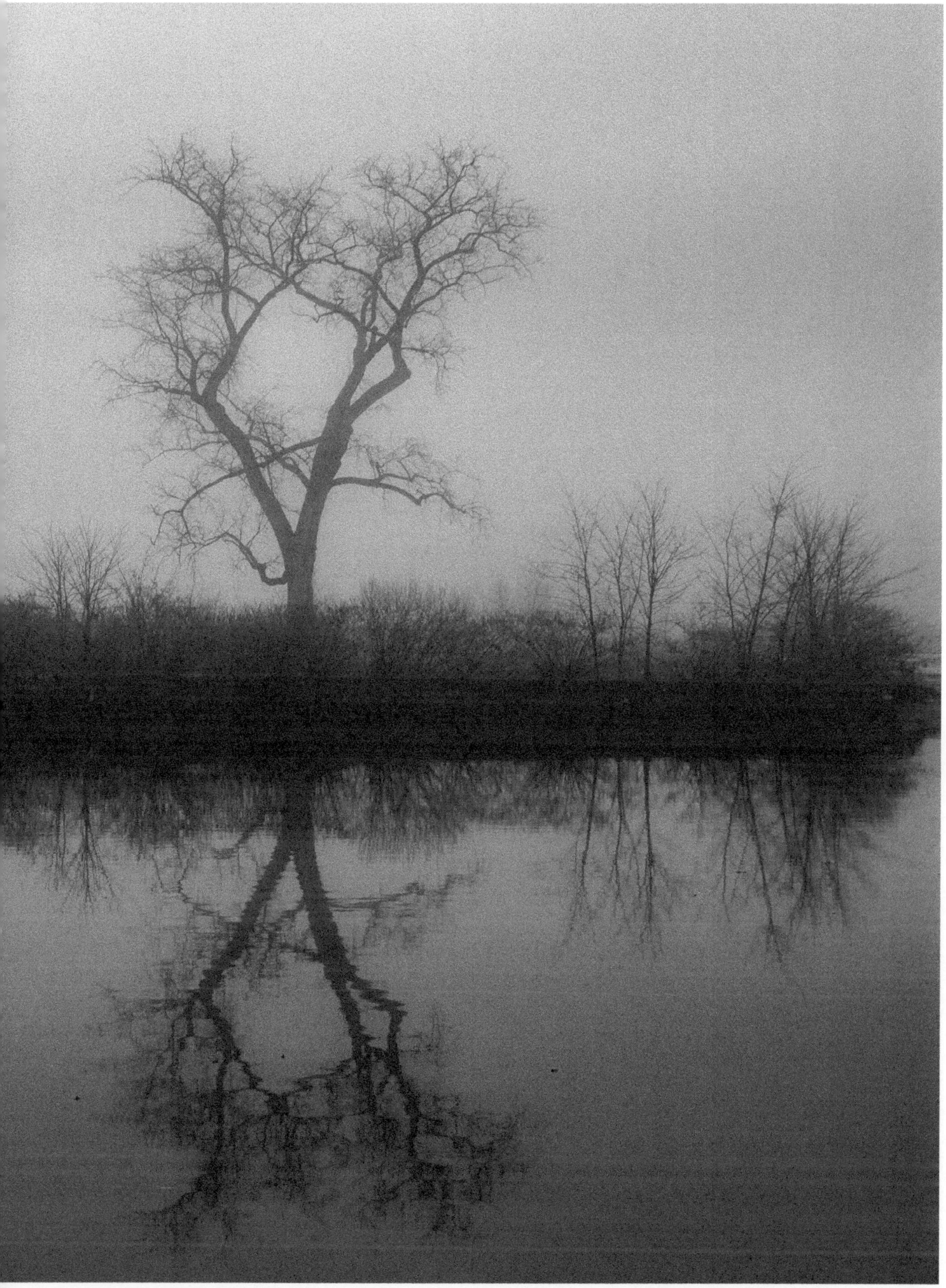

g had concealed the area's true emptiness until it was too late to turn back.
made traveling difficult.

e wandered an eerily silent forest for days.

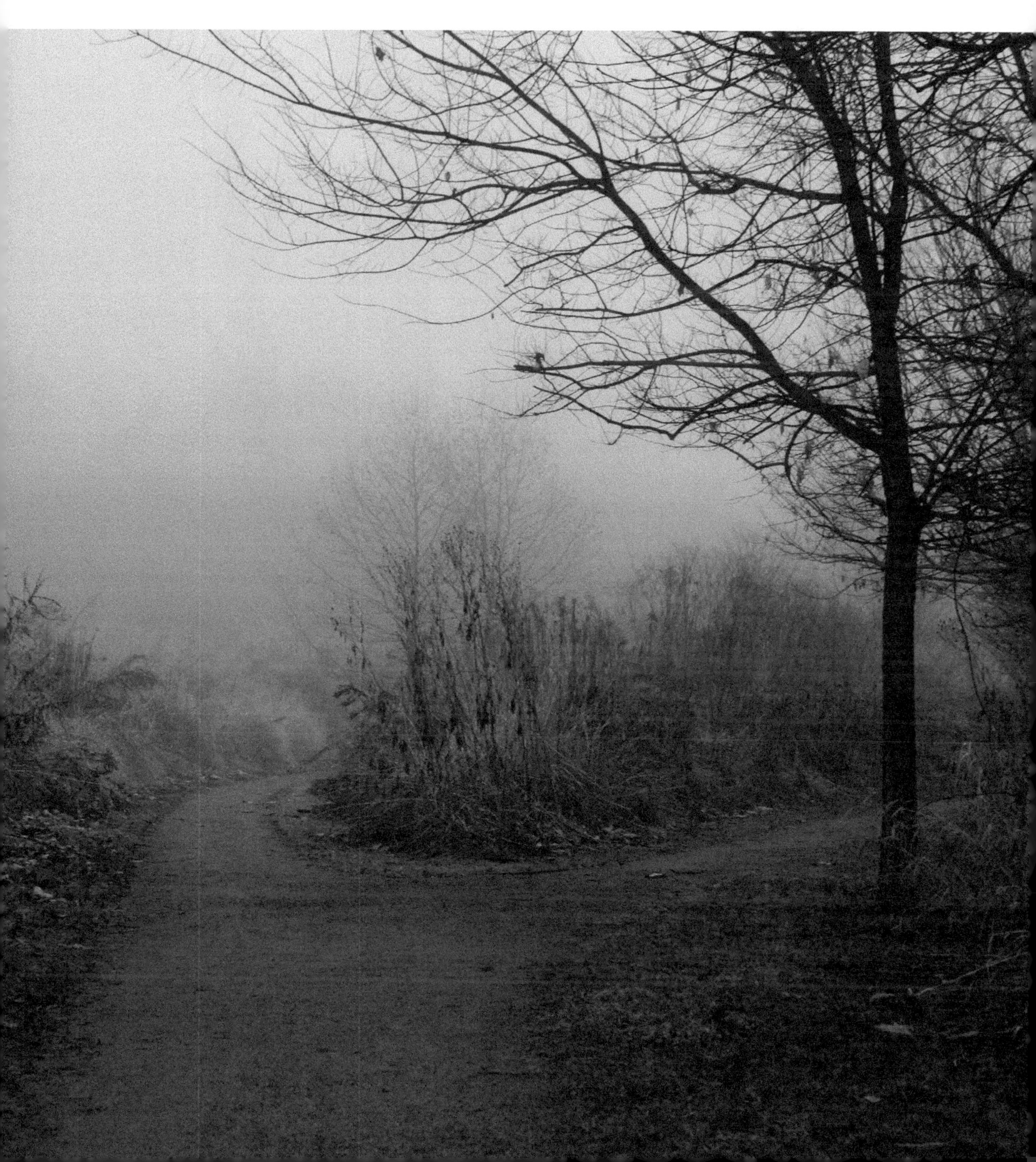

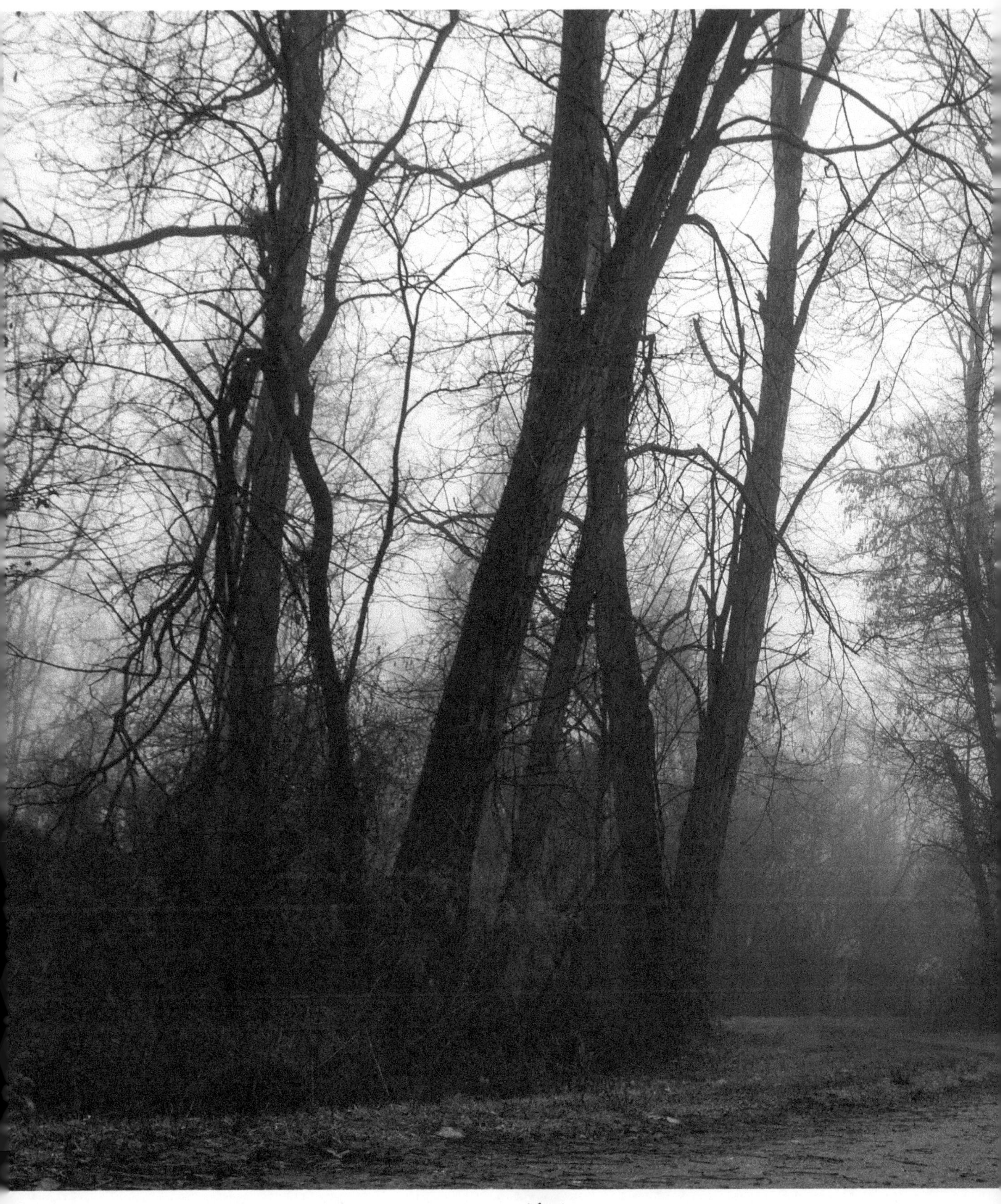

Eventually, he came across a group of people whose clothes were like flash-lights in darkness. The residents were vibrant as though bright clothes and an exuberant personally would beat back whatever caused this land to be so dreary. The buildings were about as terrifying though residents decorated them with eye-watering and often clashing colors.

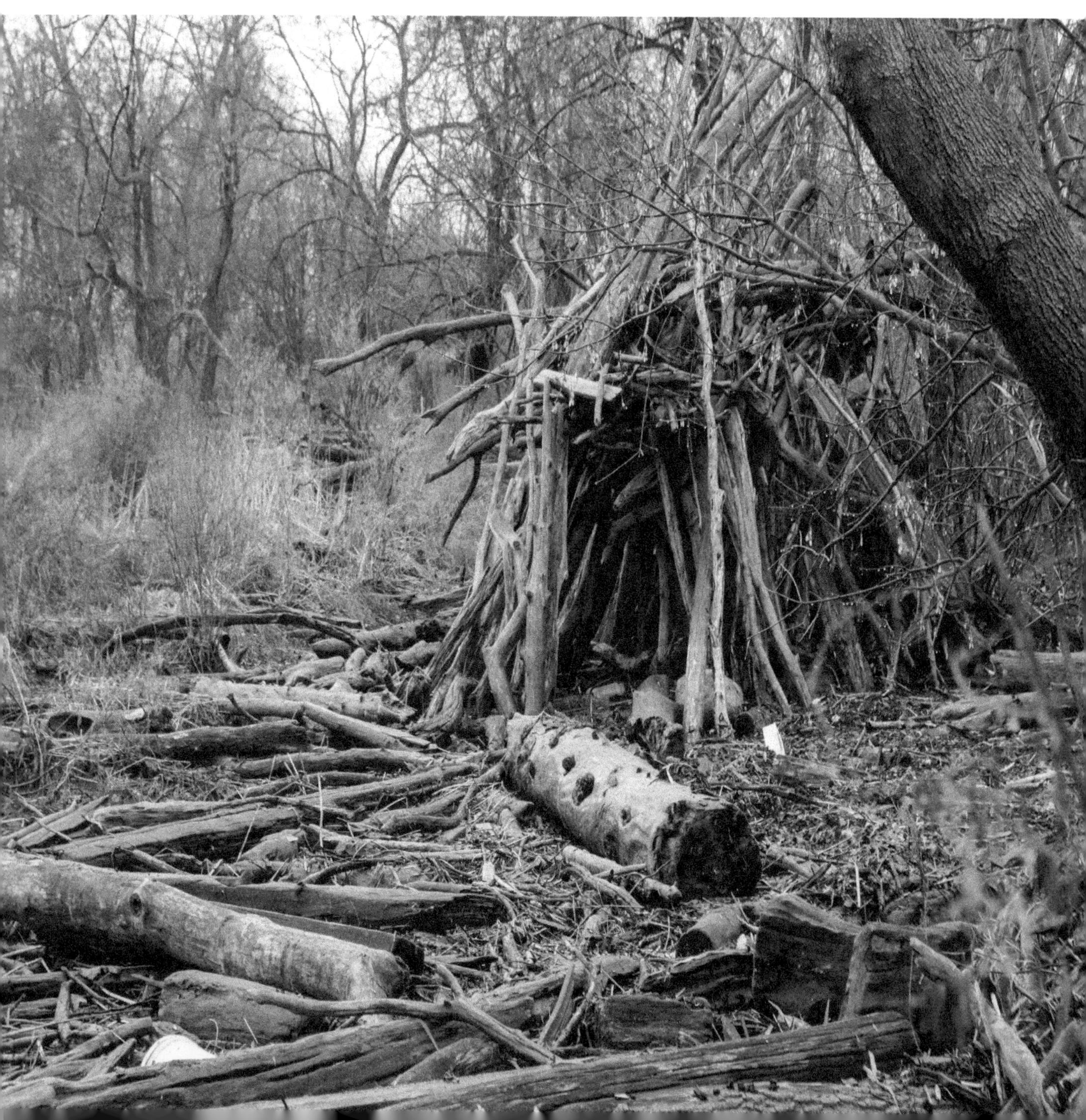

e asked about the fog but everyone danced around the topic. The residents were experts at avoiding his questions. He was often steered away from the original topic without realizing it.

Residents always traveled in groups when leaving the community. He tried joining those groups to explore the outside but he was always rejected. Politely, of course. He was encouraged to stay in town.

Despite the mystery and the fog, it was a strangely beautiful island.

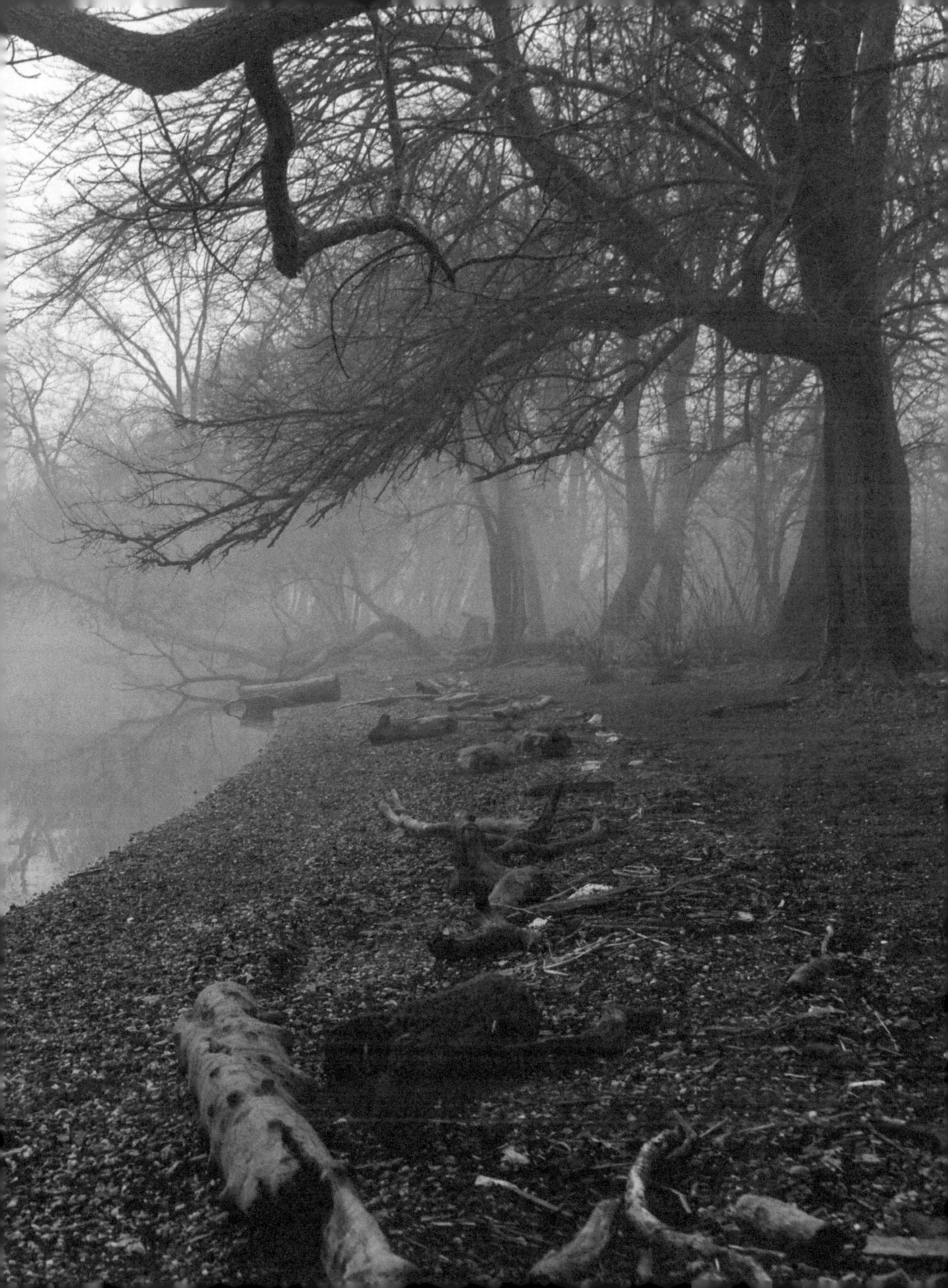

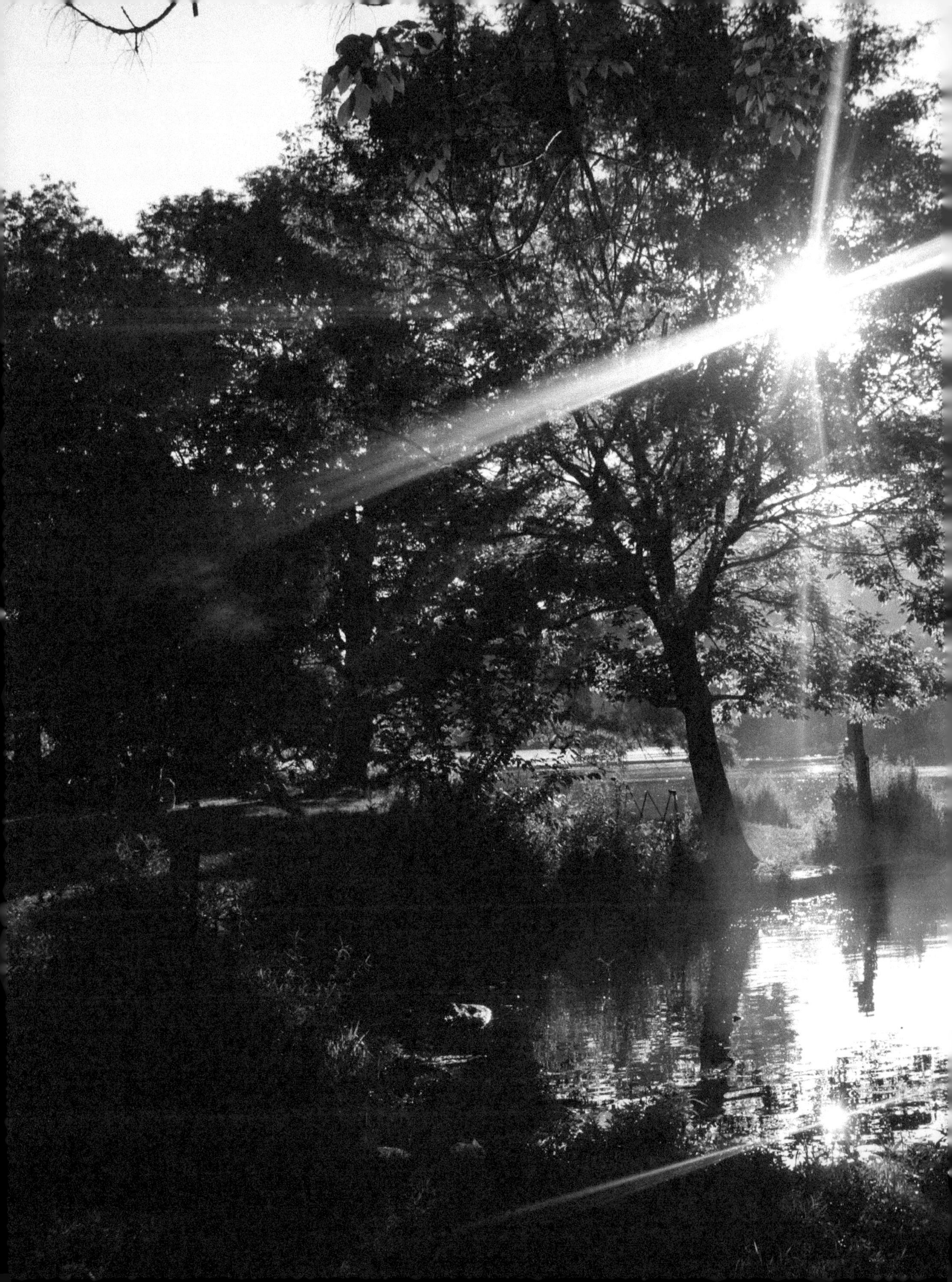

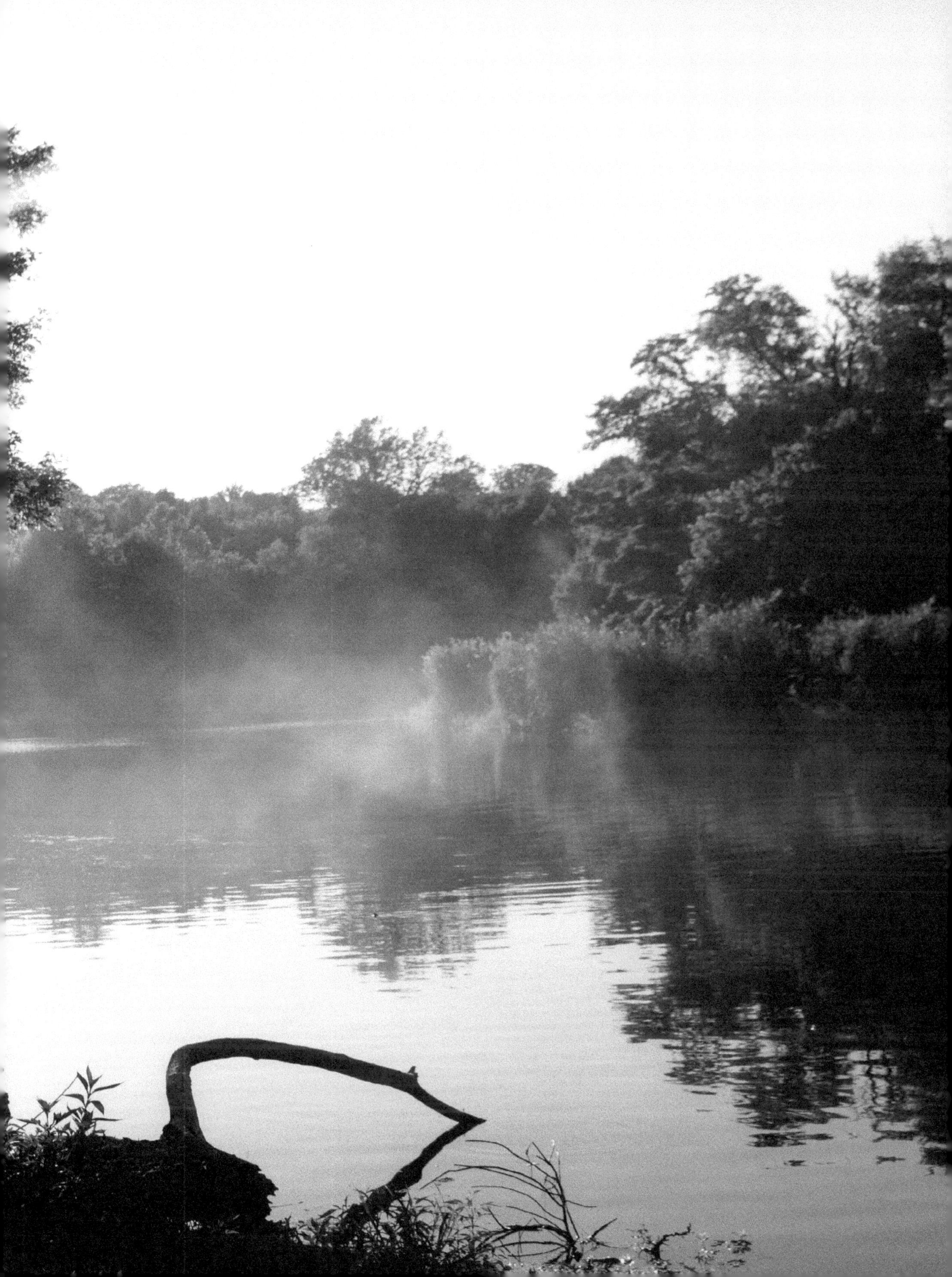

The residents were hiding something but he could not tell if it was out of malice or protection. During his travels, he grew skilled at reading people. He had to. He didn't sense anything but genuine kindness from the island's residents.

In the end, he spent three months on the island and never learned the mystery within the fog. One day, he'd return.

THE HIDDEN TREASURE

The journey removed distractions, cleaned filters, leaving him open to receiving the magic in nature.

Maybe he was running, searching for something he could never find. Trying to escape inescapable circumstances. Maybe he wasn't looking for other worlds.

Sometimes, that was okay.

These hidden wonders no one would believe. The legends and other-worldly lands. They filled him with an energy separate from the magic they possessed.

His heart felt calm for the first time in years. He felt able to roll though any obstacle.

He had searched for other worlds and found peace instead.

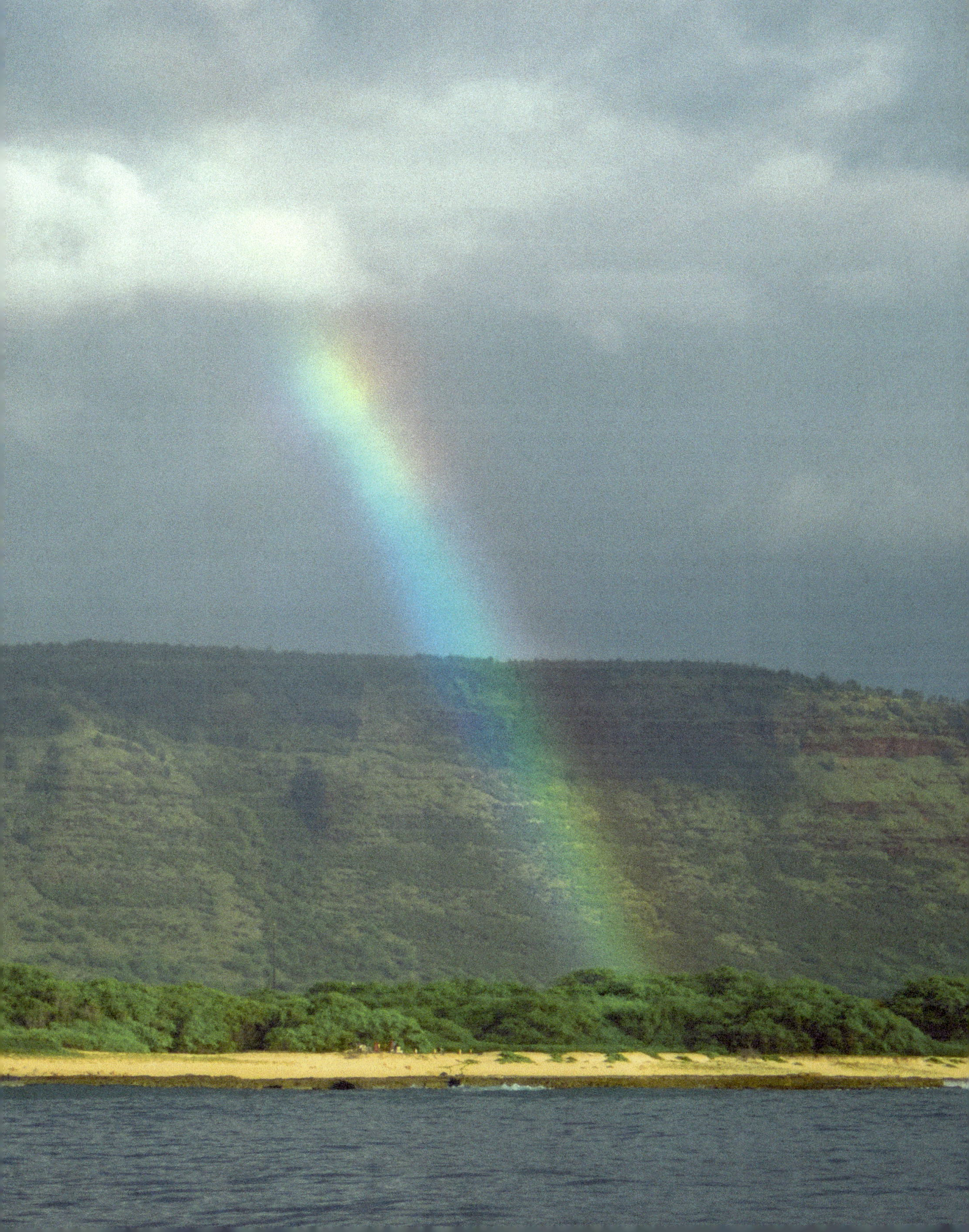

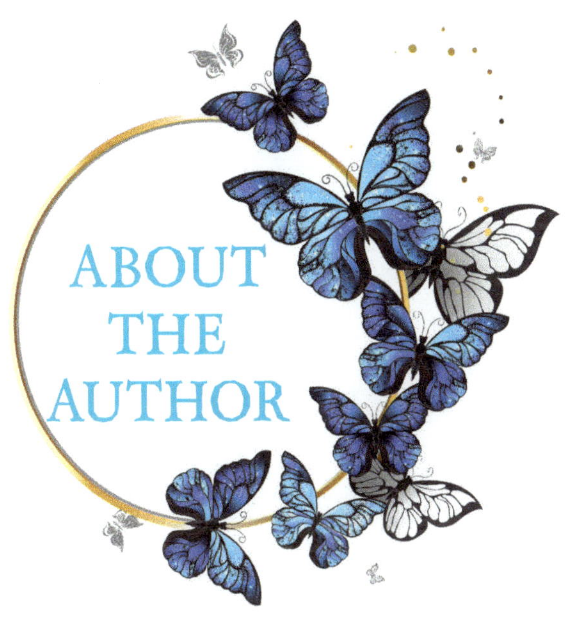

a kid, Auden created her own books by folding several construction papers in half and stapling
em down the middle, adding her own illustrations. She's an artist at heart, telling stories through
ords and photos. She holds a B.A. in English, a M.S. in Library and Information Science and
e studied Creative Writing in England. She also has a M.S. in Publishing from NYU. One of
r photos won a Muse Creative Award. She's a fantasy author and designer for Aubey LLC and
rrently lives in Brooklyn, NY with her dog Oreo. Auden has published 14 books. Find them and
ore photos on her website audenjohnson.com.

9 780996 423434